Swipe Right for Stab Wounds

Elle Kleos

For Alex, my love.

And for Evelyn Mee, who proved that age has nothing to do with a person's ability to love wholeheartedly.

CONTENTS

CHAPTER ONE

"It should be on your right, just down the street. The big gothic-looking place—you can't miss it."

"Thanks. I've got it from here."

"Good luck, Detective."

The old cruiser pulled to a stop between the painted lines. The church building towering overhead cut an imposing figure above the parking lot. The detective took one last draw from their giant coffee before throwing the car door open and stepping down onto the smooth asphalt.

Their feet settled into an easy pace as they made their way across the pavement to the corner of the parking lot that was blocked off by yellow police tape and a small army of people in navy blue CSI jackets. Ducking under the tape, the detective stood back a respectful distance and took in the crime scene.

"Homicide's here," a voice called, and several heads turned as the detective's presence was finally noticed.

They nodded in acknowledgement, but otherwise didn't attempt to interact with the forensics team, who were just as happy to ignore the detective in return. The call had come through on the dispatch less than ten minutes ago, so it was unlikely the team had anything more specific to report at this point than time of death.

From the look of the body, there wouldn't be much to analyze in this case, anyway. The victim, Father Simon D'Angelo, lay where he had fallen, cheek down on the pavement, his eyes dull and unfocused in death. His body was rigid, with one wrinkled hand still extended in a clawlike shape above his head. Had he been trying to crawl toward something? Perhaps the old Toyota parked just a few spots away? The detective tilted their head to get a better look at the object tucked in the priest's hand. The key fob did look like it could be a match for that car.

On first glance, the story appeared very simple: An older man with graying hair and a generous layer of wrinkles had dropped dead in a parking lot on a hot summer day. Hardly big news in a city of this size—even if that person was a priest just finishing up with Monday mass. But it didn't take a homicide detective to recognize the signs of a much less innocent cause of death in the priest's red-purple face and the multiple pools of vomit leading from the church's front steps to Father D'Angelo's final resting place.

Stepping up to the body now, the detective retrieved a pair of gloves from their pocket. The latex snapped into place, and the forensics photographer politely backed off a step without having to be asked. It was nice to be back in their stride on the mainland where protocol was well established and everything worked like a well-oiled machine. Their first few cases had been total softballs, but it was still good to be back in the saddle.

Hitching up their pants, the detective crouched down to perform a perfunctory examination of the body. First the key—it was for a Toyota, as anticipated—then the hands, neck, and face, which were the only areas that weren't covered by the priest's all-black uniform and white clerical collar. There were no obvious signs of a struggle, but that didn't mean much.

Patting down the body, they noted that the man's pockets were completely empty. Car keys in hand, but no wallet or phone to be found? That certainly raised a few questions.

Pulling their hands away from the body, the detective rocked back on their heels to glance around the parking lot. They didn't see any security cameras, but that didn't mean that there weren't any hiding out of sight. Failing that, there was a pawn shop across the street, and the streetlight intersection just down the road might be equipped with CCTV. Hopefully one of those sources would pan out and reveal whether their priest had indeed intended to drive away without his license or if the body had been robbed after the fact. Even if the body had been robbed, though, that wouldn't answer the bigger question here: Who would poison a priest?

There was only one way to start working toward that answer. Standing up, the detective nodded to the CSI team and took their leave. They slipped back under the caution tape and peeled the gloves off as they headed in the direction of the front stairs. Only hesitating slightly at the top of the stairs, they crossed themself once before pushing open the double doors and entering the bright space within.

The first thing they noticed was that the church was, mercifully, air conditioned. The second thing they noticed was that there was no forensics presence inside the building. That could be because the CSI team was leery about breaching the religious sanctuary without a detective there to take the heat for any missteps, but more likely it was because there didn't seem to be anything worth cataloging.

The church appeared like many others of its kind, with wood flooring, worn-down carpets, and more spare bulletins than there were seats to fill. There was no vomit on the floor, nor any sign of a struggle in here. By all appearances, Father D'Angelo had simply left the building after the morning mass, suddenly taken ill, and then dropped dead within a few steps.

But these things were rarely as they appeared.

The detective looked at the entrance to the nave just across the narrow hallway before squaring their shoulders and making their approach. The ancient door creaked open easily, and the detective stepped inside.

Fastidiously polished pews lined both sides of the room, only interrupted by the occasional ornate pillar. The eyes of the saints depicted in the magnificent stained glass windows stared down at the detective in judgement as they dared to stride down the center aisle on soft, blasphemous feet.

As they approached the altar, they pulled out their cell phone and quickly googled Saint Paul's service schedule. According to the website, this morning's mass began at 8:30 a.m. Time of death was roughly 9:45 a.m., according to the early witness report. That was an alarmingly short turnaround time if Father D'Angelo had really been standing at this altar saying mass only so many minutes earlier.

"Excuse me. No phones, please."

The detective slipped their phone back in their pocket as they looked up to see the priest who had emerged from the side door. He was dressed much more formally than Father D'Angelo had been, in a white robe and colorful stole. The old man's face was lined with wrinkles, and those wrinkles only deepened when he saw the detective standing before the altar.

The detective stood perfectly still as the priest examined them. They knew what he was seeing. The detective was either a little tall for a woman or slightly short for a man. They had brown, tidy hair and wore plain, professional clothing with no sign of tattoos or jewelry of any kind. They could politely be described as lean or impolitely as a bit on the skinny side. Despite that, they stood strong with feet planted and eyes trained on the person observing them. All in all, if it weren't for the look of calm resignation written across their serious face, the detective would be about as remarkable as any other police officer.

"My apologies, Father," the detective said, breaking the silent staring match. Ignoring the way the priest stiffened at the sound of their voice, the detective gestured to the gold shield on their belt. "I'm the homicide detective who has been assigned to investigate the murder. I was hoping to speak with you and some of the other staff members about Father D'Angelo. My name is—"

"I'm aware. You can't be in here," the priest said flatly. His gravelly voice rolled with a slight Italian accent.

"Is another service about to start?" they asked politely, despite knowing this was not the case.

"*You* can't be in here."

The detective's lips drew into a thin line. So it was going to be one of those cases.

"I'm afraid I will most likely have to enter the church from time to time during the investigation," the detective said after letting the silence hang for a moment. "But if you'd prefer, we can start by talking in your office, if that would be more comfortable."

"It would not," the old man said.

The detective frowned at his cold tone.

"I'm going to have to ask you to leave, Detective."

"That's not really—"

"Detective Sam," an authoritative voice rang out, the name echoing through the air like a thunderclap.

The detective turned in surprise to face the entrance. A stout woman hovered in the doorway. Her formal uniform and blunt haircut spoke to her no-nonsense attitude, and the unhappy twist to her mouth said the rest.

"Captain Donovan," Detective Sam responded, eyeing the woman warily. "To what do I owe the pleasure?"

"A word, Detective," the captain said simply. Her weary eyes flicked to the priest standing behind Sam, and she added, "In the hallway, if you don't mind."

Sam's expression hardened, but they kept their mouth shut. Glancing over their shoulder, they gave the priest a short nod before making their way back down the aisle. The moment they passed Captain Donovan, she turned to follow them, pulling the door shut behind her.

Sam drew to a halt in the foyer between the outer doors and the nave entrance. Folding their arms, they regarded the captain with that same look of calm resignation.

"Detective Sam," the captain repeated. Her eyes darted toward the outer doors as though she'd rather take this conversation all the way outside, and Sam's jaw tightened in response. Glancing back at Sam, Donovan said, "You got here fast."

"That's the job," Sam replied flatly.

"Right. Well, I'm sorry you had to come all the way down here. I'm afraid there was a bit of a mix-up with dispatch," Captain Donovan said, clasping her hands together. "You're not on this case."

"A mix-up with dispatch?" Sam repeated, raising an eyebrow in disbelief. And then, because that excuse really was too pathetic to let it slide, they added, "Is that what we're going with?"

"Don't make this more difficult than it has to be, Detective," the captain responded, passing a weary hand over her face. Her skin was webbed with fine wrinkles, and not the kind that came from a career full of sunshine and puppy dogs. "I've already assigned someone else to the case."

"All right. Where is he?" Sam asked, looking around pointedly, as though that would make the new detective appear.

"I'm sure he'll be here any—"

The outer doors banged open, followed by a loud "Fuck! Christ, what are those made out of?"

"Detective Mariano," Captain Donovan snapped, and the young man in the doorway nearly jumped out of his skin at the sound of her reprimand. "Please, show a little professionality. You're late, and that's no way to speak inside a church."

"Shit. Sorry—I mean, . . . sorry, ma'am," Detective Mariano stammered, looking thoroughly flustered as he stumbled through the doorway. The doors slammed shut behind him, and he winced again. "Sorry," he repeated, running an anxious hand over his short buzz cut. It was probably meant to make him look tough, but with his wide eyes and oversized ears, it just made him look like a kid playing detective.

The young man was practically shaking in his high tops with either nerves or anticipation. His shirt was half-untucked, and one shoelace trailed behind him like he had just rolled out of bed when the call came in. He barely looked to be over thirty, so maybe a pre-noon call time was a little early for him.

Sam knew Captain Donovan was seeing all the same things they were, but she just sighed deeply and gestured between the two.

"Detective Mariano, meet Detective Sam. Sam, Noah Mariano."

"Oh shi—uh, I mean, shoot. Great to meet you," Noah said eagerly. He stepped forward with a hand outstretched. "I've heard so much. Your arrest record is—wow. Legendary. And I mean, that Paradiso case? Crazy stuff. Really, really great to meet you."

Sam took his hand and gave it a single obligatory shake. Without a word to the new arrival, they gave the captain a simple nod and said, "I'll head back to the office to type up my notes. I trust you can forward them to him."

Then they turned on their heel and headed straight for the doors.

"Detective." Donovan's voice was once again a command, and Sam gritted their teeth as they drew to a halt three feet from the door. Their shoulders were rigid as they fought the urge to just keep walking and see what she would do. "Mariano is a junior detective. He's going to need a supervising officer."

"Oh my god," Noah said. To his credit, he didn't need any help connecting the dots, although he did seem to have trouble reading the room. "Are you—"

"Seriously?" Sam's sharp words cut right through Noah's excitement. They turned to face the captain. "You're benching me for making the holy water boil, but it's fine if I supervise the rookie from the sidelines?"

Noah went dead silent as Sam leveled their gaze on the captain, daring her to deny the accusation.

"You know how this works, Detective," Captain Donovan said, unflinching in the face of Sam's clear displeasure. "You're a senior member of this department. You have to take your turn supervising the new recruits. This was the right case at the right time."

"I bet it was," Sam said grimly, and this time Captain Donovan did flinch a little.

They both knew that if Sam checked the paperwork, they would see a hasty personnel change earlier today. Probably about two seconds after the church found out who had been assigned to Father D'Angelo's case.

"Nobody is being benched," the captain said placatingly. "While you're supervising Detective Mariano on this case, I've got something else for you to work on. Very high profile. We can discuss it back at the precinct."

"Great," Sam said shortly, their tone clipped in a way that said exactly how they felt about that. They were already halfway out the door when they said, "I'll see you there."

"Detective. Aren't you forgetting something?" Captain Donovan called after them, but this time Sam didn't so much as pause in their steps. "What do you think supervising means?" Donovan projected her voice so Sam couldn't ignore her needling words. "If you're going back to the precinct, Mariano is going with you."

"Then he'd better hurry up." Sam's dispassionate words floated up from the bottom of the concrete steps, where they were already disappearing out of sight.

"Wow," Noah said, letting out a low whistle. "They're pretty fuckin'—uh, freakin' intense, huh?" Grinning goofily, he added, "Still, pretty damn cool getting supervised by *the* Detective Sam."

"The Detective Sam is going to drive away without you if you don't hurry up," Captain Donovan said dryly. Noah didn't move, still looking starstruck. "Well? Start running, rookie."

"Oh, um, right." Noah glanced up nervously at the statues mounted by the church doors before crossing himself and blurting in Latin, "In nomine Patris et Filii et Spiritus Sancti. Amen." Then he kissed his fingers and bolted for the door.

The captain shook her head as she watched him trip over his own feet chasing after his new supervisor. The kid was going to need more than one rushed prayer if he was hoping to survive this partnership with his dignity intact.

CHAPTER TWO

"Hold up!"

Sam could hear the human puppy dog they had just been saddled with bouncing along in their wake, and they picked up their pace. The car was only a few feet away. Maybe they could still get out of here before he caught up if they didn't bother with the seatbelt?

Putting their hand on the door handle, Sam risked a glance back and sighed in irritation. The kid looked so ridiculous tripping over his own feet to avoid the vomit. Who the hell wore high-tops to a crime scene anyway?

This is what they got for wishing for a more complicated case.

"Shoelace."

"Huhwha?" Noah said, merging the two words together as he stumbled to a stop a few feet from the car. At least he didn't seem out of breath. If anything, he looked like he had enough energy to burn that they should make him take a few laps before letting him in the car.

"Shoelace," Sam repeated, sliding their sunglasses on and pointing to the young man's two left feet. "First lesson. If you fall on your face at a crime scene, the CSI team will take pictures, and those pictures will follow you around for the rest of your career."

"Are you . . . speaking from experience?" Noah asked, tilting his head to the side.

"Yes. The experience of seeing many, many rookies before you

9

embarrass themselves at crime scenes," Sam said flatly. "Now. Shoelace. Then get in the car."

Noah practically dropped to the deck in his haste to comply, as Sam opened the old cruiser's door and slid inside. They reached for their ever-present coffee cup only to remember that it was already empty. Because of course it was.

They had just placed the cardboard cup back down when the passenger door opened. Noah was busy typing something on his phone as he dropped into the seat and just barely managed to avoid putting a new dent in the roof with his oversized cranium.

"Jesus fucking Christ, this thing is old," Noah complained as the seat squealed in protest. "They make a senior detective drive this piece of shit?"

"No. This is my car," Sam said, turning the keys and putting it in gear.

"Why don't you use one of the department's?"

"I only drive stick."

"Oh, old school, that's pretty dope," Noah said, and Sam genuinely considered retirement for a half a heartbeat before deciding they should at least try training the colloquialisms out of him first.

"Yeah. Speaking of old school," Sam said, shifting up a gear as they took to the familiar streets, "Captain Donovan really wasn't joking about the language thing. You're going to have to clean that up if you're going to head this investigation."

"Is that Detective Sam's second rule for success?" Noah asked, sounding a little too enthusiastic as he held up his phone again. "Number one, don't embarrass yourself at the crime scene. Number two, no swearing at work?"

"Are you seriously writing this shit down?" Sam asked as the rookie's fingers blurred across the keyboard.

"OK," Noah said, amending his note. "No swearing at work, unless you're a senior detective, then some swearing OK." He shot Sam a broad grin and said, "Got it."

"You know these aren't real rules, right?"

"I know, but I'm supposed to be learning from you," Noah responded cheerfully before dropping his phone back into his lap. "And you have the best arrest record in the entire state, so if it works for you, I figure it can't be a bad idea to write it down."

"Maybe start by working on your research," Sam muttered, hitting the accelerator a little harder as the light turned yellow. They wanted to spend exactly zero extra minutes in the car with this kid.

"Wow, little tight, boss," Noah said as they whipped through the intersection.

"Oops," Sam said flatly, shifting up another gear as they hit the straightaway on Harborfront Avenue.

The road ran parallel to the coastline for several miles before heading back into the downtown core. Technically, there were shorter routes Sam could take, but habit always brought them back here. Colorful buildings flew by on either side advertising everything from seafood to fancy clothing boutiques to high-end art galleries boasting works from artists around the world.

Sam breathed in deeply and let the steady rotation of the wheels on the pavement, combined with the familiar sea breeze, remind them that this was all just part of the job. They had trained rookies before, and they could do it again.

"I only held that record in 2018."

"Huh?" Noah looked up from the phone in his hand.

Sam considered throwing it out the window but decided that might be an overreaction.

"You said you wanted to learn from me because I have the best arrest record in the state," Sam explained. "But that was only true in 2018. I've had a very average arrest record since then."

"That's still pretty fuckin' badass," Noah said, lowering the phone. "You think you'll ever pull it off again, or nah?"

"I hope not," Sam said with a reflexive frown.

Noah opened his mouth to ask, but Sam raised a hand to cut him off.

"Don't ask me about it until you've done some research, all right?" It'd be good for him to learn that when weird outliers happened in this line of work it usually wasn't a good thing.

"Cool. Cool, cool, cool," Noah said. He lifted his phone to type another note. "Research . . . 2018 . . . arrest record. Got it."

Sam shook their head in silent exasperation as they made the turn back toward downtown. Even at two in the afternoon there was a line of bumpers stretching out as far as the eye could see. Cranking the wheel, they made a sharp right onto a small side street and started zig-zagging their way through traffic in pursuit of the fastest route back to the precinct.

"Wow, you really know these streets, huh?" Noah said with wonder as Sam drew the car through the city in a complex route that only they could understand. "Did you grow up around here?"

"No."

He paused for more, but Sam did not offer any further explanation.

As the silence stretched on, Noah's fingers began tapping rapidly against his thigh. His eyes darted nervously out the windows. Sam could feel tension mounting by the second as he tried to wait them out. By Sam's count, it only took fifty-three seconds for him to break.

"You know, this whole city was pretty much my backyard as a kid," Noah finally said, glancing over at them for a reaction.

Sam inclined their head politely but did not respond.

Turning his gaze back out the window, Noah said, "My nonna's house is just up on Parliament and Broadview. The whole family still gets together like three blocks from here to fill the whole restaurant on Sundays for the game at Ricky's Diner. That's my uncle's place. Well, actually, he's not my real uncle, but you know how it is with us Italians. Everyone's family until people start getting sauced at the wedding, and then things get weird." He laughed awkwardly at his own joke. Seeing that Sam was not amused, he added, "You got a big family, or . . . ?"

"No." Sam judged the next yellow light and decided to actually hit the brakes this time. Only because there were more pedestrians in this part of town, though.

The car idled in silence, and they could feel Noah's gaze drilling into them. Unfortunately for the kid and his burning curiosity, Sam had a lot more experience not giving answers than he had trying to get them.

Just as Sam reached for the dial on the radio, Noah said, "So what's up with not carrying a gun?"

Sam sighed and dropped their hand. Technically, they were supposed to answer any work-relevant questions he had, so they said, "I do carry a gun. It's a mandatory part of the uniform."

Noah looked pointedly at Sam's belt, where there was a notable lack of deadly service weapon.

"I didn't know they made invisible guns."

"I must have forgotten it at home," Sam said dryly. Their eyes returned to the road as the light turned green.

"You—ugh," Noah grunted as his back hit the seat with the force of the acceleration. "You don't even have a holster."

"Guess I forget it a lot then."

Before Noah could pry more, Sam took the next turn hard enough to help him get familiar with the side door.

"OK, OK. Point taken," Noah grumbled, rubbing his shoulder gingerly. "You don't like carrying a gun. Jesus. No need to be a dick about it."

That got a small smile out of Sam as they shifted gears again. If he thought this was them being a dick, he was not going to enjoy being their rookie at all.

"So, do you always drive this fast, or are you just trying to intimidate me?" Noah asked casually, although he couldn't fully hide the stress in his voice when they switched lanes at Mach 10.

"How could I be driving fast? We're in rush-hour traffic," Sam pointed out, even as they peeled off into a side alley that was barely big enough to fit two dumpsters side by side. They were pretty sure he stopped breathing until they had expertly navigated their way through to the road on the other side.

"Yeah, OK," Noah said, rolling his eyes like he wasn't white in the face and clutching the safety handle for dear life. "I should write you a ticket specifically for finding a way to speed during rush hour traffic."

"You can if you want to," they said with a shrug.

"Really?"

"Sure," Sam said, picking up speed now as the traffic thinned out a little on the one-way street. "If you can remember the license plate on this car, go ahead and write me a speeding ticket."

"What? That's not fair," Noah complained, glancing at the side mirror and then flinching back as it came awfully close to the minivan attempting to keep pace in the other lane. "Why would I have memorized that?"

"Guess you can't write me a ticket, then."

Seeing that Noah was starting to look properly uneasy now, they sighed and eased off the accelerator a little.

"Listen. It's easy to be a jerk in a uniform. It's hard to be a good detective. Personally, I recommend more attention to detail and less parking tickets, but it's up to you."

"Is that why you don't carry a gun?" Noah asked, and Sam was surprised to hear him draw that connection. Maybe he wasn't totally hopeless after all.

Sam glanced at him sidelong for a moment, then finally shrugged. "Sure," they said, dropping another gear. "Something like that."

They rode in silence for a few seconds. Just when Sam thought they might actually get some peace and quiet, Noah's phone let out a sound like wind chimes mixed with a xylophone and the screen lit up with a series of bright pink and red iconography. Big, bold letters announced "You have a match!"

"Ah, shit. Sorry," Noah said, snatching up the phone and tapping rapidly at the screen to hide the hearts and confetti surrounding a young woman's face. "Forgot that was on."

"If you really want some rules to write down, here's one," Sam said, nodding at the phone as they zipped around a car attempting to turn left. "Keep the sound off. And probably save the romance for after work. It's not a good look to blow a case because you were too busy trying to find a girlfriend."

"Interesting."

Despite his business being out there for the world to see, Noah didn't sound especially embarrassed. Sam gave him a questioning look as they shifted gears, and he grinned a little in a way that Sam immediately decided they did not care for at all.

Glancing at the gear shift, Noah said, "You sped up again when I got the app notification. Is that because—"

"Don't do that."

"Do what?"

"The whole psychic detective thing. This isn't a TV show. Analyzing tells won't help you do anything except jump to conclusions." Intentionally

14

shifting to a lower gear, Sam added, "And it makes you sound like a douchebag."

"Okie dokie," Noah said, with the kind of expression you'd expect from someone who says things like "okie dokie." He took another note in his phone. "Detective Sam. Not a fan of personal questions."

Sam did not give him the satisfaction of a response. If he wanted to play this game, he was going to be sorely disappointed by the results. Sam had no interest in his personal life, and, as a rule, they didn't share any details about their own private affairs at work.

Not that there were any details to share. It would take a talented archeologist to uncover the remains of Sam's non-existent social life, forget any kind of genuine romance.

No, no hint of romance at all. Except for that one annoying text they had been ignoring for the past week. Which was definitely in no way contributing to their general crankiness.

Sam forced their hands to relax on the steering wheel as they pulled to a stop in the precinct parking lot. Yeah, they were probably going to have to work on their tells.

"Is this the part where I get the speech?"

Sam turned their head at the sound of Noah's sarcastic tone.

Noah lowered his voice as he raised one stern finger and said, "Listen up, rookie. I'm not your daddy, I'm not your babysitter, and I'm sure as hell not your friend. You're here to listen, learn, and bring me my coffee every hour on the hour." Noah had the stones to look Sam in the eye when he grinned and asked, "Did I get that right?"

"That's cute," Sam said, pulling their keys out of the ignition. "You memorize that in the mirror this morning?"

"Nah." Noah waved a dismissive hand before unbuckling his seatbelt. "It kind of just comes to me. I scored off the charts on the detective exam for dramatic speech improv."

"Sounds fun. They'll love you in the interrogation room." Sam hit the lock button as Noah reached for his door handle.

"Seriously?" Noah asked, rattling the handle pointedly.

"Just listen, OK?" Sam said. They kept one finger pressed to the lock button until he stopped trying to escape. "You're right. I'm not trying to make any friends when I'm on the clock. Sorry to disappoint. But you're not my assistant, either. You're a homicide detective now, and if you ever waste time bringing me coffee instead of working on your caseload, I'm going to be very annoyed. Sound good?"

Noah hesitated for a moment, then released the handle to pick up his phone again. "Detective Sam," he orated as he typed rapidly, "will be in the same mood as always whether you bring them a coffee or not." Flashing them another lazy grin, he said, "Got it."

"Smartass." They rolled their eyes but released the lock button. Throwing their own door open, Sam said, "Come on. Captain Donovan isn't a patient person. And she drives faster than I do."

CHAPTER THREE

"Holy shit, you weren't kidding," Noah said, and Sam shushed him as they approached the office at the end of the third-floor hallway.

Captain Donovan was already seated in her chair, looking like she'd been there all morning and not like she had just broken the sound barrier getting back here before they did. Of course, it was sort of cheating to use the sirens the whole way, in Sam's opinion, but the captain was not the kind of woman who allotted time in her schedule for traffic. Or opinions.

"Detective Sam. Detective Mariano," the captain said, waving them over impatiently as they approached her door. "I see you didn't kill each other on the way over. That's a good start."

"I'm pretty sure they tried," Noah muttered.

"That my new case?" Sam ignored Noah's whining and nodded to the fresh file on the captain's desk.

Donovan nodded back, then glanced at Noah pointedly. Sam knew that look.

Turning to face their young charge, Sam said, "Hey, rookie. Go over to my desk and count paper clips till we're done here."

"What? Ser—" Noah started to complain but cut himself off. "Wait. Wait, wait, wait." He grinned a little and raised one finger to his temple. "This is a test, right? Because I'm not supposed to be your assistant?"

Sam didn't respond, but their expression settled into something that was maybe one degree warmer than what he'd been getting from them so far.

"Right. No coffee and no counting paper clips. I'll go start working on my notes from the crime scene. And, uh, doing research."

Sam nodded in approval.

Noah had just turned to go when the captain called out, "Detective Mariano?"

"Huhyeah?" The rookie practically did a full 360 in his eagerness to turn and face the captain, who looked far more charmed by his puppy-dog attitude than Sam was.

"Work on your notes over by the front desk," she ordered. "I'm expecting my three o'clock any minute now, and I'd like her brought straight here, please."

"Do I . . . ?" Noah looked to Sam for permission, which they did find a little more charming.

"You're not my assistant," Sam said. "But you do have to listen to her." They pointed to the "Captain" part of Captain Claire Donovan's name plaque on the office door. When he still hesitated, Sam said, "Well? She said fetch. Go fetch."

Noah scrambled to obey, and Sam shook their head as they watched him go. Once they were sure he actually knew how to find the front desk, they turned back to the captain.

Sam tapped the door in question, and she shook her head. Leaving it open, they crossed the room to one of the worn chairs situated in front of her tidy desk. The clock on her shelf already read 2:58, so if she had a three o' clock, she must really be hoping to keep this short.

"Quite the rookie. Do you think he's going to be all right on the D'Angelo case?" Captain Donovan asked, her sharp eyes tracking Noah's progress down the hall before returning to Sam.

"Does it really matter what I think?"

The captain's lips pursed, and Sam sighed.

"Yeah," they amended begrudgingly. "He'll be fine."

"Good. Now, for your case." Flipping open the slim file on her desk, Donovan turned it toward Sam and said, "I've got a string of stabbings I need you to investigate. All within the last six weeks. All of them fatal."

"Mm." Sam leaned in to examine the pictures of the three women.

"Yeah, I remember this one." They tapped one finger against the bottom left picture.

The blonde woman stared back at them with the broad smile of a person who didn't know she was already dead. The pastel suit and crucifix necklace only made the image more macabre.

Sam examined the photo for a second before saying, "Cassie Adelaide. One of Martin's cases, right? The dumpster on Sixth Street?"

"Well, she's your case now," the captain said. "But yes, his notes are all in there."

"Impressive notes," Sam said as they flipped the page over to review the single sheet of text detailing what was known about Cassie's murder to date. Which was approximately nothing.

"We had no reason to think it was anything but a mugging gone wrong, until now," the captain said with a jaded shrug. "You know how those go."

Sam certainly did know. They were currently sitting on three cold cases of their own that were dead ends for exactly that reason. The sad truth was that most murders weren't the type of pre-planned, first-degree cases that could be methodically investigated and untangled. When you were looking at murder as a result of random violence, the very lack of connection between the victim and the killer was what made it nearly impossible to catch the perpetrator.

Nodding slowly as they finished skimming Martin's notes, Sam said, "So what changed?" They flipped back to the page with the pictures of the three women and added, "I'm guessing we don't think it was just an unlucky mugging anymore?"

"No," the captain confirmed. "Nikki Russo was killed just under two weeks ago. Then Alicia Hancock only three days ago. All stabbing victims."

"OK . . . " Sam glanced up at the captain and then back down at the file, examining the pictures. "Weird to have three stabbing victims so close together, but not that weird. What's the connection?" Frowning, they added, "Also, why not put Martin on this if he was already looking into the Adelaide girl?"

"Martin's caseload is full, and you were open," Captain Donovan said.

Sam did not miss the fact that she chose to answer that question first.

Hesitating ever so slightly, she added, "We also needed someone who could be a little more . . . subtle, for this one. More under the radar."

"Me—subtle?" Sam asked, offering the captain a disbelieving look. Gesturing to themself vaguely, they said, "You've seen the Paradiso video, right?"

"Once or twice," the captain said wryly.

Sam's infamous celebrity wedding arrest had racked up several million views on social media and caused the department no shortage of headaches.

"I'm going to go ahead and say that was a bit of an outlier, though, since you don't even have a Twitter account," she continued. "Martin, on the other hand, has to tell the world every time his dog takes a dump."

"Fair point," Sam conceded with a shrug. Glancing back at the file, they said, "So you need someone who can stay under the radar. Fine. Why? What do these three have in common?"

"Well . . ." the captain started and then hesitated. Sam frowned at the way she fidgeted in her seat. "It's a little . . . sensitive. It has come to our attention that all three of these young women were using a—uh, well, actually the same app at the time of their assaults. It gets complicated, you know, whenever private businesses and investigations mix." She gave Sam a meaningful look and added, "Especially businesses that Mayor Kelso has a vested interest in."

"All due respect to Mayor Kelso, but why would he care about this investigation just because of some random app?" Sam asked, not sure they liked what her tone was implying at all.

"Because the mayor met his wife on the Paths app," a new voice responded.

Sam stiffened as recognition hit them like a bolt of lightning.

They turned slowly in their chair to get a look at the speaker, and any hope that they might be mistaken vanished. The tall woman standing in the captain's doorway hesitated for half a beat when their eyes met, but she was quick to gloss over the hiccup with a beatific smile.

"My app, actually," the woman said. "And, unfortunately, the same dating app these three ladies were using shortly before they were attacked."

"Uh, Captain?" Noah said awkwardly as he side-stepped past the woman in the doorway. "Your three o' clock is here."

"I can see that. Thank you, Detective Mariano."

"My apologies for running behind," the beautiful woman said politely as she stepped into the room. She moved with all the grace of someone who had no problem being a glamorous giraffe in a stable built for work horses. "Things at the office have been a little crazier than usual preparing for the investigation."

Despite her easy demeanor, she cut an imposing figure standing there in her fashionable business attire and killer shoes. If she had been a little younger, she would have been in danger of looking more like a model than a business owner. As it was, her ebony skin and curly hair were somehow still radiant under the hideous overhead lighting, and her coy smile said she was well aware of the effect her presence had on the room. Noah could barely take his eyes off of her, and even Captain Donovan sat up a little straighter.

Sam sunk lower in their seat and wondered whether—if they just stayed still long enough—they could make themself disappear entirely.

Standing up, the captain stepped around her desk to offer the woman her hand.

"It's not a problem at all, Mrs. Fox. Thank you for coming down on such short notice." Gesturing to the empty chair next to Sam, she said, "Please, have a seat."

"That's very kind," Mrs. Fox said, placing her hand over the captain's to shake warmly. The illusion only cracked a little when her eyes flitted to Sam and she added, "But I'm, ah, comfortable standing."

"In those heels? Consider me impressed," the captain said, returning to her side of the desk.

Mrs. Fox smiled politely, but made no move to take the empty chair.

Clearing her throat, Captain Donovan gestured between her detective and the businesswoman as she said, "Mrs. Fox, this is Detective Sam. Sam, this is Vivienne Fox. She is the owner of Paths, the dating app that all three of our victims were using shortly before each was attacked. Her assistance will be an invaluable resource on this case."

Captain Donovan waited for Sam to acknowledge their new guest, but Sam remained stock-still in their chair. Probably because their brain had started flatlining about a minute ago and still hadn't come back online.

The only real coherent thought they seemed to be able to generate was that somehow, even after all these years, she still smelled the same. What kind of useless nonsense was that?

"Detective . . . ?" Captain Donovan prompted, frowning at the blank look on Sam's face.

Standing abruptly, Sam turned to face the beautiful businesswoman. They stared at each other for a long moment, in which neither of them quite seemed to know what to say, before Vivienne finally offered another glossy smile and held out one slender hand.

Sam only hesitated slightly before accepting her handshake. At least the calm and cool reception told them this little reunion was a surprise for her, too. She always had been on top of her game during a crisis.

"Sam," Vivienne acknowledged in a low voice, and Sam flinched at the familiar way their name rolled off her tongue.

"Mrs. Fox," they replied shortly, not so much shaking the other woman's hand as shaking her off. They hurriedly returned to their seat.

"Mrs. Fox is actually the one who alerted us to the connection between the three women," Donovan explained.

"I can't take any credit," Vivienne said, graciously ignoring Sam's strange behavior. "We received a . . . distressed call, let's say, from one of the victim's relatives, who was very emotional and insisted that my app had made her sister a target. Of course, we took this accusation very seriously and passed the information on to the police straight away." Her eyes were on Sam again when she added, "It's a relief to know the city is taking this situation so seriously."

"Of course," Donovan assured her smoothly. "That's why we've cleared Detective Sam's caseload. They'll be focusing all their energy on solving this case as quickly and quietly as possible. Isn't that right, Sam?"

"Right. Of course," Sam said, doing their level best not to seem completely blindsided by this information. Still refusing to look in Vivienne's direction, they said, "It sounds like we're pretty confident about the dating app angle on this case. Can we get access to the victims' online history, maybe their interactions or user habits?"

"Mrs. Fox?" the captain asked.

"Yes. I can provide any information that they entered or sent using the app from the central servers at my office," Vivienne confirmed, and Sam could feel her looking at them a little more intently now.

"Great," Sam said, a little too eagerly, as they reached for the file folder on the desk. "If you send that over, it should give us a list of people worth talking to. I'll set up some interviews and we can—"

"Not so fast, Detective," the captain said, pinning the folder in place with one finger as Sam attempted to make their escape. "We'll be taking a more subtle approach for these interviews."

"Subtle," Sam echoed. Their stomach dropped as they slowly released the folder.

"Yes, subtle," the captain repeated calmly. "Mayor Kelso has made it extremely clear that he will not be pleased if one of the city's top entrepreneurial successes ends up at the center of a media circus."

"And we appreciate his discretion," Vivienne said gratefully, as though the Mayor was doing this out of the goodness of his heart and it had nothing at all to do with protecting his image for the upcoming reelection campaign.

"Of course," the captain agreed, although she didn't take her eyes off Sam's drawn face for a second. "That's why we'll be putting Detective Sam in the field to conduct some discreet interviews as one of your clients."

"One of her clients," Sam repeated, letting the reality of the situation sink in. "Meaning . . . you want me to use the app to arrange undercover interviews by inviting the potential suspects to go on . . . dates." They hesitated and then added, "With me."

"Yes," the captain confirmed, and Sam was shaking their head before the words were even out of her mouth.

"What?" Noah blurted from his spot in the corner.

"No."

"Listen," the captain said, shooting Noah a glare that instantly had him zipping it. "I know it's not how we normally do things in Homicide, but this is fairly routine for other departments."

"No," Sam repeated, even more firmly this time.

"We've got a few members of Vice on loan to help with any questions you've got, and we're not asking you to go deep undercover," Captain Donovan said in a placating tone that had approximately zero effect on the tension mounting in the room. "This will just be the occasional cover for interviews. You're welcome to continue on with the rest of your life outside of the case."

"Ah, Captain Donovan," Vivienne interjected. For the first time her cool surface had cracked a little to show some real concern at the sound of this plan. "I know we discussed some undercover work to keep the investigation under the radar, and of course if you feel Detective Sam is the right person to head up the case, I trust your judgement . . . but are you sure they're the best choice to be . . . 'in the field'?"

"Absolutely," Captain Donovan said immediately with a confidence that no one else in the room seemed to share. "I have full faith in Detective Sam's abilities. They've been a senior detective with this department for eight years, and their arrest record is the best in house."

"I don't have the best arrest record."

"Excuse me?" Captain Donovan's expression tightened with displeasure as she saw Sam gearing up for a fight that she was clearly not interested in entertaining. "After the Paradiso case—"

"My record is tied with Detective Harrison's," Sam said flatly.

"Well, Harrison is busy with another assignment."

"And Detective Benson? Or Detective Trager?" Sam pressed. "You said you wanted subtle. My record might be stronger, but they've both done undercover work before. If you want the best, why not go with one of them? Or are they both busy as well?"

Captain Donovan considered their accusatory words for a long moment before saying, "This case has specific requirements. We need a detective who . . . well, you can guess."

"No. I really can't." Sam narrowed their eyes at her dangerously. "A detective who can what, exactly?"

"We need someone who can perform undercover interviews using Mrs. Fox's app," the captain said. Seeing that Sam was not going to let her sidestep the issue, she added, "Which means we need someone our potential suspects will agree to go on a date with."

Sam nodded slowly, and the tension in the room ratcheted even higher. Poor Noah looked like he might have forgotten how to breathe as the detective and the captain stared each other down across the desk.

"You mean a woman," they finally said bluntly.

"Yes. A woman."

"But Sam's not—" Vivienne's startled words choked off, too loud in the tense room. Glancing at Sam, who was looking damn near carved from stone, she asked awkwardly, "You're not . . . you haven't . . . transitioned? Have you?"

Sam's head snapped to the side, and the look they gave her could have peeled the paint off a car.

"All right, I didn't think you did. Just asking," Vivienne muttered.

"I'm sorry, did I miss something?" Captain Donovan asked with a frown at Sam and Vivienne's little psychic exchange. "Do you two know each other?"

Sam shook their head again, even as Vivienne said, "Yes." Ignoring Sam's sound of disgust, she added, "It's, ah, been a while. Since we crossed paths."

"All right." The captain didn't seem quite sure what to do with this information. "All right," she repeated, placing her elbows on the desk. "Mrs. Fox. I understand your concerns with having Detective Sam on this case." Glancing at Sam, who still had not uttered a single word, she said, "As a department, we are disappointed to not have more women on the force. That's something Chief Sanders and I are very passionate about correcting. Very passionate. But at the moment, Sam is our only—er, our best match for the needs of this case."

More silence met her plain assessment of the situation. Vivienne looked like she wanted to say something, but the nuclear anger radiating from Sam's corner of the room made it hard to breathe, much less speak.

"Do you have something you want to say, Detective?" the captain finally asked when the silence had stretched on for over a minute.

"Is this a fucking joke?" Sam's voice was low and positively simmering with the kind of pent-up anger that didn't come from one bad day on the job.

"Detective," the captain reprimanded with a frown. "I understand that this isn't ideal, but let's keep things professional."

"Professional?" Sam demanded sharply. "I'm sorry. You want me to go undercover—as a woman—to find a killer by, what, dating a bunch of homicidal men? And I'm the unprofessional one?"

"Well, that's a nice way of putting it," Vivienne said, sounding, unbelievably, like she was the one who was offended here. "The men on my app are just trying to find love. They're not predators."

"Obviously they are if they're using your app to murder people," Sam snapped, and Vivienne flinched in the face of their raw anger.

"All right, that's enough," Captain Donovan said tersely. Reaching one hand up to pinch the bridge of her nose, she said, "I apologize for my detective's behavior, Mrs. Fox. This is completely unprofessional. And inappropriate. Would you mind waiting in the hallway for a minute while I sort this out?"

"I—" Vivienne started, then cut herself off. She looked like she had more to say, but the look on Sam's face said they really didn't need her dumping fuel on the fire right now.

Making her way over to the door, Vivienne hesitated, then turned to look at Noah, who was still hiding in the corner and looking very much like he wanted to disappear.

"Detective Mariano, right?" she asked, and he nodded. "Perhaps you'd like to help me find the restroom?" She glanced pointedly toward the captain and Sam, who seemed about two seconds away from a full-on bloodbath.

"Uh, yeah. Sure. I can do that," Noah said awkwardly, and Sam hated that Vivienne Fox, of all people, was the person in the room most concerned with their dignity at the moment.

But here they were.

The door shut quietly behind the two of them, and Sam forced themself to remain silent. If they said even ten percent of what they were thinking right now, it would definitely get them fired. Not that they had ruled that out as an option yet.

"OK. I can see that you're angry," Captain Donovan said after a long moment, which was a laughable understatement. "And I acknowledge that this assignment is . . . complicated, given your . . . your . . . " She floundered for the right word, gesturing vaguely in Sam's general direction before settling on "situation."

"What could you possibly know about my 'situation'?" Sam demanded.

"Well," the captain said, clearing her throat uncomfortably. "I know you're not a woman, er, technically speak—"

"I am a woman."

"OK," Captain Donovan said hesitantly. Her eyes flicked down to Sam's chest and then back to their face in a way that really made Sam want to start throwing things. "But you're not—"

"This has nothing to do with what I'm not." Grinding their teeth hard enough to crack a crown under the force of their humiliation, Sam said,

"I'm only going to explain this one more time, all right? Write it down if you have to. I *am* a woman. I *am* a man. Both. At all times. *Technically speaking.* Is that clear enough?"

"Of course," Captain Donovan agreed hurriedly. "And I respect that. But—as a woman, at all times, as you say—"

"This is bullshit!" Sam snapped, and the captain grimaced. Fighting to lower their voice, they didn't manage to sound any less furious when they said, "You would never, never ask any of the other men in this department to—"

"I would." Donovan's words were ice-cold in sharp contrast to Sam's outrage. "If the victims were all male and we were looking for a female killer, I absolutely would."

"No," Sam said, shoving their chair back hard enough to tear a strip out of the cheap carpet. "No," they repeated, shaking their head and beginning to pace, because they really were going to start throwing things otherwise. "I'm not doing this."

The captain was silent for a long moment as she watched them pace. "I feel for you, Sam," she started after giving them a minute to simmer down. "As a woman in this profession, believe me, I know—"

"Oh my god."

"This is a bad situation," Captain Donovan continued right over their disgust. "And if there was another choice, I wouldn't be asking you to do this. But we need you on this case. You're the only hope these women have for justice."

Sam's pacing stopped just long enough to give her a look that was pure loathing. "Don't do that."

"Sam," the captain said with a frustrated sigh, like Sam was the one being unreasonable here, "I know what I'm asking for here isn't easy. But can you appreciate that it's not easy for me, either? This situation is a political disas—"

"No," Sam said sharply. Placing their hands on her desk, they leaned in to look Donovan right in the eye so she could see the anger written in every line of their body. "Don't pretend this is hard for you. You aren't the one getting screwed over after carrying this entire goddamned department on your back for eight fucking—"

"That's enough, Detective," Captain Donovan snapped. "You want to be mad about something?" She jabbed her finger at the folder splayed open on the desk between them. "Be mad at the bastard who's out there killing these women. But if you think you can talk to me like that, you can get out of my office right now."

"Yeah. That's probably for the best," Sam said with disgust. They were halfway to the door before she had even finished speaking. "I'd hate to say something I might actually regret."

CHAPTER FOUR

Sam shouldered their way through the rooftop door hard enough to smash the doorknob into the opposite wall. There was already a deep crack in the concrete, no doubt from years of pissed-off police officers taking their frustration out on this escape hatch.

Breathing hard from their rapid climb up the thirteen flights of stairs, they put their hands on their hips and shut their eyes. The burning in their lungs did nothing to chase away the smell of lavender oil or the sound of Captain Donovan's words echoing in their head.

Goddammit. They should have quit this job a long time ago. All the pain, all the sweat, all the years of relentless hard work they had given this city, and they still couldn't give Sam the one tiny thing they asked for in return.

Trying to shake off the anger, they headed to the side of the roof and leaned out over the edge. They just needed to breathe. The sun beat down overhead, and a summer breeze curled through the sky as Sam forced the air in and out until they felt a little less like they might really lose it. They shut their eyes again and let the breeze wash over them. Even this far into the city, the wind still carried that teasing hint of sweet ocean air.

Maybe they were loopy from running up so many flights of stairs Maybe it was all the cigarette butts and fast food wrappers up here reminding them that they were well on their way to becoming just one more in a long line of washed-up detectives with barely a shred of dignity left to their name by the time they retired. Either way, Sam found themself reaching into their pocket for their phone.

Teddy: question of the day
Teddy: if I told you I was going to be in the city for a client meeting tomorrow afternoon, would you want to meet up after?

Sent five days ago. Sam had probably read that text a hundred times in the past week but never had managed to figure out a good response. The window for saying yes had long since passed, but since they hadn't actually said no, either, they were kind of stuck now.

So that was the end of that—no more casual good morning texts, no more of his funny little anecdotes or occasional updates on whatever art piece he was currently working on. Definitely no more of his cute daily questions or invitations to "meet up" when he was around.

It was for the best. It wasn't like anything was ever actually going to happen between them.

Sam: If someone asked you to undo years of hard work, but it meant potentially saving lives, would you do it?

Stupid. So stupid. Why did they do this to themself?

Sam stared down at their phone screen for a long minute before sighing in disgust and letting it drop to their side. They should chuck it over the ledge. Maybe then they'd have a good excuse for bailing on this case. Couldn't use a dating app if they didn't have a phone, right?

"You good?"

Sam went rigid at the sound of another familiar voice. They turned and saw the woman posted silently up against the far wall, a lit cigarette in hand.

Apparently they really had offended God by going to the church today. That was the only conceivable reason they could think of for why Donya would be here, now of all times, after they hadn't crossed paths personally or professionally since she ran point for the research team on the Paradiso case.

Evidently, Sam needed to be humiliated in front of every woman they had ever slept with in their entire life before this hellish day would finally be over.

"Sorry," Donya said, quirking a thin eyebrow at whatever she saw on Sam's face. Nodding at the phone in their hand, she added, "Just looked like you were thinking about tossing that."

Sam considered the other woman for a moment, and Donya didn't flinch away from their stare. Not that she was the flinching kind. She bore her cool confidence like a suit of armor. She wasn't unlike Sam in that way. It was the kind of armor you had to develop when you weren't the sort of person who was good at "staying under the radar." And Donya, with her short, stocky build, combat boots, and collage of distinctly sapphic designs inked across her pale skin, clearly had no interest in playing it subtle.

"Yeah. Might have been," Sam finally admitted before allowing themself to slump against the guardrail. Sighing, they tipped their head back and said, "Honestly, I still might."

There was a pause, then the sound of footsteps crunching across gravel. Sam caught a glimpse of white-blonde hair out of the corner of their eye as the other woman silently settled in beside them.

"You want?" Donya's hand rested casually against the metal railing between them, the smoldering cigarette balanced between her fingers.

Sam rolled their head to the side to stare at the tempting little stress reliever for a long, long moment before finally shaking off the weakness.

"No thanks. Quit a long time ago."

Donya shrugged easily and said, "Yeah, me too," before raising the cigarette to her lips and taking a drag. Blowing out a long stream of smoke, she said, "Yet here we are anyways."

"Here we are anyways," Sam agreed, their lips quirking into a wry smile. "So, I know why I'm up here. Question is, what are you hiding from, Detective Novikoff? The boys on Vice already making you regret jumping ship?"

Donya scoffed at the teasing way they said her new title. "So you hot shots up in Homicide do get the news."

"I kind of didn't believe Vince when he told me," Sam admitted before glancing curiously over at the other woman. "What'd he do to make you flip?"

"Maybe we're sleeping together. That's the rumor I keep hearing," Donya muttered around her cigarette, and then grinned a little at the sound of Sam's startled laughter. "Nah, you know how it is. Just needed out from behind the desk. Vince is a pain in the ass, but the rest of Vice really isn't so bad." Taking another drag on the cigarette, she grimaced and added, "Obviously getting out of the office makes it easier to pick up old habits, but it's better than looking at blood samples all day."

"That's too bad," Sam said, and Donya gave them a questioning look. Shrugging, they said, "It was nice having someone in the lab who didn't take a million years to process every sample."

"Are you kidding me? That crap still took forever," Donya said, rolling her eyes. Sam had always privately thought, despite her tough-chick aesthetic, that those baby-blue eyes and her short stature made her look like an adorable doll.

"Yeah? Then how come I always got my stuff back so fast?" Sam asked with a knowing smirk.

"Simmer down, Supercop," Donya said, blowing out another stream of smoke, directly in Sam's face this time. "Your stuff just got expedited because you're currently the least terrible detective on Homicide. And that's not saying much."

"Yeah, I guess every department's got its gems," Sam agreed with a sigh, any levity instantly evaporating as they remembered the shit show that was waiting for them back downstairs.

"So what's got you so pissed off, huh?" Donya asked abruptly. She dropped the remains of her cigarette to the gravel and ground it out with the toe of her boot. "I didn't think you were capable of losing your temper, so I'm guessing it must be pretty bad to have you this worked up."

"I'm not worked up," Sam said reflexively.

Donya shot a disbelieving look at the phone they were still clenching in a death grip.

Grimacing, Sam said, "All right, I may have lost my temper a little. It's just a case Donovan wants me on."

"Must be some case."

"Yeah, it's some undercover nonsense." Sam gave a helpless laugh and shook their head. "She wants me to use a dating app to 'subtly investigate' a recent string of stabbings."

"A dating app?" Donya said, scrunching her face up in that way people do when they've had one too many negative experiences navigating the world of online dating. "That seems a little . . . "

"Yeah."

"So, what, you've got to go on these dates or turn in your badge?" she asked.

Sam shrugged, although that had been the implication.

"Damn. How'd you get the short straw? You the only single person left on the floor or something?"

"No," Sam said shortly.

"So you're not single anymore, or . . . ?"

"No—I mean, yes, I am single. I meant that wasn't why she pulled me for this." Seeing that Donya wasn't connecting the dots, they sighed and glanced down at themself pointedly before saying, "She needs someone who will interest the suspects."

"Oh shit," Donya breathed, recoiling a little at the not-so-subtle implication. "You serious?"

Sam nodded. They weren't sure they could trust themself to say more without losing it again. Not that checking their temper all these years seemed to have accomplished much, since they were still being served the same garbage they'd been treated to for the last four decades of their life.

"Well, fuck that."

Sam looked up in surprise.

Donya's expression was hard with an anger that was all too familiar as she stared out at the city. "I say you tell her to go to hell. See how she likes her star detective putting in a transfer to Vice."

"Vince would love that," Sam scoffed, as much because it was a ridiculous thought as to hide the way Donya's bold suggestion made their chest constrict with longing.

Sam was a homicide detective. They knew that. They had been made for this kind of work. Driven, observational, levelheaded, and willing to do what it took to get the right guy without losing their mind in the process. But god, some days it felt like it would be so much easier to just do something else.

"I'm being serious," Donya said, seeing the resigned look on their face. "You have a choice, Sam. You don't always have to be the hero."

"Sure. I'll think about it," Sam said agreeably.

Donya shook her head in disbelief. "Masochist," she muttered, pushing off the railing and heading for the stairwell. She wrapped one hand around the doorknob, then hesitated. She turned back and gave Sam a long, searching look.

"Hey," she said, nodding toward the phone still clutched in Sam's hand. "You still got my number in that thing?"

"Uhh, probably?" Sam said a little too honestly, not having expected the question and not at all sure how to respond. Not that getting drunk and fooling around after the holiday party hadn't been fun and all, but it wasn't exactly an experience Sam was looking to repeat while sober. "I'm, uh, not really—"

"Yeah, yeah, keep it in your pants," Donya interrupted, looking embarrassed enough for both of them. "I just meant if you're going to keep working with these assholes and you ever need to blow off some steam . . . " She shrugged uncomfortably and said, "You can talk to me. That's all."

"Oh," Sam said eloquently, because they weren't really sure what else to say when being propositioned for . . . friendship?

"Jesus. Don't pull a muscle. Just trying to be nice," Donya grumbled, then threw the door open so she could disappear down the stairwell before things could get any more awkward.

Sam watched her go, feeling a little lost, a lot confused, and sort of seen in an uncomfortable way. But weirdly a little bit better than they had five minutes ago.

The phone in their hand buzzed, and they glanced down in surprise.

Teddy: something crazy that might save lives, huh?
Teddy: not sure I'm that brave. but it sure sounds like something you would do
Teddy: :)

Sam sighed as they read over his response for the first of what would no doubt be an embarrassing number of times. Yeah, they were definitely feeling a little too seen right now.

The thirteen flights of stairs back down to the third floor felt twice as long as they had on the way up, but Sam kept putting one foot in front of the other, just like they always did.

Not wasting any time or giving themself a chance to change their mind, they made a beeline for the office at the end of the hall and knocked twice before entering.

Captain Donovan looked up in surprise.

"Detective," she said a little stiffly, inclining her head. "How can I help you?"

Walking over to her desk, Sam picked up the file and felt the heft of the three women's lives within. Just pictures on pieces of paper and bodies in the morgue now. But they had been real people with families and friends who loved them, all of whom deserved real justice. Even if that justice came at the cost of Sam's dignity.

Turning to face the other occupant of the room, Sam gave themself half a second to accept the absurdity of the situation before saying, "Detective Mariano and I can meet you at your office tomorrow morning to go over the case details. If that would be convenient for you, Mrs. Fox."

"Sure. I can make that work," Vivienne said without hesitation. Standing from her seat gracefully, she reached into the pocket of her dress and pulled out a matte business card. "There's the address. The number is for my operations manager, Beck. She can buzz you in when you arrive."

"Great," Sam said, tucking the card into their own pocket. Turning back to the desk, they nodded shortly and said with exaggerated politeness, "Captain Donovan."

The captain returned their nod, although she didn't look thrilled about it, as they took their leave again.

"Detective Sam?" Vivienne called after them, and Sam paused.

Their eyes met over Sam's shoulder, and a thousand unsaid things passed between them. Few of them pleasant.

Gesturing to the file tucked under Sam's arm, Vivienne said, "Thank you. For doing this. And . . . I'm sorry."

"Don't be," Sam said coolly, already turning their back on her again. "I'm just doing my job."

CHAPTER FIVE

Sam should have just turned on the TV. Or picked up that book they'd been meaning to finish for the last five years. Or gone to buy some goddamned cigarettes—really, anything other than this would have been a better use of their time.

But instead, they just sat there and read his text for the five hundredth time and hated themself a little more for it.

Teddy: something crazy that might save lives, huh?
Teddy: not sure I'm that brave. but it sure sounds like something you would do
Teddy: :)

It was the stupid smiley face. They had convinced themself if he just hadn't included the smiley face, they would have been able to ignore the message, but now they had to read it again because what was that supposed to mean?

Did he like that they were the type of person who would blow up their own career to save lives? Did he think that was brave? Attractive? Or just deeply stupid? Because Sam was feeling deeply stupid right now.

Groaning, they let their head fall back against the couch cushions. They were way, way too old to be obsessing over this kind of thing.

Scrolling back through their conversation history, Sam saw the last two weeks of casual texting flash by. Lots of good mornings, how are yous, charming daily questions about their various likes and dislikes—it was all fun and friendly, but that was all it was. Then his unexpected text about being in town, and radio silence ever since.

It was so stupid. If they had known they were still going to be thinking about this a week later, Sam would have just said yes and met up with him at some cheap motel so they could bang this weird little crush out of their system.

But of course they wouldn't have done that, because they already knew they were way too into him, and that was the whole reason they hadn't answered his booty call in the first place. How were they supposed to treat him like he was one of their usual hookups when they could barely have a real conversation with the guy over text message?

They should cut this thing off before they let themself get hurt. One scorching-hot night, seven great days of post-concussion companionship, and a couple weeks of friendly texting was probably the best outcome they could hope for. Pressing their luck could only lead to disaster.

Sam: Hey.

Teddy: hey

But then, what was the harm in a little disaster when he was willing to text back so quickly?

Sam: Sorry about the weird question earlier.

Teddy: does that count as your question of the day?

Sam: Pretty sure I have at least five of those banked.

Teddy: oh so THAT'S why you've been ignoring me
Teddy: saving up for a full interrogation, I see

Sam couldn't help laughing at his playful way of not letting them off the hook for ghosting him. Maybe they should have found his coyness more immature than charming—but even after weeks of texting they still found almost everything he did embarrassingly appealing.

Sam: Not ignoring. Just busy.

Teddy: busy with what?

Sam: Work stuff.

Teddy: is it a big case?

Sam: Yes.

Teddy: do you want to talk about it?

Teddy: assuming from your text earlier that it's not a FUN big case . . .

Sam: Wish I could, but it's confidential.

Teddy: I won't tell anyone if you don't

Sam: Why don't we stick with questions and answers?

Teddy: ok
Teddy: question of the day – what's the case you're working on?

Sam: Teddy . . .

Teddy: Sam :)
Teddy: should I try a different question?

Sam: Only if you actually want an answer

Teddy: hmm. ok
Teddy: how do you feel about pets?

Sam: Pets?

Teddy: like dogs, cats, goldfish
Teddy: do you like them?

Sam: I barely have time to feed myself. Definitely no pets.

Teddy: but do you LIKE them
Teddy: don't say you never thought about it
Teddy: I already know you had a dog growing up

Sam: Poor Snowball. RIP.
Sam: Death by tractor is no way to go.

Teddy: are you serious?
Teddy: that's so messed up
Teddy: did you grow up on a farm or something?

Sam: That's another question.

Teddy: I thought I had five banked?

Sam: No. I have five banked. Your questions expire.

Teddy: you know you can just say so if you want me to text you more

Sam: Maybe I want you to text me less.

Teddy: doubt it

Sam: Someone's getting cocky.

Teddy: you're the one still flirting instead of answering the question

Sam: OK. I think pets are fine, but I also think anyone who gets a pet knowing it's going to die eventually is a masochist.

Teddy: that's so dark
Teddy: I think the tractor traumatized you

Sam: You'd think, but weirdly, it's the smell of caramel corn that really reminds me of that day . . .

Teddy: now you're messing with me for sure

Sam: Maybe.

Teddy: you totally did grow up on a farm, didn't you?
Teddy: come on, just tell me
Teddy: tell me
Teddy: tell me
Teddy: tell me
Teddy: tell me
Teddy: tell me
Teddy: tell me
Teddy: tell me
Teddy: tell me

Sam: Has anyone ever told you that you are annoyingly persistent?

Teddy: has anyone ever told you that you are incredibly stubborn?
Teddy: it's really a very attractive quality
Teddy: tell me pleeeease?

Sam: That can be your question tomorrow.

Teddy: fine. I'll text you at midnight

Sam: I bet you will.

Teddy: are you going to ask me a question? or are you still too busy working?

Sam: I think I might have really offended you this time.

Teddy: why would I be offended by you ghosting me for a whole week after I asked you out?

Sam stared at the phone, their gut twisting with a potent mix of anxiety and intrigue. It was one thing to know he had been hoping to hook up when he was in town. It was another thing to think he was genuinely disappointed that they hadn't taken him up on the offer.

Sam: Sorry.
Sam: I'm just bad at this stuff.

Teddy: saying yes to dates?

Sam: That too. But I more meant the small talk.

Teddy: nobody said it had to be small
Teddy: ask me something profound

Sam: Not sure I'm any better at profound.

Teddy: don't know until you try . . . :)

Sam: OK . . .
Sam: What's the story behind your tattoo?

Teddy: which one?

Sam: Left shoulder.
Sam: The stained-glass heart.

Teddy: who says the story is profound?

Sam: I find it hard to believe any art you put on your body isn't meaningful.

Teddy: and you said you were bad at this <3

Sam: So that one is special?

Teddy: you could say that. it was my first
Teddy: why do I feel like you already knew that?

Sam: It was more worn down than the rest.

Teddy: damn
Teddy: you really never miss anything, do you?

Sam: I've seen you naked. Kind of hard to miss things.
Sam: Or to forget.

Teddy: Detective Sam.
Teddy: I really think you might be flirting with me.

Sam: And if I am? You've seen me naked, too.

Teddy: believe me, I remember
Teddy: often
Teddy: ;)

Sam: I'm still waiting on this profound story.

Teddy: I know
Teddy: I'm trying to figure out how to put it into words

Sam: That sounds like something an artist would say.

Teddy: I feel VERY called out
Teddy: ok, how about
Teddy: at that age, I really felt like my heart was made of broken pieces
Teddy: between school and parents and all the other paradiso bullshit, life really sucked for a minute after I was outed
Teddy: but it also felt beautiful somehow
Teddy: so I drew up my stained glass heart and put it on my sleeve
Teddy: it was like a dare to the world to try and break me
Teddy: it could only make things more beautiful

Sam: That's cute.

Teddy: cute?
Teddy: sam, you're really bad at this

Sam: Isn't that what I said?

Teddy: it's ok
Teddy: I like it
Teddy: makes my moves look extra smooth ;)

Sam: Good night, Teddy.

Teddy: night sam <3

CHAPTER SIX

"Hello, and welcome to Paths. You've reached Beck Fisher. How can I help you find your way today?"

Sam looked down at their phone in disbelief. The voice on the other end of the line sounded like it belonged to a sixteen-year-old hopped up on too much ADHD medication. Nobody should be that cheerful before 10 a.m. Although, considering the steel monolith they were standing outside of emblazoned with the words Paths of Love in neon light strips, Sam really shouldn't have expected anything less.

"Hello?" the voice repeated, and Sam shook their head before lifting the phone back to their ear.

"Yeah, this is Detective Sam. I have a meeting with Vivienne Fox?"

"Of course, Detective. Please come right up to the tenth floor. Feel free to take a welcome basket from the front desk."

Sam hung up the phone as the door in front of them unlocked with a gentle sound like a wind chime. Even the security measures around here were way too cutesy for Sam's comfort.

Opening the door, they gestured for Noah to enter first.

He made it exactly one step inside the building before he stopped to stare wide-eyed at the grandiose reception hall within.

"Holy shit. This place is fuckin'—"

Noah cut himself off as Sam gave him an exhausted look.

43

The only rules in the car this morning had been no talking until Sam finished their morning coffee and to keep his language clean once they got to the client's offices. Now he had managed to fail at both.

"Let's get this over with," Sam muttered, feeling a headache tugging at the edges of their brain just standing under all this fluorescent lighting.

"Which path do you think we take?" Noah asked. He looked down at his feet, where a dozen cheerful prints cut the tile floor into paths that directed visitors to different services.

"The one that takes us to the elevators," Sam replied bluntly. They intentionally avoided any of the colored tiles as they strode toward the elevator bank on the far side of the room.

Noah, on the other hand, followed the complicated blue chevron path with great concentration as it took him by the front desk with the welcome baskets before looping him all the way back around to the elevators.

"What?" he asked as he clutched the cellophane-wrapped basket to his chest like he thought Sam was going to take it away from him. "I haven't had breakfast."

Sam just shook their head and jabbed number ten. Since he had managed one whole sentence without cursing, they decided to take the win.

Unlike the reception hall, the tenth floor was tastefully decorated if you were into that ultra-modern, minimal aesthetic. The woman sitting behind the desk popped up like a cheerful jack-in-the-box the moment the elevator doors opened. She looked like a real-life doll in her powder-blue jumpsuit, which stood out in sharp contrast to the muted colors in the room.

"Detective Sam, Detective Mariano," said the woman, presumably Beck, with the same bright enthusiasm Sam had heard over the phone. Stepping up to shake each of their hands in turn, she added, "It's so good to meet you both. I'm the director of operations and client relations, Rebecca Fisher. But please just call me Beck."

"Operations and client relations?" Sam accepted her surprisingly firm handshake.

"It's a mouthful, I know. It really just means I handle the day-to-day stuff," Beck said with an easy laugh. "With a boss as brilliant as Viv, someone's got to remember to actually pay the power bill, right?" When Sam didn't seem amused, Beck cleared her throat and said, "Speaking of Vivienne, she's ready for you in the situation room."

"Situation room?" Noah looked to Sam for clarification.

Sam just shook their head. They knew at this point not to expect anything other than over-the-top drama. That was the Vivienne they knew.

Following Beck, they made their way down a small hallway that led to what appeared to be a large, conventional boardroom. Or it used to be, before it had been transformed into some kind of spy bunker mixed with a Macy's. There were screens on every surface, what smelled like a fresh coat of dark paint, and high-backed office chairs that would have looked more at home in a villain's secret headquarters than in this painfully cheerful building.

By contrast, there were at least three floor-to-ceiling shelves of shoes in every style you could imagine, and another corner was dedicated to clothing racks with approximately five million too many girly-looking outfits for Sam's comfort. Next to the gilded tri-fold mirror and fitting pedestal, there was also a bookshelf full of self-help titles that embarrassed Sam just to look at.

And seated at the head of the table was Vivienne Fox, looking positively radiant in her white suit, with her natural hair arranged like a lion's mane around her slender shoulders. Her lips pulled into a coy smile as the powerful smell of lavender oil punched Sam in the gut for the second time in less than twenty-four hours.

Jesus Christ. She had to be doing that on purpose.

Uncrossing her long legs, Vivienne drew herself to her feet. "Detective Mariano," she said, taking Noah's hand.

Noah looked like he was working hard not to drool as he gazed up at the incredibly tall businesswoman.

"Sam," she said.

Sam shook her hand, working equally hard not to roll their eyes at the way she said their name with such familiarity. So annoying. Not to mention unprofessional. And yet Sam's pulse still skyrocketed like they were nineteen again when she gave them that knowing smile.

"Vivienne," they said stiffly, deciding it was a waste of time to play at formalities. Dropping her hand, they said, "Do you have something for us to look at, or is this setup just for fun?"

She blinked her long lashes slowly in response to Sam's cold tone before offering an elegant half-shrug and saying, "Of course. If you'll look over here, I've gathered all of the information as requested."

Gesturing to the bank of monitors on the wall, she picked up a remote control and brought the screens to life. The faces of the three victims lit up, along with their dating profiles and a collection of fastidiously labeled files covering everything from "chat history" to "location data."

"Yo, that's sick," Noah said, circling around the boardroom table to take in the massive wall of information.

Sam sighed at the sound of his special brand of enthusiasm.

"What?" he demanded, gesturing to the large screens. "Even you have to admit this is a wet dream for the research department. There's enough information here to predict what these girls ate for breakfast every morning. Cross-referencing their dating history to find a killer is going to be a piece of cake."

"Unfortunately, if your research department wants to look at any of this information, they'll have to come here," Beck said from the doorway. Turning the tablet in her hands toward the two detectives, she said, "Actually, I'll have to ask both of you to sign release forms as well, stating that you won't share or make copies of any of our clients' personal information."

Seeing the frown on Sam's face, Vivienne quickly interjected. "Beck is right. We've already discussed the situation at length with your captain. The privacy of our clients is our number-one concern. Although we want to assist the investigation in any way we can, we can't put their private information at risk."

"You mean you can't risk having your clients realize that all of their data is being sold to the highest bidder," Sam scoffed, and Vivienne's polite expression hardened by a fraction.

"We don't sell anyone's information," she said, and Sam could tell that their words had really touched a nerve. "We keep it for exactly this situation. We have a dedicated team working 24/7 trying to follow up on reports of any inappropriate behavior. Checking app history after a complaint is one way we help resolve issues and remove any abusive users from the app."

Considering her for a long moment, Sam finally nodded in acceptance. They took the tablet from Beck, scrolled to the bottom of the screen, and entered the three letters of their name before scribbling out an equally short signature.

"Um, sorry. Could I get a last name?" Beck asked with strained politeness as Sam attempted to return the tablet.

"It's just Sam," they said flatly, releasing the tablet so she either had to take it or let it drop to the floor. Turning back to face the monitors, they said, "All right. Show me the vics. And tell me why you've got Donovan so convinced that these cases are all related."

"The most recent victim was Alicia Hancock," Vivienne said. She hit the remote again to bring Alicia's profile front and center. "Thirty-one years old and originally from Atlanta, Georgia. She missed her managerial shift at the bank the day after the attack, which was what prompted the initial search."

"She bled out on the way to the hospital?" Sam asked, quietly committing the young woman's face to memory.

According to Alicia's profile, she loved pugs, *Ru Paul's Drag Race*, eating way too much sushi, and a good game of tennis. And she also wanted to find a partner to spend her life with. All things women in this city should be able to pursue without fearing for their lives.

"Yes," Vivienne confirmed. "Her sister, Natasha Hancock, was the one who initially reported the situation to us. Of course, we covered all of the family's funeral expenses and offered trauma counseling services, but nobody is going to feel comfortable until the person responsible is behind bars."

"And the other two?" Sam asked. If Vivienne thought she was going to get a pat on the back, she was mistaken.

"About two weeks ago was Nikki Russo."

The image onscreen switched to feature a slightly older-looking woman. Everything about her, from her ink-black hair and ultra-thin frame to her pale skin and full tattoo sleeves, screamed that she was not a chick you wanted to mess with.

Sam's observations were interrupted by the sound of a loud bang followed by an even louder curse. Sam turned to raise an eyebrow at their young rookie and the tablet he had just managed to fumble onto the conference room table.

"Sorry," Noah mumbled as Beck quickly snatched up the tablet and checked it for damage. "I'm just, uh, surprised, I guess." Gesturing sheepishly to the dead woman on the screen, he said, "Doesn't look too much like the other chick. Aren't serial killers supposed to have a type?"

"Nobody said serial killer," Sam said, turning back to look at Nikki's sparse profile, which included such intimate and lavish details as "employed" and "30+," compared to the essay spilling off Alicia's page.

"But he is right that these two don't seem to have much in common besides their cause of death."

"Not on the surface," Vivienne said, bringing up the final girl's profile. "The third girl, Cassie Adelaide, helps bridge the gap a little."

"Right. She's the one from six weeks ago," Sam said, nodding as the bright-eyed blonde woman with the toothy grin took up the screen. Despite the crucifix hanging around her neck, Cassie shared Alicia's sharp business-chic style and Nikki's short haircut. Not exactly the damsels in distress one might expect on a case like this. "They found her in the dumpster on Sixth Street," Sam recalled. "No phone or ID, either."

"She was also the director of publicity for a local non-profit and liked volunteering at her church's food bank on the weekends," Vivienne's dark eyes reflected the light from the screen. "In case you wanted to know more about her. Before she became a murder victim, I mean."

"OK," Sam said, taking note to be a little more tactful in their analysis going forward. Regardless of any personal issues they may have with Vivienne, she obviously cared about these women who had died, presumably while using her app.

"Church volunteering aside, we have a few commonalities," Sam observed. "The missing cell phones and wallets could indicate a mugging gone wrong, as we originally assumed with Ms. Adelaide, or it could just be the perpetrator's attempt to cover up the real reason for the murders. And, of course, all three were stabbed multiple times with what appears to be the same or a similar weapon." Hesitating slightly, Sam frowned and then added, "They've got some aesthetic similarities, but that wouldn't be enough to convince Donovan that one person is responsible for all three deaths. So what's the connection? Dating history, or . . . ?"

"I got it," Noah blurted excitedly, and Sam turned, surprised to see him with his nose buried in the case file Sam had brought along from the office. Flipping rapidly through the pages, he nodded to himself before looking up with a victorious grin. "It's all in the time of death."

"Explain."

"Uh, really?" Noah's grin dropped now that all of the attention in the room had switched to him.

Sam gestured impatiently for him to go ahead.

Noah looked to Vivienne and asked, "Can we go back to Alicia's profile?"

Vivienne hit a button, and the first woman's picture reappeared on the screen.

"See this?" Noah said. "She was online and marked as active right up until 1:13 a.m. on June 14." He stepped around the table so he could point to the long string of timestamps filling the right column of Alicia's information log. "Even though there's no record of her going on a date that night or sending any messages, she still had the app open for some reason between 10:51 p.m. and 1:13 a.m. Then she goes offline." Raising the folder in his hand, he said, "According to the hospital, a street worker spotted her bleeding out in the alley and called the ambulance, but she was declared dead when the paramedics arrived at the hospital."

"Very good, Detective Mariano," Vivienne said, and he looked a little too pleased with himself when she gave him a warm smile. Pulling up Nikki's profile, Vivienne pointed to her activity log and said, "We noticed the same thing with Ms. Russo's history. Online but not active on the app from 9:27 p.m. until 11:46 p.m. on the night of her death, June 7. Then she abruptly signs off."

"And the coroner put time of death between 11:30 p.m. and 12:15 a.m.," Noah said, skimming one finger down the file in his hand until he found the information and nodded in confirmation. "So not only were they using the app at the time of their deaths—"

"But they went offline almost immediately after the stabbings took place," Vivienne confirmed.

"Right," Noah said with growing excitement. "So that was when the cell phones were stolen. The killer must have taken them right off the bodies and destroyed them to cover up whatever he was doing with the app to lure out his victims."

"Seemingly."

"What?" Some of the brightness faded from Noah's smile as Sam spoke up for the first time.

"I said seemingly," Sam repeated calmly. "As in *seemingly* that must be what happened."

"But it makes perfect sense!" Noah protested.

"It's a good theory," Sam agreed with an easy shrug. "But what about Cassie? She's marked as online not long before her time of death, but then idle for another 24 hours after her final message was sent. That sounds more like a phone with a drained battery than a phone that was purposefully destroyed."

"Maybe the killer hadn't realized he needed to destroy the cell phones yet," Noah suggested, even as Vivienne flipped back to Cassie's profile, revealing the broken pattern in her timestamps. "She was his first kill. Her cell phone wasn't with her body, so if he took it, maybe we could track—"

"Page 13," Sam said, gesturing to the folder.

Noah narrowed his eyes, then flipped through the folder. His eyes skimmed over the pages, until—

"Oh."

"What is it?" Beck asked, craning her neck to try and see inside the folder.

"Untraceable," Noah said, sounding disappointed as he shut the folder again. "She didn't have location tracking turned on, so we have no idea where the phone went after she was killed. Could have been five feet away from her the whole time, for all we know."

"Like I said, it's a good theory," Sam said, not unkindly. "She did open the app shortly before her time of death, despite weeks of inactivity beforehand. So I can see why Donovan is concerned that these three cases are tied up in all . . . this." They gestured vaguely to the building around them. "But there are still too many unknowns to start jumping to conclusions."

"Maybe we can help clear up some of those unknowns," Vivienne suggested. She placed the remote down on the conference table so she could focus her attention back on the detectives. "How familiar are you with the Paths app?"

"A little familiar," Noah admitted sheepishly.

Vivienne looked at Sam.

"Do I look like I use dating apps?" Even though they certainly had used dating apps before, Noah could learn a thing or two about the value of playing dumb.

"OK, since Sam's old school, we'll start with the basics," Vivienne said, reaching for a cell phone sitting in the center of the table. She showed them the little pink icon lighting up the screen. "The Paths app is, in many ways, like most dating apps. You create a profile, you answer questions, you provide basically as much information as you're comfortable sharing to try and attract a match." She opened the app. As it loaded, three new colorful icons popped up.

"Where things change is how you get those matches. Take Beck, for example. When she first interviewed for the Cupid Team, she was a huge skeptic."

"Honestly, my ex had just moved out, so I only went to the interview because I really needed the paycheck," Beck offered cheerfully. "At the time, I didn't feel like swiping right on random strangers just because they were handsome or whatever was going to help anyone find their soulmate. It certainly hadn't done me any good."

"Right. And that was a story I had been hearing for years," Vivienne said, and Sam could tell this was a speech she had given at a hundred investor meetings. "The point of Paths is to give our users options instead of a single method for finding love. If you want to scroll through profiles and message individual people based on your own research, you can do that. That's called the Smart Heart path. If you just want to see pictures of singles in your area and swipe right or left to indicate interest and unlock a conversation, you can go for the Swipe Right option. And if you'd rather have one of the Cupids on Beck's team do a deeper dive and use our advanced research methods to find you a solid match among our users, we can arrange for that, too."

"A 'Cupid'?" Sam asked, cringing a little at the cheesy name.

"The Cupids are what we call our research division," Vivienne said, completely undeterred by Sam's judgmental tone. "We have a 91% success rate for couples mutually deciding to pursue second dates after making a Cupid Connection. A solid 43% of Cupid users report being in a serious relationship three months after finding a match."

"Those are unparalleled numbers in this field," Beck added with real pride in her voice. "My team is really helping people find true love."

"That's . . . " Sam wanted to say "stupid." But considering that they were thirty-eight and the only hint of romance in their life was a text-based flirtation while Vivienne was wearing a diamond ring big enough to generate its own gravity field, Sam figured they should probably let her have this one.

"OK. That's interesting, I guess," Sam said. "But none of these women were using that service, right? The Cupid service?"

"Right, that's another thing they all had in common," Vivienne confirmed, turning back to the women on the screen. "They all went on a variety of dates and had a, ah, variety of things they were looking for in a relationship, I would say. But all three relied primarily on the Smart Heart method for finding their dates."

"OK. We should keep track of those similarities," Sam said. "Can you start a list?"

Vivienne nodded, picking up a tablet and opening a blank file on the screen so she could type up the notes.

"We know that they were all over thirty. All female."

"All cisgender, to be specific," Vivienne said, adding those items to the list. She hesitated slightly, and her eyes slid in Sam's direction before she added, "But Cassie did list herself as queer."

"OK, all cisgender," Sam said, ignoring Vivienne's pointed comment. "What was the job situation like across the board? You mentioned that Alicia was a manager at a bank and that Cassie was a director of publicity at a non-profit."

"I don't have access to their financial records, but Nikki listed herself as a business owner, and social media history would suggest none of them were hurting for money."

Vivienne opened a new folder and pulled up a series of photos, mostly selfies, showing the women in a variety of nice-looking outfits. Even tough chick Nikki was generally wearing something that would look more at home in a nice restaurant than the hot dog stand at Costco.

"Based on their chat history, I can say their dates were fairly typical for women in their demographic. Even first dates tend to get taken pretty seriously at a certain age. At the very least, I'd say all three tended to go for men who weren't allergic to a suit and tie."

"Any other commonalities stand out from the chat history?" Sam asked.

"Let's just say none of them were the type to go dutch," Beck interjected, and then flushed when Sam raised an eyebrow at her shrewd tone.

"Not—not saying they were pushovers or anything, but, you know. Kind of seemed like they were all playing to win."

Sam nodded their understanding, and Vivienne gave the long-suffering sigh of a woman who understood exactly what Beck was implying. Noah, on the other hand, was doing his best not to look completely lost at this point.

"She means they let the man take the lead," Vivienne explained, seeing that the poor kid was not following. "Let him make the first move, let him pick the restaurant, let him pay the bill."

Sam made a face at the thought.

"Most men don't like feeling emasculated on a first date. And given the financial status of these three, I'd say that was likely something they were all aware of."

"Because how dare women make their own money, right?" Beck added sarcastically. She looked to Noah and said, "you wouldn't believe the survey results when we ask men if they care how much their partner makes. Ridiculous, right?"

"Uh-uh," Noah said slowly, glancing between the two women and Sam. "You think I'm stupid? I know entrapment when I hear it. I'm staying out of this."

"So he is learning, after all," Sam said with a small grin before turning back to the women on the screen. "Speaking of dating history, are there any men that went out with all three of them?"

"That was one of the first things we checked," Vivienne said, pulling up yet another file. This one was a scary-looking chart attempting to organize a long list of names into different arrangements based on various factors. "There are a couple dozen who shared interactions with all three of them, whether it was a profile click, a short chat, or an actual date, but only three who ended up going on at least one date with all three of them."

"Great. Guess that's my shortlist," Sam said as Vivienne clicked a button and brought three names to the top of the list.

Brad Lu. Christian Kaufman. Jason Albertalli.

Not very murder-y sounding names, but if Sam had learned anything in this line of work, it was to spend less time trying to figure out who was and wasn't "capable" of murder and to spend more time figuring out what it would take to make a particular person snap.

"Now all you have to do is convince these men that you're a thirty-plus cisgender woman with a great sense of fashion and a decent amount of money in the bank, who also won't emasculate them on a first date," Vivienne said.

Sam stared at her balefully for a long moment, but she just stared right back, refusing to be cowed by their bad attitude. Finally, they said, "It's definitely going to be the 'over thirty' part that's hard to pull off."

That at least got a good laugh out of the room, even if it didn't ease the tension Sam was feeling.

"You can start by getting familiar with your profile," Beck said, pointing to the brand-new cell phone that Vivienne had placed back on the table. "Captain Donovan had that couriered over this morning. Your account is already set up to sync with the ops team back at your office so you can see all of 'your' conversations with the men and read up on any upcoming dates. You won't have to actually set up your own profile or, uh, proposition anyone."

"Great. The team can probably make up better answers than I can, anyways," Sam said.

They reached out to grab the phone, but when the app instantly burst to life with the sound of wind chimes, they were quick to put it back down. Yikes.

Glancing over at the fancy fashion setup at the far end of the room, they said, "I'm guessing you also need to measure me before I leave?"

"Unless you have a secret closet full of properly fitted, brand-name dresses, then yes," Vivienne said, seeing the way Sam looked uncomfortable at just the thought. "Old Navy isn't going to cut it for these dates, Sam."

"I'm not wearing any dresses," Sam said flatly.

Vivienne gave them that look that said they were being stubborn again, but Sam was unaffected. This was one thing they weren't bending on. Although they probably would have said the same thing about going undercover as a straight, cisgender woman twenty-four hours ago, so . . .

Sighing, Sam stood up and said, "Let's just get this over with."

"Uh, should I leave?" Noah sounded a little panicked as Sam started pulling off their tie without further ado.

"Relax, rookie," they said, throwing the tie down on the table and kicking off their shoes. "I'm not doing a striptease. She's just going to measure me."

Stepping up on the pedestal, Sam did their best to steel themself as Vivienne approached with the measuring tape. They stiffened the first time the tape pressed lightly against their arm, but otherwise managed to stay still as Vivienne stretched the tape from one shoulder to the other.

"Shoulders at eighteen inches," she said, and Beck quickly entered the information into a new file.

Sam closed their eyes as she wrapped the tape around their neck. Not because of how close she was standing—or not just because of how close she was standing. The idea of anyone keeping a detailed catalog of their bodily measurements in a file somewhere made them feel almost as queasy as the overwhelming smell of her perfume.

"Neck is thirteen and a half inches," Vivienne said, and Sam felt her move a little farther away before dropping the measuring tape to their waist.

"Waist is . . . " She hesitated, and Sam opened their eyes, looking down at the little tape measure she had wrapped around their midsection. Shaking her head in disbelief, Vivienne said, "Good god. Waist is 29 inches. How'd you get this skinny, Sam?"

"I don't know," they said, maybe a little more irritably than was warranted, but she should know better than to comment on that kind of thing. "How'd you end up so freakishly tall?"

"Good genetics. And really expensive shoes," Vivienne replied calmly. So maybe she had known what she was getting herself into.

Sam stiffened as she slid the tape up their body in one smooth movement.

"Arms up," she said, and they obediently spread their arms out to the sides.

The tape pulled tight around Sam's chest, and they focused their eyes on the trifold mirror propped up against the wall. Vivienne hesitated again, and this time Sam really did flinch at the feeling of her hand ghosting down their side.

"Are you wearing a binder?" she asked quietly, peering up at Sam with those dark, bottomless eyes.

"What? No. It's just—" They cut themself off, catching sight of Noah in the mirror, looking a lot like he'd rather die than be here at the moment. Scowling, Sam said, "It's just a normal bra."

Vivienne still hesitated. "Did you have a breast reduc—"

"No," Sam said sharply before physically removing her hand from their body. "I just . . ." They shook their head in frustration. "Whatever. How about we just not talk while doing this?"

Vivienne continued her measurements without any more running commentary on what she thought Sam's body should, or shouldn't, or used to look like. The silence in the room was stifling, interrupted only by the shift of the measuring tape against fabric and Vivienne announcing the occasional number.

Sam watched Noah growing more and more uncomfortable as the silence stretched on, and they hoped to god that when he broke it would be to share another annoying story about his weird family, and not anything too stupid.

"So are you guys, like . . . exes or something?" he finally blurted—and, yeah, that was pretty much what Sam had expected. Noah might be a junior detective, but he wasn't that naive.

"That's none of your business," Sam said firmly, at the same time that Vivienne said "Yes."

"Seriously, Viv?" Sam said with disgust as the other woman released the measuring tape and stepped down from the pedestal.

"I don't know what you want from me, Sam," Vivienne said, and somehow she managed to sound like the exasperated one, which was only more infuriating.

Stowing the measuring tape, she said, "You want to be mad at me, fine. But you also want me to pretend—what, that we've never met before?" Glancing sidelong at Noah, who had shrunk down in his seat, she added, "If you want to work this out like adults, I'd be more than happy to talk. But please don't expect me to read your mind."

Sam's vision flashed red at her condescending tone, and an old, familiar heat clawed its way up their throat. For half a heartbeat they were back in that sweltering kitchen with the broken AC unit, a pile of unopened bills on the kitchen table, and a crumpled napkin with ten digits written in smeared lipstick clenched in their fist. The thin walls of that sad apartment had stood no chance against the explosive fights that had filled its hallways, and Sam was sorely tempted to see if Vivienne's fancy new office would fare any better.

But that was then. And the Sam in that apartment was not the same Sam standing here now.

"Well?" Vivienne demanded, not seeming intimidated in the least by the anger radiating off of them. "What are we doing, Sam? Your choice."

Sam turned their head slightly to the side and managed to say, "Noah?"

"Uh, yeah boss?" Noah said awkwardly, having sunk so low in his chair that he was in danger of disappearing completely beneath the table.

"Go get me a coffee."

"Wha—"

"Come on," Beck cut in, saving Noah from accidentally setting off the nuclear explosion brewing in the room. Her forehead was creased in a deep frown, but she hustled over to his side and said, "Let's head down to the lobby for that coffee, OK?"

"Uh, yeah. OK," Noah said, slowly getting to his feet. Glancing uncertainly between Sam and Vivienne, he said, "I'll . . . meet you at the car with that coffee, yeah boss?"

Sam nodded once without looking in his direction. Beck's heels tapped rapidly against the tile as she ushered Noah out the door. A few seconds later her footsteps faded, and Sam was left alone in the room with their badge, their anger, and their least favorite ex-girlfriend.

"Well?" Vivienne repeated after a long moment of stewing in the silence. The defensiveness had faded from her voice, leaving her sounding more exhausted than anything else. "What are we doing, Sam?"

Sam tried to summon the right words, but as usual, they wouldn't come. They may have mastered the art of biting their tongue over the years, but they hadn't gotten any more eloquent in the process. They had plenty of other exes who could attest to that.

"Listen," Vivienne started. Sam stiffened before she could even get going, and Vivienne let out a long sigh. Dropping her gaze to the floor, she tried again. "Listen, I get it. You're mad at me. And—that's fair. More than fair. Please believe me when I say not a day has gone by that I haven't regretted the way things ended between us. But for the sake of the case, can we try to move past this? Professionally, at least?"

Sam blinked once, which was the only sign that they were still listening.

Vivienne's beautiful face twisted into a grimace, and she said, "I know it's been years. And I know it's too little, too late, but I really am sor—"

"Yes," Sam said abruptly, cutting off Vivienne's attempt at an apology. She gave Sam a confused look, and they repeated, "Yes. Let's move past it. Professionally." Sam's stance was rigid enough to snap, but their tone was perfectly calm.

". . . OK," Vivienne said slowly. "Do you want to talk about—"

"Let's set some ground rules." Sam's tone was clipped as they spoke right over her. Walking back over to the table to retrieve their tie, they wound the fabric tightly around their fist and said, "This is your workplace, which means it's also my workplace for the foreseeable future. So we'll keep things professional while we're here." Slipping their feet back into their shoes, Sam paused and then said, as clearly as they possibly could,

"Anything we knew about each other prior to twenty-four hours ago can stay outside of these walls."

"And when we're not inside these walls?" Vivienne asked.

Sam gave her a look filled with decades of unspoken resentment. Her gaze flitted away again, and Sam took that as their cue to head for the door.

"Sam," Vivienne called after them.

Despite their every intention to leave as fast as humanly possible, Sam felt their footsteps slowing to a halt at the soft, sad sound of her voice. It made them furious that it still gave them pause, even after all these years.

"I really would like to apologize. If not for everything else, then just for the fact that you got dragged into all this." Vivienne waved her hand vaguely, indicating the dresses and shoes at the far end of the room. Her voice was full of sympathy when she said, "I know it's not right. What they—we—are asking you to do. If I had known it would be you . . . I mean, I know how you feel about—"

"You don't know how I feel about anything," Sam said sharply. Turning back to face her, they made sure Vivienne could see exactly how serious they were when they said, "You don't know me at all. If you did, you'd know I don't want your apology. So let's both just do our jobs and be done with it, OK?"

"Sam," Vivienne tried again.

"OK?" Sam repeated, louder this time, in case she somehow had not gotten the message that they were done talking about this.

Vivienne was silent for a long moment as she took in the shuttered expression on Sam's face. They were sure she was remembering those volcanic summer afternoons just as clearly as Sam was in this moment.

For half a second, Sam felt a flash of sympathy for their younger selves. They had just been two broken kids clinging desperately to one another for survival in a world neither of them was equipped to handle.

But Sam was not in survival mode anymore, and the kindest thing they could do for those kids now was to leave them in the past.

"OK," Vivienne finally said, sounding at a loss. "If that's really what you want."

The sound of the door shutting behind Sam was the only answer they had for her.

CHAPTER SEVEN

Sam cursed under their breath when they exited the building and saw Noah leaning up against the side door of the old cruiser with an actual coffee in hand.

"Oh, hey. How'd that go?" he asked with forced cheer as Sam blew right by him.

Sam gave him a hard look that said exactly how it had gone before wrenching the driver's side door open and disappearing inside the car.

"Uh, Sam?" Noah said nervously. Rattling the handle, he leaned down to peer through the open window and said, "You going to let me in, or—"

"What the hell are these?" Sam asked abruptly, gesturing to the fuzzy objects hanging from the rearview mirror. Those definitely had not been there this morning.

"They're . . . dice," Noah said hesitantly, glancing at the red, green, and white cubes. "It's an old family superstition. Like, an Italian lucky charm or some shit, you know?" Sam gave him a disbelieving look, and he explained, "My great-great Nonno got them at a gas station on his way out of the city when he drove across the country to settle on this coast. He was always saying shit like, 'We are the only Italians in this godforsaken place, so we must—'"

"All right, enough," Sam snapped, and Noah's mouth shut faster than an Italian shop during riposo. Sighing, they raised one hand to press against their temple and said, "You know you can't be doing this stuff anymore, right?" Noah looked confused, and Sam gestured to the fuzzy dice impatiently. "You're a homicide detective now. You can't be showing up at crime scenes with crap like this."

"They're just dice."

"They're *Italian* dice," Sam corrected, their voice laced with frustration. "You need to understand that when you put on this badge people can't see you as an Italian guy with a job as a police detective. They need to see you as a police detective who happens to be Italian. No biases, no prejudices, no favoritism." When they looked at him, their expression was heavy with the day's events. "It's the job first," Sam said firmly. "Everything else comes second."

"I don't know about that," Noah said, glancing down at the shield on his belt uncertainly. "Seems like always putting the job first could lead to some pretty fucked-up situations."

"Yeah. It does," Sam agreed with a shrug, because there was no point in pretending otherwise after what Noah had seen back in that office. "But someone's got to do it. For them." They tapped one blunt nail against the case file tucked between the seats. "You have to decide if you want to be the nice guy with the fuzzy dice, or if you want to be the guy who can get the job done."

Noah considered this for a long moment, then reached through the window to pop the lock manually. Stepping into the car, he placed the coffee in the cup holder and then unhooked the dice from the rearview mirror. "Sorry, Nonno." He kissed each fuzzy cube once, opened up the glove box, and threw them inside before slamming it shut again.

Turning to face Sam, he said, "I think you're a crazy son of a bitch. But if you can put up with all that bullshit in there and still want to solve this case, maybe you're onto something." Then he shrugged and added, "Also, your ex-girlfriend is smoking hot, so points for that, too."

"Don't make it weird," Sam grumbled. They turned the car on and put it into gear.

"Copy that," Noah agreed cheerfully as they took to the streets. "Not making it weird."

They drove in silence for a few blocks. When they crossed the two-minute mark, Sam decided to take mercy on him.

"Tell me about the D'Angelo case," they said, and Noah let out a sigh of relief so massive Sam wondered if he had just been holding his breath to keep from talking the whole time. "You know the point of having a supervisor is so I can help you with this stuff, right? You're allowed to ask questions."

"Thank the fucking Lord," Noah said fervently. He reached into the bag shoved under his seat and pulled out a thin red file. "Have you seen this shit? It's just, like, total blank slate. How do you even know where to start?"

"What do you mean, start?" Sam asked, taking their eyes off the road for half a second to glance over at the rather meager-looking file he was holding up. "You should have a lot more than that by now."

"Seriously? It's only been twenty-four hours," Noah said a little defensively.

"So? I cracked the Paradiso case in forty-eight hours. And I had time to—well, let's just say I wasn't working the whole time." Pulling to a stop at the next red light, Sam reached for the folder. "Let's see this. Did you at least get the tox report back?"

"Oh yeah, that came in this morning. Should be at the back."

Sam flipped through to the printout at the "back" of the folder, if it could even be called that with so few pages inside.

"Get this," Noah said, clearly eager to prove that he had at least read the report. "The guy died from—"

"Cyanide poisoning," Sam read off the sheet. Raising an eyebrow as the light turned green, they tossed the folder back to him and said, "Congrats. Sounds like you've got yourself a real case of first degree."

"Not necessarily. Cyanide poisoning accidents do happen," Noah said, and when Sam seemed surprised, he added, "I did do some research, you know."

"Well?" Sam said with approximately zero sympathy for the rookie's petulant tone. "Go on, then. Tell me what you've found out so far."

"Uh, OK," Noah said, flipping open the folder again.

Sam worked hard not to react to his floundering. They knew from experience that ninety percent of being a good supervisor was just instilling a sense of confidence in the new recruits. But that was surely going to be difficult if this kid couldn't even do some basic googling without doubting his own results.

"Let's see. Um, cyanide is a super-famous poison, obviously," Noah said as he skimmed over his notes. "Kind of the comic book bad guy poison of choice, on account of the whole Nazi connection. But while it's most well known as a poison meant to, um, poison people, it also occurs naturally in some fruit pits and seeds. Although you'd have to eat something like forty apples to get cyanide poisoning that way, so unless the vic is a fuckin' horse, it'd be easier to get exposed to it through insecticides or metal polish. Obviously, if you're only exposed a little at a time, you'd only get sick a little at a time. But if you actually did get poisoned on purpose or decided to chomp through forty apples in one go, you'd get the vertigo, the flushed face, the puking, some nasty convulsions, and then . . . you know. The part where you die."

"Interesting," Sam said after waiting a beat to be sure he was finished with his report. "What do you make of all that?"

"Seems like a shit way to go," Noah said. He punctuated the blunt statement by slapping the folder shut.

"OK, but are you thinking accidental or intentional?" Sam pressed as they approached another intersection.

Weighing the options, they made a right and headed further away from the downtown core. The kid seemed like he could use a little extra motivation.

"It's gotta be an accident, right?" Noah seemed completely unaware that they were now traveling away from the precinct. "I mean, who the hell would poison someone with cyanide? Even if the guy didn't eat it in the middle of a parking lot, that's a massive red flag on any coroner report."

"If it was an accident, how did it happen?"

"Maybe the metal polishing thing? They've gotta have a lot of that fancy shit in a church, right?" The question in his voice suggested he wasn't so confident in the theory.

"Why didn't it affect anyone else at the church, then?" Sam asked. Questioning a rookie's theory was about as hard as finding holes in Swiss cheese. "And if it was a gradual poisoning from bad cleaning products, why did D'Angelo 'eat it' so suddenly on the day he died? Did he seem sick at all in the days prior to his death?"

"So . . . I shouldn't look into the metal polish," Noah said, sounding frustrated again.

"No, it's fine to pursue that angle," Sam corrected patiently. Almost patiently, at least. "You just can't pursue it blindly. Believe me, you don't want to wait until you're in the interrogation room with the wrong suspect to realize you missed something."

The streets around them were starting to look very familiar now. Or they would be, if Noah had bothered to pay more attention to his surroundings.

"What else do you have?" Sam asked.

"Uh, not much," Noah admitted a little sheepishly. "I was going to start with the metal polish angle and see where it went from there."

"Always be chasing multiple theories," Sam told him, feeling more than a little irked by Noah's lack of drive. For a guy who had made the time of death connection on the Paths case in under five minutes, this felt almost painfully lazy by comparison. "'Might be an accident' isn't a good reason to stop digging. Did he have enemies? Was there someone who would be motivated to make his death look like an accident?"

"Why would someone want to kill a priest?" Noah asked. He sounded disturbed by the mere thought.

"You wouldn't have a job if I could answer that question without doing any investigating," Sam replied shortly.

They pulled up outside the church. It towered over the car—dark, foreboding, and completely off limits to Sam. Any investigating that happened in there, Noah would have to do solo.

"A tox report can only tell you how someone died, not why they died," Sam told him, letting the engine idle. "You need to get off your ass and really start digging."

Noah was silent for once as he stared up at the church. There was a look on his face that Sam could only read as intimidation. They wanted to feel sorry for the kid, but sympathy wasn't in the cards today. Or most days when you were a homicide detective.

"Well?" Sam said impatiently, gesturing over at the church. "Just looking at it isn't going to get you anywhere. Get out and start doing your job."

"It's 11 a.m. on a Tuesday—hey!" Noah complained as Sam reached over to pop his seatbelt and then shove his door open. Taking the hint, he got out of the car, but then just stood there, looking between the car and the church uncertainly. "No one's going to be in there at this time of day," he insisted.

"Then head back to the station and start calling people at home," Sam said, not cutting him any slack. "Keep calling until someone picks up. Then set up some interviews. Don't even think about taking no for an answer."

"Are you fucking kidding me?" Noah demanded. His eyes were wide as he looked up and down the busy street. "It's a five-mile walk to the station from here."

"I guess you'll have lots of time to start working on some new theories," Sam said before reaching out to pull the passenger door shut.

"Is this another test?" Noah asked, bending down to look at them through the window. "Please tell me it's another test."

"It's not a test," Sam said. They put the car back in drive. "Consider it a lesson in taking this job a little more seriously." Leaning over so they could see his feet out the window, they raised an eyebrow and added, "Also a lesson in wearing appropriate footwear. Five miles isn't going to be fun in those shoes."

Noah watched helplessly as Sam peeled out of the parking lot fast enough to make the tires squeal against the pavement.

Sam glanced at him in the rearview mirror. He looked so pathetic standing there, backpack in hand, with nothing more than a lame little folder and no real clue about how to do this job.

Not that Sam hadn't told him exactly what he should be doing next. Not that his theories so far were even entirely terrible. He just lacked the confidence to put it all together without someone holding his hand the whole time.

Cursing under their breath, Sam eased up on the accelerator. They spotted a coffee shop up ahead, shot past, then pulled a quick U-turn so they could slip into an empty parking spot. Slamming the car into park, they sighed and sat still for a moment.

They could feel the frustration eating away at their insides. Partly with Noah for not trying harder. But also maybe just a little teeny-tiny bit with themself for letting this thing with Vivienne rattle them so much.

Knowing what they needed to do, but not wanting to face the music, Sam pulled out their phone.

Sam: Question of the Day: Is it a dick move if I make my rookie walk 5 miles for being lazy?

Sam couldn't help smiling a little when the typing icon immediately appeared on Teddy's end. Almost like he'd been waiting to hear from them.

Teddy: you're hilarious
Teddy: total dick move
Teddy: I love it <3

Sam: You're not supposed to love it. You're supposed to tell me I'm being a bad supervisor and to go easy on him.

Teddy: face it Sam
Teddy: only a good supervisor would worry about being a dick in the first place
Teddy: you're way too good of a person to actually torture that poor baby cop

Sam: Says who? I really did make him get out and walk.

Teddy: says me
Teddy: you're definitely going to go pick him up

Sam: Pass. He's not my type.

Teddy: ha ha. You're soooo funny

Sam: Damn. There go my dreams of being a standup comedian.

Teddy: question of the day
Teddy: if baby cops aren't your type, who is?

Sam: I'm pretty sure you already asked your Question of the Day this morning.

Teddy: put it on my tab
Teddy: I want to know

    Sam considered his text for a long minute. Just last week a cagey answer like that would have had Teddy backing off politely. But ever since their little texting hiatus, he had been noticeably bolder in his flirtations. Or maybe just not as willing to let them get away.

    And despite knowing it was a bad idea, Sam couldn't say they hated being pursued so determinedly.

Sam: I don't really have a type.
Sam: Physically.

Teddy: . . . but?

Sam: But I guess I don't mind people who are willing to call me out on my bullshit.

Teddy: that kid isn't even going to make it 1 mile before you show up to rescue him

Sam: Very subtle.

Teddy: really?
Teddy: my bad. I wasn't trying to be subtle
Teddy: ;) <3

Sam: I hope you realize that you're the one who's going to have to hear me complain about him.
Sam: If I decide to be nice and go get him.

Teddy: I hope you do
Teddy: I want to hear ALL the complaints <3

Sam shook their head before throwing the phone down in the cup holder. The really crazy part was, they were pretty sure Teddy meant it. He actually did want to hear them complain about their day. And that was just . . . not something Sam knew how to process right now.

But if Teddy wanted to listen to them complain, they might as well do something worth complaining about. It seemed like a better idea than telling him they were stuck working with their ex-girlfriend for the foreseeable future, at least.

Sam put the car in reverse and was just starting to back out of the parking lot when their pocket buzzed. They glanced down at their phone in the cup holder for a few seconds before they realized it was their other phone. The one for the new Paths case.

It buzzed again, then made that sound that was like wind chimes mixed with an overenthusiastic xylophone. Apparently, the ops team was already hard at work selling Sam to the highest bidder. Scowling into the rearview mirror, they pressed their foot back to the pedal.

One thing at a time. First, Noah. Then they could worry about how they were going to get through this investigation without losing their mind.

CHAPTER EIGHT

"Come on. Briefing time," Sam said.

Noah startled to attention at the sound of their fist knocking on his cubicle wall.

Raising an eyebrow at the ten whole words he had typed out on his computer screen, Sam said, "Seems like you could use a break from all that hard work."

"I don't need a break," Noah grumbled. He stretched out a kink in his neck and then lurched to his feet. "I need a real fuckin' lead."

"Witnesses not panning out?" Sam asked. It had only been a few days, but they already trusted him to follow as their footsteps traced the familiar path through the maze of cubicles carpeting the third floor.

"Can you call an old lady with more cataracts than cats a real witness?" Noah replied. When Sam just gave him a look in response to his whining, he sighed in defeat. "I don't know, man. This shit is just depressing. I still can't get over why someone would murder a priest."

"Maybe he was an asshole," Sam said bluntly.
Noah opened his mouth to protest, but Sam just waved his Catholic sensibilities away impatiently. Turning into the entrance of the break room, they grabbed a mug and filled it with stale coffee from the pot as they asked, "Well? Did all your witnesses agree that he was a saint, or what?"

"He was a priest," Noah insisted.

Sam stepped back out of the kitchenette without waiting to see if he wanted anything.

Noah hurried to keep up as Sam strode toward the elevators with steaming mug in hand. "I didn't think I needed to poll people on his personality."

"Well, there's your problem. Can't know motive if you don't know your vic." Sam took a sip from the mug and scowled at the taste. "For example, I'm going to murder whoever keeps making this watered-down crap."

"That'd be Sofía. She's still in her first trimester, and the smell was making her nauseous." When Sam gave him a surprised look, Noah just shrugged. "What? People tell me things."

"Maybe spend more time getting your witnesses to tell you something useful instead," Sam suggested.

Noah rolled his eyes at their typical warm and fuzzy attitude.

Jabbing the call button for the elevator, Sam took another sip and grimaced again. "Really? Sofía? Didn't she just get married?"

"Uh, like . . . two years ago, I think?" Noah said uncertainly.

"Huh. Good for her." Sam stepped onto the elevator and pressed the button for the fifth floor. They watched Noah fidget out of the corner of their eye. Despite their best efforts not to notice, they could see the kid was already starting to look like he could use a vacation. And he had barely dented his first case.

"Hey," Sam said abruptly as the elevator doors opened onto the fifth floor. "If this stuff is ever getting too heavy, let me know."

"Why, so you can tell me to suck it up?" Noah asked sarcastically.

The briefing room came into view at the end of the hall. With the blinds raised, Sam could see several people already gathered inside. The urge to disappear on a "vacation" of their own was overwhelming—and they'd been doing this a lot longer than Noah had.

Glancing at their young rookie sidelong, Sam considered the new circles under his eyes and said, "No. In case you need to talk to someone. I can recommend a few people who specialize in this sort of thing, if you ever need it."

"What, like some kinda shrink?" Noah asked, making a face that Sam was all too familiar with. "Uh, thanks, but . . . that shit's not for me."

"Glad you're feeling tough." Sam let their gaze track back to the briefing room and the four people already inside. Shaking their head, they reached for the door handle and muttered, "You're going to need it for this."

"Uh, what? Why?" Noah asked, but Sam was already pushing through the door.

"Nice of you to join us, Detective," Donovan said from her spot at the front of the room before Sam had made it two whole steps inside. Despite the fact that her eyes were glued to the phone in her hand, the captain didn't miss a single thing that happened in her briefing room.

A projector was connected to an open laptop on the desk in front of her. Detective Martin was bent so close to the screen that his bushy red mustache was catching the glow of the monitor. The pile of dirty laundry perched on the table beside him twisted to face the new arrivals, revealing itself to be a human being beneath layers of patchy leather and ragged denim.

"Sorry. Had to stop for some fuel," Sam said, gesturing with their mug before turning away from the three and making their way over to an empty seat on the far side of the room. Noah's footsteps followed faithfully in their wake.

"Hey," Donya said, nodding to them from where she lounged in her own seat a couple of feet from the laptop. Unlike Sam, she was smart enough not to seem completely standoffish—while still taking no interest in whatever her coworkers were gawking at on the screen.

"Hey," Sam replied, returning the nod.

Noah was looking around at all the new faces with curiosity, but Sam just took their seat in silence. They knew better than to think any sort of peace would last long in this room.

"Sammy! Our leading lady," the man perched next to Martin crowed cheerfully, as though he could hear Sam's thoughts.

Jumping down from the table, the man sauntered over to look at them with a grin that might have been charming twenty years ago. He had a thick layer of graying stubble and flat, shark-like eyes. Not many would mistake his leer for a friendly invitation these days.

Jerking his chin in Noah's direction, the man said, "Don't be rude. Aren't you going to introduce us?"

Despite the fact that the man was standing right in front of them, Sam's gaze was fixed somewhere on the hallway beyond. As far as they were concerned, anything they did have to say would be much ruder than saying nothing at all.

"Detective . . ." Donovan said warningly from her spot at the front, without so much as looking up from her email.

Sighing, Sam lowered their mug to the table. Pointing to the tough-looking blonde detective with the full body ink, Sam said, "This is Junior Detective Donya Novikoff." Looking to the man planted in front of their desk, Sam added in the same flat tone, "And this is her supervising officer, Detective Vince Renier."

"Oh, so you must be the new recruit on Vice Squad, yeah?" Noah said eagerly when Donya offered him the same cool nod she had given Sam. "Nice to meet another rookie."

"Uh huh. Likewise," Donya replied in a voice so drenched in sarcasm that even Noah couldn't miss it. If that wasn't clear enough, Vince's immature snicker certainly sold it.

"Ah, cut him a break. You know Sam probably didn't tell him shit," Martin said, although his expression looked more pitying than friendly in the face of Noah's naivete. "D's been in forensics since before you could drive, kid. She's not exactly your typical rookie."

"Exactly how old do you think I am, Martin?" Donya drawled, although she didn't seem ruffled in the slightest.

"I dunno. Forty?" Martin said with a shrug.

"Jesus. Forty? Do us all a favor and don't ever join forensics." Donya flashed those icy-blue doll eyes over Noah's slouchy clothes and nervous expression. "Even if I was forty, you'd still be wrong about him. Based on skin elasticity, I'd say this one's at least thirty-two, even if he does look like he still gets carded at the club." Flicking her gaze back to Sam, she asked, "What do you think, Supercop? Over-under on thirty-two?"

"Supercop?" Noah parroted, only looking more confused.

"I believe everyone is now acquainted," Sam said, looking pointedly over at Donovan to see if she was appeased yet.

"Not quite," Vince said. Circling around the table, he shoved his hand in Noah's face and offered that shark-eyed grin from about a foot away this time. "We still haven't been formally introduced to your new rook."

"Uh . . . OK," Noah said slowly. Accepting the greasy man's handshake with the appropriate amount of trepidation, he said, "Noah Mariano.

72

Homicide detective. Uh, junior homicide detective, I guess."

"Mariano, eh?" Vince said, looking the rookie up and down with enough sharp-eyed curiosity to have Noah looking properly uncomfortable.

"Keep holding his hand, and I'm going to think you want more than an introduction, Vince," Sam said, and both men jerked their hands back like Sam had tased them.

"Charming as ever, Sammy," Vince said with a curl to his lip that revealed the nasty edge beneath. "Tell me, are you planning to bore these guys into a confession, or are we supposed to believe you actually have a personality programmed somewhere in that circuit board?"

"Are we getting OT for this, or can we start sometime today?" Sam called to Donovan, who sighed loudly and finally stowed her phone.

"If you've got it out of your system," Captain Donovan replied, as if this little hazing session had somehow been Sam's idea. Focusing her weary eyes back on the laptop, she said, "Detective Martin? The screen, please?"

"Oh. Sure," Martin said, reaching for the keyboard a little too eagerly for Sam's liking. His fingers pressed a few buttons, and the projector came to life.

For a half a second there was silence as everyone in the room got a good look at Sam's Paths profile projected in 4K glory on the large screen at the front of the room. The profile showed one Samantha Ryder, whose coy smile was full of intrigue and whose profile was nothing short of saccharine.

It took about three seconds for Vince to break into loud, braying laughter while Noah nearly choked on his tongue. Even Donya had to duck her head to hide a grin at the description of "Samantha" as someone who "enjoyed long walks on the beach" and was "searching for her missing piece."

"Oh my god. Is that supposed to be you?" Vince demanded when he finally managed to stop laughing. Gesturing vaguely between Sam and the screen, he said, "Damn, Sammy. Do all these guys have brain damage or what?"

"Don't call me that," Sam forced out between gritted teeth.

"My bad, *Samantha*," Vince sneered.

Sam's hand clenched around the handle of their mug. They told themself sternly that they would not throw it at Vince's head. They would only picture it. In detail. At least until Donovan left the room.

"Are you finished, Detective Renier?" Donovan asked. She looked like she was regretting this career path a little more with each passing second.

"Come on, Cap," Vince said. He gestured emphatically to Sam's photoshopped face on the screen. "What guy is going to stick around when Sam shows up instead of that chick?"

Donovan sighed. "Mrs. Fox has already made the appropriate arrangements to ensure Detective Sam looks the part for her clients. I've been assured it won't be a problem." Glancing at the pretty woman in the profile picture and then back to Sam, she said a little more pointedly, "Isn't that right, Detective?"

Sam stared silently back at her with an expression that was pure loathing, but if the captain felt bad at all, she was doing a great job of hiding it.

"So that's Sam's profile. Who's the target?" Donya asked abruptly. Sam wasn't sure if she was taking pity on them or if she was actually bored with the briefing, but either way they appreciated the effort to move things along.

"Tomorrow's person of interest is Christian Kaufman," Donovan said, using the clicker to bring Christian's profile front and center.

"Ooh, restaurateur. And he likes dogs, too. What a catch," Vince goaded as Sam got a good look at their date for the first time.

Six foot one, with a generic smile and a severe widow's peak, Christian was dressed exactly the way you'd expect a self-proclaimed "amateur sommelier" and "podcast enthusiast" to look. Forty years old and no mention of a divorce or kids. Sam wondered if he'd just forgotten to settle down earlier or if there was something lurking beneath the surface that had him single so late in life.

Not that Sam could really talk.

"At least you'll be able to wear heels," Donya said dryly after it became clear that Sam was not going to be reciting any love poetry in response to Christian's profile.

"Yeah, right. I'll give you twenty bucks if they actually wear heels," Martin scoffed, and Vince snickered.

"So what's my angle?" Sam asked, just loudly enough to indicate that they did not find the joke funny. Keeping their eyes on Christian's profile, they added, "I know he went out with all three women. Have we determined what ended those relationships?"

"It would be more accurate to say they never made it off the ground," Donovan said. Pulling up photos of Cassie, Alicia, and Nikki, she explained, "According to his chat history, Christian went out with all three women a handful of times each with very little messaging between dates and total radio silence after the relationships ran their course. So while we can guess at what he's looking for in a date, we don't know what exactly is turning him off of these women."

"So he finds these women using the app, but he doesn't actually talk to them at all between dates?" Donya asked. She squinted at Christian's profile, as though trying to picture what the women had seen in him, and finally just shook her head. "Sounds like a serial killer to me."

"Old fashioned serial killer, huh? Maybe Sammy actually does stand a chance." Leaning in closer to examine the three women on screen, Vince said, "Other than having some kind of boss-babe kink, do we know how he's choosing his victims?"

"The research team did a deep dive into his dating history," Donovan said. "Christian is primarily interested in women who are over thirty, have steady employment, and are relatively new to the app. He also prefers women who seem to be of a . . . gentler disposition."

"Gentle?" Noah blurted in disbelief.

Sam shot him a glare as Vince started laughing again, obviously delighted that even Sam's rookie didn't think they could pull that one off.

"I'll remind you, Detective Renier, that the reason you're at this briefing is so you can advise Detective Sam on how best to stay in character during their time undercover." Donovan's acerbic tone instantly had Vince sobering up.

"All right, all right," Vince said, holding his hands up placatingly. Pacing closer to the screen with all the grace of a feral racoon, he examined Christian's profile a little more closely. "So what am I building here? A good girl, yeah? Someone who wants to have his babies and bring him a beer in the evening while also contributing to his retirement fund?" Grimacing at the three women, with their sharp outfits and short haircuts, he said, "I guess that explains why he goes for the whole bitchy femme-bot aesthetic."

"Detective Renier . . ." Donovan warned.

"What? It's a good thing," Vince said dismissively. "If our killer liked curvy blondes, we'd be even more screwed." Squinting back at Sam critically, he said, "I guess it's not completely impossible, looks-wise, if Sam's lady friend is as good as you say."

"She's not my 'lady friend,'" Sam said automatically, then regretted it when Vince's face split into a toothy grin at the sound of their denial.

"Come on, Sammy. If you want this guy to like you, you're going to have to be a little more agreeable than that," Vince said. Wiggling his eyebrows obnoxiously at his own rookie, he asked, "What do you think, D? Maybe this guy likes hearing about a little girl-on-girl action."

"You're disgusting," Donya replied flatly.

"Am I? The way I hear it, Sammy used to go down for more than just ballistics reports when you were still working in the lab."

"Enough, Vince," Sam said a little too sharply as Donya flinched at the largely inaccurate but persistent rumor.

Seeing the keen interest Vince was taking in the embarrassed look on his rookie's face, Sam quickly swallowed their pride and said, "That doesn't even make any sense. Since I'm only interested in men."

Vince's gaze flicked back to them with real interest this time.

Offering him a big, plastic smile, Sam channeled their inner *Samantha* as they said, "I might have gotten a little . . . distracted by my career, but you know how it is once the biological clock starts ticking. Everyone has to settle down eventually, right?"

"So you're interested in starting a family?" Vince asked, circling closer to their desk.

"Sure."

Vince frowned at their glib tone, and Sam resisted the urge to roll their eyes.

"Fine. Yes."

"How many kids?" he pressed. Placing both hands on the table, he leaned in closer. "Two? Three?"

"Uh . . ." Sam glanced to Donovan. Roleplay wasn't exactly Sam's specialty, but the captain wasn't offering any further direction.

Shifting their gaze back to Vince, Sam lifted one shoulder in a half-shrug and said, "Just . . . a lot, I guess?"

"This is a waste of time," Vince said, straightening up. When Donovan tried to interject, he shook his head and spoke over her. "No, come on. Come on! They're not even trying. No one's ever going to buy this."

"You'll be on coms all night," Donovan said. "You can feed them the right answers, if necessary."

"Right," Vince scowled. "Because this is a fucking sitcom."

Sam's lips quirked a tiny, victorious smile at the sound of his frustration.

"I don't know what you're smiling about. You're the one who's going to blow this thing by being too much of a goddamned robot to pull off the most basic undercover role of all time."

"I'll make it work."

"Will you?" Vince's lip curled again as he looked them over with poorly concealed disgust. "I'm still not convinced this guy isn't going to run from the restaurant the second he gets a look at you."

"I guess we'll find out," Sam said coolly. Because no matter how much they didn't want to do this, they weren't about to let a human trash bag like Vince see them squirm. Glancing at Donovan, who finally seemed to be realizing that she might have made a terrible mistake, Sam raised an eyebrow and said, "What other choice do we really have, right?"

CHAPTER NINE

Sam: Question of the Day: How do you deal with pre-game nerves?

Teddy: pregame? like for sportsball?

Sam: Really, sportsball? I thought you were going to study up to impress me.

Teddy: I did
Teddy: fun fact: it's 137.5 miles from the mainland marina to SoFi Stadium
Teddy: so with the way you drive, it'd only be like an hour along the coast to catch a game <3

Sam: Yeah? You're going to drive 137.5 miles to watch a "sportsball" game?

Teddy: I wouldn't really be going to watch the game . . .
Teddy: ;) <3

Sam: Cute.
Sam: I meant nerves before an important thing in general. Like before a big sales pitch or whatever.

Teddy: oh I hate that stuff
Teddy: I usually make henry handle the negotiating part. I just show up to shake hands at the end

Sam: Henry?

Teddy: best friend

Teddy: and business manager

Sam: You have a business manager?

Teddy: well I sure as hell couldn't sell this stuff on my own
Teddy: I like people, but I'm not really into the whole suit and tie thing

Sam: I would love to see you in a suit and tie.

Teddy: that can be arranged <3

Sam: You really are bad at negotiating.

Teddy: vicious
Teddy: so what are you nervous about? more case stuff?

Sam: Yeah.

Teddy: that sucks
Teddy: is it going to be bad?

Sam: Yes.
Sam: A little less bad now.
Sam: :)

Sam couldn't help smiling in real life when Teddy's return text appeared. It was just one long string of heart-eye emojis filling their entire screen. For all of Vince's goading about how they were going to blow tonight's op, maybe they were getting a little better at this flirting thing.

It probably wouldn't help them convince Christian they were a demure, pretty lady on a mission to get married and pop out some babies ASAP. But still.

Pocketing their phone with a sigh, Sam considered the Paths building looming overhead for a long moment before forcing themself to step inside. Texting Teddy offered a slight respite from their nerves, but they knew the fuzzy feelings wouldn't last long in the face of the chaos waiting for them in the "situation room."

Given their sullen mood, Sam was reasonably surprised when the elevator doors opened onto the tenth floor and revealed . . . nothing. No people, no voices, no chaos whatsoever. The only sign of life was a sticky note on the front desk with the words "Back in 10!" written in Beck's blocky handwriting.

Sam paused to double-check the date on their phone, but it was in fact June 22 at 6:00 p.m. Actually, it was 6:06 p.m. now, since Sam had spent so much time dragging their feet. According to the brief, their date with Christian was in less than two hours. But if that was the case, where was everyone?

With no small amount of trepidation, Sam slowly headed down the hallway to the situation room. They weren't sure what was happening, but they were certain it couldn't be good. They were starting to feel vaguely nauseous by the time they opened the situation room door to reveal . . . more nothing. Which was significant, considering what the room had looked like the last time Sam had been here.

There were still a dozen too many TV monitors mounted on the wall, but the girly clothing and shoe racks had all been removed. A small changing area had been curtained off in the corner alongside a single garment bag. There was also what appeared to be a portable hair station and makeup cart at the back of the room, but otherwise it looked normal. Like a regular boardroom.

The floorboards creaked to their left, and Sam finally allowed themself to acknowledge the only other person in the room. Vivienne offered them a rueful smile that Sam did not return.

"You're late," she said, twirling a small hairbrush in her hand expertly as she gave them a stern once-over. "How fast do you think I work?"

"Pretty fast." Sam glanced around once more at the thoroughly transformed room. "Where is everyone?"

"I thought a little privacy might be better," Vivienne said vaguely. Heading toward her setup at the back of the room, she called over her shoulder, "Come on. Let's get this over with."

Sam wasn't sure if they should be feeling more or less nervous if it was just going to be the two of them. But they didn't have much of a choice in the matter, so they decided to simply be grateful that Vince wasn't there to make this even more awkward.

"Hair first," Vivienne said, gesturing to the hydraulic stool sitting in front of the portable sink.

"What's wrong with my hair?" Sam reached up to touch their head uncertainly.

True, they hadn't been for a trim in a month or three. Possibly because they hadn't wanted to let go of certain island fantasies that involved a handsome young man running his fingers through their hair, but still. It wasn't that bad.

"You've got boy hair, Sam." Vivienne patted the stool a little more firmly. "I'm not sending you out there looking like a middle-aged Harry Styles."

"Now that's just rude," Sam muttered, even as they took their seat. "If you're going to compare me to a British boy band, at least make it one of the good ones."

"Whatever you say, McCartney."

An efficient silence fell as Vivienne got to work washing and drying their hair before bringing out the scissors. Sam had to squint against the bright makeup lights as Vivienne's fingers wielded the tools with the same bold confidence she seemed to bring to everything she did these days.

Try as they might to forget, Sam still remembered a time when they used to call in to the old shop on Glenview for her. They'd come up with a new creative excuse to keep her from getting fired on those days when the pressure from tests had Vivienne's hands shaking too hard to hold a comb. Her hands weren't shaking now as she ran the electric razor through their hair without a hint of hesitation. And the result was, admittedly, pretty damn good for a woman who hadn't had to pay her rent cutting hair in almost two decades.

Finishing up with the cut, Vivienne silently began prepping their face for makeup. Sam had to work hard not to cringe away from the wet paste being slathered on their skin.

"It's just primer," Vivienne said. She held up the little pot so Sam could see the clear gel she was applying to their face with the dainty little brush.

"Yeah, I do actually know what makeup is, thanks," Sam snapped. Vivienne's expression tightened in response to the sharp edge in their words, but she still didn't say anything, which had to be a lifetime record for her.

Sam felt an instant flash of guilt for their uncharitable thoughts. They could hardly judge her when they were the one so easily sliding back into old habits. At least Vivienne was trying to respect their request to keep things professional.

"So where is everyone?" Sam asked abruptly, and Vivienne hesitated with her foundation brush halfway to their face. Seeing her questioning look, they clarified, "I know there's no way Vince missed this on purpose."

"Ah. Detective Renier," Vivienne said in a tone that suggested she had had the displeasure of meeting the man in question. "He did take a little convincing. But it turns out the police don't have a lot of say when it comes to private property." Raising her brush again, Vivienne offered them a small shrug and said, "I don't think your captain was very impressed, but I'm sure she'll live."

Sam tried to process this new information as Vivienne continued to coax the feminine out of their features. A curve here. A sharp stroke there. A little softening around the edges. The Sam in the mirror transformed before their eyes with each expert movement of her brush.

Picking up an eyeshadow palette, Vivienne stepped in a little closer and said, "Close your eyes."

Sam did as they were told. But not being able to see her didn't reduce the anxiety they felt having her breath on their face and the brush of soft bristles against their skin.

"Why?" Sam finally asked.

"Hmm?"

Sam jerked back a little at the sound of her low voice way too close to their ear.

She tried to go back in with the brush, and their eyes flashed open in defiance.

"Sam," Vivienne said with exasperation.

"Why are you doing all this?" Sam asked a little more forcefully.

"Because it's my fault." Lowering the eyeshadow brush, Vivenne stroked her thumb over the bristles, sending up a plume of powder. Keeping her eyes pinned to the copper dust now speckling her skin, she said, "Those women were using my app when they were attacked. And this investigation tactic was my idea. So if there's something I can do . . . if I can make things less . . ." Her hand clenched around the brush, and she let out a weary sigh. "I have to try."

"Yeah, well," Sam said uncomfortably at the sight of her sadness. Leaning back on their stool a little, they said, "Don't, uh. Don't worry about the investigation part, at least. It's just part of the job."

Vivienne gave them that look again, and like Pavlov's bell, Sam's temper flared in response. Apparently, Vivienne was not so immune to old habits, either, because her voice was sharp when she said, "I don't know what you think of me, Sam, but you can't seriously believe this is what I wanted."

It took everything in Sam not to tell her exactly what they thought of her, but they forced the words down. The old Sam certainly wouldn't have hesitated to let her have it, and that felt like a victory in itself.

In their silence, Vivienne seemed to hear her own flaws. She blew out a long, slow breath. "I never would have suggested any of this if I knew they would put a genderqueer person on the case," she said in quiet sincerity. "If I had known . . . please. If nothing else, please believe that was never my intention."

Sam considered her silently for another moment. They still weren't sure they really believed her. Just the fact that they were here alone right now spoke to how much influence Vivienne had. Over the mayor, the captain, the entire investigation, really. She must know she could pull the plug on this if she really wanted to—but feeling bad while also denying her own responsibility was sort of a Vivienne Fox specialty.

Closing their eyes, Sam leaned forward in their seat. There was half a beat of hesitation, but then her brush flitted across their eyelids again as Vivienne continued down this path she had put them on. Whether she meant to or not.

"What the hell does that one mean, anyways?" Sam grumbled. Vivienne's hand hesitated, and they clarified, "Genderqueer. People keep coming up with new words, and I don't even know if they apply."

"You could just google it, you know."

"I shouldn't have to google my own gender," Sam insisted stubbornly.

"Still old-fashioned as ever." Despite the disparaging words, Sam could hear the smile in Vivienne's voice at their familiar bad attitude. "Is there a word you prefer using these days?"

Sam rolled her question around inside their head. It wasn't that they didn't have terms they preferred. "Nonbinary" seemed to be the one most people knew, and they didn't mind that. "Bigender" felt especially appropriate, although they'd only learned that one a year or two ago. But her question only reminded them of past labels that hadn't fit so well, and the past was a place Sam liked to avoid whenever possible.

So they just shrugged and let her continue working in silence.

"Just about done. And ten minutes to spare," Vivienne said when she was finally finished painting her masterpiece.

Sam blinked their eyes open and felt a little disoriented as their gaze landed on the two women reflected back at them in the mirror.

"Good to know I've still got it," Vivienne said, trying and failing not to sound smug as she began packing up her station.

There was certainly no denying Vivienne's talent with a makeup brush. The thought of going out there and letting their coworkers see them looking so feminine was enough to make Sam's palms sweat. It wasn't like they never wore makeup outside of work, but this was a little more extreme than wearing some lipstick to the local bar.

The makeup lights caught on a sparkling object in the corner of their eye, and Sam found themself asking, "So what's that about?"

"Hmm?" Vivienne followed their gaze to her hands. Her ebony skin was smudged with shimmering powder, but far more noticeable was the giant rock on her left hand sparkling under the fluorescent lighting.

"Who is she?" Sam asked. Not because they were stalling and knew from years of detective work that getting people to talk about their spouses was an easy way to kill time, of course. Shifting uncomfortably on their stool, they added, "If you want to talk about it, I guess."

"Her name's Harper. She's an anesthesiologist at St. Alexander's," Vivienne said. The smile on her face said this wasn't a topic she had any issue waxing poetic about. "We met eight years ago at a charity run my company was sponsoring. Of course, I rolled my ankle about five minutes in, but she stuck around to walk me all the way to the finish line and nurse me back to health."

Vivienne laughed lightly when Sam made a face at the mere concept. "What can I say? We've been together ever since."

"Sounds nice," Sam said, even though they weren't sure they could imagine a scenario they'd find *less* romantic.

"It is. She's an amazing woman," Vivienne said, and if her mushy tone was anything to go by, she didn't share Sam's reservations. Flicking her eyes in Sam's direction, she added a little more seriously, "It's challenging, too, sometimes."

Sam tilted their head politely.

"I run an app that's all about finding true love. But I've got a long history of infidelity, too. I don't try to hide from that."

"Ah," Sam said. Internally, they cursed themself for opening this topic, but it was too late now. "Well. That's . . . good of you. I guess."

"Harper makes me the best version of myself. I would never, never hurt her," Vivienne said. She gazed down at her enormous diamond ring a little wistfully. "I just wish sometimes that the past didn't cast such a long shadow, you know? Makes it hard to move on."

Sam nodded silently. They could appreciate the desire to leave the past in the past. Which was exactly why they shouldn't have broached this topic in the first place.

"If it'd help—if you wanted—we could talk about it," Vivienne said hesitantly. Reaching out to touch Sam's hand, she said, "I know what we had was a long time ago. But I'd still like to apologize for everything I—"

"No," Sam said sharply. They were out of their seat faster than a cat in cold water at the unwelcome feel of her skin against theirs. "No thank you," they repeated in a slightly more measured tone. "I should probably be getting changed. Right?"

". . . Right," Vivienne said, and if she was disappointed, Sam wouldn't know because they already had their back to her. Their body tensed when she added, "Just one more thing first."

She strode past Sam to the corner of the room with the changing stall. Pulling out a manila envelope from inside the garment bag hanging on the wall, she explained, "You've got the personality brief, and now you look . . . you know." Her dark eyes flashed over Sam in a way that did not make them feel any more comfortable. "But you're still missing the finishing touch."

"Seriously?" Sam complained when she opened the envelope to show them the transparent pieces of plastic within, each with a different artistic design printed across the surface. Reaching inside the envelope hesitantly, Sam asked, "What is this, the fourth grade?"

"Come on, it was in the brief. Both Cassie and Nikki had some pretty significant ink. It'll look good."

Sam paused their search to give her a disbelieving look, and Vivienne amended, "Well, I'm sure your date will think it looks good even if permanently coloring on yourself still seems like a strange choice to me. But you always did like tattoos."

"Yeah, on other people," Sam muttered. Their hand paused for a beat too long on one of the black-and-white designs, and Vivienne's eyes zeroed in on the movement.

"Really? That one?" she asked with disbelief. She pulled the temporary tattoo out of the pile to examine it critically under the overhead lights. "Doesn't really seem like you."

"Just reminds me of something," Sam said with a small shrug. For half a second, they almost gave in to the urge to smile when they imagined his reaction. Almost.

Burying the emotion, Sam plucked the transfer sheet from her hand and said, "Let's just do this—I wouldn't want to be late for my first date."

CHAPTER TEN

The click of high heels rang out against the pavement. The little side street was empty, save for a single sketchy-looking vehicle parked beneath the dim streetlight. Despite how ominous the white van looked, the striking woman approached with absolute confidence in her step. The sweep of long lashes cast deep, intriguing shadows across sharp cheekbones. Dark ink spilled out from beneath flowing white fabric, and the short undercut gave the distinct impression that this wasn't the type of woman who feared walking alone at night.

"Oh shit, here they come."

"Are they wearing *heels*?"

"No way. This I gotta see."

Taking hold of the van's side door, the woman only hesitated for half a second before throwing it wide open.

Cat calls and wolf whistles immediately flooded out of the van, and the woman grimaced in a not-quite-feminine way as the flash of a cell phone camera captured her image.

"You'd better delete that," Sam ordered. The eyeliner only made the glare they leveled on the redheaded detective more intense.

"No way," Martin said, a little too gleefully, as he held the phone aloft like a trophy. "Benson is going to be paying my tab for a month. Nobody thought you were actually gonna go through with it."

"Don't you mean my tab?" Donya said coolly. She opened the passenger door of the van so she could get a better look at Sam before turning her head toward Martin. "I believe the bet was $20 if they actually wore heels?"

"Oh, come on, D. That was obviously a joke," Martin whined.

"What are you even doing here?" Sam asked, even more annoyed now as a sullen Martin slapped a fresh bill into Donya's open palm. "I thought Vince was running coms."

"Sammy, that's no way to talk to your devoted team," Vince chided from where he was slouched lazily in front of his coms station. "Donovan wanted us to make sure her star detective stayed safe and sound on your little date. You know, in case our guy decides he'd prefer you out of those clothes and into a body bag."

"I think I can handle one guy on my own," Sam said.

"What, you're gonna outrun him in those heels?" Noah asked from his spot in the back of the van. Sam raised an eyebrow at their rookie's unusually serious tone. He looked a little pale in the face and thoroughly uncomfortable crammed in among the monitors and wires.

Sam looked to Donya, who carefully avoided their gaze. They didn't know why she even bothered. It was pretty apparent from her reaction how Martin and Vince had kept themselves entertained while waiting for Sam to show up.

"Who said anything about running?" Sam asked. They waited until Noah's guilty gaze met theirs and gave him an expectant look. Apparently Donya wasn't the only one who needed to work on her poker face, because Noah's eyes shifted in Vince's direction, confirming Sam's suspicions.

Frowning, Sam turned toward the other senior detective and said, "I'm not afraid of a fight. If someone's got a problem, I'm happy to set them straight. Heels or no heels."

"Ooh, I'm so scared," Vince shot back. His eyes openly roamed Sam's body in a way that made them want to put on ten more layers of clothing. Vince offered them a nasty smile and said, "Don't forget you're supposed to be playing a good girl tonight, Supercop."

"He's got a point, Sam," Martin said with oblivious cheer. "You might want to dial it back before you scare off our boy." He leaned out of the way as Donya hopped down from her seat and reached past him to grab the audio equipment off the tiny desk mounted inside the van. "Although you were making it look pretty easy, strutting around in those things. You sure this isn't how you dress on the weekends?"

"Very sure," Sam said sourly, despite the fact that Vivienne had, in fact, chosen an excellent pair of shoes. If all four-inch stilettos were this comfortable to walk in, they might actually consider wearing them from time to time.

Not that Sam was ever going to admit that to these idiots, who were leering at them like they were a stripper in a glass window as Donya clipped the tiny transmitter to the inside of their shirt. The sad thing was, the outfit wasn't even anything special. Yes, the pants were tight; yes, the heels were high; and yes, this drapey shirt was being held to their body with little more than a few strips of tape . . . but still. They just looked like a woman. A very tall, very flat-chested, very skinny woman. And if this was how these men looked at normal women, their police force needed some serious sensitivity training.

"What do you think, D?" Vince asked. He elbowed Donya, who was doing her best to look anywhere but at Sam now that she was done wiring them up. "She looks pretty hot, right?"

"She looks fine," Donya muttered. Those blue eyes flashed once in Sam's direction and then away again. Obviously she did not share their philosophy on standing their ground.

"Just fine? I don't know about that," Vince goaded. "I think I might actually know a few perps who would try to grope you if they saw you with your tits out like this, Sammy."

"Dude, no," Noah blurted from his corner of the van.

"What's that, rookie?" Vince asked, turning that shark-eyed gaze on him.

"Uh . . . "

"You don't like tits? Hm?" Giving Noah that trademark nasty sneer, Vince said, "Don't worry, I've got perps for that, too. One or two of them might even give you a reach-around if you ask nicely."

"What—? No," Noah stammered. "I'm just saying he—she—"

"Really? He-she? That's just offensive." Vince clucked his tongue with mock disappointment.

"That's not what I meant," Noah insisted, twice as loud and twice as embarrassed, but you had to give the kid some credit. He might be intimidated as hell, but that surely wasn't going to stop him from talking back. "I'm just saying, that's a fucking police detective right there. You can't talk to, uh, to *them* like they're a fuckin' hooker or something."

91

Unfortunately for Noah, having a backbone was not exactly rewarded around this particular precinct.

"Aw, does the rookie have a little crush?" Vince simpered, and Martin laughed obnoxiously despite the disgusted look on Noah's face. "You want to show her what a big, tough man you are?"

"Really nice, Vince," Sam said dryly, despite the way the little barbs, and Noah's repulsion, and Donya's damning silence were tearing away at whatever self-confidence they had managed to gather before coming out here. "I'm curious. Are you still going to feel like a man if I kick your ass in these heels? Or should I take them off first to spare your ego?"

"Ooh, and feisty, too," Martin laughed, like this was all just some good clean fun. To him, it probably was. Gesturing to Sam's killer stilettos, he said, "I bet she really could kick your ass in those heels."

"Don't," Sam snapped, feeling each repetition of that loaded word scraping away at more of their resolve. "Do not—do not call me that."

"What, feisty?" Martin asked stupidly. Sam stared back at him, daring him to see past the pretty paint and girly clothes to the person who had been sharing a wall with him for the past eight years. It took a couple of long seconds, but the lightbulb eventually went off. "Oh shit. Sorry—sorry." Gesturing to them helplessly, Martin said, "You just . . . you look like—"

"Like a woman? I am a woman," Sam said bluntly. Glaring at all four members of their so-called "security team," they said, "But if any one of you calls me 'she' again, I will tase you so hard your grandchildren will be tasting burnt toast. Understood?"

"Jesus, I said I was sorry," Martin said. His face was flushed almost as red as his hair in embarrassment. "You are dressed like a she, you know?"

"I am aware of that," Sam said slowly, feeling the relentless weight of old fears slowly pressing down on them. "But—"

"Yeah, Sammy, don't be so sensitive," Vince interrupted with a roll of his eyes. "Does it really matter if we say *they* when you're about to go on a date with someone who's going to be calling you *she* all night anyways?"

"I guess not," Sam said quietly, catching Donya's guilty gaze before she could look away again.

Like she thought maybe they wouldn't notice her telltale silence in all of this. Or the way she had misgendered them just as easily as her creepy boss did.

Backbones not rewarded, indeed.

"Come on, Sam. That's not fair," Donya protested at the look of resignation on Sam's face. Grimacing when her words caught Vince's attention, she muttered, "Look, this case is really weird. And seeing you looking so femme is also . . . really weird." Her eyes darted to the open front of Sam's shirt and then away again. As though seeing the more femme parts of them was really a big shock to her. "Just cut us all some slack, OK? We're on your side."

Sam stood silently for a moment, feeling four different sets of eyes crawling over their body. This was why they wore their androgynous masculinity like a shield. When they were twenty, twenty-five, even thirty, they used to go through this every day. If they didn't shave, it would be he for a week. If they wore anything more tinted than lip balm, it would be she for a month. They had to choose every day if they would take the hit and be a doormat or hit back and get that look every time they prioritized their dignity over someone else's comfort.

Sam glanced down at the anatomical heart design inked onto their forearm and wondered momentarily what Teddy would do in this situation. It wasn't hard to guess, really. But at thirty-eight, they just didn't have the energy he had to fight about this bullshit anymore.

Sam turned their back on all four of them and started down the street.

"Where do you think you're going?" Vince's voice cut harshly through the still evening air.

"Where do you think?" Sam called back. They felt the weight of the transmitter hidden under their shirt and the stares of their "team" tracking their retreat, but they didn't look back.

They turned the corner. The sign for Jacque's Bistro was just a few yards away on the bustling main street. And outside the brick building, waiting beneath the picturesque awning, a man in a gray sports coat with a severe widow's peak stood staring impatiently down at his phone.

Tapping their tiny earpiece to turn it on, Sam said grimly, "I'm going to meet my date."

CHAPTER ELEVEN

Recording #1: Christian Kaufman

[Testing, testing. Sammy, can you hear me?]

" . . . "

[Testing—]

"I can hear you. Now shut up. I'm making the approach."

[Copy. Recording engaged.]

"Uh, hi. Are you . . . ?"

"Oh. Samantha, right? Yeah, I'm Christian. Nice to meet you."

"Actually, it's just . . . "

"Sorry?"

"Never mind. Nice to meet you, too. Should we go inside?"

There is the sound of fabric rubbing against the transmitter as the two make their way inside. Chatter from other tables can be heard over the microphone.

"I hope you don't mind that I already got us a table. I wanted to make sure we got something by the window."

"That's nice."

[Really, Sam? Try being a little more lukewarm, why don't you.]

"If you'd prefer that we sit somewhere else . . . ?"

"Oh, no. This is . . . great. Very thoughtful of you."

There is the sound of a chair being pulled out, and then both people settle at the table.

". . ."

". . ."

"So . . . this is kind of what you do, right, Christian?"

"Pardon?"

"Aren't you a restaurateur?"

"Uh, yeah. Yeah, I manage a few places in the area."

"So eating at places like this must be like doing research for you."

"Oh, wow, you really are the Smart Heart type, huh?"

"What?"

"You know, on the app—the Smart Heart option?"

". . . Yeah. I guess that's me."

"It's not a bad thing. It's just, you do enough of these dates and you start to realize there are different types of people on the app. There are the ones who just click and show up and then there are . . . um . . ."

"The stalker-ish type that memorize their date's whole profile before showing up?"

"No—no, that's, uh, not how I was going to put it."

[Ease up. You're scaring him.]

"Oops."

[Fucking hell. Don't answer me. Talk to him.]

"Sorry if I come across a little . . . Honestly, this is my first first date in a long time."

"Really?"

"You can't possibly be that surprised."

"No, I am. You're—"

"Welcome to Jacque's Bistro, mademoiselle and monsieur. Can I start the lovely couple with anything to drink tonight?"

"Merci. Deux verres de votre meilleur vin rouge, s'il vous plaît."

"Actually, I prefer white."

[Goddammit, Sam. Did you even listen to the brief? We're going for agreeable.]

"Ah, a lady who knows what she likes. Right away."

" . . . "

" . . . "

"So . . . you speak French?"

"Not really. I'm just good at guessing."

" . . . "

"And really bad at dating."

"Uh huh. Sure."

"No, really, I am. Stay here another hour and you'll believe me."

"Right."

" . . . "

"So, what are you, really?

"Excuse me?"

"A cop?"

[Laugh like you think he's joking. Do NOT let him blow your cover.]

"What makes you think that?"

"You just answered my question with a question."

"Is it a crime to be curious?"

"You also keep saying this is your first date in a long time, but you're a beautiful divorcee with no children and an actual job, according to your profile. Either you're a cop, a serial killer, or some kind of unicorn. And I've been on enough of these dates that I don't believe in unicorns anymore."

" . . . "

" . . . "

[Say something.]

" . . . "

" . . . "

[Sam—]

"All right, you got me."

"Wait—really?"

[Don't you dare.]

"Well, no, not really. I'm not a cop or a serial killer. But I did lie on my profile."

". . . OK."

"The truth is, my divorce didn't go through last year."

"Are you saying you're still—"

"No, no, nothing like that. God, no. Actually, it's sort of the opposite of that. My husband left me seven years ago, and I . . . I haven't been on a real date since then. Until now."

"Oh."

"Yeah. Pretty crazy, right? My friend Nikki has been on my case nonstop to give this app a try, so I finally thought, what the hell. Time to rip the Band-Aid off, right? I'll show up, totally blow it, and then every date after will have to go better than this one."

" . . . "

" . . . "

" . . . "

"So, is it working?"

"What?"

"Am I totally blowing it?"

"Uh . . . honestly?"

"I love honesty."

"Well . . . it's not the worst first date I've ever been on."

"Seemingly. Just wait till I start talking about my cat."

"Very funny."

"You have no idea. I'm hilarious."

"Uh huh."

"Seriously—you should hear my John Wayne."

"OK."

"OK, what?"

"Let's hear it—this John Wayne impression."

"Ah, sorry to interrupt. Your glass of red, monsieur. And the white for you, mademoiselle."

"Merci."

"What he said. Thank you."

"Are monsieur and mademoiselle ready to order, or do you need a few more minutes with the menu?"

"Hmm. I'm not sure."

"Not sure about what?"

"If I'm ready to order. I think I need to hear this John Wayne impression first."

"Seriously?"

" . . . "

" . . . "

"If you can't do it—"

"No, I can do it."

There is the sound of someone clearing their throat, and then:

"I may sound like a Bible beater yellin' up a revival at a river crossin' camp meeting, but that don't change the truth none. There's right and there's wrong. You gotta do one or the other."

There's a beat of silence and then the enthusiastic sound of clapping.

"C'est incroyable!"

[Holy shit, Sammy.]

"Oh my god. How . . . ?"

"I guess we all have our hidden talents. Now I believe I was told we could order if I debased this fine restaurant with my Southern charms?"

"Southern charms, huh? I want to hear more about that. But, uh, how about a ribeye, medium rare, with the seasonal vegetables on the side first?"

"Very good, sir. And for mademoiselle?"

"Just a salad for me. The, uh, green kind."

"Very good. One ribeye medium rare, and one house salad coming up right away."

"Merci."

"Mercy."

" . . . "

" . . . "

"So, the accent?"

"It's not that exciting of a story. There's just not a lot to do coming up in rural South Carolina other than watching the corn grow or memorizing old westerns. I probably still know most of The Alamo by heart."

"That's incredible. You really wouldn't know it to hear you talk."

"Had to lose the accent when I moved to this side of the country. It wasn't really improving my employability."

"Really? I would have thought people would love having a Southern Belle answering the phones."

"Only if you sound like Dolly Parton and not like John Wayne."

". . . That's fair, I guess."

"You don't sound like you believe me."

" . . . "

"I know being an executive assistant isn't exactly a mind-blowing profession, but—"

"No, no—I'm sorry. Force of habit, I guess. When you go on enough of these dates, you get a bit . . . jaded when it comes to people's honesty."

"I guess I can't complain."

"At least you owned up to it. You wouldn't believe how far some people take the lies."

[Easy now, Sammy. He's warming up to you. Start moving him toward the vics.]

"I get that. You know, my friend Nikki, the one who got me on this app, she . . . she . . ."

"She . . .?"

". . . Sorry. Sorry. It just kind of hit me. She's the one who got me on this app, and . . . she passed, recently. Sorry. It's still kind of hard to talk about."

"It's all right."

" . . . "

" . . . "

". . ."

"Uh, not to be insensitive, but when you say Nikki, you don't mean . . ."

"Nikki Russo."

"Oh geez. Oh man. She's the girl who—"

"Yeah."

"I'm so sorry for your loss."

"No, I'm sorry. I shouldn't have brought her up. I guess I'm still just processing."

"Is that why you decided to try dating again?"

". . ?"

"Because she was on your case about it? And then she . . ?"

"Oh, yeah. Yeah. It felt like a good way to honor her, I guess. Kind of weird, but I figure she wouldn't want me to stop living just because . . ."

"Yeah."

"Yeah."

". . ."

". . ."

"You know, I actually went on a few dates with her. Nikki, I mean."

"Really?"

"Uh, yeah. Sorry if that's weird. We actually saw each other a few times this past year."

"Wow. That's . . . a pretty weird coincidence. What happened?"

"To Nikki . . ?"

"No, no. I meant between the two of you. You weren't still seeing each other when . . ?"

"Oh no, definitely not. We stopped seeing each other about a month ago."

"How come?"

"Uh, I don't really think that's great date conversation. It was a while ago, and I'm not one to speak ill of the dead."

[Don't let him get away.]

"No—please. I want to hear what happened."

"Uh . . ."

[Tell him you miss her.]

"I'm sorry if that's a weird thing to ask. I just miss her."

"Oh."

[Tell him—]

"I can't help feeling like it's my fault. I know that probably sounds crazy, but it's just like . . . what if I had called her that night? Or—or checked in, or—I don't know. But now . . ."

"I actually kind of get that."

"Really?"

"Yeah. I remember thinking . . . well, this is going to make me sound like a jerk, but after she told me she wasn't really looking to settle down and then she didn't show for the mixer that week, I was pretty annoyed. I assumed she was off scalping a free dinner off some other sucker. And then when I found out what actually happened that night . . . I still feel awful just thinking about it."

"The mixer?"

"Yeah, every Friday there's an evening mixer at the Paths building downtown. It's like speed dating, but with less structure and more booze. Sometimes they can even go all night. It's not a terrible way to meet someone if you're not into all that swiping stuff. Actually, that's where Nikki and I first met. She never missed one, so when she didn't show that night, I just figured she had another date."

"Right, but that particular Friday was when she . . . you know."

"So messed up, right? I was probably drunk and trying to get the number of some girl I wouldn't look at twice when she was getting murdered."

"Well, that's very charming."

"Sorry. That was rude. And you said you were the one trying to blow this date."

"It's fine. Honestly, Nikki was really into this online dating stuff, but I'm not sure it's for me. Seems kind of . . . exhausting."

"I can respect that. All the texting and the mind games aren't my thing, either."

"That must make it tough. Since most people on this app can be a little . . ."

"I just wish people would be more forthcoming. Like, if Nikki had told me from day one that she wasn't interested in settling down, she could have saved me a couple expensive nights out on the town. But instead, I try, and I wait, and in the end . . . nothing."

"Hm. Sorry to hear it was like that."

"No, I'm the one who should be sorry. She was your friend."

"It's fine. I'm the one who asked."

"Still. A real gentleman wouldn't be so candid."

"What, like admitting you went out on a date just to blow it on purpose?"

"I don't think you need to worry about being a gentleman. But I do appreciate the honesty."

"To honesty."

There is the sound of two glasses clinking together.

"So, do you have any other party tricks, or is it just good old John Wayne?"

"Convince me to stay long enough to finish this wine and we'll see about some Dolly. But no promises."

CHAPTER TWELVE

Sam lowered their coffee mug with a sigh as the hot bean juice worked its magic. Probably not a good idea this late at night, but these notes weren't going to write themselves. And after all that wine and awkward conversation, it was a necessary evil if they didn't want the temptation of sleep to override the importance of getting the details down.

Their phone began to ring, and the caller ID read "Vice Douchebag #1." Speaking of things they'd like to forget . . .

After watching it ring a few times, they finally hit Speaker Phone.

"Vince."

"Hey, Sammy! Or should I be saying howdy, Mr. Wayne?"

"Goodbye, Vince." Sam's thumb moved toward the End Call button.

"All right, all right. Don't hang up." Vince's voice managed to sound insistent even through the old phone's speakers. "We're on the same team."

"Are we?" Sam asked. They still weren't convinced they shouldn't just hang up and call it a night.

"Yes. We both want to get this son of a bitch, don't we?"

"I do. Can't speak for you."

"Well, I do."

Sam let their silence speak for itself as to how much they believed that statement.

"Listen, Sammy—Sam. Fifty percent of a successful undercover op is getting the details down in as many places as possible while it's still fresh. That means written report, verbal report—hell, I'd even take an interpretive dance. Whatever it takes to make sure we don't lose whatever connections you came up with tonight."

". . . Fine." Taking a deep breath, Sam glanced at their notes and said, "If Christian's mixer alibi pans out, he'll be off the table as a suspect, but I thought it was interesting that he said—"

"Wait, wait. Before you start—I've gotta read you some stupid shit."

"What are you talking about?" Sam asked, irritated that Vince was already veering off script.

"This thing from HR. Wait, I've got it here somewhere." Sam could hear the sound of papers being shuffled around on Vince's end. Clearing his throat, Vince droned, in the voice of someone clearly reading off of a piece of paper, "Detective Sam, I am sorry for misgendering you. My behavior tonight was unprofessional and unacceptable. The language I used was insensitive and not an appropriate way for one coworker to treat another. Moving forward, I will—"

"Ugh. Stop," Sam said quickly. They shuddered at the sound of the painfully insincere apology. "Please don't."

"No, seriously, I have to read you this." Vince didn't sound a lot happier about it than they were. "Someone complained to HR, and they're saying I'll get suspended for real this time if I don't give a formal apology."

". . . Fine. Read fast."

"Uh, let's see . . . language . . . coworker . . . oh yeah. Moving forward, I will respect your pronoun choices and personal gender expression in a way that befits the police uniform. I hope you'll accept this sincere apology and tell me if there's anything else I or the department can do to make this a more affirming work environment."

"Is that it?"

"Yeah, that's the end." They could hear Vince crunching up the piece of paper and tossing it away.

"Great. Let's move on." Sam tried to delete the last minute from their memory, because this was the very kind of humiliating nonsense they didn't want. "I found it interesting that Christian was so annoyed with the vic for dating around. I got the feeling that maybe he thought they were more exclusive than they actually were."

"Seconded. That was a lot of irritation for someone talking about a dead girl, even if his alibi does stick."

"So if Christian wasn't aware that Nikki was still seeing other guys while they were dating, is it possible one of the other two shortlist suspects also missed the memo and got jealous?"

"A serial killer with a boner for stabbing loose women? Super original."

"Occam's razor, Vince. A man killing women he meets on a dating app isn't the mystery of the year."

"And the other two guys definitely dated this chick at the same time he did?"

"According to their app records, yes. Nikki was seeing both Brad Lu and Jason Albertalli at the same time that she was seeing Christian."

"Brad's the Asian guy who looks like he's lost one too many bar fights, yeah?"

". . . He's a little rough around the edges, yes. But Nikki went out with him way more than either of the other two. She and Christian had four dates over the course of two months. She started seeing Jason just before Christian broke things off, and they went out three times. But she saw Brad at least eight times that we know about, and possibly even more, given how semi-regularly they were connecting."

"Was it like clockwork, or more random?"

"Pretty close to clockwork. Looks like they'd get together on the weekend every two or three weeks. He'd usually reach out and ask if she was free and she'd give him some canned response. Then rinse and repeat."

"So probably a go-to hookup when it was time to scratch that itch with someone comfortable."

"Seems like. Brad wasn't dating around a lot otherwise, but he did see the occasional other woman."

"Including the other two vics?"

"Yup. It was almost six months ago that he went on the one date with Cassie, but only a couple weeks ago that he and Alicia connected."

"And Nikki was the only regular?"

"According to the app, yeah. I'm thinking the next move is to learn what we can about the other two girls and see how it lines up with Nikki's dating habits."

"That hot ex of yours said in her police report that the Alicia girl's sister is the one who called this whole thing in. According to the brief, she works nights at St. Alexander's. You might be able to catch her after her shift tomorrow morning."

"At the hospital?"

"Unless your lady friend thinks nurses are working out of churches now, then yeah. The hospital."

". . . Great."

"You know, I heard you had a weird thing about hospitals. Maybe I should tag along in case—"

"No, thank you. I will be fine. And also, don't call her my lady friend. Her name is Vivienne."

"All right, all right, don't call HR on me again. It was a compliment."

"I didn't call HR."

"I know you didn't. You're not a little bitch like that rookie of yours."

"You sure it wasn't your rookie?"

"We don't take punk-ass recruits on Vice."

"That's weird. I thought you've been working Vice for over twenty years now?"

"Hilarious. You know, I've always liked you, Sammy."

"The feeling isn't mutual."

"Don't be so fucking sensitive. I'm basically doing you a favor. The more we work together, the more time you get to spend with my rook."

"I don't see how that's a favor."

"Don't play dumb, Sammy. Couple boring nights in the briefing room, couple drinks after work, and soon you'll be able to stop pussyfooting around and go back to actually getting some p—"

Sam hung up the phone. That was enough of that nonsense. And to think, they had almost believed Donya for half a second when she stood across from them on the roof and suggested life could be better working side by side on Vice.

Sam shuddered at the mere thought. They had made enough stupid decisions in their life. Leaving South Carolina with an ancient pickup truck, the clothes on their back, and pretty much nothing else to their name. Filling out the paperwork for the academy on a whim and then somehow actually getting in. Taking Vivienne back a couple dozen times too many before she walked out for good. Starting smoking at twelve, and then quitting smoking at thirty—both of which felt like bad ideas at different times, depending on their mood.

Pretty much all of their one-night stands in the last six or seven years could probably be classified as stupid decisions, since these days sex was something they only went looking for when the loneliness wore them down.

Their gaze flicked to the phone still sitting on the desk and then back to their half-assed notes. Then back to the phone. Then to their notes. And, finally, to the bold design inked on their forearm.

Running one finger along the temporary art, Sam conjured up images of their last one-night stand. The one with him. Their lips tracing the patterns of dark ink across bronzed skin. His body so soft and eager underneath them. Both of them enjoying the pleasure of getting lost in someone else for one glorious, electric night. Sam had needed the physical relief at the time, sure. But everything since then had been electrifying in a whole other way.

They stared down at their phone as their brain began to buzz with the start of another stupid idea. Beyond stupid, really. But that was sort of the Sam specialty when it came to matters of the heart, so why stop now?

Snatching up the phone, Sam snapped a picture and pressed Send before they could overthink it.

Sam: < Image Attached>
Sam: What do you think?

Teddy: whaaaaat????
Teddy: that looks AMAZING <3
Teddy: did you just get that??

Sam: I don't know, did I have it the last time I saw you?

Teddy: definitely not
Teddy: I'd have remembered that
Teddy: <3 <3 <3

Sam: Don't get too excited. It's just temporary for the case I'm working.

Teddy: oooh intriguing
Teddy: what kind of case do you have to get temporary tattoos for?
Teddy: is that like an undercover gang thing?

Sam: GIU? Yeah right. Those boys are worse than Vice
Sam: Also, I don't think the mainland has any cutesy heart tattoo gangs

Teddy: I don't know, anatomical hearts can be pretty creepy

Sam: Not the way you make them.

Teddy: ?

Sam: The vase you were working on before I got your boat blown up. It was heart shaped.

Teddy: your memory is INSANE
Teddy: I barely remember what I was working on yesterday, forget a month ago
Teddy: what did it look like exactly?

Sam: It was made out of plates. Like the fancy ones with the blue flowers, I think?
Sam: <Image Attached>
Sam: Like that.

Teddy: oooh
Teddy: that's right
Teddy: I can't believe you remember that!

Sam: I told you before, it's hard to forget.

Teddy: that night? or things in general?

Sam: Both.

Teddy: so you liked it?

Sam: The vase? Or that night?

Teddy: both ;)

Sam: Yes.
Sam: And also yes.

Teddy: I'll have to make you a new one in that case
Teddy: do you have a design preference?

Sam: Surprise me.

Teddy: dangerous words to say to an artist
Teddy: but I think I've got your number

Those stupid butterflies fluttered around again as Sam lowered the phone. How was this guy even a real person? Like he wasn't an actual artist with actual clients who paid him lots and lots of actual money to make things way grander than cute little heart-shaped vases. They wouldn't even know where to put something that pretty in this spartan apartment.

But that didn't stop them from wanting it anyway. Or his attention, for that matter. Or maybe just him in general. And that made them want to do all kinds of stupid things.

Sam: I've got my Question of the Day.

Teddy: hit me

Sam: What's something that really gets under your skin?

Teddy: what level are we talking
Teddy: like putting ketchup on eggs?
Teddy: or people who are rude to waiters?

Sam: No, more personal than that.
Sam: Like, is there anything someone could say that's guaranteed to ruin your day?

Sam raised an eyebrow as Teddy started to type . . . and then stopped. And then started again. And then stopped again.

They had tried to trip him up a few times with their daily questions, but Teddy really wasn't shy about sharing anything. He had no trouble listing the worst art commissions he'd ever taken, his most embarrassing childhood memory, or his full romantic history, but this was the question that stumped him?

Teddy: I really don't like being called papi chulo
Teddy: you know, like by dudes on paths?
Teddy: not just cause it's cheesy as hell

Teddy: I know nobody could tell just from looking at my profile, but I don't even really know where I'm from
Teddy: like, I'm probably mexican, but unless I do a 23 and me, who really knows?
Teddy: so it's kind of a crappy reminder

Sam: First, that sucks.
Sam: Second, I'm definitely looking you up on Paths.

Teddy: sam, there is a 0% chance you use paths

Sam: Because I'm old?

Teddy: because I tried to look you up about thirty whole seconds after we met
Teddy: also you're WAY too intense for paths
Teddy: I can't think of a single guy on that entire app that could handle you
Teddy: especially in bed

Sam: You did.

Teddy: guess I'll have to delete my profile
Teddy: ;)

Sam: Or I could just stick with dating women. Way easier than guys.

Teddy: really?
Teddy: I wouldn't know
Teddy: what makes it easier?

Sam: Easier for me, I meant. Girls usually have less trouble getting their head around my "situation."

Teddy: ooooh right your situation
Teddy: I guess some guys would find that intimidating
Teddy: what with your whole being extremely sexy and super smart and crazy intense thing
Teddy: their loss ;)

Sam: You're pretty good at that.

Teddy: ?

Sam: Flattery.

Teddy: I'm terrible at flattery
Teddy: I'm great at being honest, though ;) <3

112

Teddy: speaking of honesty. are you ready?

Sam: Wow. Someone's impatient.

Teddy: it's after midnight, isn't it?

Sam: 12:01am, but sure. I guess if it'll keep you awake all night.

Teddy: you get me <3

Sam: You make it easy with all of these questions.

Teddy: that's the idea
Teddy: so what does it take to set off someone as level headed as you?

Sam: A lot.
Sam: I used to have a pretty bad temper, actually. Not so much these days.

Teddy: that's bullshit

Sam: ?

Teddy: you shouldn't have to bite your tongue just because your coworkers are homophobic

Sam: That's a big leap.

Teddy: is it?
Teddy: you're a queer detective currently working a career-ruining case with a department full of what you've previously described as satan's frat boy cousins

Sam: Did I say that?

Teddy: I might be paraphrasing
Teddy: the point is, your coworkers are dicks, and you should be mad about it

Sam: If I got mad about that kind of thing, I'd be mad all the time.

Teddy: I think you probably are mad a lot of the time

Sam: Some days more than others.
Sam: But it's not the kind of thing that's going to change, so it's on me for caring.

Teddy: that's seriously fucked up, sam

Teddy: I don't know who started this story that if queer people are well behaved everyone else will suddenly decide to be nice on their own, but it really doesn't work like that
Teddy: you shouldn't be expected to ignore it when someone misgenders you on purpose

Sam: Sometimes I forget how much younger you are. Hardly anyone knew what the word "misgendered" meant when I was 26.

Teddy: 27 now

Sam: congrats

Teddy: people may not have known the word, but they knew they were being jerks
Teddy: there just weren't enough consequences for being a jerk yet

Sam: There still aren't a lot of consequences.

Teddy: sometimes you gotta make your own consequences
Teddy: I should tell you about the time I got arrested for punching a TA on campus

Sam: Arrested? Now that's a story I'd like to hear.

Teddy: not a very long story. the TA was deadnaming my friend, and I decided I cared more about correcting that asshole than getting a law degree

Sam: So hot blooded.

Teddy: is that a bad thing?

Sam: Not at all. I think it's cute.

Teddy: I'm starting to think cute means something different in sam-speak

Sam: You'll figure it out.

Teddy: Cute = <3
Teddy: ?

Sam: Maybe.

Teddy: well I think it's "cute" that you care more about being a good detective than correcting your coworkers
Teddy: but I still think you should be allowed to do both

Sam: Maybe I should just call you next time someone's annoying me.

Teddy: you definitely should

Sam: I don't think you know what you're signing up for. People annoy me a lot.

Teddy: good. if that means I get to hear from you a lot

Sam: I'm not kidding. I have to spend the day at a hospital with my rookie tomorrow. It's not going to be pretty.

Teddy: Because of the rookie or the hospital?

Sam: Both.

Teddy: Not a fan?

Sam: Jury's out on the rookie. As for the hospital . . .
Sam: You have no idea.

Teddy: I'll have to stay by my phone then
Teddy: just in case my services are needed <3

Sam: Very cute.

Teddy: god
Teddy: you make me crazy
Teddy: you should just call me right now

Sam: But I'm not annoyed anymore :)

Teddy: maybe I just want to hear your voice

Sam: Good night, Teddy.

Teddy: talk to you tomorrow, sam <3

CHAPTER THIRTEEN

"You're late."

"I know, I know. Sorry," Noah said as he stumbled his way through the hospital's revolving door. He looked a mess, as usual, but at least his shoes appeared to be properly tied.

"This better be the last time," Sam said sharply.

Noah winced as Sam turned their back on him and made their way over to the elevators.

"You can't just show up whenever you want for these things. Ms. Hancock's shift ended five minutes ago."

"Sorry. I'll set my alarm earlier next time," Noah promised, looking properly ashamed. Although that only lasted about two seconds, as Sam swallowed the last of their coffee and tossed the cup in the bin.

When they reached for the elevator's call button, Noah's curious gaze followed the path of their hands.

"What?" Sam snapped.

"Uh, how many cups are you at?" Noah glanced pointedly back at the garbage bin before stepping onto the elevator after them. When Sam gave him a confused look, he wiggled his fingers and said, "Hands."

Sam glanced down in alarm. Their hands did indeed have a noticeable tremor now that they were no longer holding the coffee cup, despite their best efforts to tamp down the panic. "Shit," they muttered, shaking their hands out and tucking them into their jacket pockets.

They could feel Noah staring as the numbers ticked up toward the seventh floor, but Sam offered no further explanation. They had almost succeeded in getting their heart rate back below ninety, despite his probing gaze. But the moment the elevator doors opened onto the busy hallway, with its white walls and beeping machinery, their pulse skyrocketed again.

"Are you—" Noah began.

"Drop it," Sam said shortly. They steeled their nerves and forced their feet to start moving again. Getting the attention of a nurse at the visitor's station, they said, "Excuse me, ma'am?"

"How can I help you?" the nurse asked, and Sam breathed in deeply before unclipping the badge from their belt. Their hands remained mercifully steady around the golden shield.

"I'm Detective Sam, and this is Detective Mariano." Voice even, strong. All good signs. Feeling a little more confident now, Sam said, "We were hoping to speak with Natasha Hancock? I believe she works on this floor."

"Oh. Um, of course, Detective." The nurse's eyes widened at the sight of Sam's police badge. "Um, uh, her shift just ended, but should I—can I page her for you?"

"Yes. Thank you," Sam said, returning their badge to its place. "We'll wait."

"Uh . . . How about over there?" the nurse suggested. Sam turned to follow her gaze and grimaced at the sight of the empty patient room across the hall. Noticing their reaction, the nurse lowered her voice and said, "I don't want to scare any of the patients if they think the police are looking into something. You know?"

"No, we wouldn't want that," Sam muttered. The woman tried to offer more of an explanation, but they just waved her off impatiently.

With their hands firmly back in their pockets, Sam strode across the hall to the empty room. Noah followed closely in their wake. Despite their best efforts, Sam still flinched at the sight of the prim little hospital bed with its stationary heart monitor and IV pole ready to receive the next unlucky patient.

"Paging Natasha Hancock. Please report to room 818."

The silence stretched on following the announcement over the intercom system. Noah was looking all kinds of curious as Sam wordlessly positioned themself in the back corner of the room. Their face was pale and their posture was rigid. Noah seemed desperate to ask, but Sam just stared resolutely out the window. They may not be able to control their physiological reaction to this place, but that didn't mean they wanted to talk about it.

Some people didn't like heights. Other people were scared of bees. And Sam happened to get heart palpitations whenever they got within fifty feet of a hospital. Those were just the facts. No further discussion required.

"Hey. What gives?" a weary-sounding voice asked from outside the room. "My shift—"

"It's the police," the nurse from earlier whispered in response. "There're two detectives in there who wanted to talk to you. I'm guessing about . . ."

"Oh."

"I'm so sorry. I didn't know—"

"It's fine. Thanks."

The sound of non-slip shoes on linoleum grew louder. A moment later, Natasha Hancock appeared in the doorway of the patient room. She shared some of Alicia's features, but none of her younger sister's fashionable aesthetic. At least not at the moment. Her microbraids were pulled back in a severe bun, and she still wore the dusty blue scrubs from the shift she had just finished. Her eyes carried the familiar fatigue of a long night on the clock.

When those eyes fell on the two detectives, Natasha's expression somehow grew even more exhausted, and Sam knew it wasn't from the lack of sleep.

"Natasha Hancock?" Sam asked. The woman in the doorway nodded. Pushing back their jacket to reveal their badge, Sam said, "Sorry to take up your time at work. We were just hoping to have a quick word."

"It's fine," Natasha said, sounding like she meant the opposite. "I assume this is about Alicia?"

"Yes. My name is Detective Sam, and this is my colleague, Detective Mariano. We're the team who've been assigned to your sister's case."

They knew they should probably offer the woman some comforting words, or at least a handshake, but their spine was in the process of fusing to the wall behind them, so this was probably as good as it was going to get.

"Well, better late than never," Natasha replied in a tone that suggested a handshake would not have been welcome anyway. Glancing between Sam and Noah, she asked, "What'd you all want to know?"

"If it's more comfortable, we could talk back at the station," Noah suggested, and when he gave Sam a look of such obvious concern that they knew he wasn't asking for Natasha's sake, Sam had to resist the urge to smack him.

"No thanks. Here is fine." If Natasha noticed Sam's discomfort, she surely didn't share Noah's compassion.

"All right. Why don't you get comfortable?" Sam suggested. When Natasha glanced pointedly around the spartan room, Sam said, "Detective Mariano?" Noah gave them a blank look, and Sam sighed irritably. Nodding in the direction of the closet, they said, "A chair for Ms. Hancock, please?"

"Uh . . . right. Let me, uh, get that for you," Noah said awkwardly. The poor kid seemed completely lost, but at least he managed to retrieve the folding chair without making things worse.

"Thank you," Natasha said coolly. Noah shot Sam a questioning look as he grabbed another for himself, but Sam just gave a small shake of their head.

"OK, Ms. Hancock," Sam started as they reached into their jacket pocket for their tape recorder.

"No fucking way," Noah said. His eyes were wide with disbelief at the sight of the ancient device. "I was sure that was just a rumor. You don't seriously use a—"

"I'm going to ask you a few questions, Ms. Hancock," Sam said right over Noah's enthusiastic commentary. Setting the tape recorder down on the windowsill, they said, "I would appreciate your honesty in answering, but this is a completely voluntary interview. You can leave or ask me to stop at any time. Does that sound all right with you?"

"Sure. If it'll help the investigation," Natasha said, although she was eyeing the tape recorder with significantly less enthusiasm than Noah had shown.

"Thank you," Sam said, reaching for the record button. "I believe it will."

Recording #2: Natasha Hancock

The red button is engaged, and the tape begins to roll. The faint sounds of life in the hospital can be heard in the background.

"Would you mind stating your name for the record?"

"Natasha Hancock."

"Do you prefer Ms. Hancock or Natasha?"

"Tasha is fine."

"All right, Tasha. What can you tell me about the night of your sister's attack?"

"OK. Getting right into it. I was just grabbing something to eat before my shift started when Alicia got home. She—"

"Sorry—let's back up a little. When does your shift start?"

"Pardon?"

"At the hospital."

"Why?"

"I'd like to establish a timeline of Alicia's day leading up to the attack."

"Uh, OK, I guess. My shift starts at ten. It was probably around eightish when Alicia got in that night."

"That seems a little late. Was it a long commute?"

"No. She'd just been working late a lot."

"Do you remember why?"

"Why would I know that? Bank stuff, I guess. I don't know. I—she'd been complaining a lot about some new . . . I don't know. Payroll system or something? I—she—"

"It's OK. Let's just take a second."

"I don't know what you want me to—"

"It's OK, Tasha."

"..."

"..."

"..."

"I don't want you to tell me anything other than what you know. And if you don't know, that's OK, too. It's my job to find out who did this, not yours. All right?"

"..."

"..."

"..."

"Ready to try that one again?"

"... Yeah. Sure."

"Do you remember why Alicia had been working late so much?"

"No. I think she mentioned something about a new payroll system that was a total pain at work. But I don't know for sure."

"OK. Did you and Alicia talk at all that evening?"

"Only a bit. She was in a rush."

"Can you tell me more about that?"

"Yeah. She was messing around on that stupid app, talking to some guy, as usual."

"You mean the Paths dating app."

"Right. I guess she finally got tired of the last guy flaking on her, so she was excited to go meet up with someone new. But that was Alicia for you."

"So you'd describe your sister's dating habits as ...?"

"Disastrous. If there was an asshole within a ten-mile radius, she'd find him."

"Did Alicia experience other dangerous situations when engaging with men she met on the Paths app?"

"Dangerous to her bank account, maybe."

"Can you tell me—"

"She just attracted a lot of losers, OK? Mama's boys, sofa surfers, beach bums, drug addicts. If they treated her like crap, even better. She fell for every sad set of eyes she ever met and put her whole heart into fixing them, and when they were finished wasting her time and money, she'd start all over again with a new loser. It's no surprise she eventually managed to find someone who . . . who . . ."

The woman's angry voice dissolved into the sound of distressed tears.

"Uh . . . Detective Sam? Should we . . . ?"

After a long pause, there is the slow sound of feet dragging on linoleum, followed by the sound of a tissue being pulled from a box.

"Here."

"Thank—thank you."

"Yeah. No problem."

". . ."

". . ."

"You're not very good at this, are you?"

"No, not really. But I'm a pretty good detective, if that makes you feel better."

"Are you going to get the guy that did this to my sister?"

"Of course they will. Sam's got one of the best solve rates in the entire state."

"Detective Mariano, please. Don't."

"Uh, sorry. My bad."

". . ."

". . ."

". . ."

"I promise I'll do what I can to find the person responsible for your sister's murder. But I'll need a little more information first, if you're up for it."

"Right. Of course. Sorry for getting all—"

"You don't need to apologize. She was your sister."

"Yeah."

". . ."

"Do you have any siblings, Detective?"

". . ."

"Sorry. Is that a hard question . . .?"

"No. Well, sort of. It's more that I'm, ah, not sure."

"Oh. I guess you're not very close with your family, huh?"

"I don't really have a family."

"Dude. That's so fucked. Were you, like, adopted or—"

"Detective Mariano."

". . . Sorry."

". . ."

". . ."

". . ."

"It sounds like you and Alicia were pretty close, though. Even if you didn't approve of her dating habits."

"Yeah. You could say that."

"If you don't mind me asking, why did she always go for guys who weren't good for her?"

"Well, she didn't do it on purpose. She would always think the newest guy was different—because he was a teacher, or he liked gardening, or he adopted rescue dogs. But in the end, they always turned out the same."

"Ms. Hancock, I'm sorry to ask, but did Alicia have a history of abuse? In childhood, or even as an adult?"

"No, it wasn't like that. She was just a magnet for crappy guys."

". . ."

"Listen, I know how it sounds, but Alicia literally had the worst luck in love you could possibly imagine. She'd spend two good months with a guy and then he'd lose his job. Or she'd go on three dates with Captain America and then it would turn out he was actually married. Or—all sorts of crazy stuff. But no matter who she dated, in the end, she always got burned."

"And she met all of her dates on the Paths app? She didn't use any others?"

"Uh-huh. Great app, right?"

"So that night. You're sure she was talking to someone on the app?"

"But according to her app history, she didn't—"

"Detective. Mariano."

"Sorry, shutting up."

" . . . "

" . . . "

" . . . "

"So, that night. You're sure she was talking to someone on the Paths app?"

"Yeah. She was all excited because this guy she'd been texting with for a while finally agreed to meet up in person. She'd been feeling really guilty because she just broke things off with the last loser, and every time that happened, she'd end up . . ."

". . ."

". . ."

"She'd end up . . . ?"

"I don't want to make her sound—I mean, Alicia was a really nice person.

Too nice, really. But she was a human being, too. So when she was sad, or heartbroken, or—"

"You're trying to say she enjoyed some casual connections as well."

". . ."

"It's OK, Tasha. No one is judging your sister."

"You have to understand. Alicia seriously had the worst luck in relationships. You can't blame her for wanting something simple from time to time."

"Like I said, no one is judging her."

". . ."

"What about the guy Alicia was messaging with that night? Was that a casual hookup or—"

"It was a date. A real date."

"You're sure?"

"Yes. She was planning to meet him at Calliope's. It's a swanky bar in the West End."

"That's a popular area for nightlife."

"Yeah, that's why she always went there for first dates. Lots of people around in case the guy turned out to be . . . not so great."

"And if she was only going for something physical? Would she still have met him at Calliope's?"

"No. She would have gone to The Imperial across the street. Also a bar, just a bit more casual."

"Right. So she liked to compartmentalize depending on what she was looking for. And you're absolutely certain she was going to Calliope's that night?"

"Yes. I'm sure. I'm the one who told her to go."

". . ."

"You have to understand. She was miserable. The last guy—Brad something-or-other—he was still texting her, promising he was going to get cleaned up and all that crap. She'd been stressed at work for weeks and feeling bad for breaking it off with him. Like she should feel bad for not wanting to be with some junkie."

"So you told her to meet up with this new guy. Did you happen to get his name?"

"Don't you think I would have said something by now if I knew that?"

"Right. And this new guy seemed normal? No red flags?"

"Of course not. I never would have—I just thought he was some tech bro with a boring desk job and cheesy pickup lines. So I thought . . . what's the harm? Can't be worse than the last guy, right?"

"Damn. Bet you wish you'd told her to hit up the ex-loser for a good time instead, huh?"

". . . yeah. I guess so."

"Detective Mariano."

"Uh, yeah?"

"I would like you to go get me a coffee."

"Uhh . . ."

"Right now."

"But you haven't asked her about Jason or Chris—"

"Coffee, Noah. Now."

A second later, there is the faint squeak of rubber soles on linoleum. The footsteps quickly fade away as a door opens and closes again.

". . ."

". . ."

"Tasha, I apologize for my colleague's unprofessional behavior."

". . ."

"If you'd like—"

"I'd like you to leave."

"..."

"Sorry. I just—I thought I could do this. But—"

"It's all right. I know it's a lot. And I am sorry for his behavior."

"It's fine. Men, right?"

There is the sound of someone beginning to sob quietly.

"..."

"..."

"Tasha—"

"Just go. Please."

"..."

"I said go."

"Right. Of course. Thank you for your time today, Ms. Hancock. I'll leave my card at the front desk in case you ever need to speak with me."

There is the sound of the tape recorder being picked up, and then the recording comes to a halt.

Sam stepped out into the hallway. The door closed gently behind them, but they could still hear the sound of Tasha's tears faintly through the wood paneling. They'd probably be hearing that sound in the back of their mind until this case was solved.

"Oh, hey. That was fast."

Sam sighed with irritation as Noah spoke up from where he stood leaning up against the wall. At least he hadn't actually gone to get them a coffee.

"Yeah. A little too fast," Sam said, rubbing the back of their neck as the sound of life in the hospital pressed in around them. Glaring at Noah, they said, "You're a goddamned idiot, you know that?"

"Yeah, I know," Noah admitted. He did look properly ashamed of himself, at least. "Did she kick you out because of me?"

"What do you think?" Sam sighed. They scrubbed a hand across their face. God, it was so loud in here. How did anyone think with all this noise?

Sucking in a deep breath, they began to move toward the windows at the end of the hall.

"So what does that mean for the case?" Noah asked. Sam knew their stress must be showing in a big way, because he was giving them one of those looks again.

"I'll have to try again another day. Although after that little stunt, I wouldn't blame her if she didn't want anything to do with the investigation."

Sam's stomach dropped as they arrived at the windows. They weren't the opening kind—just solid glass from top to bottom to let some natural light in. Feeling the tremors starting again, Sam pressed one hand to the cool pane and willed their body to just *calm down*.

Shoving down the panic, Sam continued, "In the meantime, I'll try to find out who Alicia was messaging that night and why there isn't any record of it, according to the research Vivienne gave us."

"Must be nice, getting a big, juicy lead," Noah said, and Sam twisted around to give him a sharp look. "Sorry," he said quickly. "I know you'd probably have more than just a lead if I wasn't such a dumbass."

"At least you got one thing right," Sam grumbled. They pressed their hand harder against the window as a nurse came hurrying around the corner pushing an empty gurney. A code was blasted over the speakers, and Sam felt the tension crawling down their neck and across their shoulders.

Dammit. This wasn't working.

Pushing off the wall, Sam headed rapidly in the direction the gurney had come from. "Give me an update on your case," they said bluntly. Their eyes darted around the hallway as they walked.

"Uh, well, it's going a bit better," Noah said, hurrying to keep up with them. "I've been trying to look into stuff methodically, like you do. You know—when, where, who was around, how did people feel about the guy."

"Great. Tell me about that." Sam was only half paying attention as they continued their search.

"Well, when was right after the service. Where was in the parking lot directly outside the church."

"Already knew that," Sam muttered. They paused momentarily to jiggle the handle on a closed maintenance door, but it didn't budge.

"Uh, what are you looking for?" Noah asked nervously.

Sam just shook their head and kept going. "Tell me something new," they said. They forced themself to slow down a little. Breathe. Think. Their eyes darted up to the exit signs on the ceiling marking their quickest escape.

"I guess it's a little new knowing the vic didn't go anywhere between the service and the parking lot," Noah said—a little too eagerly, in response to their distress. "I called a bunch of the regular mass attendees again, mostly older folk, but all of them said Father D'Angelo seemed like he was in a big rush that day. Like, he wasn't being rude or anything, but he definitely went straight from the church to the—whoa!"

Noah nearly collided with Sam as they whipped around the corner and pulled up short.

"Fuck," Sam muttered. They spun around and started heading back the way they had come before Noah had even come to a stop.

To the average observer, there was nothing especially disturbing in the hallway that could explain the ashen look on Sam's face. Just a young girl lying on a gurney, a couple of old people in wheelchairs, and some nurses fussing with a crash cart. The girl's parents stood nearby, speaking in quiet voices with a doctor. But by the time Noah had turned back around, Sam was already half a football field away and looking ready to jump out one of the windows if given the chance.

Glancing at the doors around him, Noah called, "Hey, boss?"

Sam's footsteps slowed to a stop. It took a tremendous amount of effort, but they managed to turn back to face him.

Noah tried the handle to the door on his right, which was labeled "staff lounge." It was firmly locked, as expected. "Cover me," he muttered as he pulled out his visitor's pass.

Despite their panic, Sam managed to raise an eyebrow at their rookie.

Rolling his eyes, Noah said, "Come on, Supercop. *Cover me.*"

Sam grimaced at the jab, but turned around and watched the hallway with nervous, flitting eyes as Noah worked his card into the crack between the door and the frame. "Our Father," he mumbled under his breath as he worked, "who art in heaven, hallowed be thy name. Thy kingdom come . . . "

It took a few seconds, but the old lock eased open before he'd finished the entire recitation. God bless public hospitals' crappy infrastructure.

Swinging the door open, Noah kissed the visitor's pass and gestured with it to the heavens before saying, "After you, Detective."

"Do I want to know?" Sam asked as they glanced suspiciously between him and the door.

"Probably not."

Sam considered their young charge for another moment before finally turning and pushing their way past him to get into the staff room. Their need for air was greater than their curiosity about his breaking and entering skills.

In the two seconds it took Noah to follow them inside and relock the door, Sam had already made their way over to the windows next to the little kitchenette. Shaking fingers fumbled with the ancient lever and jerked up hard enough to risk cracking the glass.

For a long minute, Sam just stood there. Their useless hands curled around the windowsill as they sucked in as much fresh air as their lungs could manage without actually hyperventilating. They tried to imagine they were standing on the docks at Paradiso, smelling the sweet ocean breeze and letting that island magic slow their racing pulse.

Maybe there was even a handsome young man there, running a hand through their hair and asking them questions. That could be nice, too. Nicer than being here, for sure.

Eventually the tremors began to subside, and the panic receded to a low, manageable buzz in the back of their skull.

"Thanks," Sam finally said. They took in one last deep breath before turning back to face their rookie.

"Whatever," Noah said with an awkward shrug. He lowered the phone he had been looking at while pretending not to notice their obvious panic attack. "I fucked up your interview, so . . . least I could do."

"How about you don't ask about this, and I won't ask about that trick with the card?" Sam suggested.

"Deal," Noah said, pocketing his phone. "Gave me time to catch up on all the Twitter news. Did you know that chick from Paradiso's writing a book on the whole wedding fiasco?"

"Which chick?" Sam asked as a memory reel of names and faces flashed through their mind's eye. Unbidden, they remembered talking with

Teddy about the supposed book deal on their last day together. "Must be Maggie, right?"

"Yeah, the psycho bride."

"That's a bit ironic," Sam said with a dry laugh. Noah gave them a questioning look and they clarified, "Calling her the psycho bride? She wasn't one of the four people involved in the murders."

"I mean, I guess," Noah said, making a face. "But she's still kind of . . ."

"Yeah, that whole place is kind of like that," Sam agreed with a sigh. Their lips quirked up in a half-smile, and they added, "Nice place to go for a boat ride, though."

"She's going to be able to afford one nice-ass boat. Apparently she got a six-figure deal for the memoir. They're thinking of doing a TV show, too."

"Seriously?" Sam asked. The smile disappeared as quickly as it had appeared.

"Oh yeah. They're floating the title *Like and Subscribe for Murder.*" Noah grinned at the way Sam cringed. "Kind of catchy, right?"

Sam considered their young rookie and his eager stream of gossip. Blowing interviews with his crude sensibilities, showing up late everywhere he went, and tripping over his own feet even when standing still. He stuck out like a sore thumb. They were pretty sure he shouldn't be trusted with any cases, much less a probable first-degree case like the D'Angelo one.

They really wished he didn't remind them so much of another young detective from a decade earlier.

"Are you the one who called HR?" Sam asked abruptly. They watched Noah's face closely.

"What?" he asked, and Sam could instantly see that this kid didn't even know they had an HR department, forget thinking he should go around calling them on Sam's behalf.

"Never mind." Sam smiled a little despite themself as they pushed off the wall and started heading for the door. "Come on. Let's figure out your case."

"Really?" Noah said eagerly, chasing after them as they made their way back into the hallway.

The sounds and sights were all as triggering as ever, but Sam kept that mental image of Paradiso firmly in their mind as they traced their steps back to the elevators. They could do this. And a good old-fashioned mystery was never a bad distraction.

"Look, I'm not going to solve it for you, but you're not doing half bad. You've got the information. Now you have to make the connections." Sam stopped in front of the elevator bank and looked over at him. Snapping their fingers, Sam said, "Critical thinking, Noah. All the methodical research in the world won't solve the case if you can't make the right connections."

"What, like making the 'connection' between some fancy-ass coffee and a crazy best man burning his shoes on the beach and then exploding a whole fucking boat to cover it up?" Noah asked, and Sam rolled their eyes at how ridiculous he made the whole thing sound. "Who makes those kinds of connections, Sam?" he demanded. "That's, like, some Batman-level shit."

"Well, you could start with making connections like pushing the call button when you're standing right in front of it," Sam said, and Noah jerked in surprise. He reached hesitantly for the down arrow, and Sam sighed. "It's not as hard as you think. A big part of it is trusting that you've already got the right stuff going for you." When Noah just looked more confused, Sam tapped their temple pointedly. "You have to believe that your mind is making the right connections even when you aren't sure how to verbalize them yet."

"Uh, what? Are you, like, a PhD or something, too?" Noah said as the elevator arrived with a ding. "Maybe you should be the one writing a book."

"No thanks."

"All right, all right. Trust my instincts, huh?" Noah said thoughtfully as he followed Sam onto the elevator. This time he pressed the ground floor button without being prompted, at least. "Well, first off, if we're talking gut instinct, I think the witnesses are being on the level with me."

"OK. That's good. Why's that?"

"I dunno. Just seems that way," he said with a shrug.

"What did I literally just say? Think about why it seems that way."

"All right, fine," Noah said defensively, even though Sam wasn't being nearly as snappy as they had been pre–panic attack. "I guess . . . they're all pretty old and shit. Like this one lady—she reminded me of my nonna.

Sweetest old gal you'll ever meet, but she'll gut you with her potato peeler if you try to steal a cookie before dinner." Noah laughed like he really thought the image of an old woman killing someone with a kitchen instrument was normal humor. Given his bizarre family stories, maybe to him, it was. "Most of the people I talked to were like that. And what kind of person goes to Monday morning mass and then lies to a police detective about a priest? That'll send you right to hell for sure."

The elevator doors opened on the ground floor as Noah crossed himself against the thought for good measure. Apparently he really was a good Catholic boy, despite his sailor's mouth.

"OK, so if Father D'Angelo really did go straight from the service in the church to the parking lot where he died, that does tell you something new," Sam said. They could feel their body relaxing by fractions as they caught sight of the outside world through the glass doors of the lobby.

"Yeah . . . yeah, probably definitely not an accident, then," Noah said begrudgingly as they headed over to the visitor's log near the front desk.

"Not a lot of time to sit and sniff the metal polishing kits," Sam agreed. They stood by as Noah scratched out their exit time in the log and threw their passes in the bin. "And how much cyanide did he have in his system?"

"Well over 200 milligrams. Would have taken him around fifteen minutes to die, max."

"And that means . . . ?" Sam prompted.

"Uhh . . ." Noah paused to squint his eyes in concentration halfway through writing his signature.

"If he went right from the church to the parking lot, and it only took fifteen minutes to die . . ." Sam repeated. Snapping their fingers again, they said, "Come on, Noah. Use your brain. How would a priest be poisoned during that timeframe?"

"It's the fucking Eucharist," he blurted, and then flinched hard enough to create a long squiggle on the page. Tossing the pen away, he crossed himself fervently and said, "Forgive me for my sins, Father."

"They must love you at confession."

"I may be a dumbass, but I'm not stupid," Noah said, rolling his eyes in direct contrast to his avid religiosity. "If I die tomorrow, no way I'm letting my big mouth send me to hell."

"Seemingly not stupid," Sam replied dryly. Seeing a nurse approaching, they took a quick step back from the desk and gestured for Noah to follow. "But you're right. If Father D'Angelo was poisoned while inside the church, the Eucharist does make a lot of sense."

"I can't believe I didn't think of it before." Noah didn't even seem to notice Sam holding the door open for him as he blew right through the rotating doors instead. He was too busy looking a mix of frustrated and amazed as the gears turned in his little rookie brain. "Yeah. Yeah, yeah, yeah . . . I mean, anyone coulda slipped something in his wine or in the bread. Hell, it's a miracle we don't have more dead priests on our hands."

Sam breathed in deeply as they followed him out into the sunlight. The panic was significantly less than it had been after the interview with Tasha, but the less time they spent trapped between those cold white walls, the better.

"Seemingly a miracle."

Noah glanced over at Sam in surprise.

"Father D'Angelo left in a rush, most likely after he began experiencing symptoms," Sam explained patiently. "And his phone was missing. You think your killer took the phone because D'Angelo was calling an ambulance or because he was calling the police?"

"What's the difference?" Noah asked as Sam fished in their pocket for their car keys. "It's all 9-1-1, isn't it?"

"I'm just saying, don't get blinded by the how. Especially if the how tells you something about the why," Sam said, looping the ancient leather keychain around their finger and heading toward the parking lot. "Motive is everything."

"You know, you really are wicked good at this shit," Noah said with open admiration as he followed faithfully at their heels.

"Thanks," Sam said shortly. As if today's little field trip hadn't already been weird enough without him adding compliments to the mix.

"Hey, can I ask you a more personal question?" Noah asked just as they reached the car.

Sam sighed loudly. They could not imagine personal questions from the kid being nearly as much fun as with Teddy. Even if Noah was somehow the older of the two.

"You can ask," Sam said finally, because thinking about Teddy always made them err on the side of not being a total jerk. He was annoying like that, even when he wasn't around.

"Why do you do it?"

Sam's hand hesitated on the car door handle. They gave Noah a questioning look over the top of the car.

"I mean, why become a detective?" Noah clarified. Gesturing over his shoulder to the hospital, he said, "You clearly hate going places like this. And pretty much everyone treats you like shit. No offense. What's the point?"

"Isn't being 'wicked good at this shit' a good enough reason?" Sam asked. Popping the car door open, they sighed again and said, "I don't know, Noah. Someone's got to catch the bad guys. Might as well be me."

"Yeah, but—" Noah stopped talking long enough to wrench open his own door and drop into the passenger seat. The second Sam had settled in next to him, he said, "I don't know. I guess I just think it's kind of wild that you still care about your vics so much even after doing this for so long."

"When you stop caring about the victims, that's when it's time to turn in your badge," Sam said, sliding the keys into the ignition. "There's really no point to this job otherwise."

"That's a pretty sick line. Can I steal that?" Noah's eager voice shattered the serious illusion of the moment.

Sam just shook their head in disbelief and started the car.

Ignoring their reaction, Noah lowered his voice and said in his twangiest country accent, "Ain't no point to this here work if you done stopped carin' 'bout the victims."

"Seriously?" Sam complained.

Noah had the audacity to laugh.

"I help you with your case and this is what I get? Unbelievable. I should drive this car right into the ocean."

"Don't you mean you oughta drive this here car right into the dang— ow!" Noah complained as Sam intentionally hit the speed bump on the way out of the hospital parking lot, hard enough to send the rookie's head into the roof of the car.

"Oops," Sam deadpanned in that old Carolina accent. "You know us Southern belles. Just can't drive for shit."

"Aw, come on!" Noah whined, glaring at them as he rubbed his head. "That move with the Wayne impression was a fucking trip. How the hell did someone like you come from the South anyways?"

Sam didn't reply. Instead, they pressed their foot to the accelerator and switched gears. Aggressively. So he couldn't possibly miss their little "tell."

"Copy that, boss," Noah grumbled, settling back in his seat. "Personal question time over."

"Good," Sam said simply. "Now it's your turn to help me. Start by telling Vivienne we're heading her way with some new information. I'm going to be very interested in finding out exactly how a ghost was texting with my vic hours before she died."

CHAPTER FOURTEEN

The silence in the boardroom was stifling. Normally Sam preferred things that way, but even they were getting a little uncomfortable as Donovan calmly read through the case notes from her seat at the head of the table.

Vivienne didn't seem to know what to do with herself now that she had ceded her position to the captain. She just kept spinning her pen around her fingers in increasingly anxious patterns.

Noah was watching the movement with zombie-like fascination, although Sam thought it was a real possibility that he was just sleeping with his eyes open at this point. Beck had at least had the good foresight to bring her laptop with her to the meeting and was doggedly working away like they hadn't all just pulled an all-nighter.

The urge to get up and walk until they made it back to their bed was nearly overwhelming, so Sam slid their phone out of their pocket for a distraction. It had been on silent since Tasha broke the news about her sister's non-existent beau some twenty-four hours ago.

Sam's eyes felt like sandpaper as they blinked down at the screen. There were several new emails and app notifications, but their attention focused on a single missed text. The timestamp read 12:03 a.m.—so probably right around the time Vivienne was telling her engineers that people were going to start getting fired if she didn't start getting answers.

Teddy: everything go ok with the baby cop and the hospital? <3

Sam couldn't help smiling a little. Maybe it was the sleep deprivation, but there was something very charming about Teddy checking in on them like that. Just imagining him actually staying by his phone all day in case they needed someone to talk to had them feeling more awake. Although it also made them wish they had checked their messages sooner.

"Phone away, Detective," Donovan said without even looking up from the report.

Sam pocketed the phone and made a mental note to reply to Teddy later.

The silence ticked on, twice as thick and three times as unbearable in the renewed stillness.

Finally, Donovan sighed and let the report fall to the table. "So we've got nothing," she said bluntly. The room erupted into a chorus of denial, and she raised one hand to pinch the bridge of her nose. "OK. OK! One at a time." Turning to Vivienne, she asked, "Are we sure there's no history of the victim talking to anyone before she was stabbed?"

"No," Vivienne said a little stiffly. Although she was making a valiant effort to behave with Donovan in the room, there was no hiding the irritation lurking just beneath the surface. "Alicia was active on Paths that day, but her conversation history is completely blank."

"Meaning?" Donovan asked.

"Assuming Tasha wasn't mistaken about her sister using the app that night, my top engineers could only conclude that someone must have gone into the backend and deleted the conversation history manually."

"Meaning?" the captain repeated, with some irritation this time.

"We're looking for Steve Jobs or some other kind of super-genius," Sam interjected before the tick in Vivienne's jaw could turn into a proper firefight. "Someone smart enough to break into the company's servers, anyways."

"Please," Vivienne scoffed. Her grip tightened around the pen in her hand when Sam sighed loudly. "Steve Jobs was a hack, and even if he wasn't, he couldn't have gotten into my system."

"We've been over this, Mrs. Fox," Sam said with all the patience they could muster, which really was not much at this point. "It's not a closed system. It was possible for someone to go in and—"

"And I told you. I built this system myself," Vivienne snapped back.

Sam stared her down across the table, too exhausted to argue anymore.

"I poured months—years—of my life into this. There's no way somebody could just—"

"Oh my god, how many times are we gonna go over this?" Noah burst out. The poor kid looked like he was going to fall asleep in his seat or start crying from exhaustion if he had to listen to Sam and Vivienne go another round on the same topic they'd been arguing about all night long.

"Detective Mariano," Donovan warned.

"He's right," Sam interjected bluntly. Ignoring Vivienne's glare, they said, "We know the hack happened, whether Mrs. Fox likes it or not. We should be focusing on figuring out who did it, not rehashing old news."

"And there are no other options for how someone might have accomplished this? Other than hacking in remotely?" Donovan asked. Sam could practically see her trying to figure out how to spin this for Mayor Kelso.

Sam hesitated. They looked at Vivienne sidelong, but when she didn't speak up, they said carefully, "There is one other method, but it was determined to be . . . equally unlikely."

"Less likely than our culprit being smarter than Steve Jobs?" Donovan asked dryly.

"What Detective Sam is trying to say is that, technically, I could have used my personal administrative password to delete the conversation history locally," Vivienne said. Placing her phone on the table a little harder than was necessary, she explained, "The password is only stored on this phone. It's a twenty-digit alphanumeric that not even I have memorized, and I can assure you it is more than unlikely that I would use it for something like this."

"I see."

Donovan locked eyes with Sam and raised one eyebrow in silent question. Sam didn't dare look in Vivienne's direction, but they gave a small, nearly imperceptible shake of their head.

"Seriously?"

"Oh, give it a rest, Viv," Sam groaned at the sound of Vivienne's needling voice. Donovan gave them a critical look, but Sam had zero energy left for placating anyone at this point. "Nobody thinks you had anything to do with these murders. But someone deleted that conversation history. And I understand that this is upsetting information, but it happened, so for the love of god, can we please move on?"

"It just doesn't make any sense." Beck's perturbed voice broke the silence coming from her corner of the boardroom. Her fingers still rested on her keyboard, but her gaze seemed far away. "What kind of person would be smart enough to hack the system but wouldn't think to delete the activity logs?"

"That is Detective Sam's job to find out," Donovan said. She turned that cool gaze on Sam, and somehow the stout woman appeared even more exhausted than the rest of the team put together. "I expect them to leave no stone unturned pursuing this new information. Yes, Detective?"

"Sure. Of course," Sam said. Most of them was too tired to care, but a small piece of them was relieved at the thought of finally turning this into a real investigation. "I'll start by narrowing in on Jason and Brad. Hopefully one of them can give us an idea about—"

"Well, that'd be a fuckin' waste of time," Noah interjected.

Sam turned their exhausted glare on him. If looks could kill, he would have been nothing but a pile of smoking ash.

"Uh . . . sorry," Noah corrected, shrinking down in his seat. "I just meant they're probably not worth looking into anymore, right? Since Jason's a lawyer and Brad's a gym owner, so . . . not exactly super-hackers . . . ?"

"Well, I think I'd need to actually speak with them to know that," Sam said in the slow, deliberate tone of someone who was speaking to an idiot.

"Detective Mariano isn't wrong," Beck said. "Although not because of their occupations." Spinning her laptop to face the rest of the table, she pointed to the information on the screen. "We have Jason and Brad's activity logs," Beck explained. Despite the fact that she had also pulled an all-nighter, she seemed utterly unaffected by the lack of sleep. "Unlike Alicia, Jason has a full chat history from that night. He was actually engaged in a conversation with another woman at the time of Alicia's death, and Brad wasn't online at all that entire week."

Donovan slid on a pair of reading glasses and leaned forward to squint at the laptop screen. Frowning at the blank timeline on Brad's part of the spreadsheet, she asked, "How is that different from Alicia having no conversation history?"

"Alicia has no conversation history from that night, but she did have the app open. Like . . ." Beck circled her hand in the air for a moment as she tried to find a way to explain the difference. Turning to her boss, she said, "Viv, can I see your phone?"

Vivienne still didn't look happy about it, but she slid the cell phone across the table to the younger woman. Beck quickly unlocked the screen and pressed the home button to bring up a row of Vivienne's open tabs. "You see how Viv has the app open right now?" Beck said, gesturing to the cheerful pink icon. "She's not literally using it right now, but she has it open. So if Vivienne had an account, she would be marked as online but not active."

"Ah. So Mr. Lu having no activity means he didn't open the app at all, much less use it to have a conversation," Donovan said, leaning back in her seat.

Beck nodded eagerly. "I've been giving it some thought," she said. With a few deft keystrokes, she brought up another spreadsheet. "What Detective Sam should be looking for is local men who have been active clients for at least six months, who were marked as online but inactive the night of Alicia's assault, and who might be technically competent enough to erase their activity."

Sam stared at the spreadsheet with dull, unfocused eyes. They knew they should be reading the information, or questioning Beck's logic, or something. But all they could really think was how much they regretted swearing off espresso.

"Well?" Donovan asked impatiently, and Sam startled to attention. "Are you the detective here, or is she?"

"Those parameters sound fine, I guess," Sam said. Giving their head a hard shake, they forced themself to refocus on the information spilling off the edge of Beck's spreadsheet. "This won't tell us anything about motive until we actually interview some of these guys, though." Squinting at the sheet to try and see the number at the bottom of the page, they asked, "If you sort by those parameters, how many men would that leave for me to speak with?"

"For just the first two parameters?" Beck asked. Sam nodded, and she spun the laptop back toward herself. Typing in a few rapid commands, she said, "That'd give us . . . 1,517 candidates."

"One thousand and how many?"

"Dude. I don't think you can do a thousand dates," Noah said stupidly. "That'd take, like . . ." he seemed to think hard for a long moment before finally saying, "Shit. I don't know. Years or something."

"I am not going on a thousand dates," Sam said flatly.

"You won't have to."

Sam looked over at Vivienne in surprise. Although she still didn't look happy, she gestured to Beck's laptop and explained, "The number she gave you is only that high because so many people leave the app open when they're not using it. But once we add the third parameter, that number will go way down."

"Exactly," Beck agreed eagerly. "It's not so easy as just pushing a button, but once I comb people's profiles to figure out who might have the technical competence to do something like this, I'll be able to create a new short list." Seeing the disquieted look on Sam's face, she said, "Don't worry. This city is no San Francisco. We've got a lot more beach bums trying to be Steven Spielberg than Steve Jobs."

That same fog filtered through Sam's thoughts again as they watched Beck typing away on her computer. Probably already searching keywords and search histories or whatever it was the Cupid team did to match people with their "soulmates." Only this time, Beck was using her methods to hunt down potential murderers.

Sam wanted to believe that if they were more awake they could have explained why data mining for leads felt all kinds of backwards. But realistically, with their lead tongue, it probably wouldn't have made any difference.

"How many?" they finally asked.

Beck paused in her typing to give Sam a questioning look.

"Suspects," Sam clarified. "After you're done doing . . . that. How many do you think it's going to be?"

"Kind of hard to say," Beck said with an easy shrug. When Vivienne gave her a pointed look, she hurriedly added, "But, uh, if I had to guess, I'd probably say at least fifty. Give or take a couple dozen."

"Fifty?" Noah repeated.

"No. No way," Sam said at nearly the same moment. Staring directly at Donovan, lest they be in any way unclear, Sam said, "I agreed to three dates with three suspects. I am not doing fifty dates with a bunch of random people who have no record of ever even speaking to our vics."

"You wouldn't literally have to do fifty more dates," Beck assured them. As if that was even a remote possibility. "We do a mixer every week. I could put together the list and then create an exclusive invite for the people you need to talk to. Something with a door prize or whatever that most people won't be able to refuse."

"That . . . might actually work," Vivienne said hesitantly, then winced at the poisonous look Sam gave her. "I'm not saying we should do it. Just that it's a viable option."

"It could really work," Beck insisted. "We'll get as many of the fifty in the room as we can, and you can blitz through them all in one night. It'll be like one long undercover date, instead of—"

"Are you hearing this?" Sam demanded, whipping around to face Donovan.

If they were expecting to find an ally there, though, they were sorely mistaken. Donovan was looking at Beck and her laptop like she had just discovered self-checkout at the grocery store.

"Oh, come on. You can't seriously be considering this crap," Sam complained.

"Do you have a better angle?" Donovan asked calmly.

"Yes. It's called real police work. Not data mining for leads," Sam replied. Beck immediately began to protest, but Sam just waved her words away impatiently. "Listen. If you want a computer to tell me who to talk to, that's fine. If Mayor Kelso thinks you need to put me in high heels and lipstick to solve this case for some goddamned reason, fine. But you cannot possibly think we're going to solve this case without doing any real police work."

"I appreciate your frustration, Detective," Donovan said with all the sympathy of an ice sculpture. "But these women aren't going to be the only victims if we don't find a way to narrow down the suspect list quickly."

"Just give me one week." Leaning forward in their chair, Sam said, "Look how far I got with one real interview. Imagine what I could do if I actually talked to Cassie's coworkers, or Nikki's family, or—"

"How long do you need?" Donovan asked abruptly.

"I told you," Sam said. "Give me one—"

"Not you. You," Donovan said, jerking her chin in Beck's direction. The other woman froze as the room's attention swiveled back to her. "How long do you need to arrange your plan with the mixer?"

"Um . . . well," Beck said slowly. She glanced at Sam guiltily but said, "If I don't sleep, I guess . . . I could probably have invitations out within 24 hours?"

"OK then," Donovan said. Sam's gut clenched at the definitive note in her voice. "Let's do it. I'll expect an update within the next two days and numbers on the attendees so we can keep Detective Sam's ops team in the loop." Giving Sam the steely-eyed look of a person used to disappointing people, the captain said, "is that going to be a problem, Detective?"

Noah winced in anticipation of the fireworks, but Sam just stared back at Donovan with nothing at all to say. Maybe they should have been shouting and swearing and making a fuss about this newest kick in the teeth. But in order to conjure up the energy for any of that, Sam would have to believe for even a second that Donovan would ever choose reason over speed. And she never would. Because people didn't get promoted for being *reasonable*.

"Captain Donovan," Vivienne said hesitantly. There was a real note of concern in her voice when she took in the utterly blank look on Sam's face. "While I see the value in Beck's idea, I think it might be worth considering Detective Sam's—"

"Enough. I've made my decision," Donovan said shortly. This time Sam dared to blink in response, and Donovan pinched the bridge of her nose again. "Listen. I'm not asking you to stop investigating. Use the twenty-four hours. Talk to the families. Find me some witnesses. Nothing would thrill me more." Dropping her hand, she offered the entire room that signature steely-eyed expression when she said, "Do what you have to do, and do it quickly. Or get used to more nights like this one, because this investigation is not over until I've got someone behind bars."

CHAPTER FIFTEEN

Sam stared uncertainly at the building sprawling out before them. Logically, they had known Cassie volunteered at a church-run food bank. It was written plainly in the brief, and they had looked up the location in advance. But somehow they still hadn't anticipated the large cross hanging on the front door of the building or the scripture verses plastered in every window.

Hopefully the Protestants would be a little more open-minded than their Catholic brethren. Although Sam couldn't say they were feeling especially optimistic.

Sam's hand had just touched down on the door handle when their pocket let out a loud buzz. They swore loudly enough to give a nun a heart attack. A cat nap in their car clearly hadn't been enough to fully restore their senses after that all-nighter.

Seeing the name on their screen only had Sam's pulse picking up more.

Teddy: hope today is better than yesterday
Teddy: call me if you want to talk <3

The wave of longing they felt upon reading his text wasn't entirely unexpected, but the intensity of it still took their breath away. Sam knew they were too tired and definitely too cranky for any good to come of such a call. But the idea of talking to someone who might actually understand their frustration was incredibly appealing, nevertheless.

Sadly, Donovan had only given them a day to make some progress, so instead of texting Teddy back like a normal person, they just pocketed their phone and promised themselves they would reply later. For real this time.

Right now they had the much easier task of solving a murder.

No sooner had Sam pushed their way through the front doors than they began regretting their decision to come here. Volunteers in neon-orange shirts flitted around in a frenzy as tired, disheveled people in need of a meal milled about the open hallway holding paper plates filled with questionable food combinations. The muted chaos made Sam think of a twenty-four-hour McDonald's filled with customers and staff who existed outside of time. If the overwhelming smell of competing dishes didn't make Sam want to leave immediately, the rictus smiles from the good Christian volunteers definitely did.

"Hey there," a cheerful male voice called. Sam tensed like a cat in cold water as an orange shirt with a silver ponytail at least a foot too long veered off course toward them. "You aren't the police detective I'm waiting for by any chance, are you?" the man asked.

"Yeah. That'd be me," Sam said, taking an uncomfortable step back when the man moved in a little too close in order to avoid a fellow volunteer hustling by with a food cart.

"Fantastic. Great to meet you," the man said, not seeming to notice Sam's reaction. He held out one hand and then added with exaggerated care, "I'm Andrew Tarver. He/him."

"A pleasure," Sam said dryly. Shaking his hand once, they resisted Andrew's sincere stare for a long moment before finally giving in and saying, "Detective Sam." And then even more quietly they muttered, "They/them."

"Cool beans. Come on with me, Sam," Andrew said. His ponytail was already halfway across the room by the time he turned back to call over his shoulder, "Let's chat in my office."

Not a minute later, Sam found themself standing in a glorified storage closet with a paper sign on the door that read "Volunteer Coordinator." The desk appeared to be a slab of wood propped up on a stack of cardboard boxes, and the office chair was one of those inflatable yoga balls people fell off for views on YouTube. All in all, it wasn't exactly what Sam would call an "office"—and that was coming from someone who worked out of their car most days.

"Excuse our humble appearances," Andrew said unapologetically as he squeezed past Sam. Turning to face them from the other side of the desk, Andrew gestured to the balance ball and said, "Care to sit?"

"Uh, no thank you. I'll stand."

"Geez. You should see the look on your face," Andrew said with a small laugh. His expression softened when he took in Sam's rigid stance and polite demeanor. "Just like hers the first time she showed up here."

"Just like whose?" Sam asked, although they were pretty sure there was only one "her" he would be referring to, given their brief call earlier this morning.

"Cassie," Andrew confirmed. Gesturing to Sam's business attire, he said, "She showed up looking like she was ready to file some taxes, too. But as you can see, that sort of thing doesn't last long around here."

"It certainly seems like you're all working hard," Sam agreed politely.

"Well, you know what they say. Nothing good is ever easy."

In direct contrast to his cheerful words, Andrew dropped heavily onto the balance ball with a low sigh. Despite his best efforts to be "up," the soup stains on his shirt and the sweat rings under his pits spoke to how taxing this work really was. And he was probably being paid even less than Sam to be here. So maybe they could afford to be a little more charitable in their attitude, at least.

"Thank you for taking the time today, Mr. Tarver." Sam reached into their jacket pocket and produced their trusty tape recorder, already primed with a fresh tape. Trying to channel as much sincerity as they could, they said, "I'm sure you're busy, so if you don't mind, we can just—"

"Oh, Andrew is fine," the older gentleman said with an easy wave of his hand. "You'll find we're not that kind of formal around here, Sam." When Sam hesitated, he added, "If you prefer Detective Sam or something else, that's fine, too. Just let me know."

". . . No," Sam said slowly. The whole vibe of this place was certainly not what they had expected, and it was messing with their train of thought. Or maybe that was the lack of sleep. Giving their head a shake, they said, "Sam—just Sam is fine."

"Cool beans," Andrew said. Grinning a little, he gestured to the ancient device in their hand and said, "So, a tape recorder, eh? I guess the police are working off the same kind of budget we are these days."

"Something like that," Sam said. Glancing down at the little device, they shook their head again and then said, "Would it be all right if I recorded our conversation, Andrew? It could be a big help to the investigation."

"Of course. Go right ahead," Andrew assured them. His smile held that same sad, nostalgic tint again when he said, "Anything for Cassie."

Recording #3: Andrew Tarver

There is the loud ca-chunk of the tape recorder being engaged. The sound of footsteps can be heard in the background of the recording, along with the general racket of a busy kitchen leaking in through the "office" door.

"Sorry, it's not going to be the cleanest recording."

"That's OK. This is mainly so I can focus on our conversation without having to take notes."

"Right. Got it."

"Can you state your name and how you knew the victim to get us going?"

"Sure thing. Andrew Tarver, he/him. I'm the volunteer coordinator here at Sunrise House, an affiliate of New Life Church. Cassie serves—used to serve here on the weekends as part our Meals for the Meek program."

"Thank you, Andrew. Are you OK with me asking a few questions about Cassie now?"

"Of course. Whatever I can do to help."

"You said on the phone this morning that Cassie had been volunteering here for several years. Do you remember when exactly she started?"

"Oh, geez. Maybe, like, two years and change? It was right after she started that swanky new job as the director of whatever."

"Director of Publicity at Vision for Excellence."

"Yeah, that. I know she was really good at what she did and all, but I think she also felt a bit disconnected. It's a big change to go from being in the trenches to working in the corner office."

"That's understandable. And she found volunteering here helped her feel . . . more connected?"

"I sure hope so, otherwise I'm not sure why she kept coming back."

"Maybe it was all the free food."

"Ha! You're pretty funny under the monkey suit, aren't you, Sam?"

"... Super funny."

"You really do remind me so much of her. She kept trying to fix everything for her first few months here. Like if we just added one more spreadsheet, suddenly this place would go from organized chaos to a machine of efficiency. It took her a while to figure out that that wasn't really the goal."

"You prefer being disorganized?"

"Not really. But the first goal is for everyone who comes here to get a good meal and leave with a full heart. The rest is just icing on the cake."

"Right."

". . ."

"So after a while Cassie was able to, uh, get with the program, so to speak?"

"Sure did. In fact, up until a few weeks ago, she was one of our top volunteers."

"Up until a few weeks ago?"

". . ."

"Oh. You mean—because she passed away."

"Yeah. Sorry. Sometimes we just . . . We lose a lot of volunteers, you know? People get busy with kids, or new jobs, or move farther away, and . . . it can be easier sometimes. To think of the real losses as just another missing connection."

"Ah."

"But it's better to face reality. Death is all part of Christ's plan for each of us, and even though Cassie was called home much sooner than any of us would have liked, we can still honor her life by trying to help you find the person responsible for her death."

"So you can pray for them?"

"No. So they can go to prison for the rest of their God-given life."

"I see. In that case, what else can you tell me about Cassie? We know a fair amount about her from a professional perspective, but not much about her as a person. Did she have hobbies, friends, interests, fears, dreams . . . ?"

"Oh yeah, all that good stuff. Cassie wasn't the super chatty type, but once she opened up to you, you realized how much was going on behind the curtain. She was the type who could read a book and still be having thoughts on the themes a month later. But you wouldn't know unless you asked her."

"It sounds like you really took the time to get to know her."

"I try to know all of our volunteers. We're doing soul work here, not solo work."

"How much did you know about Cassie's dating habits?"

"Uh, well, I'm a paid staff member, so I wasn't trying to get to know any of the volunteers in that way."

"Sorry. I wasn't trying to imply anything. I can see that you're married."

"Thirty-five years next month."

"Congratulations."

"You know, I tried to avoid any topics that might be crossing the line with the volunteers, but Cassie did ask for prayers regarding her search for a partner a few times during our morning huddles."

"So she was looking to find a husband?"

"Or a wife."

". . ."

"I assume you know Cassie was queer."

"I read it in her file, yes."

"Well, we were very supportive of her search. Speaking from experience, when a person is called to partnership, it can be very lonely before you find that missing piece."

". . . Sure. And Cassie never found her . . . person?"

"No. For a while there she was spending a lot of time on those apps—you know, the ones that bleep and bloop a lot about foxy singles in your area."

There is the sound of startled laughter in response to the man's blunt assessment.

"I don't think that's quite what the apps do, but go on."

"Honestly, I wouldn't know. Those things always made me uncomfortable, but I thought I was just being old-fashioned. She seemed to feel like she was getting somewhere, or at least learning more about what she wasn't looking for."

"That's an optimistic take."

"Cassie was a pretty optimistic one, that's for sure. That's why I thought . . ."

". . . ?"

"It just seemed a little odd to me after her phone stopped making all those noises. I thought maybe she had found someone to go steady with, but she seemed . . . off."

"We're aware that she wasn't actively using the app as much in the weeks leading up to her death. Does that line up with what you observed?"

"Yes. It was at least the last three Saturdays before she passed that she really wasn't seeming herself."

"And you're sure she wasn't just distracted by something else unrelated to the app? Maybe a new hobby, or long hours at work?"

". . . I'm quite sure."

". . ."

"I guess it's a little misleading to say she didn't seem herself. What I mean is, she seemed nervous. Jumpy, even. She asked my wife for a ride home after each of her shifts, even though she normally walked, and she stopped coming out for dinner with the rest of the Saturday group."

"Do you know the reason for her change in behavior?"

". . ."

". . ."

". . ."

"You can tell me, Andrew."

"..."

"..."

"She was nervous. About using the—the app thing. Ever since ..."

"..."

"..."

"I understand wanting to keep Cassie's confidence, Andrew. But it's important that I know."

"..."

"Do you think Cassie was assaulted by one of her connections on the app? Or—"

"No. No, she promised me it was nothing like that."

"..."

"You have to understand. If it was anything like that, I would have encouraged her—I would have insisted that she go to the police. But she promised me it was a—a—a mutual decision. Unexpected, but—nothing like that."

"..."

"Well, it wasn't—it wasn't what she planned, obviously. She told my wife she had been using . . . protection. But I guess something went wrong, and—"

"Oh."

"... Yes."

"Cassie was pregnant."

"Yes."

"You're sure?"

"She ran off in the middle of one of her Saturday shifts. It wasn't like her to disappear like that, so I went to make sure she was all right. When I saw her chucking up out back, well. I've got four kids of my own."

"And you're absolutely—"

"I am sure. My wife asked, and she told her honestly what had happened."

"Ah. I see."

". . ."

". . ."

". . ."

"Andrew, I know this might be an uncomfortable question, but I have to ask. Did Cassie intend to keep the baby?"

"Of course she did."

"My apologies. I didn't mean to offend."

"No—I'm sorry. I don't mean to be so . . . it just wasn't like that. It wasn't the way she planned it, but Cassie was excited about the baby."

"Excited?"

"I know how it sounds, but I promise, if she hadn't been, we would have supported her. Of course we would have. But it was like Cassie had suddenly found her missing piece in that moment."

"I see."

"I know how it must sound. Really, I do. But it's God's honest truth."

". . ."

"Do you have any children of your own, Sam?"

"No."

"Do you want children?"

"No."

". . ."

". . ."

". . ."

"I guess it might be more accurate to say it's not really an option for me. Biologically."

"Biology doesn't have much to do with wanting something."

"..."

"..."

"And you're sure that's how Cassie felt? Even though there was no one else in the picture?"

"I told you she asked us to pray for her to find someone. But when we found out about the baby, she said it felt like she had found her missing piece already. Like this was the thing she had actually been searching for."

"That's nice."

"Yes. I just wish . . ."

". . .?"

"We were all so happy for her. But it was obvious something had been weighing on her beyond just grappling with this change."

"..."

"..."

"You haven't mentioned the baby's father yet."

"You don't miss much, do you?"

"It comes with the job."

"..."

"So Cassie's sudden anxiety—I'm guessing it had something to do with the father? Did he know, or was she afraid for him to find out?"

"He knew. I believe their last interaction was when she used the app to tell him right after she found out."

"He didn't take it well?"

"To say the least. I can't imagine someone suggesting—well, let's just say the man had no interest in being a father. And he was not interested in Cassie being a mother, either."

"Ah. I see."

"She told us that she tried to talk to him at first, to assure him he wouldn't have to be involved in the child's life or anything like that. But his messages turned aggressive. She was frightened about what he might do. And then . . ."

"She was murdered."

"I wish I had taken it more seriously. I should have—gosh. I should have told her to go to the police, or asked her to come stay with my wife and I, or—or at least asked to see the messages. Anything. We just thought because she said it wasn't a big deal and she wasn't going to use the app anymore . . ."

"It's OK, Andrew. It sounds like you were being a good boss and respecting Cassie's wishes. You couldn't have known this would happen."

". . ."

"Andrew, I know this is difficult to talk about, but I need to know. Did Cassie ever tell you the name of the father?"

"No."

"You're sure?"

"I couldn't be more sure. I've thought and prayed and searched for that answer, but . . . she never told us. Or maybe I just don't remember."

"I'm sure it's that she never told you."

"I hope you're right. I pray to God you're right."

". . ."

"I'm—I'm sorry. Could you just—? I need a moment."

"Sure. Of course. Take as long as you need."

The button releases with a pop and the sound of muffled weeping fades out as the tape spins to a stop.

CHAPTER SIXTEEN

"No," Noah gasped. His eyes were wide with horror as he wrapped his arms around the back of the office chair he was straddling. "The guy really tried to force her to . . . ?"

"That was the implication."

The young rookie had taken up residence in the abandoned cubicle to the right of Sam's desk, much to Sam's chagrin. There was a reason the space had been abandoned for years. But no matter how many times they snapped at him to turn down his music or got annoyed with his inane chatter, Noah still had not taken the hint to move somewhere else.

At least having someone to go over case updates with wasn't the worst possible outcome.

"According to Cassie's boss at the shelter, our mystery guy wanted her to terminate the pregnancy, or he was going to make her regret it," Sam explained. They filed the tape from Andrew's interview alongside Tasha's recording from earlier in their cabinet. "Apparently, she refused, so maybe he made good on that promise."

"Damn. That's super fucked." Noah rested his chin on the top of the chair, looking somber at the thought. Then he immediately ruined the image by saying, "This is exactly why you gotta wrap it. Double wrap it. Whatever it takes."

"And if that doesn't work?" Sam asked with some amusement. The situation wasn't really funny, but Noah's simplistic take on things kind of was.

"Uh, it works," he insisted. Glancing down at himself with some concern now, Noah added under his breath, "It better fuckin' work."

"So, what, if a good Catholic boy like you knocked up some girl, you'd just dump her?"

"What? No. Hell no," Noah exclaimed, looking properly horrified all over again. "I'd marry her if she wanted to keep it, obviously. Wouldn't you?"

"If *I* got a girl pregnant? I don't know. It'd certainly give me a lot to think about," Sam said dryly. Martin let out a snort of laughter from the other side of their shared cubicle wall. At least Sam wasn't the only one who found the gullible rookie amusing.

"Seriously? That seems kind of . . ." Noah's impassioned words trailed off as he finally picked up the sound of Martin snickering. Narrowing his eyes at Sam's tiny smirk, he said, ". . . You're making fun of me again, aren't you?"

"You know, I think maybe you are getting smarter," Sam said, and Noah rolled his eyes at their version of "teasing."

"Worst supervisor ever," he muttered as he spun his chair back toward his computer screen.

"Hey. I still sign off on your performance reports, you know."

"Yeah, yeah. I'm working, aren't I?" Noah scooted closer to his desk and reached for the landline wedged into the corner before Sam could get in another dig. Despite the fact that he couldn't be bothered to sit like a normal, professional human being, he had no trouble snatching up the phone and dialing the number without even looking at the keypad. "Hey Doc," he said after a couple seconds of silence. "This is Detective Mariano calling you for the . . . third time this week. Call me back at the same number I gave the last two times whenever you feel like being helpful."

With that, the rookie hung up the phone with all the grace Sam had come to expect from him. He pulled up a spreadsheet and started typing.

"What was that?" Sam asked, leaning back in their chair to get a look at the case update Noah was writing.

"The guy's a tool—trust me," Noah said with a casual wave of his hand. "There's no point in being polite."

"No, I mean—who were you calling?" Sam clarified. Abandoning their own case notes, Sam swiveled to face him properly. "I haven't heard anything about a doctor yet."

"I thought I was supposed to be working?" Noah grumbled as Sam's suspicious gaze pinged off the back of his skull.

"Reporting to your supervisor is working."

"More like you're stalling 'cause you don't wanna go back to Barbie's Castle for the op tonight." Grabbing his cell phone, Noah looked at the time on the screen and added, "You're gonna be late, you know."

"Shut up," Sam said with a scowl that hid nothing about their feelings on the matter. As if the speed dating event from hell could actually be considered real police work. "Now give me an update or go get me a coffee."

"But I'm not supposed to get you—"

Noah cut off when Sam raised a pointed eyebrow at him.

"Ugh. Fine. Fine!" Noah said with all the exasperation of a teenager being asked if his homework was done. "Doc Dickhead is Father D'Angelo's PCP. The guy was on some serious meds on account of being super old or whatever, so I'm trying to figure out if a delayed release could have put the cyanide in his system right as the service was ending."

"What happened to the Eucharist angle?" Sam asked. Scrolling back in their memory to their conversation at the hospital, they frowned slightly. Noah had had a day or two to go to the church for the samples, but that seemed like an awfully fast turnaround time for the boys in the lab. "Did the stuff you tested come back negative for cyanide already?"

"Uh . . . no."

"What do you mean, uh no?"

Noah suddenly looked very interested in the report on his computer screen.

"You did get it tested, right?"

"Well, I went and checked it out, obviously. I talked to Father Nicholas," Noah said, sounding a little defensive now. "He said everything about the Eucharist is communal. If Father D'Angelo's bread or wine was poisoned, everyone in mass that morning would have been poisoned."

"Noah."

"What?"

"Are you seriously trying to tell me right now that you didn't get any of that stuff tested because Father Nicholas told you not to?" Sam demanded. When Noah didn't respond, they groaned in disbelief. "Come on. You went and asked one of the other priests whether the sacrament was poisoned, and you just believed him?"

"Of course I believed him," Noah said with a scowl that would have been more convincing if his ears weren't turning bright red. "He's a priest."

"I don't care if he's the goddamned Pope."

Noah raised a hand to cross himself at their blasphemous words, but Sam slapped his hand down before he could complete the motion.

"Don't be such a dumbass. Who would have served Father D'Angelo the Eucharist that morning?"

Noah looked away again in stubborn silence, but the answer was written all over his face.

"Answer the question. Who would have served the victim that morning?"

"One of the other priests. Probably—" Noah hesitated, then let his shoulders slump in defeat. "Probably Father Nicholas."

"So the one person with the most access to poisoning Father D'Angelo told you that was definitely not how it was done," Sam said slowly, just in case Noah hadn't realized how stupid this was yet. "And you just believed him?"

"But he's a priest," Noah repeated. "He can't fucking lie."

"Everyone can lie," Sam said firmly. "Whatever your hang-up is, I expect you to get over it and start looking into Father Nicholas. Starting now. If he is involved, I'm sure your little chat encouraged him to destroy any possible evidence, but it's still worth having the lab take a look at the chalice and ciborium, just in case."

"Oh, good. When you're done yelling at me, I'll just head over there with my baton and a burlap sack," Noah said. He scowled when Sam didn't so much as blink. "You do know I'm Catholic, right?"

"Yeah, believe it or not, I had noticed."

As if the frequent Latinisms and golden St. Joseph medallion hadn't

162

been clues enough. He was certainly more Catholic than Sam had ever managed to be, even with his sailor's mouth.

"And you still expect me to go around taking shit from a church?" Noah demanded.

"If it's evidence, then yes," Sam said unsympathetically. "That's literally your job. But if you'd rather go back to being a beat cop, just let me know. I'm happy to arrange it."

Noah flinched at their harsh words, but before he could come up with a response, the landline on Sam's desk let out a shrill ring.

Glaring over at him, Sam held up one finger and said, "Don't even think about it. I'm not done yet." They snatched the phone from its cradle and snapped, "What?"

"Uh, Detective—Detective Sam?" The female voice on the other end of the line was bright with nerves that accentuated her light accent.

"Yeah. Speaking," Sam said shortly. Seeing Noah wince out of the corner of their eye, they made a concentrated effort to dial back their ire. "How can I help you?"

"Oh, hi. This is Sofía from the front desk. Sorry to bother you, but there's a, uh, delivery here? In your name?"

"If it's something sketchy, just give it to the bomb squad. I'm sure it'll keep them entertained," Sam suggested, and Sofía laughed nervously on the other end.

"Um, I'm pretty confident it's nothing like that. You should probably come down and check it out."

"Great. I'll be down in a minute." Sam sighed, wondering what fresh hell this was going to be. Knowing their luck, it was an entire wardrobe full of glittery pink dresses for their "big date" tonight, courtesy of Vice Squad.

Sam hung up the phone maybe a little more firmly than necessary. Noah's body language was all wounded puppy dog, which only annoyed Sam more. Mostly because it made them want to tell him very loudly to grow up and stop screwing around on this case. But also maybe a little bit because they knew that when they were in his shoes, they could have used a little less yelling and a little more advice.

Letting out a slow breath, Sam finally said, "Listen. You're doing . . . fine. OK?" Noah gave them a skeptical look, so Sam tried again. "I know it's hard. And honestly, it's probably not going to get any easier. But you're going to have to do this stuff anyways, so whatever you have to do to get your head around it, start doing that."

"Geez, thanks. Great pep talk," Noah muttered. He looked surprised when Sam let out a quiet noise that might have been a laugh.

"Sorry to disappoint. They didn't exactly cover pep talks in Sunday school."

"Like you attended Sunday school," Noah scoffed.

"You better believe I did. Mass every Sunday for fifteen years," Sam replied, and Noah nearly fell out of his chair at the easy sound of that old Carolina accent. Smirking a little, Sam said, "Sometimes more often, depending how many times I got caught smoking between services."

"No fuckin' way." If Noah's eyes got any wider, they'd be in real danger of popping right out of his head.

"Just be happy you didn't grow up in my town. The nuns would have strung you up by your boots for all that cussing." Standing up from their chair, Sam stretched out a kink in their neck and said, "Now, I have to go trick some nerds into buying me a drink. And you need to quit leaning on your Catholic guilt as an excuse for not getting this case wrapped up. Understood?"

"Yeah, yeah. Understood," Noah mumbled. He looked contrite, but Sam couldn't help smiling faintly when he added a quiet, "Thanks, boss."

"Sure. I'll see you at the op tonight."

"Yeah. See ya."

Stepping onto the elevator, Sam jabbed the button for the ground floor. Now that babysitting was over, it was time to go face whatever horrors Vivienne had in store for them tonight. They had already attended two briefings in preparation for the mixer—one for strategy and the other on who they'd be targeting—but they still didn't feel any more prepared for the inevitable humiliation.

Sam's thoughts were so wrapped up in pre-planning their argument against whatever girly nonsense they'd undoubtedly be expected to wear that they nearly made it all the way out the front door before a familiar voice called, "Detective Sam?"

"Hm?" Sam said vaguely as they turned back to face the front desk.

Sofía stood there, ringing her hands. When Sam still looked confused, she glanced pointedly at the man slouched against her counter in his all-beige uniform.

"Oh. Right." Sam gave their head a shake and wandered back over to the desk. Glancing around the tidy surface, they asked, "Where's this package I'm signing for?"

"Right here, Miss," the guy said, and Sam took a step back in surprise when he shoved the enormous bouquet of flowers he was holding straight into their face.

"Oh. Um, Sam doesn't go by 'Miss,' I don't think," Sofía interjected weakly as Sam stared cross-eyed down at the spray of magnificent long-stemmed roses.

"OK. Here's your flowers, *pal*," the guy corrected, only gesturing more impatiently for Sam to take the bouquet.

"Uh," Sam said eloquently. Giving their head another hard shake, they finally managed, "These definitely aren't for me."

"Are you 'Detective Sam'?"

". . . Yes."

"Then congratulations. They're for you."

Sam found the bouquet being thrust unceremoniously into their arms, followed immediately by the guy's clipboard.

"Sign here, please."

"Uh . . ." Sam just stared at the clipboard like it was an alien object.

"You know what, I'm just going to initial it. Sound good?" The guy pulled the clipboard back to scribble something indecipherable at the bottom. When Sam continued to look too stunned to object, the man offered them a big plastic smile and said, "OK, you have a nice day now!"

Sam was still floundering for the words to explain that this was some kind of terrible mistake by the time the guy had marched across the lobby floor and straight out the front doors. Their brain was insisting this must be a joke, but if it was, they weren't sure what the punch line was supposed to be. Other than Sofía, no one was here to witness the delivery.

"Well?" Sofía burst out after a long moment. Her gaze was glued to the magnificent bouquet in Sam's arms. "Aren't you going to see who they're from?"

"Uh, right. Sure," Sam said awkwardly. Shifting the paper cone into the crook of their arm with all the grace of a person who clearly had never bought or received flowers, they muttered, "I'm telling you, they're not for me, though."

Despite their words, Sam's heart rate began to increase as they fumbled among the blossoms for the note. It was a single piece of cardstock with a message scrawled out in the prettiest handwriting Sam had ever seen. Blinking hard, they tried to make sense of the words, but for some reason it was all just gibberish. Frowning, they forced themself to read the note again. And then again, because it still didn't make any sense.

Sam,
No sabes todo lo que me haces sentir.
— T
PS. Por favor, llámame

"So? What does it say?" Sofía asked impatiently.

"I'm, uh, not sure, actually," Sam admitted. Their throat was too tight as the words left their lips. Glancing over at her, they asked, "Any chance you speak Spanish?"

"Un poco," she replied sarcastically, and Sam's heart leapt into their throat when she reached for the card. Sofía's curious gaze flicked over the words and she let out an amused giggle. "Wow. Someone has a secret admirer," she teased. Oblivious to Sam's rattled expression, she read, "'Sam, you have no idea what you're doing to me. Signed T.' And then the postscript says—"

"I know what it says. Thanks," Sam said, hurriedly snatching back the card. They didn't need to speak Spanish to guess what Teddy was writing "por favor" about. It was the same thing he'd been asking them for all week while they'd been too busy pulling all-nighters and getting lost in the pressure of the case to text him back. Or to actually press the Call button.

And apparently Teddy had decided that sending them flowers at work was the next best way to try and get their attention. Which was . . . ridiculous. And maybe a little romantic. But still completely ridiculous.

Breathing in deeply, Sam tried to force their looping thoughts back into order. They shoved the card into their pocket and looked helplessly at the flowers in their arms, then at Sofía's glowing face across the desk. "Hey. You're the pregnant one, yeah?"

"Wow. I'm kind of surprised you know that."

"Yeah, well, Noah might have told me," Sam admitted. They shifted the bouquet back into their hands and allowed themself a subtle whiff of the sweet perfume. So outrageous. Really. Flowers, at their office? What the hell was he thinking?

"That Noah," Sofía gushed, touching a hand to her belly. "He's such a sweet—oh." Her words cut off in startled surprise when Sam abruptly held the flowers out to her. "Um . . . ?" Sofía's voice trailed off in question as she tried to see past the blossoms to Sam's shuttered expression.

"Take them," Sam said impatiently. Ducking their head, they tried to sound at least a little polite when they added, "Consider them a congratulations or whatever. For the baby."

"What? But . . ." Sofía's hands wrapped uncertainly around the paper cone like she thought Sam might yank them away at any moment. Giving them a confused look, she asked, "Don't you want to keep them . . . ?"

"No."

Sofía looked skeptical at the sound of their sharp denial, and a hot flush crept up Sam's neck. Gesturing helplessly at the bouquet, they said, "I wouldn't even know what to do with something like that. Better for you to have them."

"Well, I guess I could put them in some water," she suggested hesitantly.

"Great. Sure. Do that."

"And maybe I could keep them on the front desk?"

Sam's insides lurched at the mere thought, and Sofía smiled a little more at the sight of their undoubtedly fluorescent complexion.

"That might be nice, right? So people can see them whenever they're coming and going?"

"Uh, yeah. Maybe." Clearing their throat, Sam avoided the sappy look she was now giving them and said gruffly, "I guess that'd be nice. Thank you."

Before their entire body could literally break out in hives, Sam turned and made a beeline for the door. They needed to get out of here ASAP.

First, because they really could not take one more second of her looking at them like that. Then, because they needed to spend their evening speed dating their way to catching a murderer. And then maybe, if there was still time later, they'd give this ridiculous young man a call. If only to explain the concept of professionalism in the workplace.

And maybe also to tell him how much Sofía appreciated the flowers. It was really the only polite thing to do.

CHAPTER SEVENTEEN

[Sound check.] Vince's voice was loud in Sam's earpiece as they entered the Paths lobby.

"Check one," Sam murmured to the soundtrack of their heels striking tile. They followed the hot pink LED lights guiding them toward the open doors to the far right of the elevator bank. Light and sound spilled out, indicating that the singles mixer was well underway.

"Check two," Beck said into her headset before putting on her best polite stranger smile and checking Sam against the guest list. "Welcome to the mixer, Ms. Ryder. Please take a wristband and enjoy the party."

[Check three.] Noah's voice came through the earpiece as Sam selected a neon purple wristband that was apparently for people seeking men.

If Noah was in position, he should be located at the building's back door. There were only two exits from the party room. With Beck covering the front and Noah at the back, they should have full coverage of anyone coming or going.

[Check four.] Donya's voice was barely audible over the ambient noise her mic was picking up. She had entered the mixer twenty minutes earlier to avoid any suspicion, and she was already deep into the crowd of single men and women with their multi-colored wristbands.

[All right, ladies. Let's get this over with.]

Sam took Vince's smarmy words as their signal to enter the room.

[Donya, your mic is too hot. Go offline unless you've got something.]

[Copy that.] Donya's line went dead so the only crowd noise was coming in through Sam's transmitter now.

In contrast to the rest of the ultramodern Paths building, this large room was all dim lighting and dark wood, with a crowded bar in one corner and a DJ spinning romantic mood music in the other. There had to be at least a hundred people gathered in the space.

"Seriously? Does this crap actually work for anyone?" Sam muttered through a rictus smile as they scanned the room for targets. The women outnumbered the men at least 2:1, but that still left plenty of potential suspects for Sam to talk to.

[According to our follow-up surveys, an average of thirty-two percent of mixer attendees report that they've made some kind of connection they're interested in exploring further.] Beck's voice was matter-of-fact in their ear.

[Time to make that number a lot higher tonight, Sammy. Pick a nerd and start lining up dates with any potentials.]

"Yeah, yeah," Sam grumbled. Glancing around at the pulsating crowd of other humans, they asked, "Which pair of khakis am I starting with?"

[Your hot ex wouldn't give us video. You scout any good options, D?]

Donya's mic clicked back on briefly. *[At your four is Tristan Wright.]* Sam turned slowly to take in the man with his tucked-in shirt and sky-blue wristband. *[He's the CEO of a startup that handles ad purchasing and information exchange.]*

"Great," Sam sighed. "You actually going to tell me what that means, Vince?"

[Maybe you should have actually paid attention in the briefings.]

Burying their pride for what would likely be the first of many painful introductions, Sam pulled their heel a quarter inch out of their stiletto and then stepped right into Tristan's path. He stumbled, they stumbled, and the shoe came flying off with ease.

"Oh my god, I'm so sorry," Sam gushed, hopping on one foot as gracefully as they could.

"No, no, it's my fault." Glancing down and seeing Sam's predicament, Tristan quickly dropped to the floor and snatched up their wayward shoe. "There you go, Cinderella," he said as he slipped it back onto their foot.

"I swear I've got two left feet. Thank goodness there are still some Prince Charmings out there."

Vince made a gagging noise over the coms, but Tristan didn't seem to mind the cheesy line.

Holding out one hand, Sam said, "I'm Samantha, by the way."

"Tristan," he replied. His palm was sweaty as his eyes raked appreciatively over Vivienne's latest attempt to make them look ten years younger and twice as feminine. "You can call me Prince Charming all you want, though. Can I buy you a drink?"

"Lead the way," Sam said, and when their flat tone didn't quite land right, they offered him their best doe-eyed expression to make up for it.

Mollified, Tristan took them by the hand and guided them over to the bar. It felt a little silly, since Sam had a good three inches on him in their heels, but thankfully he didn't seem terribly emasculated by the height difference.

"So, Tristan," Sam said, releasing his hand as he stepped up to the bar and confidently ordered two drinks. "What brings you here tonight?"

"What brings all of us here? Looking for love, of course," he said with a smile that was slightly more appealing, at least.

The bartender gave Sam a knowing look as she handed them their drink. Taking their glass of very convincing grape juice, Sam turned to face Tristan and offered him a toast. "To finding love," they said, and his smile grew by another degree.

"To finding love."

When Tristan finished sipping his wine, Sam said, "Why don't you tell me a little more about yourself, Prince Charming?"

What followed was possibly the most thorough lesson anyone had ever taught on why most people didn't enjoy mixers. At least when Sam went to the bar looking for a hookup, they could usually find someone interesting enough for a few hours' worth of company. But here? They pitied any girl trying to find companionship among these particular men.

Scanning the crowd around them, Sam was pretty sure that if they lost the girly getup and slapped on a blue wristband they could do some serious damage among these underwhelmed women.

". . . why you can't cheap out when it comes to server space."

"Mm. That's so interesting," Sam said. Their tone was unconvincing, but Tristan didn't seem to mind as long as he got to keep hearing the sound of his own voice. Putting down their grape juice, Sam said, "Hey, I'm going to keep walking around, but could I maybe get your number?"

"Uh, sure. I mean, yeah, of course," Tristan said, eagerly accepting the phone they pressed into his clammy palms. Peering down at the screen, he frowned and said, "What's this?"

"What?" Sam asked, then gave an irritated sigh as they looked at the pop-up on the screen. "Oh, honestly, I don't know. I'm hopeless with technology. That keeps coming up every few hours and then I have to wait ten minutes to get into my phone." Giving Tristan sad damsel-in-distress eyes, they said, "I guess I'll just have to hope I can find you on the app later?"

"Well, let me just take a look first. I bet I can fix it."

Taking the device in both hands, Tristan started pushing buttons and navigating through the phone's internal systems with the ease of a man who may or may not be a hacker, but clearly knew a little more than basic HTML.

Holding the phone up triumphantly to show them his number on the screen, Tristan said, "There you go, Cinderella. Good as new."

"Oh my god, that's amazing. You have to tell me how you did that," Sam said with all the enthusiasm of a kindergarten teacher admiring a child's artistic masterpiece.

"How about over dinner?" Tristan suggested, and Sam had to admit that what he lacked in social grace he certainly made up for in blind confidence.

"Definitely. I'll message you."

Vince's voice resumed in their earpiece as they drifted away from Tristan in search of their next target. *[One down. Twenty-nine more to go.]*

"Is it really one down if I still have to go out with him again?" Sam grumbled.

They knew the cell phone trick was their best bet for chopping down Beck's overly long shortlist, but they hated the idea that this entire night was only setting them up for more future dates as *Samantha*.

[Number twenty-nine is standing over by the door. Go talk to him before he decides to bail.]

Making a slow circle of the room, Sam took in the man standing anxiously by the door. He was taller than Sam, at least, but he looked like he was going to need an inhaler if a woman talked to him for more than thirty seconds.

"Yeah, OK, I'm on it," Sam said begrudgingly.

[At least try not to scare him away.]

Sam just ignored his nagging. Vince could keep telling Sam that they were supposed to be playing a demure, flirtatious lady until he was blue in the face, but that didn't mean they could pull it off.

A flash of white-blonde hair caught their eye. Donya was wrapping up a conversation with another young man only a few paces away. Glancing at number twenty-nine standing by the door and then back to Donya, they decided to make a quick detour before continuing with this torture.

"Going dark for a minute. Be back in a second," Sam muttered before tapping off the transmitter hidden under their blouse. They could still hear Vince complaining in their earpiece, but Vince could no longer hear them.

"Hey," Sam said, nodding to Donya subtly as they came to stand beside the shorter woman. Vivienne's team had focused more on covering up her full-body collection of sapphic tattoos than they had on dolling her up, but she still looked plenty nice enough to turn a few heads in this crowd.

They waited until the man she had been talking to had wandered far enough away and then asked, "You still muted?"

"He's telling me to turn it back on," Donya replied with a subtle tilt of her head. Vince's rant filled their earpieces. "But yeah, still muted. What's up?"

"I've been meaning to talk to you." Sam pretended to sip from their drink as they glanced sidelong at the other detective. "About the HR thing."

Donya's expression tightened at the mention, but she didn't respond. One pale finger slid beneath the purple band hugging her wrist in a way that betrayed her discomfort.

Seeing that she wasn't going to own it of her own accord, Sam said, "I appreciate the thought, but—"

"I didn't do it for you." Donya's words were quick and blunt. Her finger pulled the wristband taut for a second, then she released it abruptly. "But yeah, whatever. Won't happen again."

"Donya," Sam said quietly. They raised an eyebrow as the other woman took a long drink from her glass, which was full of ice and a clear liquid that smelled a whole lot more like vodka than water. "Is everything good with Vice? Because I can say something if you don't want it coming back on you."

"I thought you didn't want HR to get involved?" Sam felt the cut of those sharp words when Donya turned those blue doll eyes on them.

"I don't want HR to bother *me*," Sam corrected coolly. A big part of them wanted to say she had no business being so accusatory when she had hung Sam out to dry the other night. But they also understood a thing or two about what kind of pressure she was under in her new position, so instead they said, "If things are getting bad, just say so. I'm on your side, you know?"

Donya appraised them for a long second before dropping her gaze and muttering, "Yeah, all right. I'll let you know." Taking another sip of her drink, she grimaced and said, "I don't know how you're putting up with all this crap. This is the longest I've played straight since preschool, and I already want to die."

"I thought you volunteered for this?"

"Oh yeah. Super voluntary," Donya said, and Sam wondered again exactly how serious the hazing was on Vice these days. Before they could press further, she said, "You should get back out there. That guy really does look like he's about to leave."

"What a shame. Then I'll only have to flirt with twenty-eight other men," Sam said, and Donya barked out a laugh.

Sam raised their hand to the transmitter under their shirt, but before they could turn it back on, Donya said, "How does an IOU sound?" When Sam gave her a questioning look, she just shrugged and said, "To make up for the HR thing."

"Sure," Sam said, offering her a rueful smile. "I've got your number."

Vince's irritated voice filled their ear the minute Sam tapped the transmitter back on. *[Are you two done braiding each other's hair, or can we maybe get this show on the road sometime tonight?]*

Reaching out, Sam snatched Donya's drink from her hand. The other detective's eyes widened in surprise as Sam took a long, burning draw off the "water." Sighing, Sam lowered the drink and then said, "All right. Let's get this over with."

The next three hours could have easily ranked among the top thirty worst experiences in Sam's life, and that was a very prestigious list to crack. It only took about four more conversations for Sam to be pretty sure that they never wanted to talk to a straight man again. When the conversations started hitting double digits and weren't improving, they seriously started to consider walking out the front door and taking their chances with Captain Donovan in the morning.

Fourteen men had already passed the cell phone test. That was fourteen more godawful dates they were going to have to go on, at a minimum.

The crowd was starting to thin out a little as Sam reached number nine. Many of the women had given up and gone home or found someone to leave with. It made the men easier to track down in the crowd, but it also meant Sam had to be a little more subtle, in case someone they had been talking to earlier saw them repeat the cell phone test on a new, unsuspecting victim.

Just as Sam was beginning to make their approach on number nine, a familiar face caught their eye in the crowd. For a second they couldn't place him, but then the man turned a little to the side and his profile clicked into place.

"Hey, Beck?" Sam murmured. They tried not to sound like a crazy person talking to themself as they fell into step behind the man walking with purpose toward the back of the room. "Has Brad Lu been here the whole time, or did he just arrive?"

[Just arrived.] Beck's voice was anxious over their earpiece. *[He seemed kind of . . .]*

"Yeah, I saw," Sam confirmed, seeing the jittery tension in Brad's movements.

[I thought we already cleared that guy?] Sam could hear Vince shuffling papers in search of Brad's profile.

[We did. He wasn't active on the app that week] Noah's voice interjected.

"Seemingly not active on the app," Sam corrected as they began to move in Brad's direction.

[I hope by seemingly you mean not. As in, he was not active on the app that week and is not currently a person of interest.] When Sam didn't reply, Vince grew more serious. *[Sam. Drop it.]*
"I just want to know where he's headed."

[Do not approach.] Vince's words were an order Sam was happy to ignore

as they watched Brad walk up to a couple standing at the bar. *[You've only got nine more guys to go. I don't care how bored you are, you need to—]*

Whatever else Vince had to say was lost as Sam removed their earpiece. Keeping it loosely tucked in their palm, they edged their way closer to the bar so they could catch some of the conversation happening between a squirrely Brad and a rather unhappy-looking gentleman in an oversized sportscoat.

". . . don't have it," the gentleman was saying, his eyes darting around the room to see if anyone else had caught on to Brad's intrusion. Sam was quick to turn away before the guy could notice them noticing him. "Would you just be cool? We can meet up tomorrow."

"Tomorrow is too long," Brad insisted. His voice was hoarse and there were large rings of sweat under the arms of his wrinkled dress shirt. Reaching out to grab the other man's sleeve, Brad said, "Please, I need—"

"Get offa me," the man said, shoving Brad away hard enough to make him stumble back a few steps. Adjusting his coat as a few heads turned in their direction, the man held up his blue wristband and said, "I told you. I'm not interested."

A lovers' quarrel, perhaps? Sam glanced at Brad's wrist, which was free of any wristband. Clearly he had shown up tonight with a specific person in mind, but that person was already making his way swiftly toward the back door.

Glancing between Brad and his retreating companion, Sam quickly stuck the earpiece back into place and said, "Donya, I need you to cover the room."

[What? Where are—]

[Sam, what do you think you're doing?]

"Noah," Sam said, ignoring the confused chatter on the line. "There's a guy coming your way right now. I need you to tell me where he's headed. And Donya, keep your eyes on Brad. I'm going to circle back around for him."

[Don't you put one fucking toe outside that door, Sam. I swear to god, I will—]

Sam removed the earpiece again as they watched the back door swing open and shut on the mysterious man in the sportscoat. They counted to thirty in their head before shoving through the door and out into the cool night air.

"Noah," Sam said, nodding to their rookie, who stood at his post looking tense and concerned. "Which way did he go?"

"Uh, are you sure this is a good idea?" Noah practically shouted while pointing emphatically to the transmitter in his ear. "Seriously, Sam. I think you should go back inside." In direct contrast to his words, Noah pointed silently over his shoulder.

"I can't believe you won't help me," Sam said in a voice so flat you'd have to be braindead to find it believable, but Noah seemed mollified.

Hurrying as fast as they could in their high heels, Sam turned the corner into the building's side alley—and nearly ran straight into the man standing just on the other side.

"Oh," Sam blurted in genuine surprise. For a half a second they got ready to defend themself before they saw the smoke curling from the cigarette between the man's fingers. "Um. Sorry—sorry. I didn't realize anyone was, uh, out here."

"Sure you didn't, sweetheart," the man said with a nasty little smirk. Raising the cigarette to his lips, he said, "I bet you follow all the cute guys out into dark alleys at night."

"This is hardly what I'd call a dark alley." Sam did their best to match the man's casual tone, despite the alarm bells going off in their head.

The tidy alley between the Paths building and its neighboring skyscraper wasn't exactly the kind of sketchy place where girls got dragged off in the night, but that didn't mean it wasn't plenty secluded to present a real danger. And despite his sports coat and gelled-back hair, this guy was packing about twenty pounds of extra muscle compared to the next biggest guy at the party.

Offering him a coy smile, Sam said, "Is it really my fault if you left too fast for me to say hello?"

"Uh huh," the guy said. He seemed utterly unconvinced by their fluttering eyelashes. Dropping his cigarette to the pavement, he ground it out with the toe of his heavy-looking boot and said, "I'm abouta get out of here, so either tell me what you're looking for or scram, principessa."

Either this guy was an even worse flirt than Sam or he was not at this party looking for love.

Just in case they were wrong, Sam turned the question back on him. "What do you think I'm looking for?"

"From the look of you?" His lip curled again as his eyes flicked up and down their rail-thin body. "I'm guessing it doesn't take much of a bump to make you fly."

"More than you'd think," Sam responded coolly, because they may not work Vice, but they knew a drug dealer when they met one.

"All right, I see what this is," the guy said with an impatient wave of his hand. "You saw me with my friend back there and now you want the new customer special, huh?"

"You got me." Offering him an innocent shrug, Sam said, "I'm in the mood for a nice white Christmas, and I thought you might be feeling generous."

"Whatever. Get that tweaker locked up, you'd be doing me a fuckin' favor," the man scoffed, but Sam didn't miss the way his eyes darted nervously back toward the building. Looking Sam over again, he folded his arms and said, "OK, how's this? I can give you a snowball for two and a little somethin' extra if you really like to party." Kissing his lips at them obnoxiously, he added, "I promise, it'll be better than any Christmas you ever had."

"OK," Sam said. They let their eyes drop eagerly to the pocket of his oversized sportscoat. "Show me."

The man started to reach inside his jacket, but just as the baggie full of powdered white evidence started to appear, his hand froze. Sam's gaze flicked back to his face just in time to see his eyes widen in fear.

"Everything all right over here?" A long shadow fell across the two of them, and Sam didn't dare turn around, but *goddammit*.

"Yeah. We're cool," the man said. His hand was out of his jacket pocket in less than a millisecond, and the damning bag of cocaine he'd been about to sell Sam disappeared back inside. Giving Sam a pointed look, he started backing away from the sound of Noah's approaching footsteps. "I was just telling this chick—"

Whatever excuse the man had been planning to spin was lost as a piercing scream split through the night sky and then cut off abruptly. The sound was so raw and shocking that all three people in the alley froze— and then the shouts of concern started.

Taking advantage of the distraction, Sam's new friend turned and booked it out of the alley at top speed.

Cursing, Sam gave chase, but the sky-high spikes strapped to their feet

178

had not been designed with running in mind. Noah had easily caught up by the time they reached the end of the alley that turned out onto the sidewalk beyond. The loud voices were coming from the front of the building to their right, and the man's figure was quickly disappearing into the night on their left.

"Shit," Sam swore, out loud this time, as they came to a halt. Noah hesitated beside them, and they snapped, "Well? You're not wearing heels."

"What?" Noah said, looking a little panicked as they gestured in the direction of the runaway drug dealer. "You want me to . . . ?"

"Are you a police officer or not?" Sam demanded, giving Noah a hard shove in the retreating man's direction. "Go get him!"

Not waiting to see if he would obey, Sam hurried toward the growing pool of people spilling out of the building's front lobby. Their heart sank as the crowd formed a circle, and they had a bad feeling they knew what they would find at the center.

"Don't." Donya appeared by Sam's side before they had made it two steps into the throng of people. She looked a little out of breath, having apparently run to intercept Sam. Drawing in more air, she said, "You can't go over there."

"But I have to—"

"Sam. You're not—" Donya cut off with a grimace as a guy in the crowd gave them both a weird look. Dropping her voice, Donya said, "Just put your earpiece back in."

Sam gave her a long look, but the other woman was serious. Rolling the tiny earpiece between their fingers, Sam brushed a hand through their hair and used the motion to subtly slide their mic back into place.

Vince's furious stream instantly filled their head again. *[I don't care what you have to do. If you let them take one step closer to that body, I swear to god, I will come down there myself and—]*

"I can hear you again," Sam muttered, dropping their hand. "What body?"

[Oh, good.] From the genuine anger in Vince's voice, Sam knew it must be really serious. *[And here I thought you didn't want to join Vice.]*

"What the hell are you talking about?"

[While you were busy chasing that punk-ass dealer, our killer was out here claiming victim number four. Paramedics are on their way now. Do not approach.]

"And Brad?" Sam asked, turning to face Donya, who still hovered next to them. "Where was he when—"

"I had eyes on him the whole time," Donya said. "He was still inside when it happened."

"What about the other nine guys?" Sam asked, but Donya didn't have an answer. "Vince?"

[I don't know, Sam. I don't exactly have any video to monitor. Keeping track of the other guys was your job.]

Sam's temper flared, and they were about to snap right back when the person in front of them shifted to the left. For half a second, Sam had a partial view through the milling crowd. Just long enough to see a pale hand splayed out on the pavement with a trickle of blood slowly painting the woman's nails a new shade of crimson red.

"I need to get a closer look at the body," Sam said. They didn't even make it one step before Donya's hand had clapped firmly around their wrist. Sam glanced down at the shorter woman in disbelief, but her expression was stone cold.

[Don't you fucking dare. Do you hear me, Sam?] Vince's voice was way too loud in their earpiece. *[The only thing you have going for your right now is that you haven't blown your cover yet. Do not screw that up, too.]*

Sam stared at Donya's hand for a long second before turning their eyes back to the crowd. The whispers were turning from voyeuristic curiosity to real concern now. It was evident that the woman bleeding on the ground was either dead or close to it.

Sam shook Donya's hand off but didn't make another move to get closer to the body as sirens started to filter through the air. A prickle of discomfort climbed up their spine when the ambulance pulled up at the curb, but they refused to look away. Two young men in navy-blue uniforms spoke into their radios as they worked to lift the young woman off the pavement. Sam got a good look at her slack face before she disappeared inside the ambulance.

She was no one. Just another attendee at the mixer. Definitely not someone Sam would have looked at twice, despite being in the same room with her for over three hours. And now she was a limp, blood-stained body being held together with bandages and prayers as the paramedics loaded her into the ambulance.

[You better hope to god she lives, Sam.] Vince's voice was grim in their ear. *[Or you're going to be the one explaining to her family why she's dead.]*

CHAPTER EIGHTEEN

"Shut the door."

Sam obediently closed the captain's office door and came to stand in front of her desk. As they made to take a seat, the older woman's mouth flattened into a grimace.

"Don't bother. This will be fast."

Captain Donovan's weary eyes searched Sam's face for something—an apology, maybe, for dragging her back to the office in the middle of the night. Maybe regret, for the way tonight's op went. Or maybe she was just hoping Sam would make this easy by offering their hand for the slap on the wrist they were about to receive.

But Sam simply stared back at her, looking like they'd rather stand there all night than ask for forgiveness.

"Tell me what happened," Donovan finally said with a sigh. The dark circles under her eyes only accentuated the fine wrinkles lining her face.

"It'll all be in my report tomorrow morning."

"Did I ask what would be in your report?" Donovan snapped, and from the stress in her voice, Sam thought they might be in for a little more than a lecture this time. "I want an explanation, Detective. Right now."

"OK." Sam's voice was cool and measured in the face of the captain's ire. "I attended the mixer at the Paths building. Detective Renier was coordinating over coms. Beck Fisher was checking guests in and out at the front entrance. Detective Mariano was covering the exit, and Detective Novikoff was providing backup on the floor."

"And?"

"And I spoke with twenty-one potential suspects. There are fourteen who are worth investigating further." Sam paused, and when the captain didn't interject, they asked, "Do you want their names now, or can I save those details for my report?"

"I seriously suggest checking the attitude if you want to avoid suspension, Detective," Donovan said sharply.

Sam didn't think they had really been giving attitude, but obviously Donovan was not messing around.

"What happened when Mr. Lu arrived?"

"He looked agitated. I followed him and overheard his conversation with a guy who looked a little out of place at the event," Sam explained.

"Define 'out of place.'"

Sam paused before saying, with as little attitude as possible, "He looked like a textbook drug dealer. And Mr. Lu looked and sounded a lot like a user in need of a hit, which lined up with how Ms. Hancock described him in her earlier interview."

"And after the supposed drug dealer left?" the captain asked. She managed to sound impatient, even though she was the one who had asked for this briefing. Being dragged out of bed at one in the morning could do that to a person.

"Not 'supposed.' He is a drug dealer," Sam corrected. "Which I know because I followed him outside and he tried to sell to me."

"Right. But why did you follow him in the first place?"

"I was going to ask him some questions about Mr. Lu and the three victims after I had something to hold over him. But then we heard the woman screaming—"

"Kayleigh Evergreen," Donovan interjected. When Sam tilted their head in question, she said, "That's the new victim's name. She's in a medically induced coma at St. Alexander's following her emergency surgery, and there's no guarantee she'll ever wake up."

"Right," Sam said, having the decency to look a little perturbed by this information. Privately, they were simply happy to hear the woman had lived at all. "After we heard Ms. Evergreen scream, the drug dealer took off."

"At which point you told Detective Mariano to give chase?" Donovan asked.

"Yes."

"And then?"

"Well, Noah didn't manage to catch the guy," Sam said dryly. "But I waited until he circled back. Then I came straight here, like I was ordered to."

The captain was silent for a long moment. Her elbows rested on the desk and her thumbs pressed against her forehead hard enough to leave twin red marks. For a moment when she looked up at Sam, she almost seemed to be at a loss for words.

"What were you thinking, Sam?" she finally said in a tone that bordered on despair.

"Was I unclear?" Sam asked, and the captain's mouth tightened just enough for Sam to know that was the kind of "attitude" she wasn't looking for. "I wanted to talk to him about the potential connection between Mr. Lu and Ms. Russo, who he had been having regular dates with before her death. It seemed like a bad idea to keep talking to long shots when I only knew of one person in that room who definitely had a strong connection with one of our victims."

"Did you have any reason—any *concrete* reason—to think Mr. Lu or this drug dealer had the skills necessary to hack into Mrs. Fox's app and delete Ms. Hancock's conversation history?" Donovan pressed. Glancing over Sam's feminine getup, she asked, "Or did you just think chasing a drug dealer would be more fun than finishing the op?"

"No. I was following my instincts. That was all."

The captain searched Sam's face again, but if she thought she was getting nothing before, Sam was emoting about as much as a block of ice now.

"What am I supposed to do with this?" Donovan asked plaintively.

Sam didn't have an answer for her. Certainly not one that would come without plenty of "attitude," anyway.

The captain breathed out a harsh sigh and pressed her thumbs back to her forehead. "Sam, I'm trying to help you here, but you need to start helping yourself. There is a game to play, and you are running out of friends who are willing to look the other way when you refuse to play along." Dropping her hands, she leaned forward and said, "I'm going to be blunt with you."

"I would expect nothing less."

"This isn't a joke, Sam," she said tersely, even though Sam wasn't laughing. "Mayor Kelso is up for reelection, and Chief Sanders will be looking for someone to hang if we can't wrap this case up quietly. If push comes to shove, I will do what needs to be done to protect this department. Do you understand what that means for you?"

"I understand," Sam said simply.

And they did understand. It wasn't like this was anything new. There was always going to be another politician, another election, another higher-up worried about their job, or their legacy, or their upcoming promotion, or whatever else they had deemed of dire importance at the moment. The victims were nothing but folders in filing cabinets, as far as the people playing this so-called game were concerned.

"Good."

Sam could see how tired the captain was in that moment. They actually felt a little bad for her—it must be hard being an ass-kissing, spineless shill some days.

"I'm not saying it's fair," Donovan continued, oblivious to Sam's thoughts. "But I need you to suck it up and get the job done by the book, all right? Whether Ms. Evergreen wakes up or not, the body count on this case ends here."

Sam nodded silently. Their fists were clenched in their jacket pockets, but their stony facade betrayed nothing of their loathing for her in that moment.

"All right," Donovan said. She was clearly dissatisfied with their taciturn response, but not having anything else she could really complain about, she said, "I expect you back here first thing tomorrow morning, Detective. The people in this city need you. Don't let them down again."

CHAPTER NINETEEN

Sam dropped their keys on the kitchen table and jumped as they rattled against the hard wood surface. At two in the morning their tiny apartment was dead silent, save for the uneven sound of their own breathing.

They kicked off one stiletto and sent it skittering a few inches across the crappy linoleum tile. Then they sent the other one flying across the room hard enough to dent the baseboard.

Sometimes they really hated this apartment. It had seen so many sides of them. Sam, strung out after too many back-to-back shifts on the beat when they were trying to make detective. Sam, lonely and craving companionship, but too stubborn to go looking for it. Sam, huddled on the couch in the middle of a panic attack because they had to refill a simple prescription and even that was just too damn much sometimes.

And now Sam, very angry and very much wanting a cigarette. Or something they could break. Or someone they could yell at. And it only made them angrier that they couldn't do any of those things, because that would just be one more strike against them. It didn't seem to matter how hard they toed the line—when the act of existing was a rebellion in itself, anything less than perfection in every other area was intolerable.

But Sam was not feeling very perfect tonight. And that kind of made them want to do something destructive and impulsive, like punching a hole in the wall.

Or picking up their phone and pressing the Call button.

"Sam?" His voice sounded groggy and confused when he picked up on the third ring. "Is that you?"

Sam knew they were supposed to respond. But instead they just stood there like an idiot, feeling angry and conflicted and like they really, really just wanted to hear more of his voice right now.

"What time is it?"

Sam wondered if Teddy could hear how uneven their breathing was over the line.

"Is everything OK?"

"No."

"Sam, what's going—"

"I can't—it's my case. I can't share any details. Sorry."

"It's OK."

Because of course he would say that.

There was silence on the line for a moment, and then, "Hey . . . are you all right?"

"No."

"What—"

"God, this is so stupid. I'm sorry. I don't even know why I called." Sam scrubbed a hand across their face as their nerves began to fray. "I should go."

"Wait—wait!" His voice no longer sounded so sleepy. "Before you hang up, I have something I need to ask you."

"Teddy, I can't—"

"It's not about the case. It's just my question of the day." Teddy paused as if to see if Sam would hang up. Maybe they should have—but they didn't. "It's after midnight, isn't it?"

". . . Yes."

"So I can ask, right?"

". . . Fine. Ask." Sam rested their arms on the back of one of the dining room chairs. They were way too anxious to play this game right now, but it only seemed fair since they had called him.

"What's your favorite shade of red?"

"What kind of goddamned question is that?"

"Because I'm partial to cool reds, you know? More on the blue side of the spectrum." Teddy's cheerful voice didn't even skip a beat, despite Sam's snappy tone.

"I don't even know what that means."

"You know what a fire truck looks like?"

". . . Yes."

"That's warm red. And you know what a rose looks like?"

"Yes."

"That one's cool red."

Sam let out a slow breath and lowered their forehead to rest against their outstretched arms. "OK, and?"

"Well, which one do you prefer?"

"I don't know, Teddy," Sam said, and his name was little more than an exasperated sigh on their lips. "I don't really think about that kind of thing."

"OK, how about just a favorite color in general, then?"

"I really don't—" Sam started, then stopped themself. Letting out another slow breath, they tried to appreciate the distraction instead of biting his head off. "OK. I guess, if I had to think about it, I just like, uh, warm things."

"Warm things?"

"Yeah, like . . . yellow. Or, I don't know, orange."

"And warm reds?" His voice was sweet and encouraging as he coaxed them back from the ledge in his own strange Teddy way.

"Yeah. I guess that sounds right."

"Because you actually like those colors or because you hate being cold?"

"How do you know that?" Sam straightened up from the chair in surprise.

"I remember a certain investigation into all my missing socks back on the island." They could hear a cautious, teasing note in his voice now.

"That's right. It was so damn cold in the mornings." Sam's anger faded a little more as other, fuzzier feelings competed for their attention. "I guess I'm not the only one with a good memory."

"How could I forget?"

Against all odds, Sam found themself smiling ever so slightly at the appealing sound of Teddy's laughter.

"You were so cute. It would be, like, fifty-nine degrees, and you'd be huddled up on the balcony looking like you were freezing to death."

"Because fifty-nine degrees is freezing. I don't know why I have to explain that when you're the one who was born on an island."

"Yeah, and you were born in South Carolina. I may not be great at geography, but I'm confident it gets a bit colder than fifty-nine degrees on that coast."

A little more tension left Sam's body. It was easy to forget how much of themself they had already given him over the course of his daily questions.

"Why do you think I hated it so much there?" Sam said as they finally found the energy to start moving again. Making their way out of the living room, they asked, "Have you ever tried to milk a cow when you can't feel your fingers?"

"Stop it. You did not milk cows growing up."

"I swear," Sam insisted. They flicked on the light in their tiny bathroom and made a face at the stranger reflected back at them in the mirror. Switching the phone to speaker mode so they could still hear him while they reached for the makeup remover, Sam said, "Sometimes if it's really cold you have to punch the udder to get things warmed up, or you just end up with a milkshake."

"You are such a liar."

"Maybe," Sam admitted with a grin as they started scrubbing away their thick coating of makeup. Each pass of the cool cloth left them feeling a little less on edge.

"So what did you really do on the farm?"

"It was all corn. Endless, endless fields of corn. But it's still hard to shuck with frozen fingers."

"Too bad I wasn't there to hold your hand."

"Oh god. Could you imagine?" Now he had them laughing too.

"What's so funny about that?"

The immediate, stubborn response only made Sam laugh more. There was no way a born-and-bred California boy like Teddy would ever be able to wrap his head around small-town South Carolina in the 1980s. Just the thought of a guy like him in a place like that was absurd.

"Well, first of all, you would have been about three years old when I left home," Sam explained. "And second, even if we were closer in age, that town could barely handle just having me. Forget if I started going around with a guy like you."

"You make a little hand-holding sound so scandalous." They could tell from the smile in his voice that Teddy loved the idea.

"It would have been." Sam shook their head ruefully at the thought. "Sounds like exactly the sort of hell I would have loved raising at that age, though."

"If we really wanted to freak people out, I could teach them all sorts of crazy island things."

"Oh yeah? Like what?"

"Like different shades of red."

"Shut up," Sam complained, and Teddy had the audacity to laugh at them instead of being offended.

Peering at themself in the mirror again, Sam almost recognized the person looking back at them now. The only unfamiliar part was the goofy smile on their face that could not possibly belong to the same person who had entered this apartment spitting mad ten minutes ago.

Picking up the phone, they headed back into the main room. Before they could overthink it, Sam said, "Can I change my answer?"

"To what?"

"I think I actually prefer, uh, what'd you call them?" Sam dropped down on the couch and tucked their feet up underneath them. "Cool reds?"

"Oh yeah? How come?" Teddy's voice was predictably full of curiosity. Like he was ever not curious.

"Because firetrucks are loud and annoying, and firefighters really aren't all that. But roses . . ." They let their head tip back until it rested against the cushions. Closing their eyes, Sam said, "Roses are pretty good."

"Yeah? So you did like those?"

"I mean, they were . . . kind of nice, I guess," Sam admitted. Then, lest Teddy go getting any ideas, they added sternly, "You're just lucky more people didn't see them being delivered."

"Believe me, you have no idea how lucky you got. I really might have shown up in person to make sure you were still alive if Henry hadn't talked me into sending flowers instead."

"Yeah, well. It was still very embarrassing." Sam couldn't help feeling those familiar butterflies when Teddy just laughed at their surly version of a thank-you. His sweet nature made it so much easier to say, "Sorry for disappearing on you, though. I guess I, uh, wasn't having the best week of my career."

"It's OK. I knew it might freak you out sending something like that to your office. I just hated the idea that people were making you feel like—you know. And I wanted your coworkers to know—I wanted you to know—that you have someone who . . . cares. Who's kind of, uh, really into you. Just the way you are." Teddy let his words trail off nervously. "Sorry if I made things worse."

"You definitely didn't make things worse." Those butterflies were kicking up a hurricane now at the idea of Teddy being *really into them*. Not that it hadn't already been apparent after all the texting, but hearing it out loud made it feel real. Real enough that Sam admitted, "You know, in thirty-eight years no one has ever bought me flowers before?"

"Well, well, well. Always nice to be the first." Teddy sounded terribly self-satisfied, much to Sam's chagrin.

"Uh huh. Probably because most of my exes realized I'm not the type to keep a vase on hand."

Despite their dry words, Sam couldn't help feeling a pang of longing at the thought of those beautiful roses. Maybe this passionate man had a point. If they weren't so concerned with trying to make other people comfortable, those flowers would be sitting on their kitchen table right now instead of living on Sofía's desk at work.

"I guess it was kind of nice," Sam said before they could think their way out of it this time. "To feel—you know. Supported, or whatever."

There was a beat of silence following their hesitant confession. And then another. Sam was just starting to think they might have said the wrong thing when Teddy finally spoke.

"Hey, Sam?"

"Hm?"

"I really wish you would have called me sooner." His voice was low and intense in a way that made Sam think they had said exactly the right thing for once. "I miss you. I've been missing you." Teddy waited a long moment for them to respond, but Sam had never been more tongue-tied in their life. ". . . You still there?"

"Yeah, I—I'm here," Sam forced themself to say. "I, um . . . I've been missing you, too."

"Good."

It was a little unbelievable how he could get their pulse going with just one word, even from across the ocean. Maybe it had something to do with the fact that Sam was *really into him*, too.

"So . . ." Sam was sure they weren't imagining the flirtatious shift in his tone. "Do you miss me enough to answer another question?"

"Are you going to make me regret it if I say yes?"

"That depends on your mood, I guess." Teddy's voice was all innocence. "I was just wondering what you're wearing right now."

"Seriously, Teddy?" Sam said with a helpless laugh. "We're doing what are you wearing questions now?"

"Come on. Wouldn't it be nice to blow off a little steam? I know you've been having a bad week . . ."

"Oh god. First you want me to do small talk and now you expect me to . . . to . . ." A flush crawled up Sam's neck when Teddy snickered at their inability to finish that sentence. "Shut up," they grumbled. "You know I'm not good at this stuff."

"Sure you are. It's just answering questions." Despite his amusement, Teddy clearly wasn't going to let them get away that easily. "If it makes you feel better, I'll go first. Ask me what I'm wearing."

"Nice try," Sam muttered. As if they hadn't already been very aware of what he was "wearing" the moment they woke him up with this call. "I know how you sleep, so I'm pretty confident you're not wearing anything at all right now."

"You got me. Currently very naked. And turned on. And also really wishing you were naked and turned on, too."

"Who says I'm not?"

"I say you're not." His reply held just the right amount of confidence to do bad, bad things to Sam's libido. "Am I wrong?"

" . . . Not completely wrong," Sam admitted. "I'm not naked. But I am a little turned on."

"Oh por Dios. ¿Solo un poco?"

Sam couldn't help smiling a little when Teddy's words came out in Spanish, like they often did when he was feeling impatient. They were surprised to realize how much they had missed that during their text-based conversations.

"You know I still only understand English."

"You understand me just fine." Teddy's words were heated and frustrated in a way that Sam very much liked. "I can't eat. I can't sleep. I can't even sketch a damn picture. All I can do is sit by my phone and hope that you'll call."

"Hmm. Now that is sexy."

"Oh, I see. So what really turns you on is knowing that you drive me completely crazy."

"So much more than you know."

"Are you sure I can't talk you into a good time?" Teddy's pleading was shameless as ever. "If you're too shy to do it over the phone, I could just come see you."

"I am not shy," Sam scoffed. "You're just being ridiculous."

"Is it ridiculous?" Clearly, he was not interested in their attempts to deflect. "Sam. I'm being serious. Just say the word and I'll race the sunrise to your door."

"Teddy . . ."

"I swear to god. I'll do it. We could meet at the marina in less than three hours."

Sam's desire to have him battled against all the heavier things taking up space inside of them. Teddy made them want like they hadn't wanted in years. But wanting him didn't change the reality of what tomorrow would bring. Or the fact that they were pretty sure he wanted more than they could give him at the moment. If ever.

"Things are really . . . not good for me right now," Sam finally said, as honestly as they could. "I don't think—"

"Then tell me. Whatever it is that's going on, I'll listen."

"You know I can't do that."

"Then at least tell me what else I can do to make you feel better. Please." Teddy's sincerity took Sam's breath away every time. "I can't stand knowing you're hurting, cariño. I really can't. There has to be something I can do for you."

"Uh . . ." Sam's train of thought fell apart at the unexpected sound of that cute pet name.

"Just imagine I was there with you. Right now. What could I do for you that would take your mind off things?"

"Um . . . well . . ." Sam tried and failed to find the right words, as usual. "Well . . ."

"What if I wanted to kiss you? Would that be OK?"

"Uh, sure." Sam's pulse picked up at just the thought of kissing Teddy again. "Sure. Yes. That would be . . . distracting."

"In a good way?"

"Yes."

"And what if I also wanted to get you out of those clothes?"

A pleasant heat crawled up Sam's spine at the mental image that accompanied Teddy's suggestive words.

"I guess that might also be . . . OK."

"And then? If I wanted to make love to you?"

"Well, then I would need to bend you over my kitchen table and remind you that I don't really do 'making love' . . . cariño."

The sound he made in response to the slightest hint of their aggression was a sinful reminder of how incredibly easy Teddy was in bed. And they loved that he did absolutely nothing to try and hide it.

"You like that? Cariño?" Sam repeated with a small smirk. "What does that mean, anyways? Hm?"

"You know what it means, sweetheart."

"Sweetheart?" Sam made a face at the sappy term.

"Yes, cariño. You are my very grumpy sweetheart." His voice bubbled with laughter in response to their complete and utter lack of romantic spirit. "I think it suits you."

"Absolutely not. You'd better come up with something better before tomorrow."

"What's tomorrow?"

"Tomorrow is when you're going to call me again to distract me properly . . . if you still want to, that is."

"I think you'll find that I'm willing to call you exactly as many times as you're willing to pick up."

"Ugh. Are you sure you're not still concussed?" Sam complained in response to his dreamy tone.

"Very sure." Sam's heart melted a little when he muffled the sound of a yawn. "Although I have been told that I can be a little much when I've got my heart set on something. Hopefully that's OK."

"Anyone who has a problem with that is an idiot."

"Maybe I am still concussed." Teddy's sleepy voice was soft in a way that made Sam think they might be getting it right again. "That almost sounded romantic."

"Sure. But you are going to call me tomorrow?"

"Yes. I promise. You're going to be sick and tired of me calling you."

"Only one way to find out." Sam was helpless to the warmth spreading inside them at just the thought. "I guess I'll talk to you tomorrow . . . cariño."

CHAPTER TWENTY

Sam sipped their coffee as they slouched lazily against the wall outside the situation room. They could hear feminine voices chattering away inside with an ungodly amount of enthusiasm for the early morning hour. Of course, that might just be the three hours of sleep talking.

"Posture," Vivienne called out.

Sam grimaced even as they straightened their spine. They'd made the mistake of complaining that their back was sore one time, and she hadn't let it go since.

Vivienne's high heels clicked sharply on the tile floor as she somehow managed to walk, criticize, and type on her phone all at the same time. Glancing up to frown at them, she seemed to notice for the first time that they were still in regular Sam mode.

"Have you still not gone in yet?"

"I thought I was waiting for you," Sam replied with a stifled yawn.

"No, Beck is taking care of your look today." Vivienne's eyes were already glued back to her phone as she flicked a hand vaguely toward the situation room. "I have to deal with this crisis in London."

"At seven in the morning?" Sam said as Vivienne's fingers blurred across the keyboard at superhuman speed.

"It's not seven in the morning in London," Vivienne corrected with a sigh. Despite looking put together as ever, she did sound a little weary. Glancing around again she asked, "Where's Noah?"

"Sleeping, probably."

"Ah, sleep. I remember when I used to sleep," Vivienne said wistfully.

Sam hid their smirk by sipping their coffee. They, too, remembered when they used to get a full night's sleep, but they weren't exactly complaining. Things had certainly been . . . interesting since the mixer. When Teddy said he was going to call until they stopped answering, he had not been joking. And maybe it wasn't smart, but every time Sam saw his name on their caller ID, they were only more eager to hear his voice again.

Oblivious to Sam's good mood, Vivienne said, "Well, call me when Noah gets here. We can go over the notes for today." She turned away and was walking back to her office when her phone rang. "Oh god, what now?"

Sam watched as Vivienne stared down the phone in her hand like it was a snake that might bite her if she dared to ignore it. After a long moment, she pressed the Accept button and held it up to her ear.

"Hey, honey, is everything OK?" Vivienne asked with strained enthusiasm. "No, no, everything is fine, why would you think . . . No, I saw your text, I'm sorry I didn't answer. You know things are just a little busy right now with . . . No, it's nothing about that. I'm just dealing with some server issues in the London office. I'm not even working on any of that today . . . I know. I won't miss it, don't worry . . . I know. I love you too. I'll see you there tonight."

Vivienne hung up the phone with a look on her face that was somewhere between exhaustion and exasperation. Not exactly the happy look Sam had come to expect when Vivienne spoke about her wife.

"Everything all good?" they asked, and Vivienne nearly jumped out of her heels in surprise.

"What? Yes. Everything's fine." Sam arched a silent eyebrow at the too-fast response, and the other woman gave up the act with another sigh. "It's nothing, really. Harper's just been feeling a little . . . sensitive. Since the mixer."

"The mixer?" Sam said with a frown. Shifting their weight off the wall to face Vivienne properly, they asked, "Why would she care about that? You weren't even there that night."

"Right, but I did help with your makeup, and it may have made me a little bit late to our IVF appointment. When she found out what held me up, let's just say she was . . . unimpressed." Vivienne winced at the memory in a way that told them Harper had been more than "unimpressed."

200

"IVF, huh?" Sam asked. Vivienne darted a guilty glance in Sam's direction, but they just offered her a faint smile. "I can see why she wouldn't want you to miss that."

"Well, it's still early days," Vivienne demurred, but there was no hiding the way she softened at the thought.

It sort of surprised Sam to know she was considering that kind of thing. The Vivienne of years past certainly had not been interested in anything to do with babies. But if there was anything Sam had learned over the last few weeks, it was that they knew very little about who Vivienne Fox was these days.

"So, what? You got caught up working late and now Harper's too mad at you to do the baby making thing?" Sam asked.

Still looking a bit guilty, Vivienne admitted, "It's not really the working late part she was upset about. That just comes with being married to me. It's more who I've been working late with."

"Oh. You mean because of . . . ?"

Vivienne gave a short nod, and Sam's insides did a flip at the thought of Harper being jealous of them.

It was ridiculous. Why would they ever want to revisit that sour chapter in their life? Sure, Vivienne was beautiful, and powerful, and self-assured in everything she did. But could she make them stay up all night flirting over the phone? Could she leave them loopy from sleep deprivation and dizzy from the intimacy and aching to do it all over again the next day?

No, Harper definitely didn't have anything to worry about from Sam's lovesick ass these days.

Seeing that Vivienne was still waiting for their reaction, they finally shrugged and said, "Well, that's just silly. I'm pretty sure Beck is married to her laptop. I don't know why anyone would be threatened by that."

"Hilarious," Vivienne scoffed. But she did seem a little relieved by their lack of concern.

"Yeah, yeah. You go deal with your waiters or servers or whatever," Sam said, already turning back toward the situation room's door. "I'll tell Beck to call you when Noah shows up."

They didn't wait for her answer before pushing open the door. Just in time, too, because Sam's phone started buzzing in their pocket at that very moment, and it was in their hand less than two seconds later.

Teddy: buenos días, cariño <3
Teddy: also, how the hell were you sending good morning messages at 5am?
Teddy: don't you ever sleep?

Sam felt that flutter of warmth that often accompanied Teddy's insistent use of adorable pet names when he referred to them in Spanish. Cariño was one of his favorites because, according to his very long rant on Spanish grammar the other night, it could be used to refer to anyone of any gender.

The man couldn't remember his own email password, but he had taken the time to compile an entire dictionary of gender-neutral pet names to use during their late-night phone calls. Sam didn't consider themself a romantic, but goddamn. They were only human.

Sam: I'd sleep more if you'd stop keeping me up so late.

Teddy: I wouldn't keep you up so late if you weren't so fun to talk to ;)

Sam had to work hard to wipe the smitten look off their face as they exchanged pleasant hellos with Beck and the other staff. Their fingers drummed impatiently against the back of their phone as they endured the requisite hair wash and towel before finally settling in at the makeup station.

Beck started in on their face while Sam eagerly turned their attention back to their phone. Texting while getting made up was a skill they had quickly learned to perfect, because waiting until the team was done to respond to Teddy's messages simply wasn't going to happen.

Sam: Did I already ask my question today?

Teddy: You can ask me as many questions as you like as long as it means I get to hear from you <3

Sam couldn't help feeling a little self-satisfied. If Teddy had been enamored before their phone calls started, he was really making no effort whatsoever to hide how much he liked them now. Sam still thought he must have brain damage or something, but as long as he was enjoying the unedited Sam experience, they were happy to accept his glowing attention for as long as they could get it.

Sam: Cute.
Sam: I'm curious, since you're such a nice guy . . . do you stay friends with your exes?

Teddy: is this a hypothetical question, or . . . ?

Sam: Irrelevant. Answer the question, Mr. Burgess.

Teddy: well detective, I would say it depends on the ex

Sam: Meaning?

Teddy: if he broke my heart, no
Teddy: if I broke his heart, no
Teddy: if things just fizzled . . . probably also no

Sam: So the answer is no.

Teddy: I'm not against it as a concept, I just don't really see a reason why
Teddy: not unless you have kids together or something
Teddy: you don't have any kids, do you?

Sam: Not that I know of.

Teddy: ha ha. hilarious.

Sam: What if you broke up 20 years ago?

Teddy: When I was 7?

Sam: OK fine. 10 years ago.

Teddy: why did we break up?

Sam: Does it matter? It was a long time ago.

Teddy: of course it matters. if I broke this guy's heart, I wouldn't expect him to want to be friends

Sam: What if she broke up with you?

Teddy: was I heartbroken? or was it inevitable?

Sam: Both.

Teddy: hmm . . .
Teddy: are we both still single in this scenario?

Sam: She is married.

Teddy: happily married?

Sam: I think so.

Teddy: and me?

Sam: You are also occupied.

Teddy: occupied???

Sam: Answer the question, Mr. Burgess.
Sam: Is friendship possible?

Teddy: sure. anything is possible
Teddy: but I would make sure the person I was "occupied" with didn't
get jealous
Teddy: or my ex's spouse

Sam: Noted.

Teddy: ???

Sam: I didn't say it wasn't hypothetical.

Teddy: Sam . . .

Sam: No need for anyone to be jealous.

Teddy: Good <3
Teddy: <3 <3 <3
Teddy: <3 <3 <3 <3 <3 <3
Teddy: ???
Teddy: <3 <3 <3 <3 <3 <3 <3 <3 <3 <3
Teddy: ???????? <3 ???

Sam closed their eyes and tried hard not to laugh. They really did, but he was just too damned cute sometimes.

"That's quite the smile. Is that one of your boyfriends?"

Sam nearly fell out of their chair at the sound of Beck's curious voice coming from right in front of them. For a person who spent ninety percent of her day tapping away on her laptop, she was surprisingly quiet when she wasn't helping other people find their soulmates.

"Jesus, Beck," Sam complained, immediately dropping the phone. Thank god they hadn't been talking about anything more scandalous.

"Sorry." Beck laughed, which only confirmed how embarrassed Sam must look in this moment. "I wasn't trying to snoop. It's just kind of hard to do your makeup when you won't look away from your screen for more than two seconds."

"Yeah, yeah," Sam grumbled. Shifting uncomfortably in their chair, they raised their chin a little for her. "Could have just asked."

"I don't think I've ever seen you actually texting with one of your dates. Doesn't the ops team take care of that stuff?"

"They do," Sam said shortly. They probably could have just lied, and she would have believed them, but their pride wouldn't allow it. Teddy was not just "one of their dates."

"Ooh, so is that your real-life girlfriend, then?" Beck teased. She wiggled her eyebrows at Sam knowingly. "Does she know about all this?"

"About the case?" Sam asked, and she nodded as she went back to work on their face. "No. I don't share case details with anyone outside of my investigations. Also, he's not my girlfriend."

Just their lover, apparently, no matter how many times Sam insisted that you could not be *lovers* with someone you hadn't actually seen in weeks. As if that would stop Teddy from calling them cariño, or cielo, or corazón, or any number of other sappy pet names whenever he got the chance.

"Uh huh. That's a pretty big smile for 'not your girlfriend.' Or, I guess, boyfriend, in this case," Beck said. She tilted Sam's head to the side as she brushed color into their cheeks. Not that they really needed it at the moment. "It isn't my business, but if you want some professional advice, I'd tell him anyways. You wouldn't believe how many breakups could be avoided if people were just a little more honest."

"Uh, we're not dating, so we couldn't really break up. And even if we were, I don't know why he'd care. This is just work." Sam's phone buzzed loudly in their hand, and they avoided Beck's gaze in the mirror as she offered another knowing smile.

Sam moved to put the phone on silent just as she said, "Hey, are you done with that coffee?"

"Hm?" Sam glanced down in confusion at the half-full coffee mug they were still holding in their free hand. It was maybe a little lukewarm, but still fine as far as crappy office coffee went.

"Let me get you a fresh cup." Beck snatched the mug from Sam's hand before they could protest. If that was too subtle, she mimed texting as she added, "Plenty of time to make sure your guy is OK with what you've got going on today."

Sam watched her go, a little dumbfounded and a lot embarrassed. Not so much because she thought Teddy was their boyfriend, but more because she thought the interviews for this case were actual dates worth being jealous over. As far as Sam was concerned, the "Samantha" these men were going out with wasn't even a real person, much less a reflection of their own personal interests.

Their gaze flitted back to their phone when it buzzed again.

Teddy: Should I let you get back to work?
Teddy: Hope today isn't too rough. I'll call you tonight <3

Sam's heart squeezed tight with a dangerous amount of affection. Teddy really did understand them too well to be fooled by some ridiculous undercover work.

Sam pulled up the keyboard and tapped the little red heart emoji. Their thumb hovered uncertainly over the Enter key. It was stupid to feel nervous about something so small, but nothing about this thing felt small to them anymore.

Before they could make up their mind, the door swung open to admit a frazzled-looking Noah wearing the same clothes he'd had on the previous day and balancing a large coffee mug in each hand. Sam quickly pocketed the phone to focus their attention on the new stack of profiles wedged under his arm.

"Late night?" Sam asked as he let out a jaw-cracking yawn.

"Yeah," Noah grunted. He shoved one of the coffee cups into their hand, then dropped heavily into one of the boardroom chairs. When Sam raised a pointed eyebrow, Noah just scowled and said, "Don't thank me or anything. Beck told me to give that to you on my way up. Also that she hopes your conversation goes well, whatever the hell that means."

"Oh. Great." Taking a sip, they grimaced at the watery taste of the thoroughly underwhelming coffee. At least it was hot underwhelming coffee now. Glancing at Noah over the rim of the mug, Sam asked, "Is this walk of shame because you were out having a good time, or does St. Nicholas still have you burning the midnight oil?"

"Like I've got time to get laid when I'm up to my neck in liturgical red

tape and all this shit," he said, gesturing rudely to the folders he'd left splayed out on the table.

"Well, that'd explain why you're so cranky."

"Yeah, yeah," Noah grumbled. "You want to make fun of my love life, or do you want to get this over with?"

"Sam's making fun of someone's love life?" Vivienne interjected as she appeared in the doorway. Her bejeweled phone was still glued to her hand like an extension of her arm. "You must really be in rough shape."

"Gee, thanks." Standing up from their seat at the makeup station, Sam said, "How about you pass me those profiles and we get this over with before Vince starts whining about the schedule?"

"Not so fast." Sam didn't make it one step toward the table before Vivienne was cowing them back into their chair under the force of her fierce glare. "Where's Beck? And why do you still look more like Timothée Chalamet than Ruby Rose?"

"Noah?" Sam asked, ignoring the dig. "You talked to her last."

"Last I saw, she was handing me this and heading into her office for a call," he said, lifting his own coffee mug in a small salute. "Something about having cracked the Jackson account."

"Oh great. As long as Jackson finds love, everything will be just fine," Vivienne said with exasperation. "Honestly. I thought I was a workaholic."

"You hear that?" Sam craned their neck to see past Vivienne to their cranky rookie. "Workaholic. That probably means she's still single."

"Shut up and put on your stupid makeup," Noah shot back. His eyes were already sliding shut as he leaned back in his chair. "God knows I could use a fuckin' break."

"Yeah, right." Sam glanced at themself in the mirror. They actually thought this look was OK, but that probably just meant Vivienne was right. Reaching for the eyebrow pencil, Sam said, "I still want to talk about Brad Lu. Any update on what he's been up to since the dust-up with his dealer at the mixer?"

"What are you doing?" Vivienne asked at the same time Noah said, "Shouldn't you be focusing on the guys you're actually meeting?"

"Everyone's a critic."

Vivienne still looked alarmed by the sight of Sam with an actual makeup utensil in their hand.

"Well? Either I do it myself, or you have to call your wife back and explain that you actually are working on this today. Your choice."

"No, you can do it," Vivienne said quickly. Walking over to join Noah at the boardroom table, she looked down at the men's profiles spread out across the surface. "What's this about Brad Lu?"

"I think you mean Tristan Wright," Noah interjected before Sam could reply. "You know, the guy you're actually going out with today?"

"What happened to rookies listening to their superior officers?" Sam shot back. Noah scowled, but shut his mouth when Sam just raised one rounded eyebrow at him in the mirror. "I'm still going to clear Tristan later. I just don't believe questioning him is going to tell us anything new." Picking up the bronzer, Sam swirled the brush through the powder as they explained, "Not one of the guys on Beck's list has known a single thing about our victims. Most of them haven't even met one of the girls, much less all four of them."

"Seemingly," Noah muttered, then flinched when Sam tapped the excess powder off the brush a little harder than necessary. "Be pissed all you want, but Donovan's still gonna fuckin' fire you if you don't go out with these guys."

"No one's going to get fired," Sam said dismissively before leaning in to begin contouring their face into a more feminine shape. "If Donovan wants me to waste my time chasing dud leads, that's fine. But that's not going to stop me from conducting a real investigation at the same time."

"But Brad wasn't even on the app that week," Vivienne pointed out. "And unless this Jason guy could be in two places at once—"

"Seemingly in two places at once," Sam corrected. Squinting at their reflection in the mirror, they nodded and reached for the setting powder. "Our killer is supposed to be smart enough to beat your system, right?"

Vivienne grimaced, but that may well have been because of their brusque blending technique.

"Would it be so hard for someone that smart to delete Brad's activity log or input a fake chat in Jason's conversation history?"

"If they did that for Jason, why not create a fake chat for Alicia, too?" Noah asked.

"I think someone's first instinct would probably be to cover their tracks by making two fake chats instead of one," Sam agreed. They were glad to hear him thinking critically, at least. "But anyone smart enough to pull off a hack like this is probably also smart enough to know that the police would definitely speak with whoever Alicia was talking to right before her death."

"Right," Noah said slowly as Sam started digging through the tub of lipstick samples in search of something specific. "So they'd have to be real sure the person they chose to frame would go down for it. No unexpected alibi or some shit."

"Exactly." Sam hesitated over a matte tube of rose red. "If the killer had left us a suspect to look at, chances are we would have realized that we were dealing with a hacker eventually. This way, if we hadn't spoken to Tasha, we may never have made that connection."

"So you're thinking Brad and Jason might be similar, yeah?" Noah suggested as Sam began to apply the red coating with a steady hand. "Like maybe one of them didn't do it, but they know something that might help."

"It's what I'd be looking into right now if I wasn't stuck doing this," Sam said, gesturing vaguely with the tube of lipstick. Placing it back down on the vanity, they added, "Brad's got the interesting drug connection, but Jason is the only person we know of who definitely went out with all four victims. I don't have a lot of extra time, so I'll probably have to start with him."

"Really, all four?" Noah asked. "Even the new girl, uh . . . Kayleigh?"

Sam was impressed that he remembered the girl's name. Maybe he really was learning.

"It's a pretty unlikely coincidence. At the very least, it means Jason's got insight no one on Beck's short list can give us." Sam took one last look in the mirror before nodding to themself. Glancing over at Vivienne, they said, "So what do you think?"

"About looking into Jason?" she asked.

"No, the makeup," Sam clarified. Waving impatiently at their reflection, they repeated, "What do you think?"

"Is that . . . a trick question?"

"You look like a chick to me, boss," Noah called from the table.

"Deeply inappropriate," Sam replied, even as their red lips quirked up into a small smile. "But good enough. What was the last interaction the ops team had with Jason?"

"Copy that," Noah said, glancing back down at the profiles on the table. He had to shuffle through several dozen before he finally found Jason's. "Oof," he said with a wince. "That's gonna be a tough sell."

"Explain," Sam said. They turned on their stool to face the table.

"Looks like the ops team has pretty much been ghosting him since we started down the hacker road." Noah made a face at the printout in his hand and added, "Which is only gonna make things harder, 'cause he, uh . . . does not seem like the patient type, ya know?"

"What's that supposed to mean?" Vivienne asked with a frown. "Was he really that offended that they weren't interested?"

"Uh . . . I guess not . . . offended?" Noah's giant ears turned a brilliant shade of cherry red, but Vivienne still looked confused. Sam rolled their eyes when Noah looked to them in desperation.

"I think he's trying to say our guy isn't looking for romance so much as he's looking to get laid," Sam said bluntly. When Noah didn't respond immediately, they said, "Blink once if I've got that right, altar boy."

"Yeah. Seems like a total douchebag." Noah only looked more embarrassed by Sam's crude summary. Glaring at them, he slid the profile across the table in their general direction. "Just your type."

"I don't have a type, but I do generally try to avoid douchebags." Standing up, Sam crossed over to where Noah and Vivienne were gathered and picked up the meager printout of Jason and "Samantha's" chat history. "Did he send me any dick pics?" they asked as they leafed through the contents.

"Excuse me?" Vivienne demanded.

She sounded offended by the mere concept, which Sam thought was pretty funny given that she owned one of the world's largest online dating services. If she thought everyone on there was looking for true love, she was in for a rude awakening.

"Noah's the one who said he wasn't looking for romance," Sam said with an easy shrug. "Oh look. There it is." They held up the blurry bathroom selfie for the room to see in all its underwhelming glory.

"Dude," Noah complained, immediately jerking away from the nude photo. "I don't wanna see that."
"Don't be so uptight. It's just a penis," Sam scoffed.

By the time they had made their way back to the start of "Samantha" and Jason's history, Sam could pretty well see what kind of guy they were dealing with. The conversation was direct and to the point. "Hey, you look hot, wanna bone," etc. Said in a few more words than that, but the guy clearly knew what he was looking for, and it wasn't to settle down. "Samantha" had engaged a little bit in the dance, but her responses were too stiff to really get anyone going.

"Interesting . . ."

Sam flipped back to the nude photo and brought the paper even closer to their face. Noah made a sound of disgust, but Sam was unfazed as they closely examined the blurry bathroom-mirror selfie.

"That small, or are you just getting old?" Vivienne asked when Sam had been squinting at the photo for over a minute. "Because I think Harper left a pair of reading glasses in my office if you need—"

"No. I'm just trying to see something," Sam said, because they absolutely did not need reading glasses, and even if they did, they would literally have to go blind before they would admit it.

Dropping the printout, Sam grabbed their phone and typed Jason Albertalli's name into Google. The law firm of Wellesley Alexander popped up as the first result. Sam pinched to zoom in on one of the staff photos. Their guy was posing with his all-American smile and a suit that probably cost more than Sam's monthly car payments.

". . . Very interesting."

Sam returned their attention to the printout of "Samantha's" chat history with Jason. Despite her lukewarm response, it hadn't taken long for him to start sending her his junk mail. But shortly after the pictures started coming, Jason seemed to lose interest—probably because he could never get anything exciting back from "Samantha."

So maybe "Samantha" should give him something worth responding to.

"Hey, Noah," they said, barely glancing up from the printout. "Where's the phone?"

"Pretty sure it's in your pocket," he said, hardly daring to look in Sam's direction, lest they still be looking at anything that might offend his Catholic sensibilities.

"Not my phone—the phone," Sam said impatiently. Searching the cluttered tabletop, Sam's eyes fell on the little silver iPhone that allowed them to access "Samantha's" profile.

"What do you need that for?" Noah asked as Sam snatched up the device.

Their only response was to tap on the screen and load up the app. From there, they quickly located and started scrolling through their messaging history with Jason. It looked a little more real displayed across the neat little chat boxes on the app's interface. Although his cheesy nudes really weren't any more impressive on screen than they were on paper.

"Are you messaging him right now?" Vivienne asked with surprise as Sam began to type.

"Yup," Sam said, even as they deleted everything they had written so far and started over. This first message had to work, or Captain Donovan really might fire them when she found out what they'd done.

"Doesn't the ops team need to clear any messages?" Noah asked, and Sam grinned a little at the thought of anyone on the ops team clearing this kind of message. Not likely.

"They already struck out with him. Time to find out if I can do better."

They pressed Send. There was no taking it back now.

"With your legendary flirtation skills?" Vivienne said a little disbelievingly. "This should be good."

"It will be. You'll see." Even as Sam spoke, the phone made a flowery noise indicating a return message, and their lips curled into a knowing smile. "What do you know. Guess he likes me after all."

"Yeah, right. Let me see that." Vivienne circled around behind them. Sam quickly tried to hide the screen, but it was too late. "Sam!" she gasped, and Sam couldn't help smirking a little immaturely as they began crafting a reply to Jason's predictable response.

"No peeking," they said as their thumbs continued to move across the keyboard.

"You can't—you can't write that!" Vivienne insisted, sounding thoroughly scandalized.

"Why not? He likes it."

"What'd they write?" Noah asked, half-rising from his seat to try and get a look.

"Nothing you need to see," Vivienne said quickly, although Sam wasn't sure why she was trying to protect his innocence. He might like to play the uptight good boy, but they found it hard to believe he was really all that naive about the world of online dating.

"I asked him if married men still like to fuck on first dates," Sam said bluntly. They sent their reply and the typing icon appeared on Jason's end almost immediately.

"No way." Noah's eyes looked like they might pop right out of his head. "He's fuckin' married?"

"Yup. Clocked the tan line in that selfie. And he's wearing the ring in his company photos," Sam said, nodding to the abandoned printout they had been examining so closely.

"But you're not actually going to . . . ?"

Sam paused their texting to raise an eyebrow at Noah. Maybe Beck wasn't the only one blurring the lines between the case and reality.

"Now that would be scandalous, wouldn't it?" Sam teased, just to watch him blanch. Rolling their eyes at the horrified look on Noah's face, they turned their attention back to the screen and said, "Relax. We're just playing right now."

"Playing?"

Sam pursed their lips and kept typing. It was almost embarrassing how easy this guy was to manipulate. Five messages in and he was already asking for pictures. Ten messages in and he was ready to buy them an expensive dinner at a hotel in exchange for the tantalizing possibility of taking "Samantha" back to his room after.

"Sam," Vivienne said sharply, apparently disapproving of the things they were promising to do in exchange for a time and place to meet.

"Grow up, Viv. You want me to get somewhere with this case or not?" The restaurant reservation popped up in their notifications, and Sam pressed Accept on the invitation. "And . . . done." They hit Send on their final flirty text before placing the phone down on the vanity. Noah and Vivienne were both staring at them in slack-jawed amazement. "Guess I do have some game after all."

"Who even are you?" Noah demanded, looking both impressed and deeply disturbed by their stone-cold "game."

"Someone who wants to bone a married man, apparently." Sam reached out to silence the phone before Vivienne had an aneurism at the sound of their incoming messages. If Sam's suggestive texts had bothered her, she probably didn't want to know what Jason was writing to them now.

"That is not what my app is meant to be used for," Vivienne said darkly.

Her outrage felt more than a little ironic to Sam, but hey, that was good news for her wife, at least.

"I think Jason disagrees," Sam said as they glanced curiously around the room at the racks of clothing options. "We're meeting up tomorrow night after my other dates are over. What do you think a girl wears for this kind of thing?"

"I guess something kinda skimpy?" Noah suggested hesitantly. "Not something his wife would wear, anyway."

"Noah," Vivienne complained.

"What? I'm just saying, if the guy sleeps around to get his rocks off, obviously there's something he's not getting at home."

As Noah continued to put his foot in his mouth and Vivienne took him to task, Sam smiled ruefully and pulled out their personal phone.

Everyone kept saying Sam was bad at this stuff, but it was really more like Sam wasn't most people's cup of tea. Which was probably fair. Naughty text messages were all well and good, but Sam could barely string two coherent sentences together when they were trying to have a meaningful conversation with somebody. Most people found their particular brand of unromantic, tongue-tied bluntness a bit of a turnoff when it came to dating.

But on the rare occasion that they were somebody's cup of tea . . .

Sam: <3

CHAPTER TWENTY-ONE

<u>Recording #4: Jason Albertalli</u>

There is the sound of heels clicking on tile floor. The sound echoes slightly, indicating that the wearer is in an open space. The sound of chattering voices can be heard growing louder as the walker arrives at their destination.

"Hello, ma'am. How can I help you?"

"I have a reservation for two. Under Albertalli?"

"Of course, he's waiting at the table. Please follow me."

Snippets of conversation blur by as the person wearing the mic follows the server to the table.

"Hello, Jason."

"Samantha—it's nice to meet you."

"The pleasure's all mine."

There is a rustling sound as two people embrace, followed by the soft sound of lips being pressed to cheeks. Chairs are pulled out as the two settle into their seats.

"Can I interest you in a glass of wine?"

"I don't know. Can you?"

"All right. Another glass, please—actually, just bring the whole bottle."

"Of course, sir. Coming right up."

There is an electric silence as the two appraise each other across the table. The tension is palpable even over the wire.

"So. Jason Albertalli."

"Samantha Ryder. You're even more beautiful in person."

"You look like your profile picture."

"Is that a good thing?"

"It is if it means the rest of your pictures are accurate, too."

"I see you're a woman who knows what she wants."

"Is that a good thing?"

"Absolutely. Why waste time playing games, especially if we both already know what we want?"

"And what is it you want?"

"Right now?"

"Mhm."

"I kind of want to skip the formal dinner and worry about ordering room service later."

"Cute. Does that line work for you a lot?"

"That depends. How do you feel about a dinner of strawberries and champagne?"

"Are they chocolate-covered strawberries?"

"They can be whatever you want them to be."

"Hmm. Tempting. But sadly for you, I'm not that easy."

"Damn. Can't blame a guy for trying, right?"

"Don't worry. I'm sure if you play your cards right, you'll find dessert very . . . satisfying."

[Wowza, Sammy.]

"I'll have to be on my best behavior."

"I'm sure you will be."

[When you asked me to monitor a last-minute date, I didn't think I'd be recording your sex tape.]

"Your wine, ma'am."

"Thank you."

"Are we ready to order? An appetizer, perhaps?"

"Let's just skip to the main course."

"Sounds good to me."

"The usual for you, sir?"

"Yes please."

"And for you, ma'am?"

"Just the house salad."

"Very good. I'll be back with your food shortly."

" . . . "

" . . . "

"The usual, hm?"

"You know how it is at these places. They charge a million dollars a meal, so they can't afford to forget a face."

"Mhm. You sure it's not because this is where you come for all of your little affairs?"

[Damn. Way to go for the jugular on that one.]

"Well, I wouldn't really call them affairs, exactly."

"So you are married."

"It's not a secret. My wife and I have an understanding."

"What kind of an understanding?"

"She loves her work. And I . . . well, I love the company of beautiful women. This way we're both happy."

"Hmm."

"Does that bother you?"

"I guess I'd say I'm . . . intrigued. I've never been part of an open relationship. Not knowingly, anyways."

"Ah, well, I guess I should clarify—I'm not looking for a relationship. This is just . . . you know. Some fun while she's out of town."

"Thank goodness. I was afraid I'd have to break your heart."

There is the sound of amused laughter at the dry words.

"Look, if it'll make you feel better, you can see for yourself. I texted her this morning before her lecture."

There is the shuffling sound of a phone being pulled out. On screen is the name Jennifer Albertalli alongside a picture of a serious-looking woman with fine features, large glasses, and long, dark hair. Beneath the name is a brief text conversation. Jason wishes his wife luck at her lecture, and she wishes him an entertaining evening with his new friend. Both are looking forward to seeing each other again in a week.

"See? Nothing to hide here."

". . . Huh. So you really do this app stuff just to entertain yourself when she's away—teaching?"

"She's an anthropologist who specializes in human relationships. Why marriage? Why commitment? What is the social value of monogamy? She's brilliant in her field, and you can guess from the fact that I'm here what some of her theories are."

"I'm thinking it has something to do with the ratio between nudes and heart emojis in your text messages."

There is another laugh, low and flirtatious.

"You didn't seem to mind."

"Why should I mind? I prefer a man who knows how to get what he wants."

"Getting what I want has never been a problem for me."

"I bet. Let me guess: Perfect house, brilliant wife, fancy job as . . . what? A doctor?"

"Lawyer."

"Ooh. A lawyer. How sexy."

"It is when it means I can afford dinner and a room at a place like this."

"Hmm, that's true. You must work on some big cases."

"From time to time. I just wrapped up the Marcus Springer case."

[Beach house robber. Semi-big deal on the local news.]

"Wow, I actually heard about that one. That's the robber who hit all those beach houses, right? It was all over the news."

"Alleged robber. He was cleared of all charges."

"He must have had a pretty good lawyer."

"I like to think so."

"Pretty amazing. Hard to believe you've got time for this kind of thing."

"I do end up pulling a lot of late nights when things at the office ramp up. Then it's not all nice hotels and fancy restaurants, but it saves me some money taking my dates to The Imperial instead of places like this."

[That's a flag. Same bar where Alicia went for hookups and was supposed to meet her mystery man.]

" . . . "

"You don't look impressed."

"No, I'm sure a place like that—what'd you call it? The Imperial?"

"Yeah, it's an older bar in the West End near my firm. Nice ambiance."

[Shit. You might really be on to something here, Sammy.]

"Right . . . I'm sure it's fine. For other people."

"You prefer the hotels and fancy restaurants?"

"I prefer wine that comes in a bottle, not in a cardboard box."

"If that's how you like your wine, how do you like your men?"

"It's more what I don't like in my men."

"Oh?"

"Mhm. For example, I don't want some paper pusher behind a desk who's going to ask me every five minutes if I feel good. You understand what I'm saying?"

[Oh my god.]

"Crystal clear. I think you'll find I'm the type of man who prefers paying other people to do the boring stuff so I can focus on doing what I want. Which might involve a desk, but only if it's convenient."

Their conversation is interrupted by the sound of footsteps approaching and the slight rattle of plates on a serving tray.

"My apologies for interrupting. I have the house salad here, for—"

"Actually, could we just get the check, please?"

". . . pardon me?"

"The check. I'm sorry, I'm just not feeling well all of a sudden."

[Should I even tell you not to bail before you land a second date, or just assume you're not going to listen to me no matter what I say?]

". . . Sir?"

"You can just charge it to my room."

"Would you like it in a box or . . . ?"

"I don't think that will be necessary, thank you."

"Ah . . . OK, then. I hope you . . . feel better, ma'am. Sir."

There is an awkward pause, then the sound of the waiter retreating from the table.

"You're not really feeling sick, are you?"

"Look at you. A lawyer and a detective."

[Oh, Sammy. You are a naughty, naughty girl, aren't you?]

There is the sound of two people leaving the table. Hurried footsteps head out of the restaurant and back into the echoing lobby beyond. The echoes dim again as the two pairs of feet slip into a side hallway.

"You know this isn't the way to the elev—Mmm!"

The mic is filled with the sound of fabric sliding against fabric and the unmistakable sound of two people kissing heatedly.

[Holy shit.]

"Uh . . . wow. Has anyone—uh, has anyone ever told you you're really good at that?"

"Once or twice."

There is the sound of more feverish kissing that abruptly cuts off when a new set of footsteps approaches. Two people breathe a little heavily as they wait for the footsteps to fade away.

"My room?"

"Not yet."

Hands rub against fabric, and there is a low sound of pleasure as someone is pushed up against a wall.

[Jesus, Sam. At least make sure to hide your wire if you're planning to let this guy get past second base.]

"Hmm. Down boy."

"That's easy for you to say."

"Why? Do you want me?"

"Yes."

"How badly do you want me?"

"A lot."

"What would you do to have me?"

"What do you want me to do?"

"Maybe I want you to take me to dinner."

"We just left dinner."

"Exactly."

" . . . "

" . . . "

"Are—are you serious? Are you fucking kidding me right now?"

"That's no way to talk to a lady if you're hoping to have a good time."

"That's not—you can't—come on. Are you fucking serious?"

"Do I seem serious to you?"

[Damn, Sammy. That's so savage.]

"This is fucking ridiculous."

"I thought you knew how to get what you wanted?"

" . . . "

" . . . "

" . . . "

"So I'll be hearing from you about that second date?"

". . . We'll see about that."

"I guess we will."

There is the sound of one last lingering kiss over the mic.

"I'll see you around, Jason. But feel free to think of me as much as you want tonight."

CHAPTER TWENTY-TWO

A knock on the door startled Sam out of a deep fog. Blinking their burning eyes hard, they turned and saw Vivienne's skinny arm sticking through the doorway. A large takeout bag covered in curly Thai script swung from her hand.

"I come bearing sustenance," her voice called from the other side of the door. "Can I come in?"

"Uh . . . yeah. Sure."

Rolling their neck, Sam wondered how long they had been locked in. Five hours? Six? They glanced down at the papers in front of them and then toward the window at the far end of the room. They felt a jolt of surprise when they saw the angle of the sun.

"Shit," Sam muttered with some alarm as Vivienne placed the bag of food down on the situation room's table. Scrambling for their phone, they asked, "What time is it?"

"Quarter after seven," Vivienne said. She raised an eyebrow when Sam let out a sigh of relief. "What, do you have a hot date or something?"

"What? No. I just didn't realize how long I'd been here," Sam said quickly, even though that wasn't entirely true.

They glanced down at their phone again. There was still plenty of time to get home before Teddy would be expecting them to call, at least. Which was important, because after word had gotten around to the rest of the precinct about Sam's little make-out session with Jason the other day, they needed these nightly calls more than ever.

It had gotten bad enough that they had even admitted to Teddy in a fit of frustration how the "teasing" comments had driven them to work an entire afternoon from their car in 100-degree heat. Risking heatstroke was actually preferable to biting their tongue all day. To say Teddy had not been pleased with their coworkers' immature behavior would be a severe understatement. Only he hadn't called it immature. He'd called it hateful and homophobic and lots of other beautiful things that they hadn't realized their weary heart needed to hear so badly.

Vivienne tore the top off the takeout bag, and Sam's romantic thoughts were obliterated by the mouth-watering smell of piping-hot Thai food.

"Come on. Time to eat something," she said, pulling out a little white box and waving it tantalizingly in their direction.

"Is that—" Sam started and then hesitated. Glancing between Vivienne and the familiar bag, they asked, "Is that the pad see ew? From Golden Bangkok?"

"I got a couple different things." Vivienne tactfully sidestepped the question as she laid out more boxes, two sets of chopsticks, and several bottles of water on the table wherever she could find space among the printouts and fabric samples. "Considering you've been locked in here for over nine hours, I figured you could use the calories. And I wasn't sure what you like these days, so . . . You'd better help me eat some of this."

Sam considered her for a long moment before scooting their chair closer and reaching for the utensils. Snapping the little wooden sticks apart with the practiced ease of someone used to living on takeout, Sam nodded to her and said, "Thank you."

The room lapsed into silence as the two dug into the comically oversized feast of takeout containers spread out on the table. Sam couldn't help being a little amused—not because she had thought about feeding them, but because it was so painfully apparent that she had only bought all this food to obfuscate the fact that she knew exactly what they liked from this particular restaurant, even if they hadn't eaten there in almost twenty years.

Vivienne shot them a look as Sam laughed quietly at the ridiculousness of the situation.

"I don't see what's so funny," she said stiffly, which only made them laugh harder.

"Come on, Viv. Really?" Sam said, gesturing to the food covering the space between them. "Did you actually order one of everything just so I wouldn't be mad at you?"

"I have no idea what you're talking about."

"It's fine. It's—Thank you," Sam said with a shake of their head. "I guess I do sometimes still forget . . ."

"That human beings need to eat in order to function?" Vivienne suggested.

"Yeah, something like that," they said ruefully. Stabbing their chopsticks into one of the boxes, they lifted the steaming contents to their lips and made a sound of pure pleasure at the heavenly taste. "Oh my god, this is so good," they mumbled reverently around the mouthful of food. "How did I forget about this place?"

"I had half forgotten about it, too," Vivienne admitted, and she finally seemed to relax a little, seeing how much Sam appreciated her efforts. Glancing down at her own box of food, Vivienne reached for a packet of sriracha sauce and said, "I never eat this kind of thing anymore. Harper doesn't like spicy food."

Sam paused with their chopsticks halfway to their mouth and glanced curiously down at the noodles dangling from the two wooden sticks. "Spicy . . . ?"

"She thinks pepper is spicy," Vivienne explained as she dumped the packet of red sauce onto her noodles.

Sam snorted and finished shoveling the very-much-not-spicy noodles into their mouth. Swallowing hard, they said, "That must make being married to you hard."

"It may have been the source of a few arguments," Vivienne said with a fond smile.

The mention of arguments tweaked something in Sam's mind, and they instantly put down their food to reach for their notes.

"But we're much better at making up than we are at fighting."

"Cute," Sam muttered vaguely as they picked up their pen to scribble a new note in the margins of the already cramped page.

And then another note . . . and then another note . . .

"Sam."

"Hmm?" they hummed, flipping through pages as they tried to remember something one of the guys had said on one of their nerd-dates about search algorithms. Or was that user algorithms? Was that the same thing?

"Put the notes down."

"Hmm?" Sam repeated. They flipped through the pages faster now, then pulled up short as an egg roll landed right on top of their notes. "Oh, come on. What the hell?" They knocked the roll away and carefully dusted wanton flakes off the paper.

"Notes. Down," Vivienne ordered.

Sam glared at her as they dabbed hopelessly at the grease stains decorating the page.

"You need to take a break. Eat something. Maybe try sitting up straight for a couple minutes so you don't turn into a total hermit."

"I'm not—"

Vivienne cut them off with a pointed stare, and Sam quickly straightened out their back. Grimacing a little as things popped and crackled that probably shouldn't pop and crackle quite so much at the ripe old age of thirty-eight, Sam realized she might have a point. The whole point of coming here to work was so they wouldn't have to choose between getting harassed or having permanent spine damage.

Grabbing their phone, they glanced at the time again. "Fine. I'll put it away. But not because of you."

"I'm starting to think you really do have a hot date," Vivienne said as Sam began packing up their notes.

"Nope. No date." Sam's clipped words would have been more convincing if they weren't also avoiding her gaze like their life depended on it.

"You sure about that?" she asked as they crammed their notes into their bag.

"Yes," Sam insisted, settling back into their chair. Grabbing their chopsticks again, they said, "If you have to know, I'm still single, so just . . . drop it."

"Uh huh. Single."

"Yes. Single. Unattached. Not seeing anyone." Sam stabbed their noodles a little too aggressively. "Very, very single. Is that clear enough?"

"You were always a bad liar," Vivienne said. She put down her own takeout box as a big, knowing smile spread across her pretty face. "So what's her name?"

"Fuck off, Viv."

"Sam's got a secret girlfriend," she sang teasingly.

"No, I don't," Sam insisted, but to their horror, they could feel the heat crawling up their neck at the ludicrous suggestion.

As if they could have a girlfriend when they were already so busy with this case. Not that they had had any trouble making time for Teddy lately . . . but still. He wasn't exactly girlfriend material, was he?

"You're so busted," Vivienne said, her grin only growing the more Sam denied it. "Look at that blush!"

"Shut up. There's no girl."

"Come on. Just tell me," Vivienne pleaded. She dropped her chopsticks to clasp her hands beneath her chin. "I won't tell anyone. Who is she?"

"He's not—" Sam started, then cut themself off. Groaning with frustration as her ears perked up at their little slip, Sam let their head fall back against the seat's headrest. "Would you please just let it go?"

"He?" Vivienne asked, sounding far too intrigued by this information. "Now I really need to know."

"He's not—he isn't anyone. Anything. It's not a big deal," Sam insisted. They couldn't even bring themself to look in her direction as they uttered the painfully obvious lie.

Well, what was Sam supposed to say, really? They could barely engage in casual small talk with Vivienne before tempers started flaring. How were they supposed to talk about something like this and expect it to go any better?

"Are you sure?" Vivienne asked. Sam stiffened a little at the softness in her voice. "Because anyone who can make you blush like that sounds like a pretty big deal to me."

"Listen, it's not . . ." Sam started to deny again, but she just pinned them with those big, bottomless eyes. "Really? This is really what you want to talk about?"

Vivienne's expression was all silent, stubborn expectancy.

Sighing, Sam shoved aside their now thoroughly spoiled dinner. "OK, fine. If you absolutely have to know, his name is Teddy—"

"Teddy?"

"And it's really—Would you stop laughing?" Sam snapped, but to their surprise, she only laughed harder instead of snapping back.

"Teddy? Seriously?"

"Shut up. We met while I was on the Paradiso case. I was feeling, uh, well, you know." Sam waved their hand vaguely to indicate their general state of sexual drought at the time. "I guess it had been a while, and he was there, and he was nice, and he was, uhh . . . very interested, so . . . we connected. That's it."

"And by 'connected' you mean . . . ?" Vivienne prompted. Her delight in the topic was seriously unnerving.

"You know exactly what I mean," Sam said flatly.

Vivienne gave them her most innocent look, but if she thought that was going to get her the dirty details, she was all the way wrong.

"We hooked up. Happy? Story over."

"If the story is over, what's up with all the texting and puppy dog eyes?" Vivienne asked, nodding to the phone they had practically been glued to for well over a week.

"There aren't any puppy dog eyes. God."

"Uh huh," Vivienne said in that same disbelieving tone. "Wasn't the Paradiso case over a month ago?"

"Yes. What's your point?" Not that they couldn't guess exactly what her point was.

"Sam, how many times did you connect with this guy if he's still texting you a month later?"

"We were only on the island together for a week, and he had a concussion for most of that time," Sam grumbled. "I haven't even seen him again since then."

Grinning at the embarrassed look on their face, Vivienne said, "Head over heels after one week. That doesn't sound like 'no big deal' to me."

"I am not *head over heels*."

"Really, Sam? Give it up. You're not exactly the crushing type," Vivienne said, and then laughed at the sour look on their face. "You clearly have a thing for this guy. So what's he like? Is he smart? Is he sexy? Does he have a great job, or, like, a massive penis? I need to know more."

"Viv . . ." Sam sighed, running a flustered hand through their hair. They glanced across the table at her uncertainly.

Part of them knew they should just shut this conversation down, go home, and continue enjoying this small slice of happiness for as long as it lasted. But the other part of them—the same part that was secretly relieved by the sound of Teddy's outrage at two in the morning—was just so tired of pushing it all down.

"All right. You really want to know about him?"

Stupid. Very stupid. But oh-so-thrilling.

"Yes," Vivienne insisted. "Tell me everything."

Dropping their gaze to the table, Sam ran one finger along the edge of a takeout box to avoid looking at her eager expression. "OK. Well, he's an artist, so . . . I don't know if that counts as a great job. But he's pretty good at it, I think."

"Ooh, an artist," Vivienne said. She leaned her head on one hand to offer Sam an encouraging smile. "That sounds kind of sexy."

Sam shrugged shyly, because they weren't sure with her fancy dresses and swanky office building if she really meant that, but they certainly found Teddy's passion for his work appealing.

"He also lives on a boat, uh, most of the time. And speaks Spanish." Again, the words came out abrupt and disjointed, but the rush of relief that followed lit up their insides like a goddamned Christmas tree.

"Really? Isn't he from Paradiso?" she asked curiously, and Sam made a small face at the misleading association.

"He grew up there. But he's not really . . ." Thinking carefully about their next words because they knew how sensitive this topic was for him, Sam said, "I guess I don't know his exact background. But he's Latinx for sure. And not at all like the other people from around there."

"OK. All right," Vivienne said, nodding thoughtfully. "I think I'm starting to form a picture. Is he an older guy?"

Sam shook their head silently and reached for a bottle of water.

"So he's younger, then?" she pressed, and they ducked their head as those sharp eyes took in their guilty expression. "How much younger are we talking?" Sam just drank their water and avoided her gaze. Seeing that they were not going to answer that one, which was answer enough, Vivienne started to laugh again. "Wow, Sam. Who would have guessed you'd end up being into younger guys?"

"That's really not—I mean, that has nothing to do with why I . . ." They sighed, putting down the water hard enough to dent the plastic. "OK, fine. How about this. He is a . . . younger guy. But he's also super confident. And very curious." Sam peeked over at her, but Vivienne didn't crack any more jokes. If anything, she seemed even more interested now. "He's also way too honest. You could ask this guy anything, I mean literally anything, and he'll just tell you. And—seriously, if you laugh at this, I will hurt you."

"Come on, I'm not going to laugh," she said, and Sam grimaced at the lovey-dovey look on her face. Stretching her arms out across the table, Vivienne grabbed Sam's hand and said, "He's confident, he's curious, he's honest. What else?"

"OK . . . OK, the thing is, he's really, uh, sweet, I guess. Like, to everyone. All the time." Sam looked at her nervously, but when she still didn't laugh, something loosened inside their chest. Allowing a little more affection into their voice now, they said, "He's the kind of good that makes you want to try harder to keep up. And he's always saying the right thing. Or the true thing the right way. Or . . . it's like . . . like . . ." Sam cast their gaze toward the ceiling as they struggled to find the right words, even though flowery descriptions had never really been their strong suit. Finally, they just shrugged helplessly and said, "He's the person you call when you're having a bad day, and he'll pick up the phone every time. Even if he's busy, or if it's the middle of the night, or—he just will. And he'll know what to say. That's just how he is."

"Wow, Sam," Vivienne said, grinning a little at the undoubtedly smitten look on their face. "That's quite the speech coming from you. I think you might love this guy."

"Shut up. We're not even dating," Sam muttered, instantly pushing her hand away.

Because you couldn't be in love with someone you hadn't technically been on a single date with. But the butterflies kicking up a storm in their gut didn't seem to care much for technicalities, and it was enough to make Sam queasy.

"Come on, I'm just teasing you." Smiling at their defensiveness, Vivienne leaned back in her seat and said, "He sounds like a real cutie."

"A cutie?" Sam replied with a startled half-laugh. That distracted their butterflies, at least. "Uh . . . not exactly."

"Oh?"

"Well, he is very . . . attractive. Kind of long hair, and a great smile, too. But he's also a college dropout with a ton of tattoos. And a beard." They couldn't help grinning at the face she made. Sam might not have a type, but Viv sure did, and it wasn't tatted-up pretty boys who punched transphobic TAs between iced coffees. Picturing Teddy's soft, full frame now as he had looked stretched out next to them in bed with all his beautiful art on full display, they added, "Also, he's huge. I'm talking easily six inches on me in every possible direction."

"Sounds very . . . cuddly?" Vivienne wrinkled her nose as she struggled to restructure her mental image from the adorable, skinny little artist she had probably been picturing.

"He can be," Sam said with a smirk. "After, anyways."

"Oh my god, you are so into this guy," Vivienne laughed, and Sam couldn't help laughing too because it was seriously such a juvenile thing to brag about, but why not? She was the one who wanted to know.

"Come on, now you have to show me a picture," Vivienne demanded. When Sam shook their head, she said, "Don't even try that, Sam. I know you have not been texting this guy for over a month and don't have one photo you can share with the class."

Sam considered telling her that she probably didn't want to see the only photos they actually had of their eager-to-please lover, but that would probably be crossing the line in this already bizarre conversation. Instead, they rolled their eyes at her typical bossy attitude and picked up their phone.

Quickly pulling up the bio page on Teddy's website, Sam shoved the phone across the table toward Vivienne and said, "There, pictures. Happy?"

At the bottom of the page, there was a feed from Teddy's Instagram with plenty of family-friendly pictures for her to look at. It featured various photos, mostly professional shots of his work, but also of him with friends, or at fancy art galleries around the world, or mid-construction on some truly wild pieces taking shape on the deck of his new boat.

"Oh my god," Vivienne exclaimed, instantly snatching up the phone. "Is this really him?"

"Mhm."

"Wow. You weren't kidding," she said as she scrolled through the photos slowly. "This is . . . definitely not what I was expecting. Look at those curls. And that smile!" Glancing up at them, Vivienne said, "I can see how he'd be fun to cuddle up with at night."

Sam just shrugged, but there was no hiding the fondness in their expression as they watched her flip through the photos. It was impossible not to enjoy seeing Teddy beaming and elbow-deep in his art. He had that kind of infectious enthusiasm, even in picture form.

"You know, you may not have a type, but you definitely have good taste in—"Vivienne's words cut off with a gasp as she enlarged one of the photos.

"What?" Sam leaned forward with a frown to see what had her so shocked.

"Sam, you do realize this guy is . . . kind of a big deal, right?" Vivienne said, holding up the picture on the phone. It depicted one of Teddy's larger works, made entirely out of misprinted currency from around the world. "I'm pretty sure this piece is in the front lobby of my bank."

"The one on fourth street?" Sam asked, and she nodded. "Yeah, that's one of his."

"And you went with *I think he's pretty good?*" Vivienne said incredulously.

"Yeah. I think he probably is pretty good. But I don't know anything about art," Sam said with a shrug. Not that they didn't know a lot more now thanks to Teddy's avid, rambling monologues. Feeling another surge of that thrilling alien desire to disclose, they found themself saying, "If you like that, you should check out the commissions page."

"Oh my god. No."

"Yup."

"Sweetheart?" Vivienne said, reading off the simple one-word caption underneath the beautiful anatomical sculpture featured prominently at the top of the page. "Did he make this for you? Is that why you wanted the heart tattoo on that first date?"

Sam nodded, feeling the same rush of butterflies they had felt when he had first posted the piece. They had never been very good at romantic gestures, but if Teddy found their little flirtation inspiring, they weren't going to stop him from saying so in his own way. It was a stunning piece, after all.

Vivienne rested her chin in her hand and gave them that lovey-dovey look again. "You really like this guy, don't you?" Sam just shrugged again, and she rolled her eyes at their stubbornness. "All right, well, whenever you get around to making it official, you definitely have to bring him to brunch with Harper and I."

"Viv . . ." they groaned, leaning back in their chair. "Don't make me regret telling you about this. We're not even dating, forget being brunch-with-my-ex serious."

"Seriously, Sam?" Vivienne said, pushing the phone back toward them across the table. "You don't seriously think anyone does this"—she pointed to the phone—"for over a month if there isn't something real there."

"I'm not saying it isn't real," Sam said, glancing down at the phone. "Maybe this will go somewhere. Maybe it won't. But I prefer to keep things . . ." They trailed off as they stared at the phone with a peculiar expression growing on their face.

"Keep things what?"

Sam didn't respond, still staring at the phone with a faraway look in their eyes.

"Sam . . . ?"

"Private." Sam snapped back to attention as they stood abruptly and reached for the bag with all the notes. "You don't sell any of the app data, right?"

"What?" Vivienne sounded reasonably confused by this sudden change of topic.

"The data, from the app," Sam said impatiently. They dumped their notes back out on the table, taking no notice of the takeout boxes that were scattered in the wake of the avalanche. "Messaging history, people's survey results, whatever else gets entered on the app. You don't sell it off to third parties, do you?"

"No. Of course not," Vivienne said, still sounding completely lost. "Dating is a very personal process. I take my clients' confidentiality seriously."

"And that's a selling point for the app? That you never sell customer data?" They shuffled through the papers frantically in search of something specific.

"I'm not sure it's a big selling point, but sure. We say it on all the advertising."

"Right . . . So if someone wanted to, say, arrange a meeting with someone specific, they could do that and know that their messages were totally private, unlike on other messaging services or apps," Sam said. When they looked up at her, there was an intensity to their gaze that made it clear they were on to something.

"I guess so, yes," Vivienne said slowly. "Sam, what's this about?"

"Huh," Sam said, picking up the page they were looking for and straightening as they examined it carefully. "Sounds like a great way to set up a meeting you didn't want anyone to know about."

"You mean like what Jason is doing? If he wasn't in an open relationship, I mean?"

"Could be for something like that," Sam agreed before turning the paper to face her. It depicted Brad's profile—his smile a little wooden and his details rather spartan. "Considering our friend Brad here, I'm also thinking it would be a great way to arrange a meeting with a dealer." Tapping the chart below his profile that listed all of the scheduled dates he had arranged via the app with the three original victims, Sam said, "Take a look at his meetings with Nikki. Pretty much like clockwork, right? But then with the other women, he's all over the place. Almost like what he wanted from Nikki had nothing to do with what he was looking for with the other women."

"So, what, you think he was meeting with Nikki to sell her drugs?" Vivienne asked uncertainly as Sam's mind jumped three steps forward at a time.

"Other way around."

"Oh," Vivienne said, sounding a little taken aback. "Oh. Is that—what does that mean? For the case?"

"Nothing yet," Sam said with a shrug as they picked up Nikki's profile and put it together with Brad's. "And even if it does turn out to mean something for Vice, that doesn't mean it will be relevant to my investigation."

"But it might be?"

"Might be," Sam said, remembering the desperation in Brad's movements that night at the club. "Drug addiction is a pretty powerful motivator. It wouldn't be the first time a dealer was killed by a client who needed more than they could afford."

"What about Cassie and Alicia? Or Kayleigh?" Vivienne asked with a frown. "I'm no police detective, but I find it hard to believe all of them were using the app to sell drugs."

"It doesn't seem likely," Sam agreed even as they reached for their phone. "We could be looking at a coincidence. A typical cold case that would have ended up buried on someone's desk if it didn't get tangled up in the rest. Or it could somehow be tied in."

They groaned as they looked down at their screen. Nearly eight already. If they hit the road now, they could probably make it home in time for their call. But that wasn't going to happen.

Scrubbing a hand across their face, Sam muttered, "Sometimes I really hate this job."

"Can't this wait until tomorrow?" Vivienne asked as Sam started flipping through the contacts in their phone.

"What? No," Sam said, looking confused as their finger hesitated over the Call button. "I'll be lucky if I can get through to Vince tonight, but even if I can't, I still need to—"

"But do you really need to do that *right now*?" Vivienne pressed. Seeing that Sam still wasn't getting it, she said, "Vince and Brad and all of this will still be around tomorrow morning. Would it be so wrong to just relax and enjoy whatever you've got going on this evening with your guy before jumping back into the case?"

"You understand this is a murder investigation, right?" Sam said slowly, glancing between her and their phone incredulously. "It's a little more important than my love life."

"Sam . . ." Vivienne sighed with exasperation at their typical hard-headedness. Standing abruptly, she leaned across the table to place one hand over the phone. Looking them in the eye, she said, "You're a really good detective. Anyone with half a brain can see that. But you're a human being, too, all right? And it's OK to take a minute to just . . . be human."

For a long moment Sam stared at her stubbornly. Her hand pressed down on theirs, trapping it between her palm and the phone with firm authority. It made them regret opening up to her. It made them kind of glad they did.

Before they could figure out which they were feeling more, the conference room door flew open and a cheerful voice said, "Vivienne Fox. You'd better have a very good reason for missing dinner three nights in a—Oh."

The words cut off abruptly as the tall blonde woman in the doorway froze in surprise. She was wearing a well-fitted white pantsuit that complemented her powerful build and short, no-nonsense haircut. If that wasn't already screaming the obvious, then the giant rock on her finger that matched her wife's really drove home the point.

Obviously, the woman had been expecting to find Vivienne working late instead of coming home for dinner at a reasonable time. A little less expected was the sight of Vivienne leaning over a table covered with takeout boxes, making meaningful eye contact with her ex-partner. Whose hand she was also currently touching.

"Oh, fuck me," Sam muttered, quickly wrenching their hand away as Harper Fox's face clouded over with the righteous indignation of a person scorned. Sam had been that person before, and they had no plans to relive any part of that experience.

"Really, Vivienne?" Harper's voice had gone from playful to frosty in seconds. "This is your idea of working late?"

That was Sam's cue to pack up their notes and get out.

"Honey," Vivienne stammered. The word sounded lame, too nervous and too surprised to do any good against the mounting rage on her wife's face. "We—we were just finishing up. Right, Sam?"

"Nope. Keep me out of this," Sam said flatly as they swung the bag up and over their shoulder. Vivienne gave them a frustrated look, but there was no way they were getting involved in this mess.

It was sort of funny, really. Vivienne had always had a quick explanation at the ready for her suspicious behavior whenever she was stepping out in the past. If anything, her flustered response to Harper's anger should be the very thing that convinced her wife nothing was happening here. But Sam didn't expect Harper to find stories about Vivienne's previous affairs to be especially comforting at the moment.

"Finishing up what? Filing each other's paperwork?" Harper demanded as Sam started to make their way toward the door.

"No! What? No, we weren't—We were just having dinner and discussing . . . the case. Sam's been working really hard, and—"

"Where do you think you're going?" Harper snapped abruptly, and Sam froze in their quest to edge around the angry woman and out the door to freedom.

"I was thinking you two might like a moment to talk in private," Sam said as delicately as they could. When they tried to take another step toward the door, Harper moved directly into their path.

"Seriously?" Sam looked back at Vivienne with some irritation now. They weren't about to push her wife out of the way, but this felt like an extreme reaction to some not-quite-hand-holding.

"Harper, please," Vivienne said, looking embarrassed and completely thrown by the entire situation. Folding and unfolding her arms nervously, she said, "I understand that you're upset, but—let's just talk about this at home, OK? You're probably feeling a lot right now. The hormones—"

"Oh, do not talk about hormones with me," Harper said, and this time there was a shredded edge to her voice that hinted ominously at tears. Sam grimaced as panic blossomed across Vivienne's face at the earnest sound of her wife's distress. "If I'm hormonal it's because I'm trying to start a family, while you're here every night trying to—"

"She wasn't trying anything." Sam's words came out clipped and impatient. They so did not want to get involved in this, but . . . hormones. The IVF. They couldn't say nothing if this involved more than a little marital distress.

"Nobody asked you," Harper said, her jaw so tight that her lips barely moved when she spoke. Like she was afraid of what would come out otherwise.

The statuesque woman held herself rigidly, not so much blocking Sam's way as frozen in place now. Sam could almost see her teeth grinding against the desire to—what? Accuse her wife some more? Tell Sam to back off? Burst into tears and beg God why, why had she married someone who came with a heaping side of paranoia, no matter how faithful Vivienne might be these days?

Twisting around to look at Vivienne one more time, Sam sighed at the giant "SOS" sign written across her face. Yeah, some people did have a type, and Sam knew hers a little too well.

Swallowing their personal discomfort, Sam forced themself to look Harper in the eye and say as plainly as they could, "Mrs. Fox, you may not have asked, but for what it's worth, I have no interest in your wife. We were having dinner because Viv wanted to grill me about my . . . person.

Who I've been seeing. And who, frankly, is twice as good-looking as she'll ever be."

"Hey!"

"You be quiet and let your wife yell at you," Sam said, giving Vivienne another glare that had her mouth snapping shut again. "And you," Sam looked at Harper again and felt a little disarmed by the sadness beneath the anger. Shrugging awkwardly, Sam said, "Do what you want, I guess. But for what it's worth, I don't think she's cheating on you. And definitely not with me."

With that, they pushed past Harper as gently as they could. Behind them, the tension was thick in the air.

As they made their escape toward the lobby, they could still hear the women arguing behind them.

"Harper . . . Honey."

"Give me your phone."

"Really? We're doing this again?"

Sam winced and picked up their pace. This was not the kind of fireworks show that needed a witness.

"I'm sorry I missed dinner, but you heard them. There's nothing—"

"Give me. Your phone."

Their argument faded as Sam's footsteps carried them out of the war zone and straight toward the tenth-floor lobby. They were five feet from the freedom of the elevators when a new sound grated against their ears and drew Sam's feet to a stuttering halt.

Speaking of asking God why . . .

Sam turned their head reluctantly toward one of the lobby's waiting room chairs. Beck's long auburn hair was splayed out against the black leather, and her chunky glasses didn't quite reflect enough light from her laptop screen to hide the puffy state of her eyes. Despite knowing she was a grown woman who ran one of the most important departments at the company, Sam couldn't help thinking she looked very young curled up sideways in the chair like that. One pale hand lay limply on the laptop keyboard, which was disturbing enough for the chronic workaholic. Her other hand was clenched in a fist that she was anxiously gnawing on like a chew toy.

Sam shifted a little closer, curious to know what was on Beck's screen that had her so distressed. They caught the slightest glimpse of a Paths profile featuring a smiling woman with fine features, large glasses, and long, dark hair before Beck seemed to notice their presence.

"Detective," she blurted. The laptop closed and within seconds her heels were clacking back to the tile floor. Two quick swipes cleared the tears from her cheeks, and she said with forced cheer, "I thought you already left for the day. Wasn't that Harper I just saw go past?"

"No. I mean, yes," Sam quickly corrected. Annoyed at their own inarticulacy, they clarified, "No, I was just finishing up for the day. Yes, Mrs. Fox arrived as I was leaving."

"Oh. And she saw the two of you . . . ?" Beck's pretty brow furrowed deeply at whatever she thought Harper had seen. "Oh dear. Oh no, that's not good at all." Her anxious, red-rimmed eyes darted in the direction of the situation room.

"Well, she didn't see anything other than two people talking," Sam said, perhaps a little too gruffly, but really. Were their choices now getting harassed at the office, getting heatstroke in their car, or being accused of sleeping with their married ex?

"Right. Of course that was all," Beck said distractedly, and Sam would have been annoyed, but her eyes were still glued to the entrance of the hallway like Sam wasn't even there. "Of course," she muttered again. "I'm sure Harper is just being silly. Viv wouldn't do that to her. Especially not with the baby."

"I don't know about silly," Sam said, which finally seemed to catch Beck's attention. Before she could go looking any more worried, they added, "It sounds like they've got a few things to work on before starting a family. But I'm also pretty sure no one fights like that if they aren't in love, so . . . They'll figure it out."

Beck let out a nervous, half-hearted laugh. Offering Sam a flash of a smile, she said, "Are you sure you don't want to be on my Cupid team? Sounds like you've got the instinct for it."

"And become a workaholic like you? No thanks," Sam said sarcastically, and this time Beck laughed for real.

Her expression was still a little sad, but a little fond, too, as she stroked her thumb in a distracted circle against the logo on her trusty laptop. "I guess it's hard not to be, right? When you feel like you're the only one who can keep someone from getting hurt again?" She offered Sam another guilty, awkward smile. "I mean, I'm not solving murders or anything. But a broken heart is no small thing."

"Worth it though, right?"

Beck blinked in confusion, and they gestured to the laptop she was still stroking like a robotic kitten in her lap.

"The helping people find love thing. Must feel good knowing you're responsible for all those happy couples. A little more fun than arresting criminals, at least."

"Sure." Beck grimaced a little, but her voice still came out sounding cheerful when she added, "Now if only people could all learn to be selfless, faithful, and good communicators simultaneously, all my problems would be solved."

"Good luck with that," Sam scoffed.

"I guess we'd both be out of a job then," she agreed. Sighing, Beck hopped to her feet, looking the part of the competent businesswoman again. "But as long as people are going to keep being awful, I guess I'll have to keep trying to take care of the ones who aren't. Someone's gotta do it, right?"

Sam made a quiet sound of agreement as Beck tucked her laptop back beneath her arm like a security blanket. Of everyone working on the case, she was the only one who never seemed tired, no matter how many hours she put in. Sam had assumed it was because she actually liked her job, but remembering the tears on her face when she was looking at the woman on her screen, they wondered if maybe the work was just a distraction. That was something Sam could relate to, at least.

"Probably wouldn't hurt to spend some time taking care of yourself, too," Sam suggested hesitantly, and Beck made a face that confirmed their suspicions.

"Now you sound like Viv," Beck complained. Her expression softened when Sam made a quiet, rusty sound that might have been a laugh. "I guess I don't have to tell you why it's hard to put yourself out there again after . . ." Her eyes flicked in the direction of the hallway leading to the situation room. "Just. After."

Sam opened their mouth to clarify, then hesitated. They weren't sure how to explain that their romantic history really had very little to do with why they were the way they were. It was more the vulnerability and trust and disappointment and inevitability and a whole lot of other things that had Sam hesitating whenever they considered the dangerous possibility of pursuing . . . more. Not that they knew how to say any of those things in a way someone else would understand.

But maybe Vivienne was right, and it was time to try anyway.

"Well, I should go," they declared abruptly. Beck looked concerned, so Sam forced a smile despite those damn butterflies taking up half their throat again. Pulling their phone out of their pocket, they wiggled it slightly and said, "Have to call a guy about a thing."

"Oh really? What kind of thing?" Beck's eyes were sharp behind her glasses as she tracked Sam's quick footsteps heading for the stairwell.

"You know. How was your day. What'd you have for dinner. Has anyone accused you of trying to seduce your ex recently. That kind of thing."

The door creaked open, and Sam offered Beck one last half-smile. "I've heard a lot of breakups could be avoided if people were just a little more honest with each other."

"Whoever said that must be some kind of relationship expert or something." Beck's tone was light, but her bright expression was genuine, and Sam once again thought they were probably getting it right.

"Good luck, detective."

"Same to you, Ms. Fisher."

The door to the stairwell shut behind them, and Sam took a moment to appreciate the stillness in the cramped quarters. Between the potential break in the case and examining their own sluggish vulnerability, this day had already been all kinds of exhausting.

Staring down at the phone in their hand, with Vince's contact card still open and ready to absorb whatever remained of their energy, Sam sighed loudly. The sound echoed back around them eerily. Sometimes being human felt much harder than being a detective.

Vince's contact card disappeared from their screen. Opening up a new app, they looked at the uncertain person reflected back at them. A tired face floating against a backdrop of plain concrete. At least no one could accuse them of pretending to be any more romantic than they had ever

been in these situations. But they hit the Call button anyways, so that had to count for something.

". . . probably not," his voice was saying, the camera not even pointed toward him as he picked up the video call. Despite the odd angle, they could tell from his surroundings that he was standing on the deck of his new boat.

"Teddy?"

"Oh shit." Teddy fumbled with the phone until it was focused on his face. His familiar eyes were round with surprise when he saw who was on his screen. "Uh . . . hi. Hi there."

"You seem surprised," Sam said, and despite the way their heart was trying to kick its way out of their ribcage with pure nervous energy, a small smile started to tug at their lips.

"That you're FaceTiming me? I wonder why I'd find that surprising."

No concrete stairwells for him—the sky was all purples and blues over his shoulder as Teddy made his way to the boat's railing. The backdrop was probably pretty, but Sam's brain was already full-up on its ability to process *pretty* at the moment.

"I guess you finally talked me into it," Sam said with a shrug, as though that would hide the way their heart stuttered when the ocean breeze picked up and ruffled those dark, boyish curls.

Teddy was silent for a moment as he leaned up against the railing. His lips were pressed in a straight line as he took them in, and Sam stayed stock-still. They were painfully aware that, despite the photos he had sent them and the many personal phone calls, this was the first time he had laid eyes on Sam since their time together on Paradiso.

"Ugh. I can't take it," Teddy finally burst out, letting his head tip back. When they laughed at his melodramatic response, he raised his head again and let them see the massive, utterly smitten smile written all across his handsome face. "You can't just be calling me up out of nowhere looking this good. I need twenty-four hours' notice if you expect me to be able to think straight."

"Please. I look the same," Sam said dismissively.

"Isn't that what I just said, cariño?"

"Stop it. You're making it weird." They could feel the flush crawling up their neck, but it hardly seemed to matter when he was looking at them like that.

"No way," Teddy said cheerfully. "You should have known better than to FaceTime me if you didn't want me to make it weird."

"You're so ridiculous."

"And I think you're ridiculously good-looking," he replied, leaning harder against the railing as he took them in. "Especially the hair. That's definitely new."

"What? Oh, I forgot about that." Sam touched their undercut self-consciously. "It's just a thing for work. Long story."

"Hmm. Temporary tattoos and cute haircuts." Teddy was still looking at them like he wished he could teleport into the stairwell with them. "Maybe I don't hate everything about this mystery case of yours."

"Yeah . . ." Sam's brain was short-circuiting just seeing him there on their screen—so real, and still so far away. Maybe it was better that way—it certainly kept them from overthinking. "You look pretty amazing, too, cariño."

"Oh." He seemed flustered by the unexpected compliment in a way Sam very much liked. But really, how could he possibly be surprised? He was the one making them want to cough up butterflies all the time.

Before Teddy could respond properly, the murmur of new voices began to drift in around him. Sam stiffened as they caught a flash of long blue braids over Teddy's shoulder, and what looked to be a guy with bleached hair and glasses so big they dominated his entire face. Apparently, Teddy had company on his boat tonight.

"Who looks amazing?" a nearby female voice asked—presumably the partially obscured blue-haired person who had just emerged from the cabin.

"Ooh, is that the mysterious Sam?" The speaker was not the guy with glasses, so there must have been at least one other person on the deck that Sam couldn't see.

"No way. Hi, Sam!"

"Shit. Sorry," Teddy said, quickly dropping his phone into his pocket. The image disappeared, but Sam could still hear him saying, "Shut up. Are you trying to ruin this for me?"

"Are they actually FaceTiming you right now?"

"Yes. Now get out of here."

"Hey, what's going on?"

"Teddy's FaceTiming with *Sam*."

"Awwwww, really?"

"Would you all shut up please?"

Then there was the sound of a scuffle, some complaining, and a few yelps of pain, followed by the sound of a slamming door.

When Teddy finally raised the phone again, he was alone at the bow of the ship, looking awfully pink in the face. "Uh, sorry about that. Just . . . nosy friends."

"Is this a bad time?" Sam was a little flustered to realize Teddy's friends clearly knew who they were. Or they knew enough to illicit an 'aww' at the concept of Teddy FaceTiming with them, which was . . . not something Sam was prepared to process at the moment.

"No, it's fine. Unexpected, but totally fine," he said, ruffling his curls with one hand nervously. "So, what's up?"

"Can't I call just to say hello?"

"Of course. I always have time to say hello to you."

They were both silent for a long moment as they stared at one another through their screens, a little stunned and a little unsure how to do this. A laugh bubbled up in Sam's chest, and then Teddy was smiling sheepishly, and Sam really was laughing, so Teddy laughed, too, and it was all just so damn weird. This was a man they had been calling every night for almost two weeks, and Sam was still tongue-tied actually seeing him face to face.

"I'm sorry, I'm sorry," Teddy said, trying and utterly failing to hide his goofy smile. "This is . . . it's just really great to see you again."

"It's fine," Sam reassured him, feeling the awkwardness fade along with their laughter. "Are you going to give me a tour of this new boat, or what?"

"No way," Teddy said mock-sternly, even as he turned in a slow circle so Sam could see different sections of the deck stretching out behind him. "If you want a tour of this beauty, you're going to have to come see it in person."

Sam couldn't help a smile at the thought of seeing "the boat" in person.

Teddy groaned at the sight. "Uuuugh, god. That smile!" He thumped one hand against his chest hard enough that they could hear the impact

Elle Kleos

over the phone. "This video thing might have been a mistake. I'm really not sure I can take it."

"Yeah? ¿Te estoy volviendo loco?" Sam asked in butchered Spanish with a knowing grin. It was one of maybe three sentences they had learned with the help of Google Translate, and they knew exactly what it did to him when they attempted sweet nothings in his language.

"Creo que me voy a morir si no te veo pronto," Teddy replied dramatically, and Sam laughed because they had no idea what he was saying, but they understood his meaning just the same.

Sighing, Teddy said, "How about I show you some art before you really drive me insane?"

"Which piece?" Sam asked innocently. "The big one with all the takeout menus?"

"Come on. You know which piece, cariño."

"Yeah, OK. Show me," Sam said eagerly, because they really did want to see it as more than just a picture.

"All right, one second."

Teddy put the phone down on the rail, and they watched as he went to retrieve the piece from inside the cabin. They could hear him shouting something at his guests, who were presumably trapped inside and not that happy about it, but he just kicked the door shut behind him.

"OK, here we go." Teddy picked up the phone and turned to capture the light from the setting sun.

Technically, it looked exactly like the photo on the website. But "technical" was a horrible word to apply to any of Teddy's art. The sculpture in his arms was all broken bits and assorted pieces, each part lovingly sanded down, forged together to form an anatomical model of the human heart. Tiny, delicate wildflowers had been placed in each artery that extended from the sculpture, bringing beauty to what could have been macabre. And those colors—all peachy orange and yellow, with the occasional flicker of soft blues and pinks. It was like he had somehow managed to capture the world's warmest sunrise using nothing but broken dishes.

"Do you like it?" Teddy asked after a long moment.

"I . . ." Sam started, then stopped. They had never been all that good

245

with words, but surely they could figure out one nice thing to say. "Yeah. It's, uh, good."

Well, shit. Apparently not.

Frowning slightly at their own incompetence, Sam tried again. "Can I take a screenshot?"

"Sure." Teddy adjusted his grip on the sculpture so he could hold it out at arm's length and cut himself out of the image. "I put a picture on the website if that's easier." His voice held the easy cheer of a man who hadn't expected anything else from them, which Sam found amazing. And also incredibly annoying.

"No, I meant—I saw the one on the website. I wanted a picture of you holding it," they corrected impatiently. Teddy's curious face appeared back on screen, and Sam added, "It, uh, looks better that way."

"Oh," Teddy said eloquently. He glanced down at the pretty little thing in his arms, and when he looked up at them again, they were absolutely certain they could figure out how to say more nice things if it meant seeing him smile like that.

Holding the sculpture up against the raucous backdrop of his floral button-down, Teddy smiled for the camera and asked, "Are you saying you want a picture of me holding your heart?"

"You're so damn cheesy," Sam grumbled, even as they captured the screenshot that they were undoubtedly going to spend a stupid amount of time looking at in the days to come. Teddy laughed and they took another picture because, whatever, they liked seeing him so happy, and why should they be embarrassed about that?

"Can I stop posing?"

"Absolutely not. I need something worth looking at on stakeouts."

"OK, I got you, cariño," he said, tossing them a playful wink. Placing the sculpture down on the deck, he undid the top few buttons of his ridiculous shirt and rolled up the sleeves until he looked like a proper island douchebag. Shoving one hand into his hair, he gave them his best blue steel impersonation. "How's this? Good stakeout material?"

"Oh yeah. This is totally going to make the other cops jealous." Sam laughed helplessly as Teddy continued striking pose after ridiculous pose for their entertainment. Snapping more screenshots, they said, "This video thing really might have been a mistake. I'm going to miss you way too much."

"Miss me?" Teddy asked, dropping the silly pose. "Are you going somewhere they don't have cell phones?"

"Uh, yeah. Sort of." Some of Sam's good humor faded as they remembered the phone call with Vince that was waiting for them on the other side of this conversation. "That's kind of why I called."

"I figured," he sighed, leaning back against the railing.

When Sam gave him a questioning look, he just shrugged.

"The first time you texted me about anything real, it was because of stuff at work. Then the first time you called me it was because of . . . more stuff at work. It's not that hard to guess what this little video chat is about."

"You really know me too well."

"No such thing as knowing someone like you too well," Teddy said. Sam's heart tripped when he gave them one of those soft, crinkly-eyed smiles that made them acutely aware of how much they already missed him. "So how worried should I be? Like, keep an eye on the news worried, or start going to church worried?"

"What? No, neither of those things," Sam said, a little flustered at the idea of Teddy worrying about them at all. "I'm not going off to war or something. My case is just ramping up a little, and I didn't want you to think . . ."

"To think what?"

"You know. That I was ghosting you again or something," Sam said a little awkwardly. It was sort of an arrogant thing to assume, but since they had been talking pretty much every night . . .

"That's sweet. Did you think I was going to freak out if you didn't call me for a few days?" Teddy asked, then laughed as Sam scowled with embarrassment. Twisting around to lean his arms against the railing, Teddy gave the phone his best puppy-dog eyes and said, "Nah, who am I kidding. I definitely would have freaked out. You probably just saved yourself from listening to 500 drunk voicemails telling you how much I missed your eyelashes or something stupid like that."

"Really? My eyelashes?"

"Sure. Your eyelashes. Your laugh. The way you get all quiet whenever I tell you how much I want to see you again." Sighing morosely, he dropped his chin to his arms and said, "Believe me, I can get really descriptive when

I'm on a heartbreak bender, so . . . You'd better not forget about calling me after you're done chasing down bad guys."

"Yeah . . . well . . ." Sam floundered at the ease with which he said such romantic things. They only wished they had the words to explain how little he needed to worry about going on any "heartbreak benders." But Sam had always been more of a person of action, so they just said, "I was kind of thinking, uh, once I've got some free time again, maybe . . . maybe instead of a phone call you'd like to . . ."

"Yes." The word was out of Teddy's mouth before Sam could figure out how to end that sentence. The smile that broke across his face was better than any sunrise Sam had ever seen. "Definitely yes. The minute—no, the second you're done with this case, you just call me. I mean it. I will literally be checking Twitter every day for some wild story about how Detective Sam saved the day, and if I don't hear from you immediately, I will start sending you flowers every day at work until—"

"OK, OK," Sam laughed, feeling relief wash over them at his unfiltered enthusiasm. "I promise. I'll call you and we can meet up, or whatever. Happy?"

"The second you're free?"

"Yeah, all right. The second I'm free." Smiling helplessly, Sam said, "Hopefully it won't take too long."

"Do what you have to do. Just be careful," Teddy said. The look on his face was all kinds of heart-stopping affection when he added, "I'll see you soon, cariño."

CHAPTER TWENTY-THREE

"I've got eyes on Brad."

Sam raised their coffee cup to obfuscate the movement of their lips as they watched the scruffy man slinking his way into the clearing. Their position among the trees in the city's tidy urban park gave them an easy vantage point. Wincing a little at the sight of the man, Sam added, "Our boy's not looking so hot."

[Are you starting to get picky after all these dates, Sammy?]

"If expecting basic hygiene is being picky, then yes." Glancing toward the massive fountain that blocked them from seeing clean across the clearing to Vince's position, Sam asked, "Any sign of the dealer yet?"

[Nothing here. D?]

[Not yet. I'll take another lap and let you know what I see.]

Sam waited, and a second later Donya jogged out from behind the fountain. She didn't so much as glance their way as she bounded by, but the white headphones she sported fed the even sound of her breathing directly into Sam's ear.

"Brad's looking nervous. I'm going to have to go in soon whether Father Christmas shows or not," Sam said. They took one last sip of their coffee before tossing it in the trash can.

[Perfect timing. I've got eyes on a guy in a hoodie entering with purpose from the south entrance. Wasn't able to get a look at his face on my flyby, but he's coming your way, Vince.]

[Copy that. Get ready, Sammy.]

Sam listened to Vince and Donya's checks as they made their way out of the twilight-shrouded trees to approach the fountain from Brad's blind side. Despite the warm summer evening, Brad was sporting a heavy jacket, and his entire body shivered every time the wind picked up. He looked jittery enough to bolt at the slightest sound, and for a gym owner, his body was looking awfully lean.

[Eddie Romano, confirmed. Incoming from six o'clock.]

"Tell me when." Sam barely breathed the words as they kept their eyes trained on Brad.

[Give it a second. I want to see the fireworks.]

"Vince . . ."

They watched as the young man in a gray hoodie made his way around the other side of the fountain, only to pull up short when he caught sight of Brad.

"Dude, what the fuck," the man complained.

When the man pushed back his hood, Sam recognized the drug dealer Brad had been arguing with at the mixer—a man they now knew to be Eddie Romano, a low-level pill pusher, scumbag, and general stain on any community he came within spitting distance of.

"What—" Brad's words cut off with a gasp as Eddie's fist rammed into his stomach with enough force to drive the air from his lungs. Raising his hands in weak self-defense, Brad wheezed, "What—what are you—"

"Was my boy Tony not clear enough with you last time, shithead?" Eddie snarled, punctuating his words with a hard shove that sent Brad sprawling backward over the fountain bench. "You need a few more broken ribs to get it through your fuckin' skull? No service for junkies who can't be cool."

"I don't—I didn't!" Brad stammered, clearly having no more idea how he ended up in this park with Eddie than Eddie did. As he scrambled back to his feet, Brad's dark eyes were wild with fear. "Please, I swear. I'm not trying to give you any trouble. I—I was here to meet with someone else—a new dealer." Eddie pulled back his fist again, and Brad quickly reached inside his coat pocket to retrieve an envelope. "Look—look! You can have my money. I just need—"

"You just need to learn your fuckin' lesson." Eddie snatched the envelope from Brad's shaking hands. He barely glanced inside before scoffing at the meager contents. "Really? Two hundred? What you gonna buy for two hundred dollars, you fuckin' idiot?" Narrowing his eyes dangerously, Eddie crushed the envelope in his hand and said, "I swear to god, if you're wearing a fuckin' wire, cancer's gonna be the least of your worries."

"I'm going in," Sam said with a wince as they watched Eddie wind up again. Brad just cowered back against the fountain, looking incapable of properly defending himself.

[Let it play out. He might give us something.]

"Yeah, like another body for the morgue," Sam muttered before stepping out from their hiding place. Raising their fingers to their lips, they let out a piercing whistle that had both Donya and Vince cursing them over the radio.

Eddie spun toward Sam, one fist still raised in the air, and Sam pinned him with a hard stare. "I really wouldn't if I were you, Mr. Romano."

"Who the fuck are you?" Eddie demanded, lowering his fist and taking a few steps back. These were the practiced movements of a con who knew when he was busted.

"You don't recognize me? I'm hurt," Sam said. They tilted their head at him with a mock-frown. "What happened to that snowball you were going to sell me?"

"What?" he said dumbly. "Who . . ." Eddie's eyes squinted as his tiny brain worked hard to draw the connection between the woman from the mixer who had messaged him earlier in the day and the person standing in front of him now. Eddie's eyes widened abruptly as the reality of the situation sunk in. "Oh shit."

"There we go," Sam said, pushing their trench coat back to reveal the golden shield clipped to their belt. "Since you agreed to go on this date with me, why don't we sit and talk a little?"

[He's going to run.]

"Don't bother running," Sam said with a warning edge in their voice as Eddie looked around nervously. "You won't even make it out of the park."

[He's still going to run. They always run.]

"Shit. Shit," Eddie mumbled, stumbling back as Vince put down his newspaper and stood up from his bench on the far side of the fountain. Turning on Brad, Eddie spat, "You did this. You set me up. They'll kill you for this."

"I didn't—oof!" Brad's body hit the cobblestones again as Eddie gave him another hard shove and then booked it out of there as fast as his stocky legs could carry him.

[Well, would you look at that. He's running. Better get going, Sammy.]

"Me? I'm not chasing him," Sam said. They scowled in Vince's direction before reaching down to pull Brad up off the concrete. Holding him tightly by the collar, Sam said, "I've got my guy. You can chase your own leads."

[You think I'm chasing anyone on a bad knee and a half script of Vicodin? Fat chance.]

"Someone's getting old."

[Fuck you, Sam.]

"Fuck you both," Donya said, and both of their heads whipped toward the sound of her voice as she came around the side of the fountain. A dour-faced Eddie trudged along in front of her with both hands cuffed neatly behind his back.

"Good job, Rook," Vince said, clapping his hands together slowly as he strolled over to join the group. Tapping off his earpiece, he said, "See, Sammy? That's how Vice gets it done."

"Fucking pig," Eddie snarled. Vince pulled up short as Eddie spat on the cobblestones at his feet. "The fuzz in this city must be getting real desperate if they're using old men and fags to get their dirty work done these days."

"Now, now. That's some big talk for a guy who just got outrun by a girl," Vince said, his tone light and breezy as ever. But Eddie didn't look quite so brave when he was suddenly staring cross-eyed down the barrel of Vince's service weapon.

"You want to run that by me again, or are you feeling smart today?"

"Whoa, whoa, what the fuck?" Eddie shouted, jerking hard against Donya's hold. "I'm cuffed, man. You can't go waving that shit around."

"Can," Vince said, echoing his declaration with the sound of the gun's safety clicking off. "Am. And will not hesitate. Understood?"

Eddie's lips pressed together so hard they nearly disappeared into his pale face as he frantically nodded his understanding.

"That's enough, Vince," Sam said sharply. Judging by the tremor in Brad's entire body and the terrified look on his face, this situation was going to go downhill fast if they didn't redirect the momentum. Giving Vince a hard stare, they said, "You really think that's helping anything?"

"Sorry, Sammy. I forgot what innocent little flowers you are in Homicide," Vince said, making a big show of putting the safety back on. Giving Eddie his best shark-eyed grin, he said, "Here on Vice, we don't sit around all day with our hands in our pants. We go out and find someone to—"

Before Vince could complete that lovely metaphor, his expression twisted with disgust. "Ugh. What the hell is that?"

"Don't look at me," Donya said, giving Eddie a once-over as the foul smell in the air increased. "Pretty sure it's not this joker, either."

Brad let out a whimper of fear, and it immediately became clear where the smell was coming from.

"Jesus, man," Eddie swore, gagging against the putrid combination of urine and flop sweat. "Have some fuckin' dignity."

"Can it, pill boy," Donya said, but she did take a subtle step backward. Those doll eyes watered as the smell only grew stronger. "Sam, can you . . . ?"

"Yeah, all right. All right," Sam said, loosening their grip on Brad as his tremors increased.

Seeing where Brad's frightened gaze was pointed, Sam stepped in close enough to block his view of Vince and his gun. Taking Brad gently by the elbow, they guided him along the perimeter of the fountain bench until they were a few feet away from Eddie's group.

"Are you OK? Anything broken?" they asked, and he just shook his head. "No? All right, sit down." Brad half-sat, half-collapsed onto the bench. He looked utterly miserable as he curled in on himself.

Taking a knee in front of him, Sam tried hard to ignore the smell. They pulled out a picture of Nikki. "Do you recognize this woman?"

"You're not going to get anything out of him," Vince called. When Sam didn't so much as glance in his direction, he rolled his eyes but finally re-holstered his weapon.

"Brad," Sam said, reaching out with one hand. They hesitated for half a second, then touched their palm to the side of his face. His cheek was damp with sweat and scruffy from too many days without a proper shave, but the tortured look in his eyes was still fresh. "You're not in trouble, OK? We're going to help you out. But first I need you to tell me." Sam held Nikki's photo up again. Brad tried to look away, but Sam's hand prevented him. "Do you recognize this woman?"

Brad's gaze dropped to the photo. One hand crept up to press against his stomach where Eddie had punched him. Finally, he nodded, ever so slightly.

"Do you know her name?" Sam prompted gently.

"You'd better not, tweaker." Brad flinched as Eddie's threat was immediately followed by a grunt of pain. Vince's fist, unlike Eddie's, connected with the accuracy of a man who knew exactly where to hit someone if you wanted to maximize the pain without leaving a bruise.

"Say something else. I dare you," Vince said as Eddie doubled over.

Donya's stance was tense, but if she had a problem with her boss hitting a man she was holding cuffed in place, she certainly didn't say anything.

"Hey. Enough of that," Sam snapped before turning back to face Brad. Pressing their hand a little more firmly to his hollow cheek, they said, "I'm not going to let anyone hurt you. Do you know this woman's name?"

"Nikki." Brad's surprisingly deep voice was a shadowy reflection of the man he used to be. "She was . . . she was helping me get what I needed. When I couldn't afford my treatments anymore and the pain got too bad. She always got me what I needed."

"Did you know she was murdered?"

"Yes. I—I read about it. After she stopped answering my messages, I searched her name online and I found out." Brad's bloodshot eyes filled with tears, and he said, "I didn't know—I didn't—I just needed more." Looking over at Eddie, he wiped his face with one sleeve and said, "He was supposed to take over for her. After. But he raised the prices and I . . . then you messaged me, and . . . and . . ."

"Yeah. It's all right." Sam dropped their hand from his cheek. "We're going to help you out with that, OK?" Reaching one hand toward Eddie's little party of three, they said, "Vince, give me a card."

"Seriously?" Vince complained.

"Just give me the damned card."

"I don't even carry that crap anymore."

"Here," Donya said gruffly. Shoving Eddie toward Vince so he was forced to either grab hold or let him go for another run, Donya reached for her bifold. From inside, she produced a weathered business card and passed it over to Sam.

Taking the card from her, Sam fished a pen out of their jacket and quickly started scribbling down a string of numbers. "You see this, Brad?" Sam said, holding up the card. "That's the address for a free rehab clinic downtown. I want you to go there and get yourself clean. And now you've also got my phone number." Turning their steely gaze toward Eddie for their next words, Sam said, "If anyone gives you a hard time on your way there or when you get out, I want you to just call that number, all right?"

"I can't—I can't—"

"You can. You have to." Sam stood up and gently raised him to his feet. "You're going to be OK, Brad. Just get yourself to that clinic and let them take it from there, all right?"

Brad hesitated, looking utterly miserable in his sallow skin and baggy, urine-stained clothing. This was a man who had owned a business, was looking for love, and had hopes for the future not very long ago. It didn't take a lot for a man like him to fall, but it took a gargantuan amount of courage and strength to get back up again.

Sam gave him a firm nod, and Brad nodded back a little less certainly. Hunching his shoulders against the breeze, he tucked the card into his palm and started trudging away.

"He's going to be dead under a bridge before the sun sets," Eddie shouted loud enough that Brad might have heard him as he slipped down one of the park's paths.

"I sure hope not." Sam examined Eddie with a look of pure loathing. "If anything bad should happen to him before he makes it to that clinic, you're going to be wishing I let Detective Renier shoot you."

"Man, you really don't get it, do you?" Eddie said with a laugh that bordered on hysterical. "Threaten me all you want. The second you put me in that fuckin' cop car, I'm a dead man walking anyways. They'll cut my throat long before I can sing."

"Who's they?" Sam asked. They stepped in closer so they could see the man in more detail as the light continued to fade from the evening sky.

"Who do you think?" Eddie scoffed despite the blank looks all around him. "You pigs are really that dumb, aren't you? The Romanos. They run this part of town, and they don't take chances when it comes to cops."

"You know what he's talking about?" Sam asked, looking to Vince for a clue. "Some kind of gang?"

"Don't look at me. I don't work GIU," the older cop said with a careless shrug.

"Hey. What the hell are you talking about?" Donya demanded, using her grip on his cuffs to give Eddie a light shake. "Aren't you a Romano? Eddie Romano, right?"

"Might as well be John Doe when I'm wearing these fancy little things," Eddie said. He rattled the cuffs on his wrists pointedly. Seeing the look she and Vince exchanged, he nodded to Sam and said, "Don't believe me? Ask that pretty boy detective of yours."

"Who . . . ?" Sam paused to consider which "pretty boy" detective Eddie might be referring to. But of course there had only been one other detective outside the building at the mixer that night. "Detective Mariano?"

"Sure. *Mariano.* Ask him if he remembers Cousin Eddie," the man said, curling his lip with disgust. "He'll be like 'No, no, I never heard of that guy.' But that won't stop him from putting two slugs in the back of my head the second he can get away with it. Or making sure I get stuck with a cellmate who will. Or whatever it takes—the Romanos don't leave loose ends."

"What the hell are you talking about?" The first cold notes of suspicion crept into the back of Sam's mind. Which was ridiculous, because Eddie would obviously say anything at this point to stay out of jail.

But his words didn't sound like those of a crook just trying to avoid lockup. They sounded awfully closer to a plea for his life.

"Just—Fine. Just look at my arm," Eddie insisted. He shuffled awkwardly against Donya's grip so he could extend his arms out behind his back. Jerking his chin over his shoulder, he said, "Under my right sleeve. Roll it up."

Sam and Donya exchanged questioning looks. By silent agreement, with one hand still carefully holding him in place, Donya rolled up the hoodie sleeve.

Sam stepped in closer so they could examine the maze of ink decorating his hairy appendage. There were enough designs printed on his skin to fill a very disturbing picture book, but one image stood out in sharp contrast to the rest. Dominating the majority of his forearm was an upside-down chalice depicted in exquisite detail. The Latin cursive circling the rim of the cup read *sicut in caelo et in terra*.

"What am I looking at here?" Sam asked, even though it wasn't hard to guess.

"It's a gang tattoo, genius."

"I know that," Sam said, trying to ignore the way their gut was already clenching with trepidation. Still, they forced themself to ask, "What does that have to do with Noah?"

"What do you think?" Eddie taunted. "Good little Catholic boy, right? Very top-button. Probably nice to little old ladies and everything. But catch him off guard for ten seconds and you'll realize you don't know shit about that kid."

"Watch your mouth, you piece of trash," Vince snapped. Sam shot him a warning look as his hand jumped back to his holster. "That's a police officer you're talking about."

"Don't you think I fuckin' know that?" Eddie said. Gesturing emphatically with his cuffed hands toward Sam, he said, "How do you figure I got away from the club after this bitch nearly got me busted the other night? Obviously, I'm no Usain fuckin' Bolt, but baby cuz knew he'd be getting the call to handle me if I tried to roll, so he let me go." Sam frowned at the idea of enthusiastic, clumsy Noah "handling" anyone, and Eddie gave them a macabre smile. "Guess he shouldn't've bothered, huh?"

"I said watch your fucking mouth." Vince's voice was full of danger, and Sam hoped for both their sakes that Eddie would shut up soon. They really did not want to have to write a report explaining why they got in a fist fight with another cop defending some scummy drug dealer.

"Man, do whatever you want to me," Eddie said, jerking his head to the side. "It doesn't fuckin' matter."

"Yeah? What do you think we should do with this rat, Sammy?" Vince asked. Glancing over at them with that cold, flat gaze, he said, "That's your rookie he's talking about. You want to take the first swing?"

Sam considered Eddie for a long moment. Unlike Brad, he wasn't standing there pissing his pants. He didn't look like he gave two shits if Donya wanted to hold him in place while Sam knocked his lights out. Which was very bad news, because in Sam's experience, men like Eddie only displayed that kind of bravery when they already knew they were screwed anyway.

"Donya, can I see those keys?"

"What?" Donya asked. She glanced uncertainly over at Vince.

"Don't look at him, just give them to me," Sam said impatiently, holding out their hand. She hesitated, but slowly reached into her pocket.

Grabbing Eddie by the shoulder, Sam snatched the keys from Donya and quickly undid the cuffs before either Vice member could protest.

"Dude, what?" Eddie said, looking shocked as the metal slid free of his wrists.

"Listen. The way I see it, no one's read you in yet," Sam said, dangling the cuffs in front of his slack-jawed face. "You're not under arrest. Nobody will even know you talked to us, right?"

". . . Right," Eddie said. He still glanced suspiciously between Sam and the cuffs. "So what do you want me to do? I'm guessing this get out of jail card ain't free."

"Nothing much," Sam said, handing the cuffs back to Donya as a sign of good faith to both of them. "I just want you to keep doing your thing. But I want you to do it on someone else's app, OK?"

"What, the fuckin' dating app?" Eddie asked, and Sam nodded. "Sure. Whatever. That was Nikki's bag. I don't love going around lookin' like some kinda homo anyways." Glancing over at Sam, he added, "No offense, I guess. What else do you want?"

"I want you to keep Noah's name out of your mouth." Drawing on every car ride, every stupid comment, and every ounce of respect they had for the young detective, Sam looked Eddie in the eye and said, "That was a nice try, but he's a good kid. He doesn't need your lies getting him tangled up in some bullshit IA case."

Eddie's mouth flattened into a thin line, but he jerked his head in agreement.

"Good," Sam said, and then nodded toward the path. "Now get out of here."

"What—seriously?" Eddie asked. He glanced over his shoulder disbelievingly. "You don't want me to—"

"Do you want to leave, or were you hoping for an actual date?" Sam asked, and Eddie made a sound of disgust at the mere thought. "Yeah, me neither. So go on, get lost."

Eddie's movements were sluggish with disbelief, but he took one slow step away. And then another. When none of the three cops gave chase, he quickly picked up his pace.

"I suggest running," Sam called, and Eddie nearly tripped over his own feet in his eagerness to comply. "Idiot," they muttered, shaking their head as they turned back to Vince and Donya.

"What the hell was that?" Donya demanded. She still held her cuffs loosely in one hand, like she couldn't believe they were empty. "Did you seriously drag us out here just to let both of those guys go?"

"Yes," Sam said shortly. They glanced over at Vince, who wasn't looking any happier than his rookie. "You two can do whatever you want with that moron when I'm done with this case. But for now, I need him running around scared. Eddie's just a low man on the totem pole who would say anything to stay on this side of the bars. But eventually he'll run back home, and I'll find someone who might actually know what was going on with Nikki."

"So our little pill pusher is bait, is that what you're saying?" Vince said after a long beat, and Sam nodded, careful to keep their expression as neutral as possible. "Good luck with that, Sammy. If you're going crashing into GIU territory, you'd better be prepared to lose some skin over this."

"Yeah, about that," Sam said, turning back to Donya. "You still know anyone who works the GIU cases?"

"In the lab? Sure," Donya said with a shrug. She slipped her cuffs back into her pocket. "None of the actual badges, though."

"The lab is great. Anyone from research, really. I need everything I can get on the Romanos," Sam said, feeling the weight of those words settling in their gut. "If I'm going to go kicking hornets' nests, I want to know just how much hurt I'm in for."

CHAPTER TWENTY-FOUR

Sam sighed, and the sound felt too loud in these cramped quarters. They leaned their forearms against the steering wheel and stretched out their back as much as they could for ten blissfully excruciating seconds. Car rentals were useful for switching things up when tailing a suspect, but since Sam wasn't exactly mentioning this play on any of their reports, they had to make do with what they could afford on a crappy detective's salary.

They reached blindly for the folder sitting on the passenger seat beside them, flipped it open, and picked up the research summary. As they read, they kept one eye on the words and the other on the church doors. Not that they really needed the review. After three long days of stakeout, they basically had the file memorized.

The city hadn't had a strong gang presence in over two years, thanks to an aggressive pilot program and a mayor who staked his entire political career on the success or failure of the project. Sam had come out on the other side with that infamous record-breaking arrest count, and the city—well, the city had come out with less organized crime, and that was all the suits backing Mayor Kelso's reelection campaign cared about.

That was part of what made the Romano gang so notable, as it turned out. Not only had the gang managed to lay low during that bloody year, but they had been quietly retaking territory from their devastated rivals ever since. Any gang that intelligent and organized was enough to put Sam on high alert, but as long as the Romanos stayed quiet and predictable, GIU generally left them alone and instructed Vice to do the same. Based on what Sam was reading in this report, though, that might be about to change.

After years of subtle moves, there had been a notable uptick in crime around this area recently. More guns on the street, more candy in the clubs, and more local dealers turning up bloody and brutalized after going out one night and discovering that their old turf was now the property of the Romanos.

The research team had created a visual of recent incidents thought to be linked to the gang's activity over the past six months, and it read like a nuclear fallout map. Ground zero was where Sam had been hanging out all morning.

Glancing up at the massive church building towering overhead, Sam pictured the upside-down chalice tattoo that had decorated Eddie's arm. Nikki's body was long cremated and returned to her family—a taciturn Italian couple who hadn't seemed especially emotional, according to the morgue technician. Thankfully, the family hadn't taken the autopsy photos along with Nikki's ashes.

It had taken a while to work through the maze of full-body ink, but eventually Sam located the familiar chalice climbing up the side of her thigh. The design was soft and faded, like something that had always been a part of her skin.

Nicolette Beatrice Russo. That was the name printed on her birth and death certificates. But then why the Romano family crest? Those were the kinds of questions only their nervous rat Eddie could help them answer. If only he'd hurry up and do his part.

Their thoughts were interrupted by the sound of their cell vibrating inside the car's cupholder. Grabbing the phone, Sam glanced at the screen with trepidation.

As far as the office was concerned, Sam was off chasing leads on the Paths case with an embargo on any more dates until their second meetup with Jason tomorrow. True to her word, Donovan hadn't cared whether the lead came from Beck, Sam, or a magical talking panda—as long as there was progress to report. And even she had to agree that their last conversation with Jason counted as progress.

Donya was the only person who had any kind of clue what Sam was actually up to, and the only thing they had told her was that they needed a heads-up if dispatch caught word of any officers approaching St. Paul's. It turned out that Noah did have a point—being friendly with people in the office could be helpful sometimes.

To their surprise, though, it wasn't anyone from the office calling. The picture on their screen showed Teddy flexing ridiculously for the camera and offering a dazzling smile against the backdrop of the setting sun.

For half a second, Sam just stared at the incoming call notification in confusion. Since their little video chat the other night, Teddy had been respecting their need to focus and hadn't sent so much as a good morning text, which was its own kind of sweet torment. So why call now at . . . seven a.m. on a Friday?

"Hello?"

"Oh, hey. Glad I caught you." Teddy's voice sounded a little nervous on the other end. "Sorry for calling so early."

"No, it's fine. What's up?"

"Uh, well, I know this isn't really a good time, but . . . I wanted to let you know I'll be—"

"Shit." Sam's curse cut straight through Teddy's words as they caught sight of a man in a gray hoodie slinking along the perimeter of the parking lot.

The man's head swiveled like a water sprinkler as he nervously looked around for any signs of life outside the church.

Ducking down in their seat, Sam muttered, "Gotta go. Call you back," and then promptly hung up the phone.

Switching the volume to silent, they slid the cell into their jacket pocket before risking a glance through the window. The church doors were already swinging shut behind Eddie Romano's disappearing form.

Sam popped the car door open. Their joints complained heartily as they stood up for the first time in hours, but they blocked out the pain. Eddie had been by the church five times already in the past week, but every time he had only stayed long enough to retrieve a package from one of the charity bins out back before taking off again. This was the first time he had actually gone inside, and Sam wasn't about to waste the opportunity to meet whomever Eddie reported to.

Recalling the age of the church doors, Sam pressed their arm along the length of the ancient wood before easing it open without so much as a creak. The church's interior looked the same as the last time Sam had been there—about ten minutes before they had been unceremoniously booted off the Father D'Angelo case by Father Nicholas.

Sam stared at the doors across the shallow foyer and recalled the way Noah had come crashing onto the scene that day with his sailor's mouth and two left feet. It felt hard to believe that kid could be tangled up in a gang and counted on to "take care of" any potential loose ends. Hell, he couldn't even solve a murder from a highly traceable poison, apparently.

Or maybe he just didn't want to. Either way, they were about to find out.

Striding across the hall, Sam reached for the doors and stepped inside. Staring down the center aisle, they saw that the room was entirely empty. They strained their ears but didn't hear a single sound. The whole place was eerily quiet.

Just when they had become convinced that Eddie must have gone deeper into the church, their eyes caught on the altar. Despite the empty seats, the ciborium had been placed on the table, and several packets of communion wafers were stacked along the edge. A strange sight for a Friday morning with no churchgoers lining up for the morning mass and no priest in sight.

Walking the aisle on silent feet, Sam cautiously approached the altar. They considered genuflecting, but the concept of kneeling before the altar at a church that had deemed their very existence blasphemous felt wrong. Instead, they crossed themself and figured that God would get the idea.

Sam climbed three short steps to the raised altar and looked down at the neat stacks of wafers lining the cloth-covered table. One package lay open and had been partially deposited into the ciborium. It looked a lot like the Priest had been in the middle of transforming the bland wafers into holy bland wafers when he had been interrupted.

Sam turned one of the wafers between their fingers, considering the little piece of bread, before lifting their head to look at the lacquered wooden booth at the back of the church. An uncomfortable chill traveled up their spine at the sight of the confessional, but they placed the wafer back on the table and headed in that direction.

When they had gotten within a few yards, Sam started to pick up the low murmur of voices coming from within. Their first instinct was to hang back—you didn't need to grow up in a small town to know that confessional booths usually prioritized aesthetics over security, and Sam had never been one to take part in the resulting gossip. But then, they were here to investigate something a little more serious than who had painted Farmer John's prize pig bright purple the night before the state fair.

"Hey—what the—what the fuck are you—" Eddie's spluttering words cut off with a muffled grunt as Sam threw open the confessional door and reached into the booth to yank him out by a fistful of his sweater.

"Language," Sam chided, glancing up at the massive golden statue of the crucifixion hanging over their heads.

"What the fuuuhhh . . . rig are you doing here?" Eddie asked, just barely turning the curse around mid-sentence. Glaring at Sam even as he crossed himself, he said, "You follow me here or somethin'?"

"What would make you think that?" Sam replied flatly, then gave him a hard shove. "Now get out of here. I need to talk to the priest."

"What, for confession?" Eddie asked stupidly, stumbling back a few steps.

"Yeah, genius. For confession." Snapping their fingers with one hand to draw his attention as they slid the other into their jacket pocket, Sam said, "Don't think too hard about it. Just run along, all right?"

As Eddie went on his way, Sam turned back to the booth just in time to see the priest's door starting to open. Stepping forward, Sam pushed the door shut again, ignoring the muffled protest that came from within.

"Sorry, Father," they said, reaching for one of the choir chairs and wedging it under the doorknob to effectively lock the door in place. At least one thing they had learned growing up in the church was coming in handy. "Hate to do this, but something tells me you wouldn't feel like talking much otherwise."

Slipping into the opposite side of the booth, Sam settled into the uncomfortable wooden chair. The tiny space was surprisingly different from the booth they remembered in childhood. Maybe it was the little electric lights that kept the space reasonably well-lit even with the door closed, or just the fact that it didn't smell like cow manure and corn fields. Either way, Sam found it surprisingly easy to turn their head and meet the angry eyes of Father Nicholas staring back at them through the screen.

"Blood of the Holy Mother," he growled in a low, gravelly voice. "Don't you know it's a sin to interrupt a man's confession?"

"What about a woman's confession?" Sam asked, reaching into their jacket pocket for their trusty tape recorder.

"Excuse me?"

"Never mind," Sam said dismissively. "By the way, I should warn you. I'm going to record this conversation for the record."

"How dare you? This is a holy—"

Recording #5: Father Nicholas

The red button is pressed, and the tape begins to roll.

"—space. You cannot bring recording devices in here. You cannot be here at all. You're not—"

"I know, I know. I'm not welcome here. But since I'm already here and I am actually trying to help you, how about you humor me anyways?"

" . . . "

" . . . "

" . . . "

"Unless you're a murderer, of course. In which case you probably shouldn't talk to me."

" . . . "

" . . . "

"I won't take your confession."

"I wasn't offering you my confession."

"Then let me out of here, and we can talk. There's no reason to desecrate this space."

"Really? Because Eddie tells me that people who get caught talking to cops don't live long on Romano turf. I think that's a pretty good reason for you to want to stay in here while we chat."

" . . . "

" . . . "

" . . . "

" . . . "

"It won't do you any good interrogating me. I don't know the things you want to know."

"Are you sure? I haven't told you what I want to know yet."

"Is this not about Father D'Angelo's death?"

"Maybe."

"Then I don't know what it is you want to know. Father D'Angelo was a good friend and a brother in Christ, may he rest in peace. I willingly gave my full statement to the police already, and I have nothing further to add."

"Then why have you been fighting Detective Mariano every step of the way?"

"What do you mean?"

"Detective Mariano is the lead investigator on Father D'Angelo's case. He says you've been very uncooperative, even threatening to involve lawyers."

"You're referring to Noah, I presume?"

"Yes. Noah Mariano."

"I have never spoken with a Detective Mariano."

"But you do know him."

". . . As well as any other parishioner. His family attends this church."

"Are you sure his family doesn't own this church?"

"No one can own a church. It belongs to God."

"Does God own the parts that are used for packaging and distributing drugs as well?"

"How dare you. How dare you bring such accusations against—"

"Let's cut to the chase, Father Nicholas. I know St. Paul's is the headquarters of the Romanos. I know the gang has been eating up territory fast enough to raise some red flags with GIU. Up until now, your merry little band of pill pushers has been good at staying under the radar, but whenever people go from pushing pills to committing murders, it gets—"

"What merry little band?"

"The gang. The Romanos."

"That has nothing to do with me."

". . ."

"A gang member is a man of men, Detective. I am a man of God."

". . . I see. And Father D'Angelo? Was he a man of God as well?"

"I wouldn't know. My eyes are focused only on the heavens."

"And Noah?"

"I wouldn't know."

" . . . "

" . . . "

"Takes a special kind of blindness for a man of God to ignore that his church is being used to sell drugs to children."

"Yes. That man should pray for forgiveness on a daily basis."

"Why forgiveness when he could pray for strength to do the right thing?"

"What's the right thing, Detective? Breaking the confidence of the confessional only to end up lying dead in the parking lot?"

"It's not breaking priest-penitent privilege to report a confession of criminal activity."

"I would be breaking a promise to God, and to my community."

" . . . "

"And even if I were willing to break those promises, I would still end up in the same position as Father D'Angelo. What help is he to anyone now?"

" . . . "

" . . . "

"So you won't talk to me, then."

"I love God with all my heart. But I'm not ready to meet Him yet."

" . . . "

" . . . "

"Can you at least tell me about Noah?"

"What about him?"

"You said you haven't spoken to him about the investigation, but he has reported repeatedly that he has."

". . ."

"One of you is lying, Father. Why should I believe you over a fellow police officer?"

". . ."

". . ."

"How is your case coming, Detective?"

"Excuse me?"

"Your case. It's rather high profile, isn't it? Probably lots of opportunity for medals if all goes well. If not . . ."

"I'm not sure what you're referring to. Any cases I'm currently working on are strictly confidential."

"Are they?"

". . ."

"Well. My apologies. I'm an old man. It's easy to forget what someone has told me and what someone has . . . told me."

"I thought you respected the confidentiality of the confessional."

"Of course I do. I simply find it interesting that even the most powerful people tend to be very honest when speaking to a priest, no matter where that conversation happens. In the sanctuary. At a coffee shop. Or even at someone's house for dinner."

". . ."

"Did you know Christopher is Catholic, Detective? Not a member of this parish. But still . . . a friend of the family, so to speak."

"Christopher?"

"Ah. Christopher Kelso. I assumed a detective of your caliber would be familiar."

"I see. I'm afraid Mayor Kelso and I haven't had time to sit down for dinner recently."

"What a shame. His wife's baked ziti is simply divine."

"I'm not sure I like what you're implying."

"I'm not implying anything. Mayor Kelso is a smart man. And from what I've seen, your Detective Mariano is cut from the same cloth. They both know that accusing a priest of murder would be a very serious thing."

"I see. And here I thought you had me taken off the case because you were afraid the conversation would be boring. But I guess being easily intimidated was the bigger qualifier for this case."

"Keep that sense of justice, Detective. It'll serve you well—in other matters."

". . ."

"Run along now. And do let Noah know that if he ever wants to speak, my office hours are posted on the website. No need to come around uninvited."

After a long moment, there is the creaking sound of someone standing up, followed by a door opening. Something heavy is shuffled aside. Then the tape spins to a stop.

Sam stepped out of the church and held one hand up to shield their eyes against the morning sun as the city came to life around them. Across the street there was a pawn shop opening for the day. Around the corner there was a local rec center where people came to play pickup games in the evenings. A block away there was a high school about three minutes from ringing the morning bell.

And smack-dab in the middle of this thriving community was a church with a tall steeple that cast a dark shadow over all of it.

Reaching into their jacket pocket, Sam pulled out the little device they had "borrowed" from Eddie. So maybe dragging a person out of a confessional booth wasn't the most elegant way to pick a pocket, but desperate times and all that. They certainly weren't feeling much like confessing after that conversation.

Flipping open the cheap burner, they scrolled through Eddie's contacts. Lots of people in his logs, but not a lot of first and last names. As they continued to scroll, Sam picked up their own phone to punch in a number. If they were going to get serious about pursuing this lead, they were going to need some help, and clearly it couldn't be anyone from the precinct.

Sam's phone began to ring just as their eyes landed on a contact who actually had a name in Eddie's address book. One "N. Romano."

Sam's call connected as their eyes lingered over the damning entry.

"Hello, you've reached—"

"Hi, Beck. This is Sam. Can you put me through to Vivienne?"

CHAPTER TWENTY-FIVE

"Detective," Beck exclaimed. She managed to sound surprised even though she had been the one to buzz Sam up when they arrived at the Paths building. "This is a surprise. I thought your date wasn't until tomorrow."

"Different date," Sam said shortly. Glancing over Beck's shoulder, they said, "Is Viv in her office?"

"I—well—I think so, yes," Beck said, following Sam's gaze nervously.

"Great." Sam moved purposefully in the direction of the hallway, only to pull up short. Beck was walking alongside them like an overly anxious hall monitor. "Is there something you need . . . ?"

"Ah, well. Viv said she was planning on finishing up some paperwork tonight, but that Harper expected her home by eight . . ." Beck said slowly, and this time Sam heard the suspicious note in her voice.

"Guess she's going to be late."

Beck looked even more concerned at the sound of their unsympathetic tone, but Sam just started moving again. They so did not have time for this right now.

"Wait," Beck blurted, and Sam tensed when her hand tugged at their arm. Beck released them immediately, but Sam had to give her a little credit for not backing down. "I just . . ." Beck's eyes darted toward Vivienne's office again. "I know there's nothing—I know you don't mean anything by it. But I don't think it's fair to make Harper worry over—"

"Sam! What took you so long?" Vivienne's critical voice preceded the

273

woman herself as she came hurtling around the corner. Seeming oblivious to Beck's serious expression, Vivienne gave Sam a mock-frown and said, "Dinner is in less than an hour. Contrary to popular belief, I'm not actually a miracle worker."

"Uh, dinner?" Sam echoed stupidly. Between Vivienne's pasted-on smile, Beck's crinkled brow, and having recently had their job threatened by a Machiavellian priest, Sam was having a hard time keeping up.

"Dinner, they say. Like you aren't the one who called me asking for help," Vivienne chided. Her heels tapped out a staccato pattern on the tile as she hurried over to Sam's side and began propelling them in the direction of the situation room. "Don't you even think about standing him up, Sam."

"Standing who up?" Beck asked, looking as lost as Sam felt in that moment.

"Their boyfriend. Teddy," Vivienne said matter-of-factly.

"Oh. You mean . . .? He's actually your boyfriend now?" Beck gave Sam a hopeful expression, and their heart leapt into their throat at the mere thought.

"Uh," Sam said eloquently. They looked helplessly between Vivienne's knowing grin and the blossoming excitement on Beck's face. ". . . Yes?"

"Sam!" Beck exclaimed, and Sam grunted in surprise as they found themself being hugged hard enough that their feet stumbled to a halt. "I told you if you'd just call him, it'd all work out! And now a real date—that's so exciting!"

"Yeah. Very, uh, exciting," Sam replied stiffly as they subtly extricated themself from her hold. Clearing their throat, they gestured to the situation room door only a few paces away. "Well. Like Viv said—big date. Dinner. Thing. So . . . better get ready."

"Yeah, yeah. Go hyperventilate in peace," Vivienne said with a roll of her eyes. Sam scowled but didn't argue with the opportunity for escape.

"Oh my god. Why didn't you tell me?" They could hear Beck whispering excitedly even as they wrenched open the situation room door and disappeared inside.

"You know Sam. So embarrassed over the silliest things," Vivienne replied casually. It was almost scary how easily she could come up with a story just like that when her feet were put to the flame.

"Do you think I should head out? I don't want to make them nervous before their big date."

"That's probably for the best. I'll make sure they get there in one piece."

"You'll call Harper, though? So she doesn't worry about you working late?"

"Already done. Don't worry so much! Go find your own cute person to get nervous over."

"Well, I guess you're the boss."

Vivienne walked into the room and eased the door shut behind her before collapsing dramatically against the wood panel. "Geez, Sam. For someone who spent ten minutes lecturing me on the importance of discretion for this op, you are a terrible liar."

"And Beck is delusional if she actually bought that I would ever call you for dating advice," Sam shot back. Glancing around the room pointedly, they asked, "Now what am I supposed to be wearing for this imaginary date?"

"Literally anything other than that." Giving Sam a scornful once-over, Vivienne said, "Go sit in the chair. If we're going to convince any watchful eyes that you were here for the mixer, you have to at least put in an appearance. And that means not looking like . . . this."

"What's wrong with how I look?" Sam asked, looking down at themself.

"Really, a trench coat, Sam?" Vivienne said. She gestured to Sam's jacket with exasperation. "That's cliché no matter what gender you are. And it's definitely not appropriate for a mixer."

"It's got a lot of pockets," Sam said stubbornly, even as they stripped out of the coat.

"And you like that no one can tell what you look like under there," Vivienne replied. She folded her arms impatiently as Sam made their way over to the hair washing station. "No time for that," Vivienne said, pointing to the makeup chair. "Sit. I've got work to do."

"Someone's taking this seriously," Sam muttered, loosening their tie as they sat for her.

"Pretending to investigate a murder so you can actually investigate a police officer?" Vivienne said. She applied primer to Sam's face with enough intensity to turn it into an exfoliant. "I would say that's pretty serious, Sam. Do you really think Noah's involved in all this?"

"With your case? Probably not. I'm hoping he can tell me something about Nikki and what the hell is going on with that whole church situation, but I doubt he's got much to do with—uh, whoa!" Sam jerked back as Vivienne whipped out a blush brush. "Skipping some steps, aren't we?"

"I told you. We're just going for feminine enough to check in, take a lap, and get out," Vivienne said, grabbing hold of their chin. "Now hold still and tell me why I'm risking getting in serious trouble so you can look into something that isn't even relevant to the case."

"It's relevant to *a* case, just not *your* case," Sam said. They did their best to keep their head from moving as she buzzed around at lightning speed. "There was a priest who was murdered a few weeks back. Father Simon D'Angelo. Turns out the church he was working at is the headquarters for a nasty local gang called the Romanos."

"What does that have to do with Noah?" Vivienne asked. She raised a new brush and then put it down again with a sigh. "This is really too tragic. I just—I can't let you walk around like this." Walking over to the wash basin, she grabbed a spray bottle and a comb.

"Gee, thanks." Sam rolled their eyes but didn't fight it when Vivienne started wetting their hair and combing it into some kind of order.

"So, Noah?"

"A few people have suggested that he might be related to the Romanos. Maybe even blood related," Sam said, and Vivienne's hands paused in her work. "I'm not saying it's true," Sam added quickly. "But there are some things that don't add up. Like how long it's taken him to wrap up this D'Angelo case. And the fact that his number might be in a drug dealer's phone."

"Might be?" Vivienne asked, and Sam shrugged.

"It isn't the number I have for him, but I can't exactly call it and find out. I'm only going to get one shot at this before he's tipped off, so I've got to make it count."

"That sounds like a big risk to take over a maybe," Vivienne said. Her forehead wrinkled with either concern or concentration as she finished fussing with Sam's hair and went in with the mascara wand. "What's going to happen if he's innocent?"

"Even if he is, I still need to know," Sam said as they resisted the urge to blink. "He's my rookie. If the gang is dragging Noah's name through the mud for some reason, then he's in trouble, and it's up to me to fix it."

"And if he's not innocent?"

Sam tried to respond, but she was already busy applying their lipstick. They didn't miss the fact that it was the same shade of rose red they had picked out the other day.

When she finally pulled back, Sam said, "Then he's still my rookie, and I still have to fix it."

For a second Vivienne's dark eyes met theirs, and a quiet understanding passed between them. Sam had never been one to give up on someone, even when maybe they should have. But they also would never let someone get away with hurting innocent people. Who their wrath fell on in this situation would be determined by what they could discover with Vivienne's help.

"All right. Let's get you changed," Vivienne finally said.

Sam glanced at themself briefly in the mirror as they rose from their chair. They weren't so sure this look counted as "feminine," but the makeup would be enough of a social indicator to keep most people from outright questioning which pronouns they should be using. Which was annoying in its own way, but at least it was working in Sam's favor for once.

Stepping behind the changeroom screen in the corner, Sam started to take off their clothes and then hesitated at the sight of what they would be changing into. "Uh . . . Viv?"

"Hmm?"

"Are you sure this is the right outfit . . .?" Sam asked, picking up the shirt to examine it. She had put them in some interesting things over the course of their seventeen previous dates, but this was . . . different.

"Yes."

"Don't you think it's kind of—"

"Just put on the outfit, Sam."

Whatever, she was the fashionista. Sam finished pulling off their clothes and, with enough jumping and tugging, managed to squeeze their way into the new outfit.

"Jesus, Viv," they complained as they made their way out from behind the screen. "Are these the tightest possible pants you could—"

Sam's words cut off abruptly as they caught sight of themself in the full-length mirror. Blinking slowly, they took in the person reflected in the glass, unsure quite how they were supposed to feel about the image.

"You like?" Viv asked as they took a half step closer to the mirror.

The jeans were tight enough to cut off feeling to Sam's toes, which they would probably appreciate after about five minutes of walking in the stiletto boots that were currently strapped to their feet. Despite the skin-tight white tank top doing its level best to make it look like they actually had a decent rack, the shirt was probably doing more harm than good showing off their broad shoulders and straight-cut sides.

It didn't matter how much red lipstick they wore. Most women's waists curved where a man's body simply didn't. And Sam's body didn't curve. At all. Normally that was easy enough for Vivienne to hide with even the most basic of blouses, but not in a shirt this tight.

"Well?" Vivienne asked impatiently as Sam met her gaze in the mirror uncertainly. "It's closer at least, right?"

Sam nodded slowly. They weren't sure it was particularly wise to go around looking like this while in their undercover role, but that didn't change the fact that the look was . . . closer. And they did like that.

Glancing around the room, Sam spotted a rack of clothing that was slightly less garish than the rest. Walking over, they thumbed through the hangers until they found what they were looking for.

"It'd really kill you to show some skin, huh?" Vivienne teased, looking nothing short of delighted as Sam let the leather jacket settle comfortably against their skin.

"Yeah, yeah," Sam grumbled, but couldn't help a small smile as they glanced into the mirror again. Definitely closer. "At least it's more femme than the trench coat, right?"

"Sure. You totally don't look like a stereotypical lesbian at all," Vivienne said. She walked over to fuss with the collar until Sam batted her hands away. "All right, fine. Go make your appearance. And try not to turn any girls tonight."

"In this outfit? I'll do my best. No promises, though."

Vivienne headed for the elevator, and Sam made their way out onto the fire escape. Climbing down the rickety metal staircase in stiletto boots was a challenge, to say the least. They walked back into the building through the front doors and checked in with the smiling young woman who could have been a carbon copy of Beck standing at the mixer's entrance.

Grabbing the requisite purple wrist band, Sam made their way inside the dim room and took a quick lap before melting into a dark corner and setting a mental timer for ten minutes. They spent the time going over everything they knew about Noah—both what they had learned personally from working with him and what they had been told by Eddie and Father Nicholas.

On either side of the equation, there wasn't a ton of information to go on, but they had meant what they said to Vivienne up in the situation room. They wanted the kid to be innocent, even if their gut said things weren't looking good for the young rookie.

When enough people had come and gone since they had entered the party, Sam slipped back out through the front entrance. They even made a point of asking the lady at the front if they needed to return the wristband, just to be on the safe side. Once they were outside, Sam tossed the little souvenir into the nearest trash can and headed for the side of the building. They worked hard to avoid looking at the spot where Kayleigh had lay bleeding out on the sidewalk. Not dead, but not really alive anymore either. It was possible she would recover enough to come out of her medically induced coma at some point, but the odds got worse every day.

Turning the corner, they made their way down the alley between the skyscrapers. Vivienne already stood waiting at the back door of her building, looking distinctly out of place in her elegant dress and designer heels.

"So what's the plan now?" Vivienne asked. She carefully picked her way toward Sam while attempting to avoid touching anything sticky, dirty, or otherwise nature-adjacent.

"If Noah's really involved in the gang activity at the church, I'm going to need to catch him red-handed. I can't do it anywhere near there, since that would be a huge tip-off. But if I can set him up here . . ." Sam craned their neck back as they looked up at the building for potential hiding spots. Catching sight of some telltale twigs balanced precariously on the struts of the neighboring high-rise's fire escape, they said, ". . . there's a chance he'll fall for it."

Walking over to stand beneath the fire escape, they gauged the distance and said, "Can you give me a boost?"

"Excuse me?"

"Give me a boost," Sam said impatiently, waving her over. Vivienne took one look at the weedy grass and litter under the rickety structure and immediately started shaking her head. Sighing, Sam said, "Fine. Wouldn't want you to break a nail or something."

Wincing as they felt the painfully tight jeans digging into their hips, Sam took a step back and then launched themself at the fire escape. Vivienne made a high-pitched sound of terror as their hand nearly slipped off the rusty metal beam before their heel found purchase on the lowest strut and kept them from falling. After a tenuous moment, they managed to firm up their grip. Then it was just a matter of climbing the latticework of metal beams supporting the fire escape until they could reach the little bird's nest tucked in the juncture of two struts.

"Sam, when was the last time you had a tetanus shot?" Vivienne demanded from the ground.

"Did they give those in the eighties?"

They steadied themself with one arm as they reached into their jacket pocket for the small recording device they had purchased earlier in the day. According to the guy behind the counter, the camera's battery would be good for forty-eight hours, so their timeline to make this play work would be tight, but doable.

"Yes. But you're supposed to get a new one every ten—oh my god, be careful! Do you have a death wish?" Vivienne exclaimed as Sam briefly kicked both feet off the structure. Using the momentum of their swing, they reached up to shove the camera into the bird's nest where it would have a clean shot of everything happening in the alley below.

"No. I just want to clear Noah's name," they grunted as their feet slammed back onto the strut below. Thank god these heels cost more than Sam's rent, or they probably would have snapped on impact. Sighing, Sam relaxed their grip on the beam and said, "Either that or catch him—"

"What was that?" Vivienne's anxious words cut straight through Sam's explanation.

"What was what?"

"Someone's coming," she insisted, turning nervously toward the street entrance of the alley.

"Viv, relax. It's probably just—"

"My clients can't think I'm spying on them, Sam," she snapped. "Get down here right now."

Sam frowned, but when they, too, picked up the sound of approaching footsteps, they quickly climbed their way down the metal scaffolding until they were close enough to the ground that they could jump. Cursing under their breath as the impact reverberated through their knees, Sam knew they needed a good explanation for why two grown adults would be hanging out in a dark alleyway together.

Sam took two steps toward Vivienne. She let out a sound of alarm as they got right up in her face.

"Option A or Option B?" Sam asked quietly. Vivienne just looked more confused as they took her hand firmly. "You want me to kiss you, or you want me to yell at you? Your choice."

"Um . . . neither?" Vivienne's eyes widened in understanding as the approaching footsteps grew louder. Throwing Sam's hand away like it had burned her, she skittered back a step and said, "OK. OK. Option B. Just . . . no kissing. Harper would kill me."

"Seriously?" Sam replied flatly.

Vivienne flinched at the raw note of anger in their voice but didn't volley back. Sam almost wished she'd opted for the kissing—at least they knew she was good at that. But for the first time since they'd reconnected, Vivienne looked genuinely rattled. It was almost funny. Murderers, hackers, and an angry wife were all fine. But the idea of kissing her ex? That clearly got to her.

And it gave Sam an incredibly stupid idea about something else they knew she was good at.

They looked her straight in the eye and said, "We're back to that?"

"Excuse me?" Vivienne's dark eyes narrowed at the familiar words. Sam stood frozen, channeling all the fragile stillness of the scene.

"What about the past couple of days? They happened, you know." Sam's voice was laced with deep disappointment teetering on the edge of outrage.

"I—I know they happened," Vivienne stammered. Sam gave her a subtle, encouraging nod. Drawing in a deep breath, she said in a perfect, tender-voiced impression, "And they were wonderful, but they were also very irresponsible."

"Oh, come on," Sam shouted, punctuating the words with a slap of their hand against the metal fire escape. The sound echoed furiously around the alley, and Vivienne raised an eyebrow at their creative interpretation of the iconic scene.

"I have a wife waiting for me in a hotel," Vivienne insisted. "She's going to be crushed when she finds out—"

"So you make love to me and then you go back to your wife? Was that your plan?" Sam demanded, taking another threatening step closer so Vivienne was forced to slink back under the shadows of the fire escape. Well out of harm's way. "Was that a test that I didn't pass?"

"No, I made a promise to a woman. She gave me a ring, and I gave her my word." Vivienne's words came out fast and choppy. The perfect McAdams to Sam's butchered Gosling.

"And your word is shot to hell now, don't you think?" they snapped, straining their ears between the lines to see if they could still hear the footsteps. Only partially because they weren't sure how much more of the scene they had memorized.

"I don't . . . I don't know. I'll find out when I talk to her."

"This is not about keeping your promise, and it's not about following your heart." Sam paused for dramatic effect. Still no footsteps. Had this actually worked? "It's about—"

"Hey," a low voice interrupted, and Sam froze at the sound. "Everything cool here?"

"Oh shit," Vivienne breathed.

Well, that wasn't the next line in the script. Although at the sound of that voice, Sam couldn't even remember what movie they had just been quoting from. Or why they had been doing it. Or what a movie was.

Sam turned slowly to get their eyes on the intruder and felt their heart stop when they realized they weren't just imagining it. That really was Teddy standing there, looking very confused and very out of place against the backdrop of the dark alley in one of his hideous floral shirts.

"Sam?" Teddy said in a way that told Sam he was just as surprised to see them as they were to see him. At least his brain didn't seem to be flatlining.

Well, what were they supposed to think? This was impossible. There was no way they were both in this alley right now by accident. The odds were simply too astronomical.

Unless "the odds" had a little outside help.

As Sam spun back around abruptly, Vivienne winced at their suspicious glare. That was all the proof Sam needed.

"Viv," they asked slowly. "What did you do?"

"You're Vivienne?" Teddy echoed, disbelief coloring his voice. "Vivienne Fox?"

"Yes. That's me," Vivienne said. Remarkably, her voice came out quite cool and professional for someone who had just gotten caught planting a camera on her own premises. But that was Viv. Always prepared with a story.

She stepped back out from under the fire escape and brushed by Sam to offer Teddy her hand. "You must be Mr. Burgess. A pleasure to meet you."

"Uh . . . likewise?" Teddy said. His voice was thick with curiosity as he accepted her handshake. Seeing the way Sam was glaring at their connected hands, Teddy quickly let go and said, "Sorry if I was interrupting. I called the office, and the lady on the phone said I could find you out here. But I wasn't expecting . . ." His gaze was soft and excruciatingly uncertain when he gave Sam a sidelong glance. "Well. This is all just a little unexpected."

"Viv," Sam repeated in a low voice. They didn't dare meet Teddy's gaze. "You'd better tell me what's going on. Right. Now."

"Did I not mention I was hiring an artist to design a new piece for the office?" Vivienne asked innocently.

"Goddammit," Sam swore loudly as the reality of the situation became increasingly apparent. Teddy raised an eyebrow at their furious response, and Sam felt a hot flush crawling up their neck. "What is the matter with you?" they demanded. "Why—why would you—why?"

"OK, so maybe I should have told you—"

"Well, that's a fucking understatement."

Teddy shifted uncomfortably, and Sam pressed a hand to their temple. They could barely even look at him, they were so embarrassed.

Apparently one long-distance lover plus one meddling ex-girlfriend plus two murder investigations involving a potentially dirty cop equaled one mess of a situation.

"Uh . . . this seems like a bad time. Should I come back tomorrow, or . . . ?" Teddy asked, tightening his grip on the strap of his bag.

"Yes. I mean—no," Sam corrected, then groaned in frustration. "This isn't—this isn't what it looks like. We're just working on a case together. The one I haven't been able to tell you much about. We're not . . ." Sam gestured helplessly between themself and Vivienne while still keeping their eyes glued to the pavement.

"Well, yeah. Obviously."

Sam's head jerked up in surprise. A rueful smile played across Teddy's lips as their eyes finally met for more than three seconds. "I've heard of Shakespeare in the park, but *The Notebook* in the alley is a new one for me."

"Oh," Sam said lamely. Ducking their head as though that would hide their embarrassment, they mumbled, "Guess I shouldn't be surprised you know that one."

"Probably not. Although your Gosling could use some work." Teddy offered them that soft, crinkly-eyed smile. "I didn't buy that you were in love with her at all."

Sam breathed out a small, helpless laugh, and Teddy smiled a little more at the subtle sound. And maybe they smiled a little back, because despite the insanity of this moment, he was here right now and that felt like not the worst thing in the world, according to their racing heart.

"Oh my god. You two are so cute," Vivienne said, clasping her hands together. Hearts all but poured from her eyes as she watched the two of them smiling shyly at one another.

"Shut up." Sam's almost-smile instantly became a scowl.

"Come on. Are you seriously mad about this?" Vivienne asked, gesturing emphatically to the handsome young man she had clearly tricked into being here.

"I said *shut up*."

"Am I missing something?" Teddy asked. He looked lost again as the two turned on each other.

"Just . . . I'll explain. Just give me a minute," Sam said as their embarrassment returned in full force. Just the idea of trying to explain this stupid situation that Vivienne had caused made them want to die. Turning their glare on the other woman, Sam took a threatening step toward her and said, "Don't think this is over. If you ever tell anyone about this, no one will ever find your body. Got it?"

"Well, you know I'll have to tell Harper," Vivienne responded smugly. "If you want to tell it your way, you'll just have to come to brunch sometime. Maybe bring a guest, if you feel like it."

"I hate you."

"You're welcome," Vivienne said cheerfully, not daunted in the least by their ire.

Shaking their head in disbelief, Sam turned on their heel and started walking away. Grabbing Teddy by the arm as they passed him, they set a determined pace for the street where their car was parked. Probably ticketed, too, with their luck today.

"Wow, you're really fast in those heels," Teddy said. He practically tripped over his own feet trying to keep up with their swift steps. "Um, where are we going, exactly?"

"I'm taking you home," Sam said shortly.

"I'm actually staying in a motel on—"

"Then I'll take you there," Sam said, tightening their grip on his arm. "We need to talk."

CHAPTER TWENTY-SIX

"Just up there, on the right." Teddy's voice sounded loud in the stifling silence of the car's interior.

Sam could feel the leather jacket sticking to their skin despite the ocean breeze drifting in through the windows as they pulled over on the quiet side street next to the motel. The neon sign flickered overhead. If this were a movie, that would probably be a bad omen. But then again, they had already spent the last fifteen minutes too tongue-tied to get three sentences out, so they weren't sure how much worse this could get.

The car rocked gently as Sam put it in park. For a second, they both sat there with the weight of a hundred unsaid things pressing in around them. Finally, Sam blurted, "Really? This place?"

"What's wrong with this place?" Teddy asked, and Sam felt a tiny amount of tension release. Enough to breathe again, anyway.

"Nothing, I guess," Sam said, although any establishment with a neon-pink sign got a hard pass from them. "Isn't there a nicer hotel like a block away?"

"Who needs some fancy hotel? This place has a bed and a shower. It's not like I've got much more than that on the boat," Teddy replied with an easy shrug.

For half a second, Sam was a little dazzled by that simple shrug. It was just so Teddy. Of course he could afford the fancy hotel with staff waiting on him hand and foot, but why not stay at the sketchy motel instead? Why waste money on things he didn't really want or need?

Why sit here in this car with someone he'd spent one night with six weeks ago looking a whole lot like he was feeling the same electricity Sam was in this moment?

Teddy reached to unclip his seatbelt, and Sam looked away again. Moment over, apparently.

"So. Vivienne's the theoretical ex, huh?" Teddy asked. His voice was so intentionally light and casual that Sam was already cringing with embarrassment when he added, "She seems nice."

"Only if you can get past the extreme bossiness," Sam muttered, then winced when Teddy gave them a questioning look. "Look, Viv is . . . It's not what you think."

"So you two just happened to have that Notebook routine memorized?" he asked with disbelief.

"No. I mean, yes, obviously she is my ex," Sam said, then sighed at the sharpness in their own voice. Why couldn't these things ever be easy? Trying for a more measured tone, they explained, "I just meant she's not that kind of ex. She's married and we only reconnected because of the case. No lingering feelings or anything."

"But you are friends now," Teddy clarified. Seeing Sam's grimace, he quickly added, "Not that it matters. Just trying to figure out exactly how I fit into this equation."

"Hell if I know. This wasn't my idea," Sam grumbled. They raised a hand to rub at their tired eyes, only to remember they were wearing makeup. Great.

Catching the disappointed look on Teddy's face, Sam let their hand drop to their lap.

It wasn't supposed to go like this. They were supposed to have more time. A plan, an outline of what to say—at least a chance to buy some goddamned flowers or something. The idea of meeting up had been thrilling when they shared that sweet video call last week, but now all the words Sam wanted to say felt like static electricity in their throat.

"Well, I guess I shouldn't keep you."

By the time Sam's heart had sunk all the way to their toes, Teddy was already reaching for the car door.

That was definitely not the way this was supposed to go. Sam might not be good at relationships, but they were very familiar with how they ended, and they knew if Teddy got out of this car right now, their little romance was toast.

As though reading their panicked thoughts, Teddy offered Sam a tepid half-smile and said, "It's all good. I know you said you were busy. And I don't want to throw off your case or anything, so—"

"Wait—wait," Sam blurted. Teddy froze in surprise as Sam scrambled across the seat to fumble for his hand. "I don't care about the case." Sam wasn't even totally sure the words were audible over the sound of their heart pounding in their ears. Swallowing hard, they squeezed his hand tighter, probably too tight, and repeated, "Please, just wait."

Teddy considered them for a long moment. Sam wished they could know what he was seeing. Probably some super-attractive combination of stressed out and desperate. But it was worth it, because that familiar smile was pulling at Teddy's mouth, and his free hand was quick to release the door handle.

"If I wait, are you going to tell me what's going on?" he asked. Sam's pulse went from way too fast to downright supersonic when Teddy turned his hand over to let their fingers tangle with his. When Sam didn't balk, Teddy smiled a little more and said, "I would be very interested in knowing if your ex actually wants to hire me or if this was all some elaborate setup to get us holding hands in your car."

"I don't know, honestly. I didn't ask her to do this," Sam said with a helpless shrug. When that smile flickered, they quickly shifted a little closer in their seat and added, "But, uh, it's probably on me for oversharing."

Teddy gave them a questioning look, and they ducked their head in embarrassment. "It was stupid. We got to talking after work sometime last week, and I guess she noticed I was, uh, excited to get home, I guess. So she asked why and . . . I told her."

"About us?" Teddy asked. His voice was still carefully neutral, but Sam didn't miss the way he drifted a little closer in response to their honesty.

"Well, no. I wouldn't even know what to call . . . any of this," Sam admitted, gesturing vaguely to their entwined hands and all the weirdness that represented from these past few weeks. Looking at him sidelong, they admitted quietly, "I did tell her about you, though."

"Oh."

His hopeful expression instantly took their breath away. How were they supposed to resist making a fool of themself when he insisted on being so transparent in what he wanted?

"I, uh, told her you were an artist. A good one. And young—younger than me. Which she found very funny." Sam scowled at the memory, which only made Teddy look more smitten. "I also told her you're always curious. Never afraid to tell me what you're thinking. And honest. Too honest, really. Way too easy to talk to. Very—uh, very, very nice to look at and do . . . other things with. Obviously. And a good listener, too. Much better than me."

Sam knew they were not imagining the heat in Teddy's gaze as they choked out their reluctant confession. Hearing the words out loud, it was no wonder Vivienne had been convinced she needed to deliver Teddy to Sam's front door ASAP. Sam couldn't have sounded any more lovestruck if they tried.

"Anything else?" Teddy asked, and Sam could barely breathe when his thumb traced slowly over the back of their hand.

"Uhh . . ." The electric sensation was doing bad things to Sam's ability to remember how words worked. "Uh, not much, I guess. Just that you're . . . good."

"Good?" His thumb stopped stroking, but they couldn't be too disappointed when he tugged them a little closer across the center console.

"Yeah. Too good for someone like me," Sam mumbled. Teddy's hand curled under their jaw and their body immediately and aggressively insisted that that was enough talking. "Too patient. Too sweet." The words were clumsy on their tongue as they leaned in close enough to breathe him in. Their body felt liquid when his gaze dropped to their lips, and they knew he was thinking that was enough talking, too. "Too good at understanding what I'm trying to say, even when I—"

Teddy's mouth found theirs with an eagerness that said he understood exactly what they were trying to say. He pulled back just long enough for Sam to let out a sigh of relief—and then they were pulling him back down because one kiss after six long weeks seriously was not even going to scratch the surface of their need.

"Sam," he breathed against their lips when they paused just long enough to fumble with their seatbelt.

"No," they replied stubbornly, flinging the belt away. It cracked loudly against the window, but they didn't care. Teddy looked so incredibly perfect with his cheeks flushed and Sam's hands tangling in his curls. Sam thought their heart might stop if they didn't kiss him again right now. So they did. "Not yet," they murmured between kisses. "Please."

Well. Sam had said he was a good listener, and Teddy was more than happy to prove exactly how good he could be.

When they finally managed to disengage, it was only to appreciate how lovely Teddy looked having been thoroughly and properly kissed silly.

"It's called dating," Teddy said, after giving them a long moment to revel in the self-satisfaction.

"Hmm?" Sam hummed, still not very interested in the whole talking thing. They tried to pull him in for another kiss, but he held back.

"You said you didn't know what to call this thing we've been doing these past few weeks," Teddy clarified. Reaching up to pluck Sam's hand from his hair, he pressed a kiss to their knuckles and said, "I think the word you're looking for is dating."

That brought Sam back down to earth like a bucket of cold water to the face.

"What? No." Sam's hands retracted from their embrace so quickly it might have been offensive if Teddy wasn't already laughing. "That's ridiculous," Sam insisted. If they had been flushed from the kissing before, then they were undoubtedly fluorescent now. "We're not . . . dating."

"No?" Teddy asked, still looking terribly amused by their predictably skittish response. "What would you call it when two people spend all their free time getting to know each other romantically and pining whenever they're apart?"

"Who says I do that?" Sam demanded. Although it wasn't very convincing when Teddy dimmed his eyes at them and they instantly swayed back into his orbit.

"I say so," he replied with just enough of a smirk to make Sam's entire brain flatline with desire.

This time when they kissed him, Sam made sure there was no misunderstanding their plans for what was going to be happening tonight. Their fingers curled in the collar of his hideous yellow shirt, and they had to fight the urge to rip it right off his body. *Dating.* They weren't sure a single word should turn them on this much, but their lovesick, sex-starved brain really did not care about *shoulds* at the moment.

It didn't help that Teddy's hands were just as eager, pulling roughly at their clothes until the leather jacket was lying in a heap on the floor and their shirt was rucked up under his fists. His warm hands slid greedily against their bare skin, and his kisses only grew more passionate as he reacquainted himself with the hard planes of Sam's body.

"OK," Sam finally breathed when they could no longer stand one more second of kissing him with this much clothing on. "Let's do it."

"Yes please," he agreed enthusiastically. "Your place or my place?"

"No. I meant—"

"You're right. My place is much closer."

Teddy had already wrenched the car door open and sprung to his feet before Sam could protest. They had barely even registered the fact that he was gone before he was opening their door and leaning down to scoop them out of the driver's seat.

Sam found themselves laughing helplessly as Teddy wrapped one hand around their belt and started towing them with a purpose in the direction of the motel across the street.

"Teddy," they chastised with another laugh. When they dug in their heels, he just tugged harder.

"What? Motel sex not good enough for you?"

Releasing their belt, Teddy circled around behind to wrap Sam up in his arms. His hands were all dirty promises hooking around their hips and pulling them firmly against his body. "Come on," he murmured when their breath caught at the sensation of him pressing up against them so shamelessly. "Just try and tell me you haven't been fantasizing about this."

"Please. You're not even going to be able to spell motel by the time I'm done having my way with you tonight."

Before Teddy could go getting too cocky about it, Sam smacked his hands away and stepped out of his embrace. Smirking a little at his helpless whine of need, they turned and hooked one finger into the top button of his shirt to pull him close. The awful fabric really was ruining the view. Teddy swallowed hard as Sam's finger curled and the button gave way with ease.

"That's fine," Teddy managed, despite looking a little like he might pass out as their finger slid to the next button promisingly. "I was never very good at spelling, anyways."

"Mhmm. We'll get to the good part," Sam assured him as another button released under their playful touch. "But first we need to settle this dating thing."

"There's nothing to settle," Teddy insisted, leaning in until the words were a thrilling whisper against Sam's lips. "I told you. We're already dating."

"And I told you we're not," Sam replied, very much enjoying the way Teddy all but stopped breathing when they skimmed blunt nails down his exposed chest. "Not until we've had at least one date."

"Right now?"

"Well, if you really want, I could take you out for dinner first, but . . ."

"Sam." Their name was a curse, brief and urgent on his tongue at the sensation of their hand sliding all the way down his body with bold, lascivious intent. Pulling their wandering hand away, he gave them a positively stunning glare and said, "You are such a problem, you know that?"

His hands found their waist, and Sam quickly found themself spun around and pinned between the car and a whole lot of extremely turned-on man. Which was really very, very OK with them. Sliding one hand under their chin, Teddy kissed them once, slowly. Then again, with more passion. And again, until Sam thought they might melt right into the concrete at his feet.

"Sam," he repeated in a murmur, tracing one thumb over the curve of their lips. "I like you *so much*. And I absolutely want to go on that date. Tomorrow. But tonight, I really, really want to have sex with you. Can we do that, please?"

"Is it bad if it turns me on knowing I could make you beg right now?" Sam asked, and Teddy groaned in disbelief.

Sam's breath caught as Teddy trailed one hand slowly down their thigh. Just low enough to get a good grip and wrench them up onto their toes. They weren't so sure he was going to be the one doing the begging when he used the leverage to lay them out against the car and kissed them with the passion of a man who really did not care about where as long as it was happening right now.

Not that Sam was going to stop him. After all those late-night phone calls, Teddy knew exactly what this kind of shameless indecency did for them.

"Sam," Teddy breathed, emboldened by their reaction when he pressed one thigh between their legs. "Please. Come to bed with me. I want you."

"Only want?"

"Need. I need you. Please."

"Again," Sam demanded, even though their whole body was begging them to hurry up and get to the being naked part. "Like you mean it this time."

"Sam, I swear to god," Teddy said, tugging helplessly at their belt as Sam's lips found his neck. When their tongue traced the pattern of ink curling across his collarbone, they felt every inch of his body react. "Come on," he pleaded, the heat in his voice thoroughly shattering their resolve. "You can watch while I take a cold shower or take me to bed and do anything you want with me. But you have to choose. Now."

"Yeah. OK. Let's—the second one. Let's go."

They raced across the street together in a mess of limbs and kisses and giddy laughter. Teddy's hands were on their body, and Sam was kissing him everywhere they could reach as they stumbled up the stairs to the rooms on the second floor, too love-drunk to be anything but all over each other.

Teddy pushed them up against his door, hard and hot and needy as he fumbled with the keys, and Sam nearly popped the remaining buttons right off his shirt in their haste to get him undressed. Teddy grinned as the key finally turned and they eagerly dragged him inside by their grip on his open belt.

The door slammed shut behind them, and they proceeded to make sure the entire motel knew exactly how enthusiastic they were about being back in each other's arms.

CHAPTER TWENTY-SEVEN

Sam's lungs were burning. Their entire body was tender to the point of sweet agony, but they couldn't stop now. They were *so close*.

The pavement disappeared beneath their feet as they turned the final corner and their low-rise came into sight. One hand grasped the ancient metal railing on the first landing, and they really thought they might pass out, but Sam forced their feet to keep going. Just three short flights of stairs and then finally, *finally* they came to a stop outside their front door. Their hand reached for the doorknob, then froze when they remembered that, for the first time in a long time, there was actually someone else inside.

Doubling over to try and catch their breath, Sam let their hand slip from the metal knob. Maybe they would wait until they sounded a little less like they had just run a marathon before they went back inside.

Their whole body protested the physical punishment, between last night's ambitious activities and this morning's workout, but the discomfort was just as satisfying in its own way. And against all odds, Teddy had still been fast asleep by their side when Sam rolled out of bed this morning, so the fun wasn't over yet. And if the sound of them showering just so happened to wake him up . . .

With their mind full of distracting fantasies, Sam was reasonably confused when they opened the front door to see Teddy sitting at their kitchen table, fully dressed. He looked sleepy and rumpled and stupid attractive sitting there in the soft morning light with a cup of coffee in one hand and his curls gathered in a wild tangle on top of his head.

He also looked quite relieved to see them, which was equally confusing—until they pushed the door the rest of the way open and saw the real reason their sweet lover wasn't still waiting for them in bed.

"Good morning, Sam," Vivienne said cheerfully from where she stood leaning up against their kitchen counter.

Naturally, she looked twenty times too put-together for an early morning visit, and the smirk on her face said that wasn't an accident. At her side, Beck was tapping away on her phone as usual, but she glanced up to give Sam a friendly wave before returning to her work. Teddy, on the other hand, was looking a little ambushed and a lot happy that Sam was back to deal with their unexpected visitors.

"Viv," Sam growled, wiping sweat from their face as they let the front door slam shut behind them. "What the hell are you doing in my apartment?"

"It's not like I broke in," Vivienne protested, pressing an innocent hand to her chest. "Can't an old friend stop in to say hello?"

"No," Sam said bluntly. They kicked off their running shoes and headed over to the sink to grab a glass from the dish rack. They filled it with tap water and chugged it in three long gulps.

Looking over the rim of the glass at Teddy, Sam tilted their head at him in silent question. If it had been up to them, they would have just told Vivienne to get lost. But, of course, that wasn't Teddy's style. Teddy was the type of man who got out of bed at 7:00 a.m. to open the door for his lover's ex-girlfriend and make her coffee. And despite the rude awakening, Teddy's smile was still all soft understanding as he tilted his head back at them.

Putting the cup down with a sigh, Sam said, "All right. Tell me why you're really here." And then, because that sounded a little too friendly, they added, "But if it's just to snoop, you can leave now."

"Someone's a little cranky," Vivienne said, raising an eyebrow in a way that made Sam wish they had just thrown her out. Pursing her lips at their sour expression, she said, "I was just trying to find the wayward artist I hired. I did go to the motel first, but the nice clerk said he checked out late last night."

"We figured he got a better offer," Beck added with an immature giggle as Vivienne looked pointedly at the kitchen table where Teddy was sitting having clearly spent the night in Sam's bed.

"Sure did," Teddy confirmed cheerfully, and Sam rolled their eyes at his utter lack of subtlety.

Not that there was really any point in being subtle when just the sight of him filled Sam with the sort of primal self-satisfaction they were sure everyone in the room could sense. But still, they'd be dead in the ground before they'd thank Vivienne for her meddling ways.

"Speaking of offers," Teddy added casually, only pausing slightly to sip his coffee, "was this whole commission thing just to help your ex get laid, or do you actually want to see these proofs? Because I've got them here if you're interested."

"Are you serious?" Vivienne asked as Sam choked back a startled laugh at the ease with which he approached the conversation. Subtle, indeed.

"Are *you* serious?" Teddy shot right back. Glancing over at Sam, he offered that familiar crinkly-eyed smile and said, "I already got what I came here for. So if you want to back out now, you can. Otherwise, you're looking at one very expensive parent trap."

"No, I definitely want to see them," Vivienne said eagerly at nearly the same time Beck said, "How expensive?"

"Oh, I don't know. Couple zeros or something. You'd have to call my manager for specifics," Teddy said dismissively. Reaching into the leather messenger bag lying on the table, he produced two clear clamshell cases and explained, "Henry manages the business part of things. I just make the stuff."

If Beck had anything to say about that, it was lost under Vivienne's gasp of delight upon seeing the delicate product samples nestled in the unassuming plastic carriers.

"Oh my god. They're even prettier in person," she gushed, immediately reaching for the first case before pulling up short. "May I . . . ?"

"Be my guest. They're your samples."

Sam edged closer for a better look as Vivienne carefully popped the lid off the first container. Inside, a perfect miniature bouquet of paper roses sat upon a pillow of something that glittered in the weak natural lighting.

"They're made from the same brand of napkin?" Vivienne asked, tracing one finger along the edge of a flower petal.

"Yup. Same ones you use at the mixer," Teddy confirmed. "As long as you've got a couple thousand of those lying around, I should be able to do my thing."

"And the glass?" Vivienne hesitated as her fingers brushed over the small, colored pieces filling the bottom of the container. "Will you have enough? I know it's a big piece."

"Sure will. That part is actually sourced from a stained-glass window that broke during a recent wedding gone wrong," Teddy said, and he smiled faintly when Sam startled in recognition. "I thought it'd be poetic."

Vivienne's fingers dipped into the pile of glittering debris. As she lifted the first piece, the entire thing began to uncoil like a bejeweled snake until she was holding a long line of copper wire dotted with sparkling pieces of blunted glass spaced out between the paper napkin blossoms. The wire spun lazily between her fingers, and Sam could only imagine how much more enchanting it would be showcased in the Paths lobby instead of their crappy little apartment.

"It's not to scale, but picture a whole bunch of those in front of something like . . ."—Teddy reached into the larger case and produced the second mockup—". . . this."

Vivienne's eyes looked like they might fall out of her head as he settled the Paths logo, formed out of more paper flowers, on the table. The wire ran in front of it, and Sam could picture a curtain of the sparkling lines hanging in front of a jumbo-sized version of the display.

"Wow," Beck said, and honestly, that single word really did capture it.

"Oh my goooood. Sam!" Vivienne exclaimed. She spun to face them and gestured emphatically with the piece she was still holding. "You seriously think this is just pretty good?"

"What else do you want me to say?" Sam grumbled. They ducked their head slightly when Teddy gave them a questioning look. "I said he was a good artist, and he is."

"You are so clueless sometimes," Vivienne scoffed. Eyeing up the proof with obvious delight, she muttered, "Pretty good. Maybe you do need glasses."

"I can see fine," Sam replied irritably. As if their aching body needed any more reminders that they weren't twenty-seven anymore. "My memory might need some work, though, because I don't remember asking you to—"

"Hey, hey. Nada de pleitos hasta que salga el sol," Teddy chided lightly. Sam's mouth snapped shut and they gave him a frustrated look, but Teddy just held his coffee mug toward them in a language they understood perfectly.

Sam was across the room in half a heartbeat. Teddy took their hand and kissed their knuckles sweetly before pressing his cup into their palm.

"Better?" he asked with some amusement when Sam practically stuck their whole face into the mug to inhale the familiar scent of rainforest beans.

"I guess," they mumbled vaguely around short draws of the heavenly liquid.

Instantly, some of their tension released. Sam considered that their caffeine addiction might be a little out of hand. Not that there was any chance of that changing if Teddy was going to continue keeping them up late and making them morning-after coffee. Which was absolutely fine by them.

Teddy's arm came up to slide around Sam's waist, and Sam let their weight settle against his shoulder with familiar ease. It only took two more sips before they relaxed enough to place their free hand gently on the crown of his head.

Vivienne seemed awfully pleased to see the two getting all cuddly, but Teddy's happy sigh chased away any irritation as Sam's fingers worked through his curls in slow circles.

"So, what do you think?" Teddy asked. He seemed completely comfortable, like conducting business from his lover's embrace was a perfectly appropriate thing to do. Somehow Sam thought in Teddy's mind it probably was.

"I think it's perfect," Vivienne said, and Sam pointedly ignored her little smirk. "But," she continued, a little more seriously, as she placed the beautiful sample back in its case, "I also think if your business manager is half as good as his client, you're already booked up from now until next year."

"That's probably true. I'm sure Henry could move my schedule around if I really wanted him to, but," Teddy glanced up at Sam hopefully, "I'd need a pretty good reason to ask him to do that for me."

"Isn't a bunch of money a good enough reason?" Beck asked, even as Sam choked a little on their coffee at Teddy's suggestive words.

"No. I've got plenty of rich clients."

Vivienne's eyebrows nearly shot off her face at his blunt assessment, but Teddy only had eyes for Sam.

"Time in one place, though . . . that's a little harder for me to come by."

"Ah. Hm. I see," Sam mumbled. The flush painting its way up their neck could probably be seen from outer space. Their free hand tightened in his curls and then released just as quickly. "And how—how much time are we talking about? Exactly?"

"Maybe a month or two," Teddy said easily, like those words didn't nearly send Sam into cardiac arrest. Instead of being put off by their nervous response, he just grinned a little and added, "Should be long enough to start working off that debt you racked up last night."

"Debt?" Vivienne asked. She exchanged a baffled look with Beck, who seemed equal parts amused and confused by Teddy's teasing words.

"What exactly were you two doing last night?" Beck asked.

"Nothing. He's just joking," Sam muttered into their coffee, which was pointless when they could already feel Teddy's quiet laughter vibrating against their side.

"I absolutely was not joking." Teddy only seemed more pleased when they tugged warningly at his hair. Shooting Vivienne a playful wink, he said, "I told them my nanny didn't raise a whore, and that they owed me one date for every time we—"

"Shh. Could you be a little less honest for one minute?" Sam complained as Vivienne burst into spluttering laughter at Teddy's shamelessness.

"I thought you liked that I was honest?" Teddy teased. "And sweet, and curious, and good-looking, and—"

"Yeah, OK, OK," Sam said, trying to pull away as Beck giggled at their obvious embarrassment. "Just call your damn manager."

"After you take me for breakfast?" Teddy insisted. He didn't so much as budge when Sam put all their weight into their attempted escape.

"Right now, if you don't want me to default on that loan," Sam replied with a pointed glare at Teddy's restraining arm.

"Well, can't have that," Teddy said smartly, and Sam staggered a little as he abruptly released his hold on them. Whipping out his phone, Teddy had dialed the number before Sam could even begin to regain their balance. It rang loudly twice on speaker phone before the call connected.

"So now you know how to use your phone." The irritated voice on the other end seemed incongruous with the picture of the beaming young man with the large glasses and bleached-blond hair on Teddy's caller ID.

"Good morning, my darling Henry," Teddy sang cheerfully as he held the phone aloft in one hand. "How's my favorite manager today?"

"Terrible."

Sam raised an eyebrow at the man's blunt response, but Teddy just seemed amused. Something told them he was not nearly as surprised as they were by his manager's cranky tone.

"I'm guessing I forgot something?" Teddy said.

"If only there was a way to know." Henry's words were the dry refrain of someone who had had this conversation many times before. "Have you even looked at your calendar today?"

"I don't know why you're always asking me that. You know I don't know how to check that thing," Teddy said dismissively, and Sam rolled their eyes. That, at least, they did not find surprising.

"Do you know how to check your voicemail? Because I've tried to reach you three times since you took off yesterday."

"Oops. Guess I got a little distracted," Teddy said, not sounding sorry in the least.

"Yeah, I bet you did, you lying little shit."

"How dare you? I would never lie to get out of a meeting," Teddy insisted so unconvincingly that Beck burst out giggling and Vivienne had to shush her.

"You think I can't tell when you've gotten laid? Hm?" If Henry knew he was on speaker phone, he surely didn't care. "I know you're blowing me off to shack up with Sam."

"What? *No.*"

"*Yes.*" Henry's reply was all exasperation as Vivienne and Beck continued to shake with silent laughter.

Teddy mouthed a dramatic "sorry" in response to Sam's glare.

"You told me you were going to the mainland to meet with a potential client, and now you're calling me from Sam's bed to beg for vacation time."

"Kitchen, actually," Teddy replied. "You'd be proud—I'm wearing clothes and everything."

"Jesus, Teddy. Do you care at all about this business?" Henry sounded slightly anguished, and Sam wondered if torturing his business manager was how Teddy stayed so happy-go-lucky.

"Hey, come on. I did meet with a client, too," Teddy said, pressing an offended hand to his chest as though he thought Henry could see him. "I can multitask, you know."

"And how much money is this supposed client offering? Because your schedule is already—"

"However much money you write on the contract," Teddy assured him. "She's the inventor of Paths, and she wants a full piece for the front lobby. She's already seen the samples and she loves them, so go crazy with the quote."

Vivienne gave him a look, but Teddy just shrugged expressively. So maybe he was a better salesperson than Henry gave him credit for.

"Of course she loves them. That's the goddamned problem, you overbooked little . . ." Henry's grumbling faded, and they could hear the sound of papers shuffling on the other end. After a long moment he asked, "You said Paths, yeah?"

"Yup. Imagine the PR." Teddy's smile grew when Henry remained silent on the other end. "Imagine introducing Ky to her in person."

Another long moment passed with only the sound of a mouse clicking and rapid keyboard tapping before: " . . . Fine. Just send me the proofs and the number for her people. I'll have a draft over within an hour." Then the line abruptly went dead.

Negotiation over, apparently.

"And now you've met the effervescent Henry Cheung," Teddy said cheerfully. Pocketing the phone, he said, "Sounds like you'll have yourself a deal shortly, Mrs. Fox."

"Only if the price tag isn't too marked up, Mr. Burgess," she replied primly, and Teddy just laughed.

"I wouldn't worry about that. Hen's a big softie, you'll see," he assured her. Giving Sam a fond look, he reached for their hand and said, "A little prickly, a little sweet. Definitely way too good to me." Sam looked away quickly when Teddy pressed his lips to their knuckles just tenderly enough to elicit a mushy noise from Beck at his lack of subtlety. "He met his fiancé on the Paths app, you know."

"Oh, really?" Beck asked, sounding all kinds of thrilled by the stubborn romantic bent in this conversation. "Was it a Cupid connection, or just a lucky swipe?"

"Don't know. You could ask him, though." Vivienne gave him a questioning look, and Teddy just smiled softly as Sam shuffled closer to his side again. "Like I said, Henry sets the prices, so . . . if you're looking for a discount, I'd start by doing something nice, like taking his fiancé out for a fancy dinner or something. I'm sure Ky would love to tell you all about how he met the love of his life, thanks to your app."

"You have a very interesting way of doing business, Mr. Burgess," Vivienne said. She looked a little bewildered and a little impressed by Teddy's complete lack of self-interest. It was a look Sam thought Teddy probably inspired often.

"So?" Teddy asked, tugging Sam's hand a little more pointedly. "I called him. Breakfast now?"

"Soon, cariño," Sam assured him. The pet name rolled off their tongue so naturally that it was only when Vivienne's eyebrows shot up in surprise that they remembered to be embarrassed. Jerking a thumb in their guest's direction, Sam said, "Give me a minute to talk to her about the other thing first." Teddy tilted his head, and Sam sighed. "The thing you interrupted last night?"

"Oh. That thing." Teddy's face scrunched up a little in a way that Sam did not mind seeing one bit.

"You actually told him?" Beck asked, eyeing Teddy with a healthy amount of suspicion. Apparently Sam was not the only one who had noticed his reaction. "And you're not . . . upset?"

"About their rookie being a gangster?" Teddy asked. Beck frowned, and her meaning seemed to dawn on him. "Oh, you mean about the fake Paths profile thing. No, that's fine." Sticking Sam with those big puppy dog eyes, he said, "I just want them to be careful. No getting in gunfights or anything."

"I'm more likely to die from papercuts than a gunshot," Sam grumbled. Still, they brushed one hand lightly along his cheek in a fleeting, tender gesture. "You're probably just going to have to listen to me complain a lot."

"There's nothing I'd rather be doing than listening to you complain."

Teddy trapped their hand against his face, and in that moment, all Sam could really think was that they hadn't had a chance to kiss him yet today and that suddenly felt totally unacceptable.

"You don't mind listening to them talk about their dates with other men?" Beck asked.

"I don't think an undercover interview with a potential serial killer really counts as a date," Teddy said, and Sam's mouth twitched into a faint smile at the undercurrent of annoyance in his voice.

"It definitely does not count," Sam said firmly. Leaning down, they brushed their lips against his despite their audience. Doing their very best to ignore Teddy's smitten expression, Sam gestured to the bedroom and said, "Could we please get this over with before I have to start calling this brunch instead of breakfast?"

With enough moaning and groaning from Vivienne about not wanting to see the aftermath of Sam's "night of passion," Sam managed to shepherd her and Beck into their perfectly tidy bedroom. It wasn't really necessary, since they'd already read Teddy in on most of the details last night, but they figured they should at least pretend to be professional about it. Especially if Noah did turn out to be guilty.

"Are you sure you still want to do this?" Vivienne asked the second the door closed, and Sam had to conjure up the memory of that delicious coffee to keep their irritation in check. "We could always put a pin in this until—"

"Yes, I'm sure I want to do my job," Sam said flatly. Vivienne winced a little, but it was a lot better than outright losing their temper. Pulling out the burner phone they had taken off of Eddie at the church yesterday, Sam asked, "Were you able to get me the account password?"

"Beck said she talked to one of the engineers," Vivienne said, turning to face the other woman.

"Here," Beck said. She reached into her large purse to pull out a scrap of paper with Eddie's password written on it. When Sam tried to take it from her, she hesitated to let go. "Don't do anything too obvious when you're in there, OK?" she said, glancing anxiously at Vivienne. "If he checks his account and realizes someone else has access, it could be really bad for—"

"Trust me, no pill pusher is going to go blabbing to CNN about cybersecurity leaks if it means exposing his own operation," Sam assured her before tugging the paper out of her hand. Not that they needed it, with Eddie's brilliant use of "Password1" to encrypt his super-secret drug dealing operations. They quickly entered the password and had his account loaded up within seconds. "Now all 'Eddie' needs to do is convince our N. Romano to show up in person."

"And get his confession on tape," Vivienne added.

"Not too worried about the confession part. More concerned with getting him in front of the camera in the first place," Sam said, already several weeks deep in Eddie's scant messaging history.

It was all very vague and spartan, which made sense. No matter how secure the Romanos believed the Paths app to be, they still weren't going to be totally stupid about what they put in writing.

Sam's eyes snagged on a familiar name. Apparently, Eddie often invited his "dates" to a local Italian diner called Ricky's just two blocks away from the Paths office. As memory served, Noah's family just so happened to eat at a restaurant by the same name every Sunday.

"So what are you going to write? 'Hey, wanna buy some drugs?'" Beck asked as Sam lowered the phone thoughtfully.

"Not unless I was trying to tip him off," Sam scoffed. "The way Eddie put it made it sound like he's a low-level pill pusher and Noah is something else. An inside man or an enforcer, maybe. I think the only way those two meet up is if I convince Noah that Eddie's in trouble and might roll on the family."

Switching over to the Connections panel, Sam quickly scrolled through to find the same "N. Romano" Paths profile that matched the number in Eddie's address book. They had a weird moment of déjà vu as they considered the little keyboard and tried to figure out what to write. Unlike with Jason, though, this situation was a little more complicated than dick pics from your average potential serial killer.

Eddie: caught some heat. need to talk
Eddie: 2 @ Ricky's

"There. It's done," Sam said, snapping the phone shut and placing it back in their pocket. "If he takes the bait, we should be on for this afternoon."

"That's it?" Beck asked, still seeming a little confused by how this whole shady criminal enterprise thing worked.

"Pretty much. Gangsters aren't really the chatty type," Sam said with a shrug. Seeing Beck's anxious expression, they sighed. "Hey. Would you stop looking so worried?"

"It just feels a little risky. The date with Jason. Tricking Noah into meeting." Beck adjusted her large glasses, and Sam had to remind themself that homicide investigations weren't within most people's comfort zones. "If this whole thing is actually about the gang, do you really think it still makes sense to—"

"Always chasing multiple leads, remember?" Sam said firmly. "Jason definitely dated all four of our victims, and he definitely met Alicia at the bar where she was later attacked. Noah and the Romanos may or may not be involved in this case, too, but you don't need to worry. I'm going to get the right person, either way."

Beck lowered her gaze to the floor and nodded. She still looked anxious in a way that reminded Sam why they couldn't afford to lose focus now. Having a cute guy around didn't mean there wasn't still a killer on the loose.

The phone buzzed loudly, and Sam flipped open the burner to read N. Romano's response:

N. Romano: OK

Not exactly poetry, but good enough.

"All right. Looks like I've got my two o'clock," Sam said, shutting the phone again. When the other women didn't immediately hop to, Sam flapped one hand toward the door and said, "Well? What are you two still doing here? I've got places to be."

"You mean breakfast with your boyfriend?" Vivienne obviously couldn't help getting one last shot in, even as Sam pushed past her to reach for the doorknob.

"None of your business. Now get out of my apartment," they said, opening the door and gesturing her on her way with one finger.

"You're really very ungrateful." Vivienne's nose crinkled pertly at Sam's indelicate response to her meddling. When she crossed them in the doorway, though, she laid a gentle hand on their arm and said quietly, "For what it's worth . . ."

"Yeah, yeah, I know," Sam mumbled, shaking her off quickly.

They were sure Teddy could hear them—had probably heard the entire exchange through these thin apartment walls. They didn't need Vivienne spelling out how amazing he was on top of everything else from this bizarre morning.

Nevertheless, they offered her the faintest, tiniest amount of gratitude in the form of a half-smile and said, "Now get out of here. I'm hoping to get through at least one date before he realizes he can do better."

CHAPTER TWENTY-EIGHT

Sam's mouth quirked up in a knowing smile as Teddy stared at them suspiciously across the table. Raising a hand to cover their lips, they continued to whisper to the waitress. The young woman nodded along, her wide eyes flicking between Sam and Teddy with interest.

"What are you up to?" Teddy asked the second the young woman darted away to serve another table. The small café hosted several other patrons, but it wasn't too busy at this early morning hour.

In fact, the most remarkable thing about the quaint restaurant was the glowing couple who had been flirting animatedly on the front patio for the past hour. More than once, Sam had caught a warm glance or curious whisper from a passerby. Honestly, they couldn't even blame people for staring.

Sam looked like . . . well, like themself outside of work. Jeans. T-shirt. Freshly shaved and showered. It had taken them five whole minutes to get ready after Vivienne had finally left. Teddy, for all his badgering about getting to breakfast, had needed another thirty minutes to "look fresh" for their date and ten more minutes of flattery after that to soothe his horror when he discovered that Sam didn't own a hairdryer. Then he'd suggested that they really ought to buy one if they expected him to stay over more often, and Sam had immediately started searching online, and then . . . well, then they had needed another twenty minutes before they were ready to even think about leaving the bedroom again.

Fast forward to Teddy sitting across from them now, looking positively radiant and a million miles out of their league with his damp curls shoved back from his face in a way that showed off his perfect smile, and his perfect beard, and his perfect little gold hoop earrings. *Earrings.* Honestly.

He was already twelve years younger than them, and now he insisted on looking all fancy for a simple breakfast date? It was so unfair.

But then again, if he wanted to look nice and let them stare at him for an hour, no one was going to catch Sam complaining about it.

"Who says I'm up to anything?" Sam finally asked, reaching for their mug. Giving Teddy an innocent look over the rim, they said, "I already bed you, fed you, took you for a walk. All the books say that's how you keep a man." Sam grinned at the sound of Teddy's laughter. Glancing down at his hand, which rested casually on the tabletop next to his empty plate, Sam said, "Or maybe I was just warning her not to let you get away with paying for anything. Considering *I* asked *you* out."

"Can't fool the great Detective Sam, huh?" Teddy said. He moved his hand and revealed the glossy black credit card hidden in his palm. "You do know I'm a millionaire, right?" he said, reaching out to tap their plate of half-eaten toast with the card. "I can afford a date with someone who eats like a bird."

"Yeah, but since I'm so hot and young I have to make sure no one thinks I'm a gold digger," Sam said sarcastically as he put the card back in his wallet.

"That's fair." Looking them over with exaggerated care, Teddy added, "It does seem a little suspicious that someone so amazing would want to romance me."

"Oh yes. I am famously very romantic."

"I don't know. Kind of seems that way," Teddy insisted, resting his chin on one hand. "Cute café. Good food, great conversation. Excellent view." Shooting Sam a playful wink, he asked, "How much better can a first date get?"

"Has dating changed in the last ten years?" Sam asked, and Teddy laughed at their exasperation. "I'm serious," they insisted, looking past him and raising their hand in a brief beckoning gesture. "I've been dumped at least three times in my life for not being romantic enough, and even I can do better than that."

"What are you looking a—" Teddy began to twist in his chair just as their waitress reappeared, looking a little breathless, but triumphant. "Oh, um. Thank—thank you," Teddy said, tripping over his words a little as she thrust a single cellophane-wrapped flower into his hands. "What . . . ?"

"Thanks, Lila," Sam said, and Teddy stared in disbelief as Sam passed the girl a healthy tip for her effort.

"No problem. Phil moved his cart, so I even managed to get some cardio in," Lila chirped, pocketing the money. Nodding to Sam's half-empty cup, she said, "I'll be back with a refill."

Sam shook their head fondly as they watched her scurry back to the kitchen before the other staff could notice her detour. "Good kid." Teddy was still quiet, and Sam raised an eyebrow as they noticed his bright pink face. "What?" Sam teased, seeing how embarrassed he was. "You don't like roses anymore?"

"No, I do," Teddy said quickly. Glancing down at the delicate red petals, he said, "I just, uh . . . I guess my dates don't buy me flowers very often."

"Hmm," Sam hummed thoughtfully. Stretching out across the table to take his free hand, they said, "I guess I can see why that would be." They weren't really sure his face could get any more pink as they lifted his knuckles to their lips and kissed the rose inked there. Grinning a little against his skin, Sam said, "It is a little intimidating to buy someone flowers when they're already covered in much prettier designs."

"OK," Teddy said a little weakly. "Now I know you're—"

His words were cut off by the chirp of Sam's phone from their jacket pocket. Wincing apologetically, they released his hand to reach for it. "Sorry," they muttered, glancing down at the caller ID. They frowned as Captain Donovan's name appeared across their screen.

"Go ahead. I won't listen," Teddy assured them. Sam shook their head with exasperation as Teddy made a big show of holding his hands over his ears, but they still pressed the Accept button.

"This is Sam," they said shortly.

"Detective. I hope you're enjoying your Saturday." Donovan's voice was equally brisk on the other end of the line. "Kayleigh Evergreen is awake and ready to talk."

Frowning now, Sam said, "Awake? I thought the doctors said we shouldn't expect any good news at this point?"

"Don't sound so disappointed. If it were my case, I'd prefer a witness to a vegetable."

"Well, obviously I'm glad she's not brain-dead," Sam muttered.

"Good. Then you need to get to St. Alexander's right away. The doctors have spoken with her a little, but of course she'll have questions—and hopefully answers."

Sam made the mistake of hesitating for two whole seconds.

"Unless you need me to send Vince?"

Sam's shoulders bunched and their voice became even quieter. "No, I can do it. His bedside manner is terrible. I can be there in . . ." Their eyes flitted up to meet Teddy's, then away again. "Uh, probably in an hour. Around ten, I think."

"The poor girl just woke up from a coma. I know it's a Saturday, but maybe a little hustle is in order?"

"Sorry. Unless someone invented teleportation overnight, ten is the fastest I can do," Sam said a little more firmly. Their gaze was drawn back to Teddy like a magnet, and his knowing smile was sweet relief.

"Glad you're in a good mood." Donovan's dry tone normally would have been enough to have Sam seeing red, but for once she was right. They were in a good mood. "I expect to hear nothing but reports of excellent professionalism, Detective. I don't think I need to remind you why she's in that hospital bed in the first place."

"Because someone stabbed her in the kidney," Sam replied flatly. They knew that wasn't exactly the shining example of professionalism Donovan was hoping for, but with Teddy's bright eyes on them, the thought of rolling over under the unfair criticism suddenly felt unbearable. "I have to go now, but I'll be there at ten."

Donovan started to respond, but Sam just said, "Yes, I understand. I—Yes. I'll keep you in the loop. Goodbye."

Shaking their head again, Sam shoved the phone back in their pocket and said, "Sorry about that."

"Mhm. The dangers of dating a badass detective," Teddy said, and only looked more smitten at the sight of their scowl. "I'm guessing that was work calling you in?"

"Soon. Not yet. My coma patient is awake and ready to talk, apparently," Sam explained. Sighing, they looked at their half-finished coffee and muttered, "Great timing, as always."

"Why not yet? Aren't you supposed to be there in an hour?" Teddy asked. When Sam gave him a look, he quickly added, "Not that I was listening."

"No, of course not," Sam said. Taking a sip of the coffee, they raised an eyebrow at his concerned expression. "Well, it's not going to take me an hour to walk three blocks, is it?"

Teddy's gaze followed as Sam gestured toward the brick monolith that was St. Alexander's peeking out above the low-rises to the east. The captain certainly would not have been impressed to know they could have been there in an easy ten-minute stroll, but Sam figured what she didn't know wouldn't hurt her.

They had put in their overtime, their sleepless nights, and more than enough humiliation these past six weeks. She could give them this single hour of freedom to enjoy a quiet breakfast with a man whose mere presence made everything else a little more bearable.

"Oh," Teddy said, looking flustered all over again. He glanced toward the hospital and then back to Sam, who continued to calmly drink their coffee. Tilting his head a little, he asked abruptly, "Hey, can I ask you a serious question?"

"Sure . . . ?"

"Have you just been messing with me this whole time?" When Sam frowned, Teddy clarified, "Like, are you secretly really good at dating, and you've just been holding back until now so you could sweep me off my feet in person?"

"What? No," Sam said, a little taken aback. Lowering their mug so quickly it thumped against the tabletop, they said, "This isn't—it's not—I'm just trying not to mess this up, all right? I'm a little rusty at this romance stuff, but I am trying, so . . ." They trailed off uncertainly. "Is it . . . working . . . ?"

"Is it working?" Teddy repeated with a startled laugh. "Sam, you just hung up on your boss so you could finish having breakfast with me. Who would that not work on?" Giving them the kind of look that got Sam's heart racing ten times out of ten, Teddy said those familiar words that they were now pretty sure they would understand in any language: "No sabes todo lo que me haces sentir."

Sam's brain flatlined like it always did in these situations. Investigating crime scenes? They could do that with their eyes closed. Interrogating murderers? No problem at all. Figuring out what to say when a man twelve years too young for them was unabashedly baring his heart? Absolutely nothing. Crickets.

"This is the part where you say . . ." Teddy prompted.

"I still don't speak Spanish," Sam said automatically. When Teddy made a telltale face at the glib response, Sam ducked their head a little and added, "But I'm, ah, really enjoying myself, too."

"Are you enjoying yourself enough to see me again tonight?" Teddy asked. Before Sam could even begin to respond, he was already waving a dismissive hand and saying, "I know, I know. You've got work, and it's bad timing, and I should probably at least pretend to play this cool, but . . . forget all that." Leaning forward to take their hand, Teddy gave them that scrunchy-eyed smile and said, "I'm terrible at playing things cool, and I really want to spend more time with you. As soon as possible. So what do you think?"

"Well," Sam said slowly once their brain started working again. "I think it is terrible timing. Honestly, I think this is probably going to be one of those all-time bad days where I'd normally call you and complain for hours after it's over, anyways." Teddy's smile only grew, and Sam softened helplessly. "But yeah. If you think that sounds like fun for some reason, I'm in."

"Hmm," Teddy hummed sympathetically. Stroking his thumb over the back of their hand in a gesture that was quickly becoming addictive, he asked, "Is there anything I can do that would make today less terrible?"

Sam was quiet for a long minute, and Teddy didn't rush them for a response. He just kept holding their hand, and at some point Sam realized that was all they really wanted.

"Today isn't terrible yet," Sam finally said. Offering him a tiny smile, they squeezed his hand and said, "And if it does go wrong, just knowing you'll be there at the end will be . . . good."

"Done," Teddy promised. Reaching up to tug playfully at the collar of Sam's jacket with his free hand, he said, "You know, I can do better than just being there for you. If you give me a key to your place, I could even have dinner ready for when you get home. Maybe some candles and flowers, if you ask extra nicely."

"Teddy," Sam laughed with exasperation, although they didn't try to stop him from reeling them in a little closer. "You can't ask someone for a key to their place on the first date."

"Well, I'll give it back tomorrow," Teddy said, as though that was really the problem here. "Come on," he cajoled. His knuckle traced the curve of Sam's cheek, and Sam thought their heart might explode. "What's so wrong with letting me spoil you, hmm? Doesn't that sound nice?"

Sam wanted to say it did sound nice. Too nice, actually. There was no way a guy like Teddy should be content to wait around for them at the end of the day. They wanted to ask him not to tempt them so much with things that couldn't possibly last.

Instead, they threw those thoughts to the wayside, along with the rest of their willpower, and released his hand so they could reach inside their jacket pocket. Teddy only drew them in closer as Sam fumbled with their key ring until they could loosen the spare key. The dull metal disappeared inside Teddy's pocket the second Sam pressed it into his palm.

Then Teddy was leaning in, and Sam was on the very edge of their seat, and they were kissing over the scrambled eggs with all the eager gracelessness of two teenagers on a first date. Only Sam was not a teenager—they were an adult with an apartment that had been very empty for a very long time. If this sweet man wanted to make it a little less empty for a while, that was a fantasy they would gladly indulge in for as long as it lasted.

"Sam?"

A familiar, disbelieving voice shattered that fantasy like a bolt of lightning on a sunny day.

"Shit," Sam cursed, pulling back from the kiss so quickly that their chair rocked beneath them. Teddy looked a little dazed, and Sam quickly scrubbed a hand across their face, hoping against hope that they didn't look quite so lovestruck.

When they dared to look over at the street, they saw Noah, of all people, standing there on the sidewalk next to the patio railing. He looked as casual as Sam did this Saturday morning in his hoodie and jeans. The professional part of Sam took in the way Noah's shirt didn't quite lie flat against the small of his back and how his tightly laced sneakers contrasted sharply with the tripping hazards he normally strapped to his feet. The less professional part of them saw that his jaw was practically on the pavement, and they hoped to god for an excuse to arrest him so he could never tell anyone at work what he'd seen.

Glaring over at him, Sam asked, "What the hell are you doing here, Noah?"

"Noah?" Teddy echoed sharply, and Sam had to force themself not to react.

As if they weren't already very aware something was wrong here. It wasn't even 10 a.m. yet—still hours from when Noah was supposed to be meeting with "Eddie"—and yet here he was hanging out mere blocks from the rendezvous location. Maybe he was smarter than Sam thought, and he was here to scope out the area for any traps. Maybe he was just doing some Saturday morning grocery shopping.

All Sam knew for sure was that if Noah hadn't gotten wise yet, they couldn't let him get suspicious now. At least this time they probably wouldn't need to do the entire Notebook routine to shake him off.

"Yeah, this is Noah," Sam said gruffly. Leaning into their embarrassment, they flicked a glance between Noah and Teddy and said, "He's a coworker. I think I probably mentioned him to you before."

"Wow. Didn't know I was so popular," Noah said cheerfully. Sam still found it hard to see the gangster under the goofy smile in response to having obviously busted Sam in the middle of a real date.

Noah stuck his hand out to Teddy over the patio's fencing and said, "I'm Sam's junior officer, Noah Mariano. And you are . . . ?"

"I'm their boyfriend, Teddy," he replied, and Sam nearly fell out of their seat. Teddy just offered Noah an easy smile, like some kind of undercover pro, and accepted the offered hand. "Nice to meet you, Detective Mariano."

"No fuckin' way." Noah shook his hand, but his eyes were glued to Sam's undoubtedly fluorescent face in disbelief. When Sam didn't deny it, he dropped Teddy's hand and said, "You've had a secret boyfriend this whole time?"

"If I told you, then I guess it wouldn't really be a secret anymore, would it?" Sam muttered, and Teddy had the audacity to laugh at their not-so-fake embarrassment. Jerking their chin toward the street corner, Sam said, "Now do me a favor and get lost, kid. I already see enough of your face at work."

"Copy that, boss," Noah said cheerfully. Making a juvenile cross-my-heart gesture, he added, "Don't worry—your secret's safe with me!"

Then he nearly tripped over his own feet spinning around to face the busy intersection. Some bone-chilling criminal he was.

"Oh my god. *That's* the baby cop?" Teddy snickered under his breath the second Noah's back was to them. "He's way too cute to be a gangster."

"He is not cute," Sam grumbled. Resisting the urge to look over their shoulder, they asked, "What's he doing right now?"

"Uh, waiting for the light to change?" Teddy said, although it came out more like a question. Squinting a little at the rookie fidgeting on the corner in his unseasonably warm sweater, Teddy stared for a long moment before suddenly leaning back in his seat. "Oh my god. Under his shirt—is that a—"

"Don't," Sam said sharply. Teddy's eyes widened in surprise, and Sam made a conscious effort to gentle their tone. "Just don't need anyone panicking," they murmured quietly. Teddy still looked nervous but managed not to say anything that would cause a scene on the sleepy restaurant patio.

"Nothing bad is going to happen," Sam assured him as they reached into their jacket pocket for Eddie's burner phone. "I'm just going to talk to him. But first, I need you to head inside to pay the bill."

"But if nothing bad is going to happen, why—" Teddy started, and Sam's hand flashed out to touch his arm warningly when his voice began to rise with concern.

"I know, I know, I said I was going to pay. I told you I'm terrible at this dating thing," Sam said lightly. Teddy settled again, and Sam flashed him a tight smile as they began punching a text into the phone. "I'll make it up to you, I promise. But for now, I really need you to go inside, OK?"

Teddy looked at them for a long moment. And then another. Sam could feel the seconds ticking by as their finger hovered over the Send button, but they refused to rush him. They would rather let Noah walk away than risk Teddy ending up with so much as a paper cut.

"Please be careful," Teddy finally said. Standing up from his seat as casually as a person of his size could on the cramped patio, he paused to pin Sam with those warm puppy-dog eyes. "I'm really counting on that second date, you know." Patting his pocket with their spare key, he said sternly, "So you'd better make it home in one piece, or you're going to have one very unhappy secret boyfriend."

"I would never stand you up, cariño," Sam promised, and despite the lighthearted exchange, they couldn't help letting their eyes flutter shut when Teddy reached down to touch their cheek ever so lightly.

By the time they had opened their eyes again half a heartbeat later, Teddy was already making his way inside like they had asked. Their stomach clenched with a potent mixture of anxiety and relief. It was all a little too much to unpack at the moment, so they turned their attention back to the burner and hit the Send button on their text.

Over on the street corner, the light flipped to the Walk sign, but Noah hesitated before crossing. Oblivious to his audience watching from the restaurant patio, he reached into his hoodie pocket. The second he produced the vibrating burner phone, Sam felt their stomach drop to their toes.

Eddie: Busted.

Noah's head whipped around just in time to see Sam aiming a finger gun directly at him and squeezing the imaginary trigger.

"Sorry, Rook," they called over to him calmly as they stood from their seat. "Looks like you're still not smarter than me."

"Shit." The single syllable was a long, drawn-out hiss as Noah recognized the phone Sam was holding. He took a quick, stumbling step backward and his hand reached automatically for the weapon concealed under his sweater.

"Hey," Sam barked, and half the heads in the café turned in the direction of the commotion. Sam kept their eyes laser-focused on Noah's frozen position. The frightened, almost baffled look on his face said innocent rookie. The hand reaching for his hidden Glock screamed danger.

"You drop that hand right now, or I will put you in the ground, you understand me?" Sam's voice was sharp with warning.

Noah remained stock-still except for his wide eyes, which slid almost imperceptibly toward the busy intersection that represented his easiest means of escape.

"Don't even think about it," Sam warned. Their hand tightened around the metal railing that separated the patio from the sidewalk. "I don't know what kind of mess you're caught up in, but—"

Noah broke before they could even finish their plea. Those normally clumsy feet hit the pavement at a dead sprint, and Sam let out a loud curse. It was better than outright drawing on them, but not by much. Some part of Sam had still wanted this to be a big misunderstanding, but that hope was disappearing around the corner along with the rest of their fleeing rookie.

Noah might be a dumbass, but he wasn't stupid. He knew as well as Sam did that a person who started running rarely got to stop. Especially when said person was registered as a cop in every database from here to New York City.

And yet he was running anyway, which could really only mean one thing.

Not pausing to worry about optics, Sam used their grip on the banister to vault the metal railing in one easy move. One patron let out a startled cry at the sudden movement, but the disturbance dissipated in their wake as Sam put all their energy into giving chase.

A car screeched to a halt as they darted across the street with barely enough time to avoid becoming roadkill. Sam swore under their breath again as they caught sight of the alley where Noah had disappeared. If he really wanted to hurt them, he could be waiting right there with gun drawn. They could only hope he wouldn't make a liar out of them less than thirty seconds after they promised Teddy they'd make it back for that second date in one piece.

Cranking up the pace, they whipped around the corner just in time to see that Noah had almost finished dragging a heavy-looking dumpster across the alley to block their path. Catching sight of Sam coming toward him, he quickly turned and booked it again.

Stupid kid. What did he think was honestly going to happen at the end of this little cat-and- mouse game, even if he did manage to shake them today?

Jumping up on top of the dumpster, Sam rolled their way across at least ten too many smelly bags of god-knows-what before landing on the other side. Noah was hesitating at the far side of the alley, and they knew why. Left was a much longer journey back toward the church. Right was a shorter path to his Uncle Ricky's diner, where he'd be guaranteed to find some friendly faces and a place where Sam couldn't get him without a warrant.

"Hey!" Sam snapped, and the kid jumped half a foot in the air at the sound of their voice gaining on him.

Cocking their arm back, Sam chucked Eddie's burner phone as hard as they could. It smashed off the wall to Noah's left about a million miles away from actually hitting him, but it had the desired effect. Noah dodged right toward Ricky's, and Sam knew they had him now.

Realistically, there was no chance that Sam would ever catch him in a foot race. Noah was younger than them, faster than them, and even with two left feet, he simply had the energy to keep up this killer pace a lot longer than Sam could. In a fair race, he would win every single time. But unfortunately for him, this wasn't a fair race.

The next time Noah made a turn, Sam kept running straight. From here, there was only one direct route to Ricky's, and Sam was willing to stake their badge on him not taking any detours. Their lungs were burning, their hips felt like they were full of broken glass, and they were seriously regretting everything after round two last night, but they knew Noah wouldn't be slowing down with the finish line in sight, so they couldn't let up either.

Thank god for shortcuts.

Ducking down an alley most people wouldn't dare drive down, Sam dodged fire escapes and hurdled garbage bins. They nearly wiped out on the hairpin turn back to the next street over, but they managed to keep their feet. Way past the point of being polite, Sam barreled into the little hair salon that occupied one of the bottom units on a towering office building.

"Ladies," Sam managed as the women inside shrieked in surprise.

They didn't stick around to explain as they made a beeline for the stairs at the back of the shop. Each step was a cruel reminder of this morning's run. They threw open the door to the second floor, revealing a dreary office building.

So close. *So close.* They just needed to pick up the pace a little more and this might actually work.

At the back of the office, the tantalizing Exit sign hung over the heavy-duty emergency door. Jamming their shoulder into the push bar, Sam stumbled out onto the fire escape landing beyond. For a second, they were disoriented seeing the Paths building from this angle, but catching sight of Noah's blurry form still moving at a good clip on the street below was all the motivation they needed to get reoriented.

Taking the stairs three at a time, Sam hit the cracked pavement with enough impact to send them stumbling forward. Their eyes were focused only on the narrow entrance to the building's closed alleyway. With one last burst of speed, they sprinted the final few steps and arrived back on the main street just in time to intercept their fleeing rookie.

Sam didn't have the energy for anything fancy, so instead they just stepped right into Noah's path and took the impact directly on their shoulder. They cursed loudly at the crunch of bone on bone, but they locked their knees and absorbed the hit.

Noah should have known from the second his ass hit the pavement and Sam managed to stay upright that the fight was over, but Sam had to give it to the kid—he had no quit in him. They let him almost get back to his feet before their fist connected solidly with his jaw and sent him right back down again.

Grabbing him by the collar, Sam hauled Noah back into the alley and sent him sprawling onto the pavement. Again Noah staggered to his feet, and again a booted foot to his gut sent him stumbling backward. This time he managed to keep his feet, at least. He quickly twisted around in search of new escape routes that didn't involve getting his ass kicked, which was a rookie move if there ever was one. Darting forward, Sam snatched the gun out of Noah's waistband and used his forward momentum to send him tumbling back to the ground.

"Stay down," Sam ordered, pointing the gun at Noah's prone form with steady hands.

Well, maybe steady hands—Sam didn't dare take their eyes off of the kid to be sure as their vision tunneled. Every gasping breath felt like a knife was being driven into their ribs, but Sam gritted their teeth and forced their arms to stay up.

"Or what?" Noah challenged. Despite the fact that he was lying on the ground with his hands up, he didn't quite look intimidated by the sight of Sam swaying on their feet after that little sprint.

"Or I'm going to shoot you in the kneecap."

"Yeah, right. Do you even know how to use that thing?" Before Sam's sluggish brain could even think of a response, Noah had rolled back to his feet in a flash.

"You're not going to shoot me," he said, sounding a little more confident when his kneecaps remained intact. "You haven't even taken the safety off."

Sam stared at him for a long moment before letting their arms drop. "'Course I'm not going to shoot you," they said. Before Noah could go looking too excited, they gestured with the gun to the fire escape behind him and said, "Your dumb ass has been on camera from the second you stepped into this alley. Including the part where I took this unregistered .43 out of your pants."

"What?" Noah nearly did a full 360 in his haste to see where Sam was pointing. "Where?"

"Bird's nest."

"Shit. Fuck," he swore, sounding a little more like his usual frazzled self as he caught sight of the little camera poking out of the struts beneath the fire escape where Sam had put it last night. They could see real panic on his face when he turned back to face them this time. "OK. OK. I know this looks bad, but this isn't—"

"This isn't what it looks like. It's not what you think," Sam mocked, then let out a small cough.

Noah's eyes darted toward the street, and Sam lifted the gun a threatening inch. They weren't planning to shoot him, but they weren't above throwing it at his oversized cranium, either, if he decided to run again. They surely didn't have the energy left to give chase.

"I've heard that before," Sam said, and despite their thin voice, Noah still looked plenty frightened. "Tell me something new."

"I don't know—"

"Oh, 'I don't know what you're talking about?' That's a classic, too." Gesturing at Noah with the gun, Sam asked, "Where is it?" When he didn't answer, Sam narrowed their eyes. "I asked you a question, kid. Where's the gang tattoo?"

"What's the point?" Noah muttered.

Sam was surprised to hear the defeat in his voice.

Noah glanced over his shoulder at the camera and said, "You're not going to believe me. And I'm already fucked anyways."

Sam considered him for a long moment. They weren't sure what they'd expected from this confrontation. Maybe for him to drop the bumbling rookie act and reveal the cold-blooded criminal beneath. Maybe some super-easy explanation for how this was all one big misunderstanding.

But as with most things in life, it seemed like easy wasn't on the table.

"That reminds me of something my last perp said," Sam said as they ejected the clip and the bullet from the chamber with ease. Noah's surprised gaze jerked back to them. Maybe he really was dumb enough to think they didn't know their way around a gun. "Your cousin seemed to think he was pretty screwed after I busted him, too. Only he said it was because you'd be putting two bullets in the back of his head before he could even think about talking to the cops."

"*Eddie* said that?" Noah demanded in a voice full of disbelief.

"So he is your cousin."

"By blood, maybe," Noah scoffed. When Sam raised a silent eyebrow, he scowled and said, "Obviously we're not that related if he seriously thinks Uncle Nico could talk me into doing his dirty laundry."

"Uncle Nico?" Sam echoed. Noah stiffened but didn't answer the implied question. "That the name Father Nicholas goes by when he's catching the game at Uncle Ricky's?"

"Well, he is a real priest, so Sunday morning football is kinda out of the question." Seeing that Sam was not amused, Noah released a small sigh. "Yeah. Uncle Nico. Father Nicholas. Padre Romano. Whatever you wanna call him, he's the top dog." His expression was bitter when he looked away and added, "Not over me, though. Not that I expect you to believe me."

"I would have twenty-four hours ago," Sam said, and Noah flinched a little at the disappointment in their voice. "Little harder now knowing you're the kind of guy who can look at a picture of his family member on a metal slab and pretend not to know her. Makes the trust thing a little shakier, you know?"

"Nikki had nothing to do with any of this," Noah snapped. Sam gave him a look, and that guilty expression returned to his face. "OK, she was a dealer for her dad, but I swear to god that had nothing to do with what happened to her. I talked to Nico myself. He—he was devastated. He said—"

"Her dad?" Sam asked sharply. "I thought Nikki's last name was Russo?" Noah's mouth snapped shut, but it was too late. Observing him coolly now, Sam said, "For that matter, yours actually is Mariano, according to your record."

"Dude. You ran a background check on me?" he protested.

"Of course I did. You've been lying to my face for six weeks straight," Sam said without an ounce of sympathy. "About Father D'Angelo. About Father Nicholas. Nikki's occupation, and letting Eddie go after the mixer. Jesus, Noah—is there anything you didn't lie to me about?"

Once again, Noah fell silent. Sam wished he didn't look like such a kicked puppy. It would have made this a lot easier if he could have just been the conniving villain his actions made him out to be.

Hardening their resolve, Sam asked, "How'd you become a police officer in the first place with connections like that?"

"Easy. I don't have connections like that," Noah said, although Sam thought the bitter note in his voice wasn't really directed at them. "I'm not part of the gang. You can strip search me if you want. I don't have the tattoo. Hell, you said it yourself, I don't even have the Romano name. Mom gave me hers to keep me out of . . . all this."

That bitter note had doubled in potency, and despite their best efforts to remain stone cold, Sam felt the faintest twinge of sympathy. Nobody had to tell them how heavy a last name could be. But then again, they had never gotten tangled up in any murders, despite their own family history.

"How'd your dad take that?"

"How do you think? The asshole made her pay for it for the next twenty years." Noah glared at the wall of the Paths building like he was picturing his old man's face right now. "GIU practically threw a party on his grave in 2018. Mom probably woulda joined in if she wasn't already lying next door."

"I guess that left a bit of a void in the family."

"For ten whole seconds, maybe."

Sam gave him a pointed look.

Noah threw up his hands in exasperation. "Look, I don't know what you want me to say. Nico is a bad guy. He was just as happy as GIU when my dad bit it. But I didn't choose to be his nephew, and Nikki sure as hell didn't choose to be bastard offspring number three. Sharing a bloodline with that creep doesn't make either of us guilty."

"No, but becoming a cop to help clean up his messes from the inside does."

"I told you, Eddie doesn't know what he's talking about," Noah muttered, once again retreating under their sharp scrutiny. "I'm not saying Nico wouldn't do something like that, but he wouldn't ask me. He knows I wouldn't do it."

"Are you sure he knows that?" Sam pressed. Weighing Noah's unloaded .43 in their hand, they said, "Covering up a murder is only one step away from pulling the trigger yourself. And he already knows you'll do that for him."

If Sam hadn't already been sure, the guilt that flashed across Noah's face was more than enough to confirm their suspicions.

"Seriously, Noah?" Sam said, their voice thick with disappointment. "What the hell were you thinking? You thought if you stayed away from GIU and Vice that you could be a cop and still have dinner every Sunday with a bunch of gangsters and not get yourself in trouble?"

"I was thinking I wanted to make this city a little less shitty. Maybe make up for some of the lives my old man ruined before GIU finally got him."

Despite the fierce words, Noah still looked completely defeated. That, more than anything, made Sam believe him when he said, "I just wanted to make a difference."

"Then why the hell didn't you say anything?" Sam demanded. "You must have known what he did. Father Nicholas—Uncle Nico, whatever you want to call him—you must have known the second you set foot inside that church, if not sooner."

"I didn't—" Noah started.

"Then you strongly suspected," Sam said firmly. "And yet Father Nicholas is still giving the Sunday sermon, and Father D'Angelo is in the ground with your parents. Is that your idea of making a difference?"

"Of course not. I was just—I made a mistake, all right?" Noah's voice cracked a little, and Sam's insides twisted at the sight of him getting emotional.

Talk about mistakes. Sam should never have come here alone. They should have told Vince, or Donovan, or anyone else, really. It was foolish to think they'd be able to stay objective when they'd basically been holding this stupid kid's hand for the last six weeks.

"I was fucking shattered when I found out about Nikki, OK?" Noah continued. "Drug dealer or not, she is—she *was* my baby cousin. And then Father D just a few days later? I thought Nico might know something, so I went to ask before I was ever even assigned to the Paths case." His voice was gruff as he scrubbed a hand across his eyes like he was angry at them for betraying his emotion. "Only it turns out, Nikki got stabbed because she boned the wrong creep on that stupid app, and Father D, he—" Noah's hand dropped limply to his side. Angry. Sad. And ultimately helpless. "Well, I guess he heard one confession too many. Nico was convinced he was going to the cops, so he took care of the problem." Looking Sam in the eye, even knowing the camera over his shoulder was capturing his every word, Noah confessed, "He told me so himself."

Mistake. Mistake, mistake, mistake. Sam's brain was screaming at them to get it together. Puppy dog eyes were no reason to go soft now. He was literally confessing to covering up a murder—a murder that he himself had been assigned to investigate.

And yet instead of arresting him on the spot, Sam found themself asking, "Why'd you cover up for him?"

"Because he knew there was no way for me to prove it," Noah said flatly. His gaze was far away and full of bitter regrets. "I didn't know what else to do. It would have been my word against his, and Nico—he's got friends. Powerful friends."

"Friends like Mayor Kelso, you mean," Sam said bluntly, recalling Nico's transparent threats in the confessional booth the previous day.

"Yeah. Like Kelso. And a whole lotta others," Noah confirmed. "I'm sorry, boss. I know I fucked up. I know I should have found a way to—I don't know. To get the evidence, or at least tell you, but . . ." His voice cracked again, and he cleared his throat impatiently. "Anyways. I know what I did, so . . . do what you gotta do. I'm ready."

He didn't look ready. Not that anyone was ever really ready to be arrested for covering up a murder—even one he couldn't realistically have closed, given the lack of viable evidence.

If they played this by the book, it would be the wrong move for Sam to help him out of this tough spot. But leaving their rookie to drown in his own mistakes would feel twice as wrong. And Sam had never really been a fan of following rules that made no sense.

"When it comes to taking down a connected guy like Nico, you have to be sure you've got the smoking gun. Something so bad and blatant, even the most powerful allies wouldn't risk protecting him."

Noah's head shot up at the sound of Sam's careful words. It gave Sam a dizzying moment of déjà vu to that moment back on Paradiso when Teddy had been so sure Sam was going to arrest him for withholding the master key. Two people who had done stupid, boneheaded things that Sam had been stuck cleaning up. Two people who maybe deserved to face the music, but who they simply didn't have the heart to turn their back on.

Apparently, they did have a type after all.

"Don't you think I would if I could? I woulda done anything—anything—to get the evidence for Father D. But it's long gone now," Noah said in a voice laced with heartache and frustration. "I've got nothing but my word against Nico's. No one will ever believe—"

"I'm not talking about Father D'Angelo's murder. You'll never get him for that," Sam said impatiently.

Feeling the weight of the .43 in their hands, Sam gave Noah a long, hard look. Then they took two swift steps closer so they could grab his wrist roughly. His eyes widened in surprise when they pressed the gun into his hand. He tried to pull back, but Sam just placed their hand over his and curled his fingers around the grip forcibly.

Looking him dead in the eye, Sam squeezed hard and said, "Sometimes the only way to prove someone is willing to shoot is if you hand them the gun yourself. You understand me?"

Noah swallowed hard at the sound of their serious words. He still looked scared, but also like he understood exactly what they were saying. Maybe he had known all along that this was his only option for taking Nico down but had lacked the courage to do it on his own.

Sam wasn't sure. But they knew Noah wasn't alone now. And building a rookie's confidence was all part of being a good supervisor.

Slowly, Noah nodded, and Sam released his hand. The gun remained in his grip, empty and not pointed at anything, but still cutting an intimidating image against the backdrop of the alley. The perfect illusion.

Nodding back, Sam said grimly, "Good. Now, tell me what it'll take to make Nico pull the trigger—and you'd better be right."

CHAPTER TWENTY-NINE

Vivienne: I'm here with Kayleigh. Text when you get here.
Vivienne: Are you on your way?
Vivienne: She's asking questions, Sam. Where are you?

Sam glanced down at their phone as they pushed through the hospital's doors. Vivienne's messages had come in over an hour ago. They had already blown well past their optimistic arrival time of 10:00 a.m., but there wasn't a lot to be done about it at this point.

Sam: Here now. Which room?

Vivienne: Thank god. What took you so long?
Vivienne: 721

Sam shoved the phone back into their pocket and headed for the elevators rather than answering. It had gone against their every instinct to leave Noah prepping for this afternoon's op on his own, but it was the only choice. They needed to get their head out of his mess and back into their own case.

Kayleigh Evergreen had been stabbed at the mixer. She was now awake. If they were really lucky, she might even have some answers about her attacker before Sam's rendezvous with Jason tonight. If they were really, really lucky they might even be able to help Noah and take down Kayleigh's would-be killer all in one day.

A nurse hurried to try and catch the elevator, and Sam jabbed the Close button three times in rapid succession. They felt nothing but relief as the nurse's irritated face disappeared behind the steel doors. Followed by a wave of bitter self-loathing.

Who were they kidding? They'd be *really, really lucky* if they could just make it through this interview without hyperventilating.

Cramming their shaking hands into their jacket pockets, Sam stepped off the elevator and made their way directly to room 721. The moment they turned the corner, they caught sight of an anxious-looking Vivienne pacing back and forth in front of the closed door. She looked much as she had at Sam's apartment earlier. The statuesque woman leaning against the wall next to her was a new addition, though.

"Sam!" Vivienne called the moment she caught sight of them. Hurrying in their direction, she asked, "Where have you been? Did something happen?"

"What?" Sam replied, and her anxious scrutiny did little to make them feel less tense in this already stressful environment. Drawing to a halt several feet away, Sam said, "Everything's fine. What are you even doing here?"

"Oh, well, I'm personally footing Kayleigh's medical bills, so . . ." Vivienne said with a vague wave of her hand.

"Right. And I'm sure your wife working here had nothing at all to do with you getting the tip-off," Sam said, and Harper grimaced in response from her spot up against the wall.

It made sense that an anesthesiologist would be alerted when a patient in a medically induced coma finally improved enough to be woken up, but Sam doubted that was the reason she was still hanging around like Vivienne's personal guard dog.

"Yes, I did call her when it became evident you wouldn't be arriving anytime soon," Harper said stiffly. Vivienne gave her a sharp look, and she forced a smile. "I just thought the patient could use a friendly face while she waited. And I knew Vivienne would want to offer her sympathies."

"Right," Sam repeated slowly. "That was . . . nice of you. I guess."

"What took you so long, anyway?" Vivienne asked with a frown. "Last I heard, you were taking Teddy out for—"

"Detective Mariano needed my help on his case," Sam said quickly, before she could finish that thought. Vivienne's eyes widened in surprise, and they clarified, "Nothing serious. I handled things, but it did put me behind schedule, so . . ." Looking uncertainly to Harper, they nodded at the door to her right and said, "Would it be all right for me to speak with Ms. Evergreen now?"

"Yes. She's only been awake for about three hours. We've gone over all the basics of her injuries and how she ended up here, but she might still be a little overwhelmed," Harper said shortly.

"OK," Sam said. They drew in a slow breath as they sized up the closed door. "OK. Thank you."

For a long beat, there was silence as all three of them waited for someone else to make the next move. Sam knew they were supposed to go into the room now. They should just do it—for Christ's sake, talking to a girl in a hospital bed shouldn't be harder than accusing their rookie of covering up a murder.

But their boots remained firmly rooted to the polished concrete floor.

"Harper, honey," Vivienne said after a long moment, and Sam gritted their teeth against the soft understanding in her voice. Vivienne laid a gentle hand on her wife's arm and said, "Could you maybe give Detective Sam a minute? I'm sure they've got a lot to sort through before—"

"Viv." Harper cut Sam a glare, and Sam rolled their eyes. They were way too anxious to play this game right now, but they didn't need Vivienne covering for them, either.

"Would you just relax?" Sam said. Wrenching their hands out of their pockets, they unfurled their fists so the whole hallway could see the way their hands shook violently. "She's not sending you away to make a move or something. She's just worried that I'm going to have a panic attack if I go in there." Giving Vivienne a pointed look as they let their hands drop, they added, "But I'm *fine*."

"OK, fine," Vivienne said, folding her arms crossly. "First Teddy, now this. I should just stop trying to help."

"No, you shouldn't," Harper said, and Sam was surprised to see a hint of tenderness on the stony woman's face. Her eyes were only for Vivienne when she touched her wife's shoulder gently and said, "It's amazing how much you care." Giving Sam a look perhaps two degrees warmer than what they'd been getting so far, she added, "If you think you might need assistance during the interview . . ."

"Uh, no. That would be the opposite of helpful," Sam said, feeling their gut clench at the thought. They quickly tucked their hands back into their pockets and admitted, "Not a big fan of doctors, you know? No offense."

"Sure."

Sam had to admire Harper's professionality, if not her bedside manner.

Giving them a short nod, Harper said, "If you or the patient do find yourself needing help, it's the red button."

Sam nodded back silently, and Harper took that as the signal that she could leave. Vivienne immediately began to follow, but Harper stopped her with a firm hand. Glancing over her shoulder at Sam, she murmured, "It's fine. Stay. Take care of your friend." Then she pressed a firm kiss to her wife's forehead before disappearing down the hallway.

Well. Sam couldn't blame Vivienne for looking a little dazzled. Brooding didn't even begin to describe the icy monolith that was Harper Fox, and Sam had to admit there was something a little swoon-worthy about the whole act.

"Shall we?" Sam asked when Vivienne looked like she was back to earth again. Even if she wasn't, there was no time to lose. Sam reached past her for the door to Kayleigh's room.

When they stepped inside, Sam couldn't help but be struck by how all hospital rooms somehow managed to look exactly the same. The familiar sterility of the blank white walls had Sam breaking out in a cold sweat. They reminded themself that Kayleigh needed them to keep it together right now. They could not afford to have a panic attack. Besides, nothing in this place could hurt them. Not anymore.

Not that any amount of logic was going to make that panic attack less likely.

Instead, Sam appealed to emotion. Focusing on Kayleigh's pale, wide-eyed face as she turned to see her visitors, Sam reminded themself of what it felt like to wake up in this place. Alone. Frightened. Not sure what had happened or what would happen next. And it gave them the strength to breathe deeply and approach her bed.

"Kayleigh Evergreen?" Sam asked.

"That's me," the woman in the bed said quickly. Her voice was dry and tight from nearly three weeks of sleep. "Are you the detective? Can you tell me what's going on here?"

"Yes. My name is Detective Sam," they said, holding one hand out to her. Kayleigh's grip was soft, but her eyes were sharp as she accepted Sam's trembling handshake. Offering her a rueful smile, Sam said, "I will warn you, I'm a homicide detective, so while I'm grateful to have a victim who's alive, my bedside manner might be a little rusty."

"Oh," Kayleigh said. She looked a little uncomfortable, but at least no longer concerned with Sam's tense disposition. "Why a homicide detective? Or . . . how does that even work? Is there such a thing as just normal detectives?"

"There are general criminal investigators, yes," Sam told her as they pulled up chairs, first for Vivienne, then for themself. "Normally that's who would be assigned to your case. But because we're currently examining a string of incidents that may or may not be related, including the attack on you, the department felt it was best to have one senior detective taking point on the entire case."

Kayleigh was quiet for a moment as she considered Sam's words. Finally, she said, "So you're saying this has happened to other women." Her eyes looked a little unfocused as her arms curled gingerly around her body. "The—the stabbing. And not everyone else . . ."

"That's right. Several other women have been assaulted, and so far you're the only survivor," Sam said, because there was no point in dancing around the truth. "We don't know for sure that your case is related to the rest, but we have to explore every possibility."

"What makes you think the cases are related? Just the stabbing?" Kayleigh asked. Touching her side, she asked, "Is it the weapon? Or clues at the crime scene, or—"

"Are you a big fan of murder mysteries, Kayleigh?"

"I may have listened to a few true crime podcasts," she admitted. "I just never thought I'd be the subject of one. I mean, I'm no one." She gestured down at herself, as though that would explain her point. Sam just saw a nice-enough-looking adult woman. Probably better than nice-enough-looking once she'd had a chance to shower and put on something other than a hospital dressing gown. But obviously Kayleigh didn't see herself that way, because she said, "I'm just a sad, single corporate lawyer with no personal life and a mountain of student debt. Why would anyone want to attack me?"

"That's part of what I want to talk to you about," Sam said. They shifted slightly in their chair as they reached for their trusty tape recorder—which wasn't there, of course. Stupid last-minute interviews. Pulling out their phone instead, Sam said, "You mentioned being single. That's something all the victims have had in common so far. In fact, you all used the same dating app."

"You mean Paths?" Kayleigh made a face, and Vivienne stiffened out of the corner of Sam's eye.

"Yes, that's the one." Gesturing to the beautiful woman sitting next to them, Sam explained, "This is Vivienne Fox, the owner of the Paths app.

We're trying to make sure no one is exploiting her app for anything other than its intended purposes."

"I am so sorry for what happened to you," Vivienne said the moment Kayleigh's eyes landed on her. Sam could see what Harper had meant when Vivienne offered Kayleigh the kind of sincere gaze that went beyond surface-level sympathy. "The police have our full support in getting to the bottom of this. If my app was the reason—or even just the tool to facilitate this violence—we will do anything within our power to ensure no one else gets hurt. And in the meantime, please consider our resources at your disposal while you're recovering. If you need food, or entertainment, or—"

"The police appreciate Mrs. Fox's generosity," Sam cut in before Vivienne could get too carried away promising Kayleigh the world. Holding up their cell phone, Sam said, "We don't want to jump to any conclusions, though. Would it be all right if I asked you some questions and recorded your answers to help out the investigation?"

"As long as you promise it's not for a podcast," Kayleigh said, and Sam smiled at her sardonic sense of humor. Hopefully she'd be able to hold onto that when these questions got a little more personal.

Recording #6: Kayleigh Evergreen

The recording begins with the soft tap of a finger on glass. The sound quality is crisp and clear, with no discernible background noise other than the beep of a heart monitor. Overall, it's much less satisfying than if it were, say, a tape recorder.

"Would you mind stating your name for the record?"

"Kayleigh Marie Evergreen."

"Do you prefer Kayleigh or Ms. Evergreen?"

"I'm already thirty-six and single. If people start calling me 'Ms.' outside the boardroom, I might save this guy the trouble of having to stab me again."

There is the sound of a startled half-laugh.

"All right, Kayleigh. We'll do our best to avoid any more stabbings. Can you tell me what you remember about the night of the mixer?"

"Sure. It kind of feels like it was yesterday, but I guess it was . . . three weeks ago . . . ?"

"That's correct. It's July now. Mid-July, actually."

"Wow, that's . . . so weird. Because I remember before the mixer thinking it had been weirdly cool out that week, but that I should wear something lighter to the party so I wouldn't end up smelling like I just came from the gym. The room where they hold the mixers gets so hot when everyone starts showing up."

"So you'd say the experience would be better if the temperature control was improved?"

"Mrs. Fox . . . "

"Sorry, sorry. Not relevant."

"What happened after you got to the mixer?"

"I don't know. I just talked to some guys, I guess? This was only the second mixer I'd been to. I wasn't even sure I was going to go that night, since . . . "

"Since . . . ?"

"Sorry. It's just messing with my mind a little. I had just been out the night before with this guy I was seeing—before all this. Nothing serious. But now . . . I don't know. I guess he probably thinks I ghosted him or something."

"What was the guy's name?"

"Why, do you think he stabbed me because I was at the mixer?"

"That would be one motive. But this is more about confirmation. We've already seen your dating history."

"What? I thought that stuff was private?"

"Not during murder investigations."

"Oh . . . I guess that makes sense. It is kind of creepy, though. You didn't read my messages, did you?"

"I did."

" . . . "

" . . . "

"Well, I don't love that."

"I don't love it, either. But it's the only way to make sure we're observing every possible connection between the victims."

". . . Right."

" . . . "

" . . . "

"So, can you tell me the guy's name?"

"Jason. Jason Albertalli. You don't think he did this, do you?"

" . . . "

"Oh god, you do. Great. I can't even have a casual hookup without the guy turning out to be some kind of psycho. Why would I even think—"

"Did you see Jason that night? At the mixer?"

"What? No. That wasn't really his scene."

"So you only ever saw him on dates? Never any other time?"

"Well, no, obviously not never."

" . . . ?"

"We both work over in the West End. He's at Wellesley Alexander's, and I'm with Langstaff and Sons, and they're practically across the street from each other."

"So you didn't meet on the app?"

"No, we did. I didn't know him before we matched on the app, but after I found out he worked in the area, I did notice him in passing a few times."

"Did you ever stop and say hello? When you saw him in passing."

". . . sometimes? I don't know. Like maybe a wave hello, yeah."

"Did he say hello back?"

"I guess? Would be pretty rude not to."

"Interesting."

" . . . "

"How many dates did you and Jason actually go on?"

"Don't you already know?"

"You sound a little defensive."

"I spend all day reading contracts for a living. I know how to spot the small print when I see it."

"Fair enough. Let me be more direct. Were you aware that Jason is married?"

" . . . "

"It's not a judgement. I just need to know for the sake of the—"

"Yes. I was aware."

"All right. And that didn't bother you?"

"No. He was upfront about being in an open marriage. He knew I was looking for something more serious, but as long as we were on the same page that what we had was just for fun while I kept looking, it worked for us."

"So you weren't concerned that he might get . . . attached?"

"Uh, no. The guy was way too into his wife to worry about that."

"Really?"

"Big-time. It kind of made me—"

" . . . "

" . . . "

"It made you . . . ?"

"I don't know. I guess I found it a little inspiring. It's easy to fall into a relationship, but it's hard to find something that's worth trying for, you know? It was kind of nice to meet someone who had figured out how to make it work."

"Interesting. So you really got the sense that Jason loved his wife, and it was a genuine open relationship?"

"Honestly, I think she kind of got off on it, too. It all tied into her research or something."

"Did you ever speak with Mrs. Albertalli? Or . . . meet her?"

"If you mean did she ever join us in bed, then no. I did hear him talking to her on the phone one time, though."

"And?"

"And what? It was all just 'I love yous' and 'see you soons.' Normal married stuff. Like I said, it was kind of inspiring."

". . ."

". . ."

"Did Jason ever seem dangerous to you? Manipulative, or aggressive, or . . . ?"

"Not really. I guess he was pretty physical, but that was sort of the point. I wasn't expecting flowers or anything."

"Right. And you're sure he wasn't there the night of the mixer?"

"No. I would have noticed. The guys that night weren't exactly all-stars."

"That's true."

"How would you know? Are there cameras at those things or something?"

"Absolutely not. We would never film our clients without their express permission."

"Mrs. Fox is correct. I was at the mixer that night interviewing any men who might have connections to the other victims."

"I didn't see anyone being interviewed . . . ?"

". . . They were very casual interviews. Do you remember anything from the actual attack?"

"Sort of. It's a little blurry, but I remember leaving since the crowd was thinning out and the best conversation I'd had so far was with this stuck-up tech exec who wouldn't shut up about his boring-ass job, so . . . it was that kind of night."

"And after you left?"

"I was standing by the curb, waiting for my Uber. It was only a block away when I heard the door open behind me. Then someone grabbed me by the shoulder from behind, like—like this. Pulling me backward."

"You're sure your attacker came from inside the building?"

"I heard someone come out. I guess I can't say that's who stabbed me for sure, though."

"Did you see who it was? When they pulled you backward?"

"No. All I remember after they grabbed me was this white-hot pain in my lower back, like nothing I had ever felt before. I have bits and pieces of lying on the sidewalk after, but mainly I just remember being so cold. It felt like . . . I don't know. Like being trapped under ice. I kept wanting to get up and say I was fine, but I couldn't move. And then I was waking up here three weeks later, so . . . guess I wasn't fine."

"All right. That's very helpful."

" . . . "

" . . . "

"Did I say something wrong?"

"No. That's just the face they make when they're thinking."

"That's a pretty pissed-off thinking face."

"I'm not pissed off. I'm just trying to figure out how this information lines up with everything else we know so far."

"Well, I . . . maybe I can try to remember something else? I don't know, maybe—maybe I did see something. Or maybe Jason was there, and I just missed him? Or—"

"Kayleigh."

" . . . "

"You don't need to remember anything. You only saw what you saw. And more importantly, you're the victim here. It's my job to solve the case. Your only job is to focus on getting better. All right?"

"OK . . . OK. But . . . what if . . . what if whoever did it comes back?"

"I told you, it's my job to solve the case. That means getting this guy before anyone else, including you, can get hurt. Whether that person is Jason or someone else entirely, you're going to be perfectly safe as long as I'm around."

" . . ."

"How about we start from the top again? You can tell me everything you remember from that day, and maybe we'll jog something else loose."

"Yeah . . . OK. I guess that might help."

"All right. Let's go back a little further this time. What do you remember from that morning?"

"Well I—I think I slept in a little? Or maybe I just forgot to set my alarm. I was out pretty late the night before. Jason and I met up at this little bar called The Imperial, and I guess we lost track of time after the first few drinks . . ."

CHAPTER THIRTY

". . . do this?"

"Huh?" Sam asked, snapping back to attention.

"I asked if you're going to be all right to do this?" Noah repeated, with a frown at the sight of their unusually pale face. "You kinda look like you're about to pass out, boss."

"I'm fine," Sam said too sharply for someone who was 'fine'. Looking down at the little blue inhaler in their shaking hand, they said, "Are you sure this is going to work?"

"I dunno. I'm not a doctor. McBride thought it might help stave off the effects a little longer," Noah said with a shrug.

Sam's hand clenched around the inhaler. Breathing in deeply, they tried to convince themself that they had to do this. It was logical. It made sense. It was just a regular puffer that wouldn't do anything bad to them. If anything, it might increase their odds of survival.

But they already knew, after spending three torturous hours in the hospital with Kayleigh earlier, that *maybes* weren't going to fly today.

"Fuck it." Sam tossed the puffer down in the car's cup holder. "Let's just do this."

"But—"

"Don't," Sam said sharply. "I'm here saving your dumb ass. Don't ask me for anything else."

Noah clamped his mouth shut, and Sam blew out a long breath. These stupid cases were definitely going to land them right back in therapy, considering how stressed out they'd been lately. Going under cover as a cis woman, chasing down gangsters, spending way too much time in hospitals, willingly putting god-knows-what in their body . . .

Christ. Maybe Noah's family could foot the bill as part of Uncle Nico's plea bargain.

"You know, you don't have to do this." Noah's quiet words cut through Sam's moody thoughts. "I—I can go to the captain. I'll tell her what I did, and—"

"Noah, enough," Sam said with exasperation. "We're doing this. We're doing it now." Looking out the windshield toward the church steeple that loomed over the parking lot, Sam said grimly, "We have to put the gun in his hand. Right?"

"Right," Noah echoed nervously. Glancing down at the little inhaler, he said, "And you're sure you don't want—"

"Just don't miss your cue," Sam said. They kicked their car door open and stepped out onto the pavement. The sound of Noah's protest was cut off by the door closing behind them.

Tapping the transmitter under their shirt on so Noah could track their progress in his earpiece, Sam set off for the church. No point in wasting time. At least having a recording of the whole bust would make for an easy homicide investigation if things went sideways.

Stepping inside the building, they glanced down at the time on their phone. 3:45 p.m. Exactly fifteen minutes until afternoon mass was set to begin. They made their way into the quiet room. There were a surprising number of people in attendance, although most were quite elderly. Sam wondered if the faithful gathered today had any idea what kind of church they were really attending.

Sam stepped into a pew near the back. Placing the kneeler down, they gingerly lowered themself to their knees. The act still sent lightning bolts of pain through their lower back, and Sam wondered if that was God's sense of humor at play, considering the various activities that had gotten their body into this state. Did chasing another Catholic person across the city to stop him from committing any other crimes counteract having unmarried sex with an agnostic Protestant?

"Dear God," Sam spoke out loud over their clasped hands, just in case their presence had not been noticed yet. "I have a question. What is Your Holy Opinion on—"

Sam's words cut off when a large hand closed over their shoulder, yanking them from the pew.

"Hey, what gives?" Sam complained loudly as a burly-looking man they had yet to meet frog-marched them out the door.

An equally big guy waited for them in the hallway along with Father Nicholas. In his elaborate robes, the man didn't look much like a gang leader—although the giant bodyguards did help a little.

"Detective," Father Nicholas said in that deep, gravelly voice.

"Father," Sam replied with exaggerated politeness. "Is there a problem here? I just wanted to attend mass."

"I believe I was very clear," Father Nicholas said, not amused at all by their false naivete. "You are not welcome here. Not during off hours. And certainly not during services."

"Are you denying me communion, Father?" Sam asked. The priest's expression hardened, and Sam smiled faintly. "Forgive me if I'm a little rusty on church doctrine, but I thought any baptized Catholic not prohibited by law could not be denied communion?"

"If you were really Catholic, you would know that you cannot receive the holy sacrament if you have not repented of any mortal sins," Father Nicholas replied. "And since I have recently seen your behavior in the confessional booth, I am assured you have done no such thing."

"Then I want to give my confession," Sam insisted.

"Confession is on Saturday mornings from ten to eleven. Come back then, if you must, Detective." Flicking his fingers at the big guy on his right, Father Nicholas turned to go. The man put his hands firmly on Sam's shoulders. "Now, if you'll excuse me, the service will be starting shor—"

"Hey, Father Nico."

They all turned to face the church's front doors. Sunlight from outside streamed in, making Noah appear for one blazing second like the silhouette of some angelic creature. Then the doors shut behind him, and he appeared just as he always did. Or maybe there was something different to the way he held himself. Sam wasn't quite sure.

"Noah. What are you doing here?" Father Nicholas didn't sound all that happy to see his nephew.

"I'm here for the service. It's been way too long since my last mass," Noah said, crossing himself and inclining his head to the statue of the Virgin Mary that hovered over their heads. Clapping a hand on Sam's shoulder, he added, "It's been even longer for my friend Sam here. Should we go in?"

"Your friend has not attended confession for some time," Father Nicholas said stiffly. His sharp blue eyes narrowed at the sight of Noah's hand on Sam's rigid shoulder. "I'm afraid they cannot receive communion today."

"Ah, don't be ridiculous, Father," Noah said with a casual wave of his free hand. "They can knock out a confession in five minutes and be back in time for the service."

"That really won't be n—" Sam started.

"No. I insist. Communion is important for the soul," Noah said firmly, and the casual authority he exuded in that moment was genuinely impressive. Giving Father Nicholas a strange half-smile that Sam didn't recognize, he said, "Come on. Spending every day taking down murderers? Drug dealers? Gangsters? Can't live on the edge and not take every opportunity for communion. You never know when God might decide your time is up. Right, Father?"

". . . Yes. I suppose that is right," Father Nicholas said slowly. His eyes locked with Noah's for a long moment before he finally gave the slightest of nods and said, "The faithful can meditate on the virtue of patience today. Come. I will see to this confession."

Turning, Father Nicholas swept away in his fancy robes. Sam wasn't sure what came next, but Noah just squeezed their shoulder a little too tightly and said, "Let's get you to that confessional. I'd hate for you to miss the service."

Sam thought he might be laying it on a bit thick, but when Noah jerked his chin at the giant man blocking Sam's way, the guy easily stepped aside. So maybe he did know what he was doing.

Offering a quick prayer that Teddy would forgive them if they never made it home for that second date, Sam allowed Noah to steer them down the hallway. A few quick turns had them walking parallel to the nave until they arrived at the end of the hall in front of a side door. Father Nicholas stood outside and gestured them through to the confessional booth. Sam hesitated, but Noah shoved them forcefully. It wasn't the most graceful entrance, but it worked to sell their trepidation as they slunk over to the booth.

At least it was empty this time when they slipped inside. The old wooden chair creaked as they settled into the musty little box. Noah shut the door firmly behind them—or so it would appear to any onlooker. The dollar bill he used to keep it from sealing completely was a clever sleight of hand, and it reminded Sam of his breaking-and-entering skills back at the hospital. For a guy who wasn't "that kind of family," he certainly seemed to have picked up a few tricks.

They waited until his footsteps creaked away before daring to ease the door open a fraction more. Just enough to pick up the sound of murmured voices from the side hallway they'd just exited.

". . . bringing a cop here." Nico sounded angry. His deep voice wasn't hard to pick up, even from several feet away.

"I had no fucking choice." Noah's reply was petulant and nervous, much as Eddie had been in the park the other day. Maybe that was the attitude Nico expected from his underlings.

"You will watch your tongue in the House of the Lord."

"Sorry, *Father*."

Did Sam detect a hint of bitterness to Noah's tone? They wished they knew more about his history. How well did Nico know his nephew? Did he respect Noah as a man? Fear him as a cop? Or see him as disposable, like Eddie?

"I told you I didn't want a part in all this. You shoulda had them assign someone else to Father D." Noah's voice wavered slightly. "They figured out—about Nikki. After I let Eddie go. And now they're onto us about—"

"Us?" Sam flinched at the cold condescension in that single word, and it wasn't even directed at them. "There is no us. If you were a tenth of the man your father was, you wouldn't have exposed the family for Eddie's sake."

"I know, but—"

"I could have taken care of him like Simon, and no one would have batted an eye. But a cop? Your softness will be our undoing if the police even begin to suspect my involvement."

"I said I know, OK?" They heard Noah suck in a deep, shaky breath.

Sam's heart nearly stopped as they strained their ears for his next words. Nico had said the magic phrase: *like Simon*. Sam had heard it, which meant the transmitter they were wearing would have picked it up, too. In theory, a vague confession like that might have been enough to put the average murderer away. Less certain with a connected guy like Nico, but still. They wouldn't blame Noah for wanting to bail on this risky play.

But Nico was right about one thing—Noah was nothing like his father. He came from his mother's line. And he would do what needed to be done, even if it meant paying for it later.

"I can fix this." Noah's voice was so quiet, Sam could barely pick up the words. "I can make sure no one will ever know. Just like with Father D. I just need you to make this go away first, OK?"

There was silence for a long moment. Then there was the sound of footsteps on polished wooden boards, and Sam hurriedly pulled the door shut.

Their heart beat in their ears, and they felt like a little kid in the confessional booth again at the sound of Father Nicholas settling in on the other side of the screen. Only this time, they had more to worry about than getting caught smelling like cigarettes.

"My apologies for the delay." Father Nicholas's voice was stiff, but not overly concerned. "If you're ready, Detective."

Taking a deep breath, Sam forced themself to settle. They needed to focus. Nico needed to believe that they were a problem worth getting rid of. Not that they had ever had trouble convincing a priest of that before.

Crossing themself once, Sam began with the words their tongue still remembered well: "Bless me, Father, for I have sinned. My last confession was three—three years ago? No. Four years ago."

"And what do you wish to confess?"

"Well, I have definitely cursed a few times since my last confession. I'm not sure I have an exact number. I have also committed blasphemy in taking God's name in vain. Again, not sure how many times."

"So noted. Anything more serious?"

"More serious than cursing? Well . . . I did interrupt someone else's confession, which I've been told is a bad one. And I guess I've brought dishonor on my family and the church for the last thirty-eight years. I'm not sure I can properly repent of that, but it does remind me of another question."

"Ask."

"I've been trying to figure out what I should confess to exactly. See, I know I've had impure thoughts and engaged in, uh, self-gratification, which is . . . sinful. Very sinful. But then there's the premarital sex, and I'm not quite sure what to confess to with that."

"Premarital sex is a sin."

"No, I know. But I'm not sure if I should be confessing to homosexual acts or plain old fornication."

"Was the premarital sex with a man or a woman?"

". . . In the last four years? Both. Not at the same time, though."

"And were you born a man or a woman?"

"Also both."

"I meant physically a man or a woman."

"I know what you meant. The answer is still both."

"Ah, I see. Then I suppose you must confess according to your conscience."

"All right."

". . . Whenever you're ready."

"Hmm. See . . . I'm just not sure."

"God will understand your intention, either way."

"No, that's the problem. I'm not sure my intentions are exactly . . . pure, in this regard."

"What do you mean?"

"Full disclosure? There's a really hot guy waiting for me at home right now, and if he's into it, I am definitely going to take him to bed tonight."

"Then you must repent and resist these sinful urges."

"I don't think you understand the situation I'm in here, Father. He's really, really hot. And I'm only human."

"Do you think this is funny, Detective?"

"Funny? No. This is very serious, Father. I'm trying to save my soul here."

"Either give a true confession or leave."

"All right, fine. In addition to the cursing, blasphemy, and general sexual impurity, I guess I do have one other sin to confess."

". . . Fine. Speak."

"I'd like to confess to breaking a promise, Father."

"What promise is that?"

"I swore I would never join Vice squad, but now I'm considering going back on my word."

"Vice?"

"I know, I know. They're not the most ethical people, but you can't say they don't get the job done. And they've promised me a great deal of resources I don't have on Homicide to get justice for Father D'Angelo's death."

"I thought that was Detective Mariano's case."

"It is. But sadly, he hasn't been able to solve it for some reason. And that got me thinking that if people are getting away with murdering priests in my town, it might be time for a proper reckoning."

"Tread carefully, Detective. Wrath is a sin."

"So is murder, but that didn't stop someone from poisoning Father D'Angelo. Or from flooding these streets with the kind of drugs that ruin lives and rip families apart. I'm not going to sit back and let that happen, even if it means joining Vice."

"I don't think you know what you're getting yourself into. This isn't a fight you can win."

"I'm a queer person from the South. I was born looking for fights I can't win."

"And nothing will dissuade you from this path? Not even knowing how it will affect your career?"

"Get used to seeing me in your pews, Father. I'm not going anywhere until I feel like justice has been served."

". . . So be it. In light of these sins, I assign you the penance of fasting. You must not eat or drink anything after receiving communion here today until the sun rises tomorrow. Do you accept this penance?"

"Yes. I accept it."

"Then I am ready to receive your Act of Contrition."

"My God, I am sorry for my sins with all my heart. I firmly intend, with your help, to do penance, to sin no more, and to avoid whatever leads me to sin. Our Savior Jesus Christ suffered and died for us. In his name, my God, have mercy."

"I absolve you from your sins in the name of the Father, and of the Son, and of the Holy Spirit. Amen."

"Amen."

When Sam emerged from the booth, they couldn't say their soul felt any lighter. They were a pretty piss-poor Catholic, but even they knew that goading a priest into murder wasn't the best way to get into heaven. But since they were also trying to take down this particular priest before he could kill anyone else, hopefully God would understand.

Circling around to re-enter the worship space, Sam made their way up the aisle until they caught sight of Noah kneeling in a pew at the very front of the church. He was hunched over his hands like he was deep in prayer—or like he was trying to hide the brick-red shade of his oversized ears after learning more about Sam's sex life through his earpiece than he had probably ever wanted to know.

How he could oscillate between the cool, confident person they had seen earlier and the prudish, bumbling young man present here, Sam wasn't sure. But they sure as hell hoped some combination of the two would be able to pull off this plan.

Settling into their pew, Sam followed along with the service on autopilot. Normally, there was a certain comfort to the familiar routines and prayers, but Sam wasn't in the mood to enjoy their biannual dose of religion today. Maybe it had something to do with the way one hulking bodyguard appeared to stand in front of the confessional exit right around the breaking of the bread. Sam didn't need to turn around to know his friend would be guarding the doors at the back.

One by one, the people around Sam got up to join the line for communion. Father Nicholas stood imperiously at the altar, allowing each faithful person to approach and kneel to receive the Eucharist. Sam waited until the last person had passed before joining the end of the line.

The smile on Father Nicholas's face was clue enough that this was a terrible plan. But it was too late to turn back now. Sam's knees touched the pillow at his feet, and they looked up at the priest with as much contrition as they could muster.

"The Body of Christ," Father Nicholas intoned, holding up a wafer seemingly identical to all the rest. Opening their mouth, Sam looked him dead in the eye as he placed the tiny disc directly on their tongue.

The wafer dissolved, bitter and damning in their mouth. Still, Sam did not flinch as they swallowed and said, "Amen."

Offering them the chalice, Father Nicholas tilted it toward them and said, "The Blood of Christ."

Sam obediently drank from the cup. The wine was weak and did little to cut through the rancid aftertaste of the wafer still coating their tongue.

"Amen."

Father Nicholas's smile was cold and easy as a timer began to tick down in Sam's head.

Their legs were steady beneath them as they rose to their feet and returned to their pew. They knew Father D'Angelo had made it through the end of mass and almost all the way to his car before succumbing, so Sam figured they could at least last the ten minutes it would take for Father Nicholas to finish droning through the final prayers.

". . . hear me. Hide me within Thy wounds. Never permit me to be separated from Thee. From the malignant enemy defend me. At the hour of my death call me, and cause me to come to Thee, that with the Saints . . ."

. . . but then again, ten minutes might be a little ambitious given that Father D'Angelo had weighed 197 pounds at the time of his death, and Sam barely clocked in at a buck thirty. Considering that their diet lately had largely consisted of granola bars and caffeine doses between all-nighters, even that number was probably just wishful thinking.

Maybe they should have taken that inhaler when they had the chance.

Blinking sweat out of their eyes, Sam tried to focus on Father Nicholas's words of dismissal. Their lips parted to repeat the response along with the rest of the congregation, but no sound came out. So that was not a great sign.

Drawing a shallow breath into their lungs, Sam moved toward the

Elle Kleos

end of the pew on unsteady legs. Grasping the end of the bench to stay upright, they staggered out into the aisle.

"Hey—You OK, Detective?"

They could hear Noah's voice come from somewhere behind them. Or above them. Or somewhere else entirely. Hard to say, really, as their vision began to tunnel and the church blurred into a rainbow smear of stained glass and worried faces.

"What the hell? What did you do to them?"

The air felt fuzzy all of a sudden. No, wait. That was the carpet under their hands, not the air. They must be lying on the floor now.

". . . call 9-1-1. They're not . . ."

Sam vaguely recalled what Kayleigh had said she felt in the last moments before going under. Cold. Unable to speak. Like being trapped under ice.

". . . even fucking think about it. Nicholas Romano, you're under arrest for . . ."

Sam was pretty sure they weren't going to make it to the coma part. They didn't feel cold. They felt hot. Boiling hot. Like acid was filling their lungs and pouring out of their throat.

". . . Sam? Stay with me, Sam. The paramedics are right outside. Just stay with me. Sam—Sam!"

CHAPTER THIRTY-ONE

Sam's eyes shot open as their lungs heaved for air. Oxygen began to make its way back into their bloodstream, and the world around them slowly came into focus.

Three silver walls. A shrill beeping sound, a long tube, and a blinding smear of over-exposed blue. Something hard and unyielding beneath them. No—two silver walls, a roof, and an open doorway. A stretcher beneath them. They were inside a parked ambulance.

Sam's head rolled to the side. A blurry figure was hovering over them. They blinked hard to resolve the image, even as adrenaline began to spike through them. A man in a paramedic's uniform with a nametag reading "McBride" came into focus along with the syringe in his hand. He was preparing to insert the needle into the IV bag that hung over Sam's gurney. A line descended from the bag all the way into Sam's arm.

His hand moved toward the bag and Sam tried to say *no*. But the words wouldn't come. Why wouldn't they come?

Sam tried to lift their arms, but they barely moved. Their entire body was incredibly sluggish, even as their pulse ratcheted up a level. Something tugged uncomfortably at their ears, and after a long moment their muddled brain finally realized that they were wearing an oxygen mask.

No. No, no, no, no.

Sam forced their hands to rise, forced their numb fingers to curl into the elastic straps binding the mask to their face. They pulled hard, ignoring the sharp stabbing pain in their arm where the IV dug in. Oh god, the

IV. The panic kicked them hard in the chest, and they shook their head as hard as they could, desperate to dislodge the oxygen mask even while grasping for the tube connected to their arm.

"Whoa—whoa!" McBride's surprised voice echoed from somewhere overhead.

Sam's vision was tunneling again as McBride grabbed their arm, and they began to hyperventilate. Their lungs were on fire, and they tugged desperately at the plastic mask with their free hand.

"Dude, you need to relax. The mask has to stay—oof!" McBride's voice cut off with a harsh exhalation as Sam brought one leg up to kick him viciously in the gut.

"What the fuck are you doing?" another voice called, but the person might as well have been speaking from the moon for all Sam could tell.

Currently, every pulse of their heart was sending the same panic message to their entire body on repeat, overwhelming every other instinct. Their fingers clawed at the needle in their arm, dislodging it one determined millimeter at a time. Their eyes flitted wildly around their prison in search of any possible escape route.

"Shit. You were supposed to restrain them, you moron."

"They were unconscious—"

"Do they seem unconscious to you?"

The speaker came barreling onto the ambulance through the open back doors, and Noah's pale face swam into focus above Sam's head. They thrashed their IV arm in pure panic as McBride followed right behind him, syringe still in hand. Blood was streaming down their forearm now and the overhead lights seemed to pulse brighter as they slammed their head back against the gurney hard enough to finally knock the oxygen mask off entirely.

"Shit. Shit!"

"Should I sedate—"

"Just give them the next injection. Come on, do it!"

No. No, no, no, no, no, no—

Sam kicked, clawed, and fought with all their strength, but it was like there was an anvil sitting on their chest. Noah pinned them down on the gurney, and no matter how hard they tried to stop it, they couldn't. They couldn't speak. They couldn't move. They couldn't stop McBride from inserting the new mystery drug into the IV line. Straight into their body.

No. No. No. NO.

Something hard and cold pressed against their face, and Sam's body shuddered as sweet oxygen flooded their lungs. This might not have been for the best, though, because it only gave them the energy to lash out blindly with their free arm.

"Ow. Stop that," Noah snapped, curling his body away from their blows while pinning their other arm in place.

His words barely even registered. With a little bit more room to maneuver, Sam was able to reach for the mask again, yanking aside the hard plastic with pure, panic-driven determination.

"You have to leave it on, Sam," Noah ordered.

He climbed right up on the gurney to pin their thrashing body with his knee, while his hands were occupied keeping their IV arm and oxygen mask in place. A guttural, animal sound worked its way out of Sam's throat as they clawed at Noah's fingers and wrist with their one free hand.

"Ow. Stop it—stop fighting me! You have to leave it on. You're going to die, you fuckin' idiot. Leave—it—on."

"Blood oxygen is starting to level off. Do you want me to sedate now?"

Sam's entire body went rigid with fear, and their harsh breath fogged the mask. They were screaming at the top of their lungs, but all that came out was a strangled, terrified noise at the thought of being forced back under.

". . . No. No sedative."

"Dude—"

"I promised them I wouldn't," Noah said firmly. His eyes locked with Sam's, and he repeated, "No sedative."

Sam let out a rattling breath as those words sunk in. No sedative. No sedative. There was no sedative in the mask. Just oxygen. Nothing else. Just oxygen.

"All right, it's your funeral."

"It wouldn't be my fucking funeral if you had just restrained them in the first place like you were supposed to!"

Just oxygen. Just oxygen. Sam forced their lungs to expand, sucking in the sweet, clean air and feeling a little lightheaded as it rushed straight to their brain. Spots danced in their vision and the panic eased back just enough for them to realize that their arm *really* hurt.

Their bleary eyes fell on the bloody IV line jutting out of their skin, and Noah immediately tuned back in when he felt Sam's body tensing up for another fight.

"No way. No you don't," he muttered. He risked releasing the oxygen mask to stretch a hand back toward McBride. "Give me the kit—no, not that. The kit, *the first kit*, you moron." Shoving the little white box with its spent vile directly in Sam's face, Noah said, "Sam. Can you hear me? You're getting the second dose of the Cyanokit. It's the antidote. Look at it, all right? It's just the antidote."

Sam tried to read the description on the box, but the letters all blurred together. Sucking in a ragged breath, they forced their fuzzy brain to try again. They had to read the words at least three times before their mind accepted what they were seeing. Then they read it three more times, just to be sure.

Finally, their head fell back on the stretcher, too exhausted to keep fighting. Their breathing was still ragged, but it wasn't quite so hard to fill their lungs as the drugs began to take effect. Drugs they *had* agreed to take before walking into that church and allowing Father Nicholas to poison them.

After another long minute, Noah eased himself off the gurney. His hands hovered over them cautiously as he waited to see if they would panic again. Sam gritted their teeth against the urge to immediately rip the IV out of their arm, but they had enough oxygen in their brain now to resist. Instead, their hands curled around the sides of the gurney in a white-knuckled death grip, commanding their nerve to hold.

Another minute passed. Then another. Their breathing was almost normal now, thanks to the lifesaving antidote. Raising one shaky hand, Sam pulled the oxygen mask away from their face. Calmly this time.

"Sam . . ." Noah said warningly. His hand reached for the mask, and Sam flinched away.

"Don't touch me." Their voice was little more than a harsh, threadbare whisper.

Pressing the oxygen mask back to their face, they made sure Noah saw as they inhaled a deep breath. His hands lowered slowly.

Turning their eyes on McBride, Sam drew in another breath and then removed the mask to ask, "How much longer?"

"For—for the IV?" the paramedic asked. His gaze kept flicking nervously to Sam's feet as he hovered just out of kicking range. Sam nodded, and he glanced over at the monitor listing out their vitals. Swallowing hard, McBride said, "Should be no more than ten minutes."

Sam's free hand fumbled inside their pocket until their fingers managed to close around their brick of a phone. It took an excruciatingly long time to navigate the screen with their violently trembling hands, but they finally managed to set the timer for ten minutes. Their body was limp with exhaustion as they rolled over to curl up around the phone. The screen filled their vision, showing the numbers steadily ticking down.

"It's better for your oxygen flow if you lie flat," McBride's voice said from somewhere above them.

Sam ignored him. Some things were more important than oxygen flow. The next swell of panic was less powerful than the last, but it still took all of their energy just to keep their body in check.

The timer read 7 minutes, 36 seconds when they finally pulled the oxygen mask aside and asked in a slightly stronger voice, "Did we get him?"

"Yeah. Had to grab Tony as well since he decided to try and knock my lights out, but we got Nico," Noah said with a grimace, rubbing the rapidly purpling bruise on his jaw. Meeting Sam's tired gaze, Noah added, "Between the monologue he gave on his way to the squad car and everything he said outside the confessional, I think we got more than enough."

Sam let out a slow breath and nodded. "Good."

The timer continued to tick down. They could sense Noah fidgeting beside them, but they didn't have the energy to either give him the answers he wanted or tell him to get lost.

"Are you OK?" Noah finally blurted when the timer read 5 minutes and 13 seconds.

"No."

"Uh," Noah said eloquently. He seemed disturbed to see them in such a distressed state, even though Sam had warned him it would go like this. It would have been much less dramatic if McBride had just restrained them while they were still unconscious like they had suggested before the op. "Is, uh, is there anything I can do? To help? Or—maybe I could call that guy you were with earl—"

"What's your plan?" Sam asked abruptly, cutting off his floundering attempts at compassion.

"What?" Noah echoed stupidly.

"With your family. What's the story you're going with?"

Noah's eyes nervously tracked Sam's movements as they rolled onto their back. Just over four minutes to go. Drawing in a deep breath, Sam forced their weakened body up into a sitting position.

When McBride stepped forward to restrain them, they snarled, "I said don't touch me," and brought up one threatening foot. They weren't that weak. McBride wisely backed off, and Sam raised the oxygen mask to their face for another steadying breath. With their eyes still closed, they said, "Come on, Noah. There's going to be questions. What's the plan?"

"Right, right. There's—there is a plan," Noah insisted.

Sam made an impatient gesture as they continued to breathe into the mask.

"Uh, right. So I figure my family is going to know I asked for the hit on you."

Sam's hand jumped to their chest to feel for the transmitter that had been hidden there.

"It's off. I disabled it and made a copy of the audio right away," Noah assured them. Fishing in his pocket, he produced the tangle of wires for them to see.

Sam nodded. That was smart at least.

Clearing his throat nervously, Noah continued, "I know they're going to know I ordered the hit. But everyone also knows that Uncle Nico and I got into it before about doing Father D so publicly. I told him then that he was getting too cocky. GIU isn't going to care that he's in tight with the mayor if we start poisoning cops in broad daylight. So I did what I had to do to protect all of us." Noah's gaze flicked away before he added, "Just like my dad would have."

"And you think people will buy that?"

"I hope so. I can spin Tony to my advantage, too," Noah said, touching the bruise on his jaw again. "If I don't press charges, he'll walk. That should work as a sign of good faith to convince any doubters where my loyalty lies."

"Is that what you want?" Sam asked. Dropping the oxygen mask onto the gurney, they gave a light cough and then said, "A sign of good faith might help you out now, but it also guarantees people are going to expect more favors going forward."

"I'll handle it," Noah said with a helpless shrug. "What other choice do I have?"

Sam searched Noah's drawn, pale face for a long moment before finally nodding. They weren't so sure he did have it handled, but this was the path he had chosen to walk between family and his conscience. Only time would tell if he had the strength to withstand the opposing forces.

The timer started to ring out, and Sam's hand flew straight to the IV line. They were calm enough at least that they didn't panic when McBride stepped in to assist. Pinching the skin gently between practiced fingers, he dislodged the crooked needle while keeping firm pressure in place. Blood oozed up from the puncture, and he quickly wrapped the wound in gauze and a tight bandage.

"Blood oxygen levels look good. Really good, all things considered," McBride said, glancing over at the monitor again in disbelief. "You're going to have one hell of a bruise on that arm, but you're going to be fine."

"Great," Sam grunted. They flexed their tender arm to test the bandage and judged it good enough.

Scooting to the foot of the gurney, Sam took a deep breath and threw their legs over the side. Their entire body felt like it had just taken a beating, but they weren't having much trouble breathing anymore, at least.

"Whoa—whoa!" McBride exclaimed. Noah stepped in to try and stop them, but one glare from Sam had him backing off again. "Dude," McBride said nervously as Sam forced themself to stand on shaking legs. "You just survived a lethal dose of cyanide. You really need to go to the hospital for observation."

"I'm not going to the goddamned hospital," Sam muttered even as they unclipped the fingertip oximeter and flung it to the side. "I'm fine."

Their first step saw them wobbling so precariously that they nearly went straight back down. The next step was a little steadier. The third step was also good, but then Sam found themself staring down the small gap between the ambulance's deck and the pavement below. They wavered uncertainly, unable to trust this stupid, weak body they were trapped in to catch them if they jumped.

"All right, all right. Don't be such a stubborn asshole." Noah elbowed past them and hopped down to the pavement below. Like it was that easy. He held out one hand, those big ears bright red as he deliberately avoided Sam's gaze. "Just let me help you, OK?"

Sam's expression hardened as they stared at that outstretched hand. Noah's eyes widened in surprise a second later when he felt the hard jumble of Sam's key ring landing in his palm.

"I don't need help."

Noah started to protest, but Sam was already jumping down to the pavement below. The impact set off sparklers behind their eyes and sent white-hot agony through every joint in their body, but sheer willpower kept them up.

"You want to be useful?" Sam glared at Noah despite the sweat breaking out on their forehead from just that small exertion. Nodding to the keys in his hand, they said, "Get me over to the Paths building in the next ten minutes. That would be useful."

Noah's mouth worked open and shut in disbelief at their stubborn pride. Turning away, Sam fixed their gaze on the far side of the parking lot. Their car seemed an insurmountable distance away, but a little pain had never stopped them before.

"Is this really a good idea?" Noah asked as Sam took their first shaking step. Then another. And another. Noah trailed uncertainly behind them.

"Letting you drive?" Sam huffed through gritted teeth. Acid burned in the back of their throat, but they kept going. One foot in front of the other. "Probably not. But I'm pretty sure it's not legal for me to get behind the wheel right now. And I've got a date to get to."

CHAPTER THIRTY-TWO

[Tick-tock. Better pick up the pace, Sammy.]

"I know. I'm working on it," Sam grumbled. They tugged harder at the sleeve of their blouse as they hurried toward the hotel on the street corner.

Vivienne had done what she could to mask the pinkish glow to Sam's skin post-poisoning, and to cover the bandage wrapped around their arm. Of course, that was easier said than done, when they were also supposed to be dressed like they were trying to get some. All in all, it was not the most comfortable Sam had ever felt in their life.

[I don't think our boy is going to be feeling too patient after you blue-balled him last time.]

"Too bad. I can only walk so fast in these heels."

Sam could feel an acute ache in their left hip with each step they took in these stupid deathtraps Vivienne called shoes. She had subtly placed a bottle of ibuprofen on the vanity while she got to work on their skin, but Sam didn't think she was especially surprised when they didn't take any. Willingly putting drugs in their body, even painkillers they desperately needed, was difficult for Sam on the best of days. And today was not the best of days, so limping as fast as they could would just have to do.

[Why so grumpy, Sammy? Not feeling guilty for sneaking around on that little boyfriend of yours, are you?]

"What the hell are you talking about?" Sam drew to a stop as the lights separating them from the hotel flipped to red. Pushing the Walk button impatiently, they asked, "Did you hit your head falling asleep at your desk again?"

[*Don't be shy. Word on the street is you were getting frisky at a crime scene with some hunky young papi chulo this morning.*]

"You heard wrong. There was no crime scene," Sam said flatly. Just a minor disturbance that the uniformed officers had been left to scratch their heads over. They could have left it at that, but because they liked Teddy more than they disliked having their personal business out there, Sam added, "And don't call him papi chulo."

[*Oh, Sammy! And here I thought you only liked to get down with the ladies. If I knew you played the whole field, I wouldn't have bothered throwing Donya at you so often. With dick on the menu, I can offer you all sorts of different op—*]

"Enough. Enough!" Sam snapped loud enough to draw a look from the man walking his dog across the street. Vince's voice fell silent in their ear as the walk sign came on. Hurrying across the street, Sam said, "Just shut up, all right? I'm so done with this." Pausing outside the hotel doors, they said, "No more jokes. No more bullshit. I'm going in there to finish this, and I don't want to hear another word from you for the rest of the night unless it's case relevant."

[*. . . Geez. Someone's feeling sensitive.*]

"That's me. Super sensitive," Sam said grimly as they shoved the door open. "Now shut up and let me work."

Their heels clicked loudly against the tile floor as they made their way into the restaurant. It only took a second for Sam to locate Jason sitting at the bar. After some flirting back and forth on the app, he had agreed to meet again for drinks to "see where things went." Sam was pretty sure he wasn't going to have any complaints about where things went tonight.

Not at first, anyway.

Sidling up behind him, Sam tapped him on the shoulder. "Hey there."

"Hmm? Oh, h—" Jason's greeting was cut off when Sam leaned in for a passionate kiss.

After a moment of surprise, Jason encircled Sam's waist with greedy hands and kissed them back with 100% more tongue than Sam had ever wanted from a potential murderer in a hotel bar. Hopefully they didn't still taste like cyanide.

"Well, hello to you, too," Jason said when Sam finally extracted themself from the kiss. Looking Sam up and down with great interest, he asked, "Can I get you something to drink?"

"God, no," Sam said, and Jason's eyes widened in surprise when Sam wrapped their hand around his tie and jerked him in close. Pressing their cheek against his, Sam brushed their lips to his ear and whispered, "I'm just here to fuck."

"Uh, OK," Jason said, his voice pitching upward slightly as Sam's hand squeezed his thigh beneath the bar top. Reaching for his drink, he drained the glass in one gulp, then stood up from his stool. "Lead the way, beautiful."

Sam's hand tightened around his tie, and they turned to drag him out of the restaurant, paying no heed to the scandalized looks they were getting from other patrons. By the time they arrived at the elevator, Jason was looking thoroughly red in the face and plenty aroused.

Shoving him onto the lift, Sam turned back to smirk at the young couple who had been waiting and said, "Maybe get the next one."

The doors slid shut in their slack-jawed faces. Not three seconds later, Jason's arms snaked around Sam from behind. Sam's body stiffened as Jason ran a trail of scratchy, stubbly kisses down the side of their neck, his hands pawing them over like a rack of discount clothing.

"Come on. Relax a little," Jason murmured against their collarbone as his fingers fiddled with the buttons on their shirt. "I thought you were the one who wanted to fuck?"

"I do, I just . . ." Sam shut their eyes, fighting off a repulsed shudder as Jason's hand slid inside their shirt. Grabbing his wrist to stop him before he could stumble across the transmitter hidden inside their bra, they said, "Did you hear about that girl? Kayleigh Evergreen?"

"Excuse me?" Jason's pulse spiked beneath their thumb, and Sam smiled faintly.

"That girl, Kayleigh," Sam explained, shifting against him with deliberate discomfort. "She was using the Paths app, and she got attacked by her date. She's been in a coma for over three weeks. It was all over the news."

"I'm trying to get laid here," Jason said incredulously, although he did finally stop trying to undress them. "What would I get from stabbing you?"

"That's interesting."

The elevator doors let out a ding as they arrived at the top floor, but Sam didn't try to get off. Jason made a startled sound as Sam shoved him up against the elevator wall. For a guy that seemed to like a strong woman, he still seemed surprised to find himself at their mercy. Reaching out to hit the doors shut button, Sam pressed their body up against his, close enough to feel his breath on their face.

Offering him a knowing smile, Sam said, "I never mentioned anything about stabbing."

"You should be a lawyer," Jason replied. He strained a little against their hold. Resisting the urge to roll their eyes, Sam let him "overpower" them and walk them backward until their shoulders touched the elevator doors. Giving them a big, self-satisfied smirk, Jason said, "You'd be good at it. Although I don't think watching the news is a crime in this case."

"Yeah?" Sam asked, grabbing hold of his belt and pulling him tight against them. "Maybe I should cross-examine you first. Just to be safe."

"Would that turn you on?"

"It really, really would."

The elevator doors slid open, and they tumbled out into the hallway. When Jason stopped making out with them long enough to unlock the hotel room door, Sam quickly reached inside their bra and tapped on the transmitter. The transcript from tonight would no doubt haunt them for the rest of their career, but if it helped catch a murderer, so be it.

<u>Recording #7: Jason Albertalli</u>

The recording begins with the sound of a door closing. The mic picks up the familiar sound of frantic kissing and hands pulling at clothes.

"So how do you plan on doing this cross-examination, Counselor?"

"Hmm. That depends. How do you feel about being tied up? For my safety, of course."

"You are a naughty girl, aren't you?"

"You're about to find out just how naughty I can be. Now take off your belt."

"Take it off yourself."

There is the sound of a buckle coming undone. The mic picks up a low, masculine laugh that quickly changes to a yelp of surprise when the smack of leather against fabric rings out.

"Whoa! I don't know about all that."

"Aw. You scared of a little foreplay?"

". . . No."

"Good. Now go lie down on the bed for me."

The mic picks up the sound of bed springs squeaking as someone climbs into the bed. Leather groans as it's pulled tight.

"Tight enough?"

"Tighter."

"And you're calling me naughty."

There is a sharp inhalation as the belt is pulled taught before the buckle is secured in place around the bedpost. The mic is filled with the sound of more heated kissing.

"God, this is hot. You'd better take some of those clothes off before you overheat."

"Yeah? You want to see me naked?"

"Yes."

"That can be arranged. But first you're going to have to answer a few questions for me, Counselor."

"I swear to tell the truth, the whole truth, and nothing but the truth."

"So help you God, you'd better hope you do."

There is a sound of pleasure as the weight of another body settles on top of his.

"Tell me, Counselor. How many sexual partners have you had in the past year?"

"What?"

"You heard me. How many?"

". . . Before tonight? Twelve."

"Twelve different women?"

"Yes."

"And how many of these women got to enjoy the ride more than once?"

"I don't know. Some of them. Not the ones who just wanted to talk all night."

"So impatient. I thought you wanted me to be turned on?"

"You like hearing about the other women I've had sex with?"

The bed springs creak suggestively. There is the sound of shirt buttons popping and then the light patter of plastic dropping on the floor.

"Jesus. I guess you are into that."

"Guilty."

"All right—OK. Uh, I've had sex with twelve—twelve women so far this year. Not including my wife, obviously. And I probably went back for seconds with, like, three . . . no, four of them?"

"And was one of those women Kayleigh Evergreen?"

"What?"

"Was one of the women you hooked up with multiple times Kayleigh Evergreen?"

"How—how—"

"Answer the question, Counselor. Unless you're feeling guilty."

"I'm not—I mean, we—we hooked up, like, a few times, sure. But I didn't know her. I definitely didn't stab her."

As the man's voice grows nervous, there is the sound of a zipper being undone. His breath catches as fabric drags against skin.

"Mhm. And why should I believe you?"

"Because . . . because . . ."

"What's wrong? Having trouble coming up with a good alibi?"

"No. It's just hard to concentrate when you . . . uh . . . when you're . . ."

"Should I stop?"

There is the sound of clothing landing in a pile on the floor.

"No. God, no."

"Then you'd better start talking."

"Fuck. Fine. When—when did she get . . . Do you know?"

"It was June 27. Around 11:00 p.m."

"Jesus. How do you—"

"I was there. That night. It happened right outside the mixer."

"That's messed up."

"More messed up if I'm about to fuck the person who did it."

"No need to worry about that. June 27? It couldn't have been me."

"Oh?"

"Yeah. I was at a work event. Some charity thing for a client who's really into manatees or something stupid like that. I remember because . . ."

"Because why?"

There is the creak of leather as someone shifts uncomfortably against their bonds.

"Because that's, uh, that's where number eleven and I, uh, connected. In the bathroom between dinner courses."

"That's quite the alibi. Do you think number eleven would remember you?"

"Every girl I sleep with remembers me."

[Bad news, Sammy. Wellesley Alexander's did have a charity event for ocean conservation that night.]

"Are you fucking kidding me?"

"Uh . . . no?"

[Afraid so. We can call his office to confirm that he was there, but unless he knows you're onto him, I don't see why he'd lie.]

" . . . "

"Well? Come on. Are we doing this or not?"

[Up to you. If his alibi checks for the 27th, he can't be your guy from the mixer. But if he just did the other two—]

"So how do you choose them?"

"Excuse me?"

"All these women who are supposed to remember you. You do the Smart Heart thing, which means you're choosing. Is that so your wife can get off on helping you pick your next victim?"

"What—victim? You mean who I hook up with? Jen doesn't care about that stuff. She just likes to know I'm taken care of while she's—"

"Then why Smart Heart? Why not Swipe Right?"

"Well, I was trying to avoid hurting anyone who was looking for something serious, but apparently I should have been screening for drug dealers and paranoid people, too."

"Drug dealers? You mean Nikki Romano?"

"Romano?"

"Russo. Nikki Russo. She's probably number eight or nine on your list."

"How the hell do you know that?"

[Careful. If you blow your cover, I am not going to be the one explaining to Cap why one of her homicide detectives got caught interrogating a man in a hotel bedroom.]

" . . . "

"Did Nikki put you up to this?"

" . . . "

"She did, didn't she? This is some sick revenge thing because I told her not all lawyers want to sleep around and do blow."

"No. You just like the sleeping around part."

"Is that what this is about? She's mad I didn't want to sleep with her

368

psycho ass anymore after I realized she was just using the app to sell—"

"I've heard it's not tasteful to speak ill of the dead."

"What the hell are you talking about? Dead?"

" . . . "

" . . . "

"Shit. You're really don't know, do you?"

"Know what? That Nikki is a crazy bitch, and you clearly are, too?"

"No. I meant you don't know that she's dead."

"What?"

"Nikki was murdered over a month ago. Stabbed to death, actually. You can see why that would make a girl suspicious."

"All right, I don't know what's going on here, but this is some bullshit. You'd better untie me right fucking now, or I—"

The angry words are cut off by the sound of a phone ringing.

"Sorry, I have to get this. Don't go anywhere."

"Fuck y—"

"Hello? Whoa, slow down. What—"

[What's happening, Sam?]

"Beck, you need to slow down. What's this about?"

A faint, broken-up voice can just be heard over the recording, but the words are not audible.

"She did what?"

" . . . "

"No. No, that's not possible. I just saw her this morning. She was fine, she—"

" . . . "

"But I was there. Vivienne saw her, too."

" . . . "

"Because that's bullshit."

" . . . "

"I'm not—OK. OK, fine. Just calm down. I'm on my way."

There is the sound of the phone being hung up.

[What the hell was that?]

"Hey—where the hell are you going?"

[Sam?]

"I'm going to the hospital. Kayleigh Evergreen is dead."

"What the—get back here! Untie me, goddammit!"

"Oh, relax. It's just a belt. You should be able to break out of that in under five minutes."

"You bitch! What's the matter with you? I should—"

The man's threats are cut off as the sound of a door slamming rings out and the recording comes to an end.

CHAPTER THIRTY-THREE

"I'm aware. I'm aware that it's late, but I need—a woman is dead, Linda. I don't care if it's one in the morning. I need that security footage."

Sam paced back and forth on the concrete strip outside their apartment door. Their head was throbbing, their hands were shaking, and if one more person put them on hold, they were going to lose it.

"Are you serious? A warrant? A person is dead, and you want me to wait for a warrant?" Sam demanded. A light flicked on in the neighbor's apartment. Sucking in a deep, calming breath, Sam made a concentrated effort to lower their voice before saying, "I understand that the hospital believes this to be a suicide. But it's my job to make sure that's true. Can you at least check the visitor's log and tell me who—no, do not put me on hold! Do not—"

The line was filled with cheesy pop music, and Sam let out a sound of pure animal frustration.

"Would you keep it down out there? Some of us are trying to sleep."

Some choice words danced on the tip of Sam's tongue as pure frustration set their blood to boiling. They barely, *barely* managed to keep the words in, but they seriously could not take much more of this. They needed a drink, and a cigarette, and a goddamned vacation, stat.

First Noah and the cyanide. Then Jason and that stupid bedroom interrogation that led absolutely nowhere except back to square one. And now Kayleigh was dead, supposedly by her own hand, but it made no sense, and they were so damn tired of things not making sense on this insane case.

Wrists cut. With a scalpel of all things—how did she even get a scalpel? Were they really supposed to believe this was a coincidence?

Cursing under their breath, Sam reached for their keys and jammed them into the lock. They threw the door open and stepped inside, only to nearly face-plant over a well-placed pair of shoes. A very large, very salt-stained pair of shoes that looked like they had probably been rescued from a Goodwill about ten years earlier.

"Hey, honey. Welcome home."

"Jesus Christ," Sam swore, nearly jumping out of their skin at the sight of the man leaning up against their kitchen counter.

"Sorry," Teddy said, although the little grin on his face really didn't make him look all that sorry. "I kind of thought you knew I'd be here."

"My bad," Sam said sourly. They cradled their aching arm to their aching side as they slammed the front door shut hard enough to feel it in the rest of their aching body. "Forgetfulness must be one of the side effects of cyanide poisoning."

"Long day, huh?" Teddy said, raising an eyebrow as Sam stomped through the apartment looking very much unlike the flirty, happy person who had agreed to a second date this morning. Or actually yesterday morning, at this point.

"Yeah," Sam snapped, wheeling around to face him. "It was a really long fucking d—" They choked off the fiery words when they saw how taken aback Teddy was at the sound of Sam's infamous temper on full display.

"Ah . . . shit," Sam groaned, feeling the fight go out of them as suddenly as it had flared up.

Their exhausted body dropped like a rock onto the ancient sofa. Glancing over at the kitchen table, Sam could see that it had been set nicely—there were even candles, like Teddy had promised. And at the center of the table was a beautiful anatomically heart-shaped vase, complete with fresh flowers.

Dragging one hand down their face, Sam shook their head and muttered, "*Fuck.* I'm such an asshole."

Why were they like this? Why had any part of them been stupid enough to think they could get through more than one date without completely blowing this thing? It was never going to work. They didn't have the patience, the words, the anything needed to make a relationship work. Not the kind of relationship someone like Teddy deserved, anyway.

Sam ground the shaking heels of their palms against their exhausted eyelids. "I'm—fuck. I'm sorry. You should just go."

For a long minute the apartment was silent, save for the sound of Sam's slightly raspy breathing. They probably should have asked McBride how long that was going to last when they had the chance, but they'd been a little distracted rushing off to meet Jason at the time. Not that that had really worked out, either.

"Do you really want me to go?"

Sam's eyes flew open in surprise. They were so busy wallowing that they hadn't even heard Teddy moving closer. Now he stared down at them with a funny little smile on his face that their sluggish brain couldn't even begin to comprehend. What they could comprehend was that he looked very warm and very comfortable and like it would be so easy, god, *it should be so easy* to just tell him how much they needed his gentle kindness right now.

"No," Sam finally mumbled. A potent mix of guilt and longing filled their chest the longer they stared up at him. "But you should really want to go."

Despite their stubborn words, Teddy's smile only grew at the sight of Sam being vulnerable in their own, strange Sam way.

"Nah. I've got a better idea," Teddy said. He held out one hand to them. "Come with me." When Sam hesitated, he leaned down even further to nudge their shoulder insistently. "Come on. Get up."

"Teddy . . ." Sam groaned, pressing their hands back to their face. "Please. I'm so tired."

"Oh, well, if you're tired . . ."

Sam cracked one eye open suspiciously at Teddy's playful tone and then gave a very manly yelp of surprise when he bent over to scoop them up in his arms. Sam immediately tried to twist free, but Teddy just laughed and adjusted his grip so he could lift them, bridal-style, off the couch.

"You're really going to have to let me cook for you sometime," Teddy teased as he carried them straight through the apartment and into the bedroom despite their squirming. "You are seriously underweight, cariño."

"Put me down," Sam demanded as Teddy kicked the bedroom door shut behind him. "I swear to god, Teddy," they growled as he carried them over to the foot of the bed. "You'd better put me down right—"

"OK, OK. Calm down." Teddy placed Sam gently back on their feet. Grinning at the fierce, defensive glare they were giving him, he said, "Was that really so bad?"

"Yes. I can walk just fine," Sam insisted stubbornly, and Teddy rolled his eyes.

"Really?" He reached out one hand to poke them in the side. A helpless whine of pain slid from between Sam's gritted teeth. "That doesn't sound fine to me," Teddy observed. "If you take your shirt off, I promise I can make you feel better."

"Teddy . . ." Sam said with anxious exasperation. Their whole body hurt at just the thought of what he was suggesting. "I know I said this morning that we could meet up later, but I just—after today, I'm really not in the mood for—"

"God, you have such a one-track mind!" Teddy exclaimed, and Sam was a little surprised to hear him actually sounding exasperated for once. "Would you just trust me for two seconds?" He reached out and pressed Sam's face between his palms. "Come on, Sam," he pleaded. "Just let me help you. Shirt. Off."

Sam hesitated for a long moment. The rejection danced on the tip of their tongue because they didn't need his help. They didn't *need* anything other than a good night's sleep and a strong cup of coffee to hit the ground running again tomorrow. Thirty-eight years had taught them that they didn't need much at all to keep on existing one sunrise after another.

But when Teddy looked at them with those big, concerned puppy-dog eyes, it was a lot harder to think about what they needed when what they wanted was standing right there.

Keeping their gaze locked with his, Sam reached down and grasped the hem of their shirt. Rucking the fabric up, Teddy let go so they could tug it off over their head and toss it down on the bedroom floor. Sam's arms twined nervously around their body, which was stupid, because he had seen them a lot more naked than this, but this felt . . . different. They weren't tearing each other's clothes off or blissed out on a post-coital high right now. This was a much rawer form of nakedness, and Sam did not care for it at all.

"Come on," Teddy repeated. His hand was gentle on theirs as he coaxed them over to the side of the bed. "Sit down with me." When Sam hesitated, Teddy sat first and then guided them down beside him.

Sam's back was rigid with tension when Teddy touched their right shoulder to turn their body away from his. "Relax," he whispered, and Sam nearly jumped out of their skin at the feel of his breath on the back of their neck. His hands pressed gently against their lower back. "Just relax. Tell me what you need."

"I don't nee—uuuuuh."

Sam's stubborn words cut off with a groan that came from somewhere deep inside their soul when Teddy's thumbs pressed hard into their sore muscles. Just when they thought they couldn't take it anymore, his hands shifted into a new position, and they made a second noise even more embarrassing than the first. But god, *who cared* as long as he kept doing more of that.

"You like that?" Teddy's voice was amused in Sam's ear. His left thumb dug a little harder into a particularly knotted muscle.

"Mm-hmmmm." Sam wasn't sure they could still remember how to form whole English sentences. Their brain was totally overwhelmed by the excruciating waves of pain and pleasure coursing through their entire body. "Where—where . . . how . . . uhhhh."

"My first serious boyfriend changed majors at least three times while we were dating," Teddy explained, easily interpreting their disjointed thoughts, as usual. "But when we met, he was really into massage therapy. I think that's half the reason I started dating him."

"Thank god," Sam breathed, and in that moment, they were pretty sure they were a little in love with Teddy's first boyfriend. "Remind me to send him a thank-you card when you're d—uh!" They let out an embarrassing squeak when Teddy's thumb found the tender underside of their shoulder blade, where there was a knot that had probably been forming since the early 1980s.

"Is that too much?" Teddy asked, instantly releasing the pressure.

"No. *More*."

Teddy laughed softly, and Sam's muscles finally began to release as he dug in harder. As always, he seemed to have no problem understanding what was working just by paying attention to Sam's body language.

"So I take it today was not a lot of fun," Teddy ventured as he felt them starting to relax.

"Mmm. Not really," Sam said. Their fuzzy brain tried hard to grasp their anger from earlier. It was still there, but dulled by the pleasant endorphins pulsing through them. "Had to do that undercover date, which was all around pretty terrible. Not even because he was a murderer. Just a regular douche."

"Oof. Been there," Teddy said sympathetically.

"Oh?"

"Massage therapist guy was a lot less fun once he got into political science instead."

"You ever leave him tied up with his own belt to a hotel bed?" Sam asked, and Teddy let out a startled laugh.

"No, you didn't!" Teddy said. His hands paused in disbelief. Sam twitched their shoulder impatiently, and Teddy laughed again with delight. "Oh, you really did, didn't you? That's amazing."

Sam laughed, too, because it really was too absurd, but then they groaned, because it had actually happened. Apparently, this was the sad state of their life right now.

"Believe it or not, my day actually would have been a lot better if that guy had turned out to be a murderer," Sam sighed. They could feel the weight of the investigation settling across their shoulders again despite Teddy's soothing efforts. "I really don't know how much longer I can keep this up. If I have to go on one more crappy, pointless date, I'm going to lose my mind."

"Mhm. Pretty sure I can fix that."

"Fuck," Sam swore, arching into his touch. "That feels amazing."

"Here?" Teddy asked. He pressed one knuckle into the spot just above Sam's bra clasp.

"A little . . . a little to the left."

Teddy's hands followed their directions obediently. "Better?"

"Mm-hmmmm. That's . . . Mm!" Sam's voice peaked sharply at the excruciating sensation. "That's good."

Teddy pressed a little harder under their encouragement. After all, he knew by now that they had no problem verbalizing when they enjoyed something.

"So, just the date, or . . . ?" Teddy asked with such painfully fake indifference that Sam couldn't help a small smile. "Did I hear you mention . . . cyanide poisoning?"

"Mm, yeah," Sam said. The muscles in their injured arm spasmed ever so slightly at the memory. "Had to help Noah close his case."

"By taking *cyanide?*"

"Yup. Didn't have any evidence from the original case, so we had to make some new evidence," Sam explained, as if that made the whole thing perfectly reasonable. "We did get the guy in the end, at least. I'll have to keep an eye on the kid, but I think he's going to be all right."

"I mean, that's great, but still—cyanide poisoning? And you just walked that off?" Teddy asked, still sounding a little incredulous.

"It wasn't as bad as I expected, actually," Sam said with an uncomfortable shrug, because the poison itself really hadn't been the bad part. "Just thirty-ish minutes of antidote and I was good to go."

"Still sounds pretty rough." Teddy's hands paused against their shoulders, and Sam let their eyes slide shut.

"Yeah." Pushing their pride aside, Sam forced themself to say, "It was kind of rough. But that's no excuse for being a dick about it. Sorry."

"If it takes a literal near-death experience to make you lose your temper, I don't think you've got anything to apologize for."

Sam was silent as Teddy's right hand trailed slowly down their bare arm to touch the massive bruise already blossoming on the inside of Sam's elbow. Despite their very best effort not to react, Sam still flinched away at the phantom sensation of the needle in their flesh.

"Are you OK?" Teddy asked softly.

"It doesn't hurt too much," Sam replied in a low voice. They forced their body to hold still as his fingers ghosted over the bandaged puncture wound at the center of the bruising.

"I didn't ask if it hurt," Teddy said, although he was quick to pull his hand away when Sam's body began to grow tense again. "I asked if you're OK."

"Yes. I'm fine."

"Sam . . ."

"I am. I'm . . ." Sam felt the denial die on their tongue as that familiar cold crept back in the moment Teddy's touch was no longer distracting them. Wrapping their arms tightly around themself, Sam said, "All right. No. Not really. Or . . . I don't know. This was . . . is . . . helping."

Sam glanced over their shoulder at him shyly, and Teddy met their vulnerability with a soft smile. He scooted a little closer on the bed and they let out a sigh of relief as their back met the familiar warmth of his chest. Maybe he pulled them in. Maybe they leaned back of their own accord. It didn't matter. Sam closed their eyes and allowed themself to just enjoy being held.

"Do you want to talk about it?" Teddy asked after a long moment. Sam tensed again, and Teddy leaned in a little more to nuzzle his cheek against theirs. "You don't have to. You really, really don't have to. Only if it would be helpful."

Sam's hand slipped down a few inches to touch the coarse bandage wrapped around their elbow. They weren't sure talking about this stuff was helpful, exactly, but if they were going to yell at him about it, they should probably try anyway.

"Let's just say I really don't like letting anyone—anything—have control over me. Over my body." Clearing their throat, Sam clarified, "When I was growing up, things were different. There weren't the same rules about medical consent, especially for children. So if you weren't born right . . ."

"Oh my god." Sam felt their gut clench at the horror in Teddy's voice and immediately wished they could take it back. But then: "Born *right?*" His words vibrated with beautiful, raw outrage against Sam's skin. "That's horrible. That's—why? Why would anyone even say something like that? Forget actually . . ."

"It was the eighties," Sam said with a stiff shrug. They could feel the tension coming off of Teddy everywhere their bodies touched, and it was more comforting than he could possibly know. "When I was born, the doctors said I was broken. So they decided I needed to be . . . like this. Surgically. Because it's easier to make a girl than a boy. But it's not—it isn't—that's not how it works. You can't just take a knife to a baby and think that will . . ."

Sam took a deep breath, letting the sentence fizzle instead of trying to find the right words. They had learned a long time ago that there weren't any right words for explaining something like this.

"The older I got, the clearer it was that I would never be the girl anyone wanted me to be. But the people who raised me couldn't accept that.

So . . . they kept trying. Whatever the doctors said would make me 'normal.' Hormones, and therapy, and blockers, and—and lots of other things. Things I didn't get any say in. So when I got old enough, I did the only thing I could do."

"You ran."

Sam flinched at the simplicity of that statement. It wasn't like they hadn't already told him as much. Except, the last time Teddy had asked what was bad enough to send a fifteen-year-old fleeing across the country, the fear had been so intense that they'd hung up on him rather than explaining themself. Of course, he'd called them back five minutes later and cheerfully picked up the conversation like nothing had happened. Because he was a goddamned angel. But they knew the time for leaning on his compassion had passed.

"Yeah. I ran. As far as I could get from that place without literally ending up in the ocean," Sam finally said. "That was twenty-three years ago. But it's still hard for me to be OK. With medication. Hospitals. Anything that could be used to put me under or make me even—less. Doctors, or needles, or . . . you get the idea." Sam felt their words growing smaller with each painful confession. "It is what it is. But now you know."

Teddy made a soft, sad sound as he dropped his chin to Sam's shoulder and squeezed them a little tighter. His fingers brushed ever so tenderly against the thick scar stretching across their abdomen, and Sam let out a shaky breath.

Sam knew logically that there was no way Teddy hadn't noticed they were intersex by now. It would have been impossible to miss over the course of their love making. But they also knew better than most that naming it out loud could make things . . . different. More real. Too real for some people.

But Teddy was nothing if not tenderhearted, and a part of Sam already knew they couldn't scare him away with this kind of thing, even if they tried.

"You know that makes you pretty badass, right?" Teddy said quietly after Sam's breathing had evened out again.

"Hmm?" they hummed vaguely as he dropped a comforting kiss to their bare shoulder.

"That you took cyanide to catch a bad guy, which most people definitely wouldn't do, and you did it knowing you'd have to deal with some traumatic stuff after," he clarified. His beard was soft against Sam's skin when he cuddled them closer.

"Someone had to do it," Sam said with a tight shrug.

Teddy pressed another kiss to their shoulder and let his lips linger this time. "Like I said," he whispered against their skin. "Pretty badass."

". . . I guess so."

Sam didn't feel particularly badass. But they didn't feel quite as rattled anymore, either.

Reaching up with their good arm, they hooked one finger under their bra strap. Teddy immediately froze in place, always prepared to be a gentleman. It was so lovely and frustrating. As Sam slid the strap down their shoulder, Teddy laid a merciful trail of sweet kisses in its wake, and Sam sighed at the sensation.

Their skin felt alive everywhere his lips touched, and the idea of having anything between them suddenly felt unbearable.

Their good arm twisted behind their back, but whichever sadistic monster had invented bras clearly hadn't accounted for those situations where surviving cyanide poisoning left the wearer's dominant hand indisposed.

"Hmm?" Teddy hummed against their shoulder at their quiet huff of frustration. He touched the band of their bra and asked, "You want this off?"

"Mhm."

Normally Sam might have felt embarrassed to need someone else's help, but in this moment, they felt nothing but relief. His deft fingers made quick work of the clasp. With sure and confident hands, he slid the straps down their arms, taking extra care not to jostle their tender elbow.

Sam turned to look at Teddy over their shoulder as the bra made its way to the bedroom floor. "That was pretty fast. You been practicing that somehow?"

"No."

Sam raised an eyebrow at his too-quick response, and Teddy flushed a little at their disbelieving look.

"I, uh, may have googled it. Among some other things."

Sam laughed softly at his painfully honest answer and leaned in to press their forehead against his. "You're really too damn cute, you know that?"

"Yeah? Is it 'cute' that I like making you feel good?" he asked, stroking one hand slowly down their bare back.

"Very cute," Sam assured him. They turned all the way around to face him.

"And is it working?" Teddy asked as their arms coiled around his neck.

"Hmm?"

"Am I making you feel good?"

Sam's breath caught in their throat as his thumb pressed hard into a tender spot on their back. They nodded slowly, then leaned in to kiss him as romantically as they knew how. Sam didn't have Teddy's hands, or his sweet words, but the way his arms tightened around them said they were getting their point across just fine.

Although Sam did have the advantage of not needing to google anything.

When Teddy pulled away, it was to give Sam a look of pure adoration. Taking their face in his hands, he pressed another soft kiss to their lips before murmuring, "I think I'd better go before you start giving me bad ideas."

Considering Sam was the one asking to be undressed, they were pretty sure they were past the point of worrying about bad ideas. But the thought of letting him leave now, with their skin still itching from the vulnerability and their heart in their throat, was unbearable.

Despite Teddy's words, Sam only had to let out the smallest dissatisfied noise and he was back in their arms. Those strong hands found their waist and Sam climbed right up in his lap to look down at his lovely, flushed face. When even the simple intimacy of eye contact felt like way too much, they coiled their body around him tighter than a spring.

Sam's lips parted, and they tried to speak. To say . . . but they couldn't even think of what they wanted to say. He just made them feel so much, all at once. Most of it good and all of it terrifying.

"It's OK," Teddy said softly.

Sam's eyes blinked back at him in silent morse code, praying he would somehow understand their exhausted telepathic message.

"It's OK," Teddy repeated. His hand stroked soothingly down Sam's spine. "Just take a minute. You're good, cariño."

Sam lowered their forehead to his shoulder with a shuddering sigh of relief. It felt ridiculously juvenile to be this worked up over a little basic vulnerability. Some faraway part of their brain knew it was only because they were running on fumes.

Or maybe it wasn't. Maybe they were just really tired for an entirely different reason. Either way, letting him hold them right now seemed like a great idea.

"Tell me something," Sam mumbled into Teddy's collar after a long minute. "Something true. Please."

"Something true, huh?" Teddy mused. His breath was warm and familiar against their ear. "Like something . . . personal?"

Sam gave a tiny nod followed instantly by a wave of shame at their own selfish need. It was wrong to demand vulnerability from him just because they had offered him a glimpse into their mess. He didn't owe them that. But Teddy was nothing if not eager to please.

"OK." Gathering Sam close, Teddy fell back against the mattress and pulled them down on top of him. For half a second, he just buried his face in their neck, and Sam's guilty heart was thrilled that this wasn't easy for him, either. "OK," he repeated after a long moment. "I guess I don't have much to say that's super deep. But, uh, I've been thinking lately . . ."

"Hmm?" Sam prompted when he shifted beneath them nervously.

"I, uh." His hands squeezed them tighter and then released just as quickly. "I think I might be bisexual."

"What—seriously?" Sam instantly pulled back to get their eyes on him, because that was not what they had been expecting. "You mean because of . . . this? With me?"

"No," Teddy denied. When Sam gave him an incredulous look, he flushed bright pink. "I mean," he corrected, "yes, obviously your being bigender got me thinking again. But it's not like I never . . ." Teddy's words trailed off, and Sam couldn't help melting a little at the nerves in his voice. "I guess I, uh, know *who* I like. But the rest of it has always been sort of . . . complicated."

"Mm," Sam hummed sympathetically. They reached down to run a hand through Teddy's curls, and when his anxious eyes fluttered shut at the sensation, it filled them with self-satisfaction. "It was kind of like that for me in my twenties."

"Really?" Teddy's eyes flew open, and Sam's heart stuttered with that potent combination of nerves and anticipation. "You didn't always know you were . . . ?"

"Kind of." When Sam scowled at the memory, Teddy just smiled in a way that made this whole *vulnerability* thing feel not quite so bad. "I guess it would be more accurate to say I never felt like I was one or the other. But I didn't always know that both was an option, either," Sam explained. "Didn't exactly have Google in the eighties, you know?"

"Yeah . . ." The word was little more than a sigh on Teddy's lips. His head tipped back against the sheets, and Sam watched in fascination as at least three different emotions flickered across his face in rapid succession. Sam was pretty sure they'd never get tired of seeing his big heart on display like that.

"It's nice, being able to look up all the options," he said finally. "But it's still . . ."

"Complicated?" Sam suggested. They wound one of his curls around their finger, and he nodded bashfully. "That's OK," Sam assured him. Leaning down, they kissed him lightly on the lips before murmuring, "Complicated works for me."

Sam found themself being tugged insistently down on Teddy's chest, and they didn't fight it when he returned their kiss twice as eagerly. The painfully honest conversation felt strangely familiar. Their late-night phone calls hadn't been so different—even the part where being vulnerable kind of turned him on. But being rewarded with kisses and petting after was definitely something Sam could get used to.

Their lips parted, and Teddy sighed, long and sweet. Then he was rolling them over so they were both lying on the bed in a tangle of limbs. He pressed his face into their neck again and mumbled, "I think I really like complicated, actually."

"You probably shouldn't," Sam said, but it wasn't very believable when they were positively melting into his embrace.

"Too late."

"Teddy—"

"It's too late. It was too late, like, twenty phone calls ago." He laughed helplessly against their skin. "Look at me," he said, releasing them just long enough to gesture down at their entwined position. "I'm crazy about you, Sam. Completely crazy."

"I—" Teddy gave them those puppy dog eyes, and the denial died on Sam's lips. "OK. Yeah. Me too," they admitted, enjoying the rush of relief that accompanied that simple confession. They knew Teddy felt it too when his smile only grew.

"You'd better be." Teddy reached out to touch Sam's face, and they shifted a little closer on the bed so their bodies could curl toward each other.

"Tell me one more thing," Sam breathed when Teddy gave them another one of those looks that put his whole beautiful heart on display.

"Anything."

God. He terrified them, and it felt so, *so* good to be this nervous around someone again.

"How the hell are you still single, Teddy Burgess?"

"Oh. That one's easy, Detective." Teddy offered them a knowing, scrunchy-eyed smile. Leaning in a little closer, he whispered, "I'm not single. I'm actually very. Very. Taken."

Well. There was really only one appropriate response to that.

Sam's throat was full of butterflies, but they didn't need words for this. They kissed him with every ounce of passion roaring through them at the thought of him being taken. By them. Because he wanted to be with *them*.

Sam's body was beyond exhausted, but they still needed him to know. They spoke through the short, flirtatious skim of skin brushing against skin, followed by longer, exploratory touches as their bodies settled together with sweet intimacy. Sam reveled in the feeling of being held in Teddy's sure embrace. The firm pressure of his hands on their body and the softness of their lips coming together was an experience Sam could easily get addicted to.

Sam's leg came up to hook around Teddy's hip, and his thick thigh pressed eagerly between their legs. Sam's hands shoved his shirt up as they kissed him even more urgently, their bodies warm and sensual against each other.

"Teddy," Sam whispered as the mood notably shifted. Their hands knotted in his shirt, and they said, "I . . . I want . . ."

They weren't even sure what they were asking him for. Not sex, exactly. Just more. More intimacy. More of this. More of him. Even though they were too tired, and it was a bad idea, and they absolutely should not let themself fall any harder, Sam still just wanted more. Even if that meant letting him have more of them in return.

Teddy sat up just enough that Sam could tug his shirt off, then used the momentum to settle them back in the sheets. Despite their desire, Sam tensed up again as Teddy's hands started working the buttons on their jeans.

"Relax. Relax," Teddy breathed as he leaned in to kiss them deeply. Sam slowly let go, dizzy with the romance and allowing themself to trust him. "I've got you, baby," Teddy murmured against their lips as he finished undoing their pants and tugging them down. "Just relax. Let me take care of you tonight." With those promising words, Teddy slipped down their body to settle between their legs.

Sam's breath caught as he paused there, waiting for their permission. Their heart was beating in their ears, but they nodded slowly, and Teddy lowered his head. Sam let their eyes flutter shut, enjoying the warmth of his hands wrapping around their hips, his kisses oh-so-tender down their stomach . . . along their inner thigh . . . and then . . .

"Teddy."

His name was a sigh on their lips as his mouth dipped into that intimate space between their legs, and oh boy. He really had been googling things.

"You like that?" Teddy asked, pulling back a little.

"Mhmm."

His mouth returned to their bare skin, steadily getting them there with each sensual stroke of his tongue. Sam let out an involuntary whimper and arched into him as his hand joined his tongue between their legs. Sam's fingers curled helplessly in the sheets, because they hadn't done anything this intimate with a lover in years, and the idea of just lying back and letting him pleasure them was—*god*, but he just made them feel so . . .

Teddy stopped doing that amazing thing he was doing with his tongue just long enough to guide Sam's hands into his hair as their breath hitched noticeably.

"That's good, baby," he murmured. His eyes closed with pleasure when Sam's fingers tightened in his curls. "Tell me what you like."

Sam guided his mouth back down, and it didn't take long after that, because there was absolutely nothing he was doing that they *didn't* like. Their hips lifted off the bed and they gasped his name as he eagerly took them over the edge into sweet, orgasmic bliss.

When he was sure they were completely satisfied, Teddy slowly kissed his way back up their body, greedily absorbing every jagged breath and shiver of pleasure along the way. Pressing his cheek against theirs, he asked, "How was that?"

"Good. Uh, very—very good," Sam managed, a little bit not convinced that he had learned how to do that from "Google" but also really not caring how he got educated, because damn.

Teddy laughed low in his chest, and when he shifted his weight against them, Sam could feel how turned on he was.

"Um. Do you need me to . . . ?" Sam reached down to touch his leg hesitantly.

Pulling back a little, Teddy gave them a soft, knowing smile and said, "Don't worry about me. Just let me take care of you tonight, OK?"

Sam nodded shyly even as their heart raced, maybe more from the intimacy of his romancing than from the orgasm itself.

"Do you need anything else? Something to eat, or drink, or . . . ?" Teddy asked, and Sam just shook their head silently.

Teddy took this as his cue to move off of them, and Sam drew their knees up to their chest as the anxious pressure of words they didn't know how to say pushed against their insides.

Smiling, Teddy reached down to grab one of his shirts off the floor and offered it to Sam. For once he wasn't perfectly understanding their Sam-speak, but that was probably because they were currently too tongue-tied to actually say anything. Sam pulled on the oversized shirt anyway, and in those three seconds Teddy had already stood up from the bed.

"All right," he said gently. When he leaned down to press a kiss to their forehead, Sam felt their heart sink. "How about I give you some space? Get some rest and you can call me when you're ready for that second date."

Teddy started to turn away, only to pull up short as a slight pressure tugged at his waist. He glanced down and tilted his head at the sight of Sam's finger hooking through one of his belt loops.

"Stay," Sam blurted before they could chicken out.

Teddy gave them a questioning look, and they felt a fierce, hot flush crawling up their neck, but it was too late now. "Stay the night," Sam repeated. "Please. I don't want space. I want . . ." Their forehead pressed to their knees as their pulse skyrocketed at the thought of what they were asking. Swallowing hard, they mumbled, "Please stay."

There was a beat of silence followed by the sound of a zipper being undone. Sam started to look up just as the mattress dipped and a very smiley, very naked Teddy crawled right back into their bed.

"Of course, baby." He grabbed hold of them and wrestled them playfully down into the sheets. "I'll stay for as long as you'll let me."

"God, this is so embarrassing," Sam complained, even as he dragged them under the covers for some good and proper cuddles.

"Hey, you knew what you were getting yourself into. This is just how I sleep." Teddy's naked body curled around them affectionately. "No need to be embarrassed about it."

"That's not what I meant, and you know it," Sam grumbled.

"Ooh, you meant asking me to stay the night was the embarrassing part?" Teddy said with a big fake gasp. "My bad, I couldn't tell."

Sam rolled their eyes at his teasing, which only encouraged him to start peppering them with enthusiastic kisses.

"Is it still embarrassing? Hmm? Is it? How about now?"

Teddy didn't let up his onslaught until Sam was laughing, and he was grinning, and they were both feeling the kind of wild, romantic insanity that came from being new lovers.

"You are so ridiculous," Sam protested before shoving him determinedly over onto the other side of the bed. "If you want to stay, you can stay, but you've got to be quiet and let me sleep."

Teddy stayed put for about thirty seconds—just long enough for Sam to curl up and start getting comfortable—when they felt him start sneaking closer again.

"Teddy . . ." Sam growled as his arm slid beneath their pillow.

"Nice try. You're the one who asked me to stay," Teddy said, tucking his other arm around their middle so he could spoon them properly. And that was . . . hmm. That was not terrible, actually.

Sam let out a jaw-cracking yawn, and Teddy made a soft, contented noise as he snuggled up against them.

"Yeah, OK, OK," Sam mumbled. His body wrapped around them was soft and warm and so very impossible to resist. "Don't go getting any ideas. It's just this one time."

"Mhm. We'll see about that," Teddy whispered. Sam felt the softest of kisses brush against their cheek. "Now get some sleep. Something tells me tomorrow is going to be a much, much better day for you, cariño."

CHAPTER THIRTY-FOUR

"Helloooo . . . Sammy? Earth to—"

"I can hear you," Sam grumbled. They picked their chin up off the conference room table as they continued to stare down the board of information. Names, dates, and numbers all ran together in a blur of cramped handwriting. Rubbing their eyes irritably, Sam said, "I just don't get what I'm missing."

"And you still haven't heard anything from the hospital about security footage or the visitor's log?" Donya asked. Sam shot her a look so scathing she immediately recoiled. "OK, just asking. Someone's cranky."

"I am not cranky," Sam snapped. They blew out a long breath and said in a slightly more measured tone, "OK. If I'm cranky, it's because I was on the phone until one in the morning, but the hospital wouldn't give me anything. I've filed for the warrant, but you know how it goes. There's no guarantee the judge will even grant it unless the coroner's report agrees that there are signs of foul play."

"You want me to swing by later, boss?" Noah asked from where he stood adding notes to the already crowded board. "Maybe the white coats would be more likely to give us something in person."

"That's not a bad idea," Sam said with a nod of approval. "They weren't very forthcoming when I was there last night, but maybe you'll have better luck."

"Yeah, because they thought you were going to burn the place down," Vince said dryly. The grizzled older cop leaned back in his chair as he appraised Sam with those cold shark eyes. "Word on the street is that

389

you put on quite the fireworks show when they wouldn't hand over the footage."

"You shouldn't believe everything you hear," Sam said flatly, even though his information was dead-on as usual. Their temporary ban from the premises was a little inconvenient, though, so they turned back to Noah and said, "I doubt the front desk will give you anything. Maybe try the floor staff. Show a few people Jason's photo and see if anyone recognizes him."

"Jason?" Noah asked. He glanced at the man's name, which was crossed out with the conservation charity alibi written next to it. "Are we still on him?"

"Yes. No." Sam sighed and scrubbed a hand across their face. "I don't know. He's got the alibi, but there's just something . . . not right with him."

"You gotta trust your instincts," Noah said wisely, tapping the marker cap against Jason's name. "Your mind is making the right connections. You just haven't figured out how to put them into words yet."

Sam made a face as the rookie quoted one of their early lessons back at them. "Instincts, huh? Don't know how sharp those are right now."

"Maybe you need some coffee," Donya suggested as Sam shoved back in their chair. "I don't think I've ever seen you go this long without drinking something that would kill a normal person."

"Just not feeling like office coffee today." A tiny ghost of a smile pulled at Sam's lips as they stood up to approach the board of painstakingly organized information.

They were pretty sure no crappy office coffee would ever be able to satiate them again. Not after experiencing the pure bliss of an expertly pressed Alturo brew sipped slowly in the arms of a man who wanted nothing more than to hold them for as long as possible. Or maybe a little longer than was possible.

Not that anyone here needed to know exactly why Sam had been twenty minutes late today and was still floating around like a lovestruck idiot.

But still.

Despite the pleasant memories, Sam's smile faded as quickly as it had appeared when they found themself standing before the whiteboard. Their eyes roamed the columns of information and found countless patterns and connections—but they were all nonsense. False flags generated by a mind desperate to deny that this case was beginning to go cold as their best leads continued to alibi out.

"How can we have all this information and still have nothing?" Sam muttered. They reached out to place the pad of one finger over Jason's entry. Dragging their finger down the whiteboard, they watched as a streak appeared through all the useless information spooling out beneath his name.

"Hey, I spent all morning on that," Noah complained. He batted Sam's hand away before they could mess up any more of his carefully written notes. "Maybe we need to go back to the beginning," he suggested, frowning up at the board.

Sam found it both humorous and alarming that Noah was more focused than they'd ever seen him, while they could barely concentrate for five minutes before their thoughts began to drift.

". . . had an alibi for Nikki, right? So Christian was ruled out before we knew to look into the hacking angle. And Jason has an alibi for Kayleigh's assault, but neither of them have alibis for Alicia or Cassie, so maybe . . ."

Useless. So useless. Sam wasn't even listening to what Noah was saying. How could they be standing here thinking about coffee and cuddling when there was a murderer on the loose? Sam couldn't even remember the last time they had been this distracted during a case.

They just needed to be able to focus.

"You're right."

"He is?" Donya said at nearly the same moment Noah said, "I am?"

Ignoring Donya's scornful look, Noah said eagerly, "So, you actually think we might be looking at multiple killers working to—"

"No, not that part. That's nonsense," Sam said dismissively. Giving their head a hard shake to clear out the static, they started glancing around in search of something. "I'm saying we're not going to solve this case by looking at a bunch of statistics. That's what got us into this mess in the first place." Sam's eyes finally landed on the whiteboard eraser. They picked it up and weighed it in their hand as they took in the information spread across the board. "We need to go back to the beginning and figure out where we lost the thread on this thing."

Noah made a pained noise but knew better than to try and stop Sam as they began scrubbing away all the meticulously organized information. After watching them work for a few seconds using only their uninjured arm, he grabbed a tissue and helped them clear the other side of the board.

Snatching up a dry erase marker, Sam uncapped it with their teeth and attempted to start writing with their left hand.

"When this whole thing started, we had three victims who had all gone out with the same three men," Sam said, writing out the women's names across the top of the board in messy cursive.

"Here, let me," Noah said. He grabbed the marker right out of their hand and elbowed them aside.

Sam started to protest, but caught the look of keen interest on Vince's face and shut their mouth again. Tugging the rolled sleeve of their dress shirt down to cover a little more of the hideous bruising from the IV debacle, Sam said, "So we've got Cassie, Nikki, and Alicia, each going out at least once with Christian, Brad, and Jason."

Noah obediently listed the three men's names beneath each of the women, then added, "And aside from dating history, all three of our vics also had weird activity timelines, yeah? Like, online but inactive before their time of death or whatever because of the hack?"

"Right," Sam confirmed. "Although we didn't know anything about the hack until after Christian had already alibied out for Nikki's murder."

"Alicia's sister is the one who turned you on to that," Donya observed. Her pale eyes tracked the movement as Noah struck off Christian's name. "She claimed Alicia had been messaging with some guy that night. But there was no record of a conversation, just the weird activity logs."

Noah's marker hesitated next to Alicia's name. "Uh, what was the sister's name, again?" he asked sheepishly.

"Natasha Hancock."

"And we're sure we believe the sister?" Vince asked as Noah jotted down the name. Sam gave him a look, and he shrugged unapologetically. "Just saying. Grief makes some people loopy."

"Alicia's body was found in the alley between the Continental and Calliope's, which is the bar where Tasha said she was going that night," Sam explained. "And the hack also helps explain the strange activity patterns for all three women."

"Cassie's was a little different though, right?" Noah asked, tapping the marker next to the first victim's name.

"Because she was also . . . ?" Donya gestured down at her own body vaguely, and Sam grimaced in silent confirmation. Donya let out a low whistle. "Stabbing a pregnant woman. That's quite the first kill for our perp."

"That assumes our guy even knew she was knocked up," Vince said in his typical shrewd fashion.

Noah turned to give him a disbelieving look. "According to Cassie's coworkers, she was scared for her life after she broke the news to her baby daddy. They even said she used the app to communicate with him. That's seriously supposed to be a coincidence?"

"Well, when you put it like that . . ."

Noah scowled at Vince's sarcastic tone but didn't try to stop him when Vince rocked forward out of his seat and prowled over to the board. Tapping the blank spot to the right of the three women's names, he said, "This is your outlier. The fourth vic."

"But—" Noah started.

"Our guy took out three more women after girlie number one bit it, and none of them were pregnant," Vince said right over Noah's protests. "That's a coincidence doing its best to look like a clue. But the lawyer chick—she was different. If she didn't get taken out two seconds after leaving the mixer, I'd be tempted to say her case was entirely unrelated to the other vics."

"But—"

"He's right," Sam agreed. They backed up a step to take in the much emptier board, and possibly to avoid the injured look Noah was giving them. "All three of our original women went out with the same three guys, have the same weird activity pattern indicating that their chat history was scrubbed, and were all stabbed in secluded areas near traditional date locations." Sighing, Sam repeated, "No matter how you cut it, he's right. Kayleigh is the outlier."

"Maybe the answer is in the differences," Donya suggested. Now she, too, got up to approach the board. Holding out one hand without even looking in Noah's direction, she said, "If our guy changed up his MO, it has to be for a reason, right?" The marker landed in her palm without question, and she scrawled Kayleigh's name on the board in line with the others. "What do we actually know about this chick?"

"She didn't date Christian or Brad, but she did have several dates with Jason, including one the night before her initial attack," Sam said, and

Donya jotted down the information. "She only used the app that day to access the evite for the event. Otherwise, she was offline and inactive the entire day."

"And then the biggest outlier," Vince said. "Getting stabbed in the middle of the street instead of in an alleyway like a proper cliché." He scratched his stubble as he stared at the board of information. "Maybe our guy panicked. Thought you were on to him because the mixer was a set-up."

"Maybe," Sam said with a frown. "Beck did stack the event with potential suspects, but there's a reason you can't data mine for solid leads. The men there that night were a match on paper, but none of them panned out in my follow-up interviews."

"But you could have missed something, right?" Noah asked.

Sam gave him a look, but he seemed determined to win his participation award in this investigation. Snatching the marker back from Donya despite her sound of protest, Noah started writing out the names of Sam's previous dates underneath a new column labeled "mixer suspects." The fact that he could remember the names of seventeen dud leads but not the victim's sister was only more exasperating.

"You're the one who kept saying undercover dating was a shit way to interview somebody," Noah said when he was done writing. Gesturing to the seventeen names and then to the three original suspects who had all alibied out, he said, "Obviously, it'd be nice if our perp was stupid enough to leave evidence that he went out with all our vics. But we already know Evil Elon Musk can delete conversation histories, so for all we know, he was smart enough to erase any trace of his relationship to these chicks."

"Evil Elon Musk?" Vince echoed.

"Yeah, our perp is some kind of super genius or some shit. Smart enough to hack into a secure app remotely, anyways," Noah explained, utterly oblivious to the malicious glee in Vince's tone.

Evil Elon Musk. This kid really was thirty going on thirteen.

Sam tuned out Vince's mocking as their unfocused eyes took in the board of information. The three men who shared dating history with the vics. The seventeen men who had no shared dating history but did have the skills to pull off an elaborate hack. Their perp should be somewhere in the crossover between the two groups, and yet that crossover seemed nonexistent.

Could it be that Noah was right and their hacker was just that good?

"He knows saying 'evil Elon Musk' is redundant, right?" Donya said over top of Vince and Noah's quarreling. She glanced at Sam sidelong, and a faraway part of Sam's brain registered that they were supposed to react.

"Seemingly," they muttered. Their eyes were still pinned to the board as their pulse slowly started to increase.

Two groups. One with motive, the other with means. So where was the missing opportunity?

"Really? You're defending Tesla?" Donya responded. "I didn't think you'd be a fan of a car that doesn't even have a proper steering wheel."

"No, anything without a manual gearshift isn't a real car. I meant . . ."

Donya gave them a curious look, but before she could ask, Sam's mind had already leapt three steps ahead.

"Hey."

Noah froze mid-argument at the sound of Sam's command.

Holding out their hand, Sam said, "Give me the marker."

"But your arm—"

"Give me. The marker." This time, Noah seemed to grasp the importance of the situation. He fumbled to hand over the marker, and Sam wasted no time approaching the board again. Pointing to the first group of men, they said, "We've got one group here with potential motives, but they all alibied out, right?"

They wrote the word "motive" above the first group—or the closest approximation they could form with their left hand. Vince started to speak, but Sam continued right over him. "Our other group has the potential means to pull off the hack, but no motive."

The word "means" appeared above the group of seventeen men. Then Sam drew two lines connecting the two groups and tapped the marker aggressively against the junction between them.

"What we need is a third option that would give a perp with motive the means and opportunity to pull this off. And since we're certain about when and where the murders took place, that means our missing piece lies in the means."

"I think you really do need another coffee, because that sounds a lot like the same thing we've been saying all morning," Vince said.

"No way," Noah breathed almost before Vince had finished speaking.

"You still got something to say, rookie?" The older cop asked with a frown at the wide-eyed look on Noah's face.

"No fucking way," Noah repeated, with no interest whatsoever in Vince's heckling now. His shocked gaze flipped to Sam and then back to the board again. "Come on, dude. You can't seriously think . . . ?"

"Think what?" Donya asked impatiently. Clearly not pleased to be a step behind her fellow rookie, she demanded, "What the hell are you two talking about?"

"The master password," Sam said grimly. Noah was already shaking his head, but Sam pressed on. "Think about it. We've been looking for a master hacker, but Vivienne told us herself that she keeps a password on her phone, which would allow someone to go into the backend and alter anything they wanted."

"OK. OK," Vince said. A peculiar smile began to twist across his face as he followed Sam's logic. "Now this is some good shit. To be clear, your brilliant new theory is that your ex-girlfriend committed a bunch of murders and then used her own business to cover it up?"

"No," Sam said shortly. "I'm saying Vivienne's *password* might have been used to cover up the murders."

"Yeah, but she also told us it's some crazy-long alpha-pneumonic combination or something," Noah protested.

"I think you mean alphanumeric," Donya corrected.

"Whatever. Point is, our perp would still have to be some kind of fuckin' super genius to memorize all that after just one glance."

"Password's on her phone?" Vince asked, and Sam nodded. "And it never changes?" Sam nodded again. Vince's flat gaze flicked to the board again. Sam might not like the other cop, but he wasn't stupid, and they knew he was seeing all the same connections they were.

Looking back to Noah, Vince asked, "Well? How secure is your personal phone, Officer Dumbass?"

"Shit," Noah swore as the pieces clicked for him just a beat behind the more-senior officers. Pulling out his phone, he looked down at the cracked screen and said, "So—shit. Anyone who could get into her phone coulda just, like, taken a screenshot or something? Damn. That's—damn."

"Like I said. No hacking required," Sam confirmed.

"So then the real question is, who has easy access to your friend's phone?" Donya asked. "Other than her, if you're really sure she didn't do it."

For a long moment, all four cops stared at the phone in Noah's hand like it might contain the answers.

"I'm not sure of anything," Sam finally admitted. Slipping their own phone out of their pocket, they were already selecting the most recent name off the caller ID when they said, "But I've got some theories."

"Tell me you're calling her right now," Vince said. His voice was positively brimming with delight at the mere concept. "Oh my god, this is going to be so good. Please tell me you're going to—"

"Would you shut up for once in your life?" Sam snapped.

"Uh. Pocket dial or am I in trouble?" The voice on the other end sounded more amused than concerned.

"Oh, hey baby," Sam said automatically. Wincing a little at their own lovesick honesty, they turned their back on the rest of the room and said, "Sorry about that. Just my coworker being an asshole."

"Baby?" Vince's voice echoed in disbelief from somewhere behind them.

"Your Captain again?" Teddy did not sound impressed at the thought.

"No, not her. One of the Vice douchebags," Sam assured him. Despite the stressful situation, Teddy's voice instantly slowed their racing train of thought. "Listen, I don't have long, but I wanted to ask you something that might help with my investigation."

"Any excuse to hear your voice, cariño."

"Mhm." Sam felt a helpless smile pulling at their lips again. And they were calling Noah unprofessional. Forcing their scattered thoughts back into line, they said, "I was actually wondering about Henry. I know he's your manager, but he's also your employee, right?"

"Technically, yeah." Sam could hear the rustle of papers being put down on the other end, and they knew they had Teddy's attention now.

"So he gets paid out of your account."

"Yes?"

"But he also manages your business accounts," Sam pressed.

"I sure hope so. It's not like I ever look at them."

"Is there anything of yours he doesn't have access to?"

"Nope. If I dropped dead tomorrow, he'd pretty much get everything."

"Jesus. You two are practically married," Sam said with a helpless laugh that was half humor and half heartbreak.

"Don't let his fiancé hear you saying that. Ky would not be above pushing me off a cliff if he thought for even one second that I was making a move on his man."

"Sounds a little intense."

"He is. You're going to love him when I introduce you."

"Yeah. Probably will," Sam agreed. And then, because the last thing they needed to be thinking about was what it meant to be meeting Teddy's friends, they said, "OK. I think that's all I need for now. You good there?"

"Yup. Just busy counting down the hours till I see you again."

"It's really very distracting when you say stuff like that, you know?"

"Good. Then we'll both be distracted. ¿Te veo esta noche?"

"Yeah. Te veo en la noche, cariño."

Sam hung up the phone as their pulse accelerated an unhealthy amount. And not just because they were sure that phone call was going to haunt them around the office for the next three months. They were more concerned with what the immediate future held.

To their surprise, it was Donya who broke the silence first. "What the hell was that about?"

"None of your business," Noah said. Clearly, he was taking his "cross-my-heart" promise from their chance meeting at the café pretty seriously, and Sam couldn't say they hated it.

"It's fine," Sam assured him as they turned back to face the room. Gesturing with their phone to Donya, they said, "That was a friend of mine who I thought might have some insight as a business owner."

"Sounds like you have a lot of good friends, *baby*," Vince sneered, but

Sam just ignored him and approached the whiteboard again.

"If we're not looking for a hacker, we're looking for someone who had access to the master password. And if it wasn't Vivienne, it'd have to be someone close to her," Sam explained. Picking up the marker again, they wrote out two more names on the board at the junction between the two groups of men. "Someone close enough that she wouldn't think twice about letting them look through her phone."

There was another long silence. The two names in Sam's messy cursive were tiny on the board, but they seemed to fill the entire room with the implications. Sam glanced to Noah before tapping one of the names silently. Noah looked pained, but for once he had nothing to say other than nodding in agreement.

The answer was clear. But that didn't make it any easier to accept.

"You sure about this, Sam?" Vince asked when the silence became overwhelming. Even he sounded serious for once. "Anything this personal is guaranteed to have some nasty fallout."

"Can you get the warrant?"

"Give me a couple hours, but yeah. I can get it using this," he confirmed, nodding to the board full of information.

"Then yes, I'm sure," Sam said simply. Looking to Donya, they added, "I am going to be needing that IOU to pull this off, though."

"Copy that, Supercop," she said. Those pale blue eyes cut through Sam, but they didn't flinch. Sam knew they weren't wrong about this, and they could tell she knew it, too, because she asked, "What's the plan?"

"I'll have the details lined up soon," Sam promised. They replaced the marker and headed back over to the table to grab their jacket. No part of them wanted to do this, but if they had to, then they wanted to get it over with. Already striding toward the door, they said, "There's someone I need to talk to first."

"Sam," Noah called out before they could disappear. Sam hesitated in the doorway, hearing the concern in his voice. "Uh, you sure that's really the smartest thing to do, boss?"

"No. Probably not," Sam said with a helpless shrug. "But it's the human thing."

CHAPTER THIRTY-FIVE

The ornate front door finally swung open, and Sam let their fist drop to their side. "I was starting to wonder how long you were going to make me knock," they said lightly, despite the way their gut clenched at the sight of her.

Sweatpants. Hair tied up in a silk wrap. Expression caught somewhere between surprise and suspicion to see them standing there on her front step.

"Just wanted your knuckles to match your knees," Vivienne shot back, and Sam felt their insides coil tighter. Her glib response should have annoyed them, but all they felt was guilty.

God. This really was the worst job in the world sometimes.

"OK, I'll bite," Vivienne said when Sam didn't even react to the playful jab. "What are you doing here? Did you need something for the case?"

"Yeah. No. Sort of, yeah," Sam said with all the coherency their brain normally brought to these situations. Shaking their head slightly, they asked, "Is Harper home?"

"Harper? No, she's at the hospital until at least six. Unlike me, she doesn't get to work from home whenever she feels like it," Vivienne replied as though her comfortable getup wasn't clue enough. "Did you need her for something?"

"No." Looking past Vivienne's shoulder to the massive house sprawling out behind her, Sam said, "Listen. I know this would piss her off, but can I . . . ?"

"You mean . . . come in?" Vivienne asked uncertainly. When Sam offered a short nod, she looked even more disquieted by their odd behavior, but she stepped aside to let them in.

Sam followed silently in her wake as she led them down the hallway with the vaulted ceilings to a large, tastefully decorated room filled with a myriad of seating options. When Sam hesitated in the doorway, Vivienne politely gestured them to a wingback armchair that had the approximate surface density of a concrete slab.

The large clock in the corner ticked loudly as Vivienne settled on the rigid-looking sofa opposite Sam's chair. For a long moment they just sat there in awkward silence, regarding each other from opposite sides of the room. Somehow, without the glitz and the glam, all Sam could see when they looked at her was that uncertain young woman who had taken up space in their bed, and in their heart, and then in their furious thoughts for all those months after she broke their heart.

It was ridiculous, really. She had caused them so much pain, and yet here Sam was, chewing their words and trying to find a way to spare her from this. How horrified would the old Sam be if they could see how soft they'd become?

"Oh, god," Sam finally groaned. They leaned forward to place their elbows on their knees. A half-laugh escaped their lips and Vivienne gave them a peculiar look, which was probably fair. "Sorry. It's just—it's kind of funny, isn't it? Could you have pictured any of this when we were kids?" They waved vaguely at the beautiful mansion surrounding them.

"We were hardly kids," Vivienne scoffed. Her words were confident, but her eyes told a different story as they drifted around the room. "Although based on the number of mouse traps we went through that year, we probably shouldn't have been allowed to make our own decisions," she admitted.

The memories were so vivid Sam could practically hear the snap of the trap and imagine the tears on Vivienne's face as Sam did away with the poor creatures. Just animals trying to survive in a cruel world that didn't want them.

Sam's gut twisted with regret as they remembered the shouting matches that would follow. Or really, it would be Sam shouting and Vivienne crying and both of them just getting more and more frustrated as everything spiraled. Then rinse and repeat the next week.

What a mess.

"Do you ever miss it?" Sam asked quietly.

Vivienne offered them a sad smile. "No. Not really."

"Yeah," they said. The word felt too small to explain the ache they felt for those lost, broken kids, but they didn't have the words to explain it any other way. Leaning back a little in their seat, Sam gave her a long, appraising look before venturing, "It was a pretty shit apartment, wasn't it?"

"It was," Vivienne agreed.

Broken AC. Broken front step. Broken stove, broken everything.

"It was a pretty shit relationship, too."

This time Vivienne didn't manage to hold their gaze. Still, she offered them a silent nod.

"You really messed me up for a long time, you know."

Her eyes flicked back to them, and for half a heartbeat Sam wanted to take the words back when they saw the hurt on her face. But still they forced themself to continue.

"After everything I shared with you. You knew opening myself up like that was—well. It was really pretty fucked up of you to step out on me after all that."

"I—" the first note of an excuse caught on the tip of Vivienne's tongue, but she choked it off before the words could form. She grimaced hard before saying in a measured tone, "You're right. What I did to you was . . . wrong. I won't say I didn't have my own demons to deal with back then, but that's no excuse. I hurt you—knowingly. Repeatedly. And I can't ever change that, but I am deeply sorry for what I put you through."

"Yeah. Well." Sam let out another long sigh that tasted a lot like regret. "Like I said, it was a shitty relationship. But I was a pretty terrible partner, too, so . . . I guess we can both be sorry."

Vivienne nodded in acceptance of their apology, but had the humility to say, "It's a little different. You never cheated on me."

"That's true." Sam scrubbed a hand down their face as the momentary relief of closure was replaced by the weight of what they knew was coming next. "God," they muttered under their breath. "What the hell were we thinking?"

"We were probably thinking we were in love."

"Were we?" Sam asked.

"I think so. Or as close as we could get back then, anyways," Vivienne said with a delicate shrug. "It wasn't like either of us had a reason to expect something better, right?" Offering Sam a weak smile, she said, "But look at us now."

"Yeah," they echoed dully. "Look at us now."

The clock continued to tick as the two lapsed back into solemn silence. Sam hoped that giving her the chance to release the past would bring her some solace. But they doubted it.

"Just say it," Vivienne finally said into the stifling silence.

Sam winced, even as Vivienne sat up straighter in her seat. They could see the cool businesswoman falling back into place as she tucked an errant curl behind her wrap and folded her hands over her knee. Strong. Professional. Ready to handle the next crisis.

Sam didn't think anyone could be ready for this.

"Whatever you really came here to say," Vivienne insisted. "Let's just get it over with, OK?"

"OK," Sam said slowly. Drawing themself up, they found themself staring at a point just past her shoulder as their mouth formed the words they'd been dreading. "We made a break in the case. This morning."

"OK," Vivienne said. "It seems like that would be . . . good news."

"It is. Of course it is," Sam agreed quickly, although the words weren't quite convincing. "You remember what we talked about with the strange time stamps on the victims' profiles?" they asked. "We couldn't figure out why the hacker didn't erase the activity logs when they deleted the conversation history."

"You said the killer didn't want to set someone else up in case they had a lucky alibi," Vivienne recalled.

"That was why they didn't create a fake conversation history. But I never could figure out why someone smart enough to delete the conversations didn't also delete the activity logs." For half a second, they felt that exhilarating high that always came with breaking a case. But then they saw Vivienne's puzzled expression, and the excitement faded again. "It's not the kind of detail an experienced hacker would overlook when covering their tracks," Sam explained.

"Well, I don't think an inexperienced hacker broke my program," Vivienne said, and despite the situation, she still managed to sound a little offended.

"But that's exactly it. We thought we were looking for some kind of genius, because only someone incredibly smart could beat your security system." Sam hesitated for half a beat to see if she would make the connection. When she didn't, they added as gently as they could, "We weren't considering that someone might just be smart enough to borrow your phone for a minute."

"My—what?" Vivienne recoiled a little. Clearly, whatever she had thought they were going to say, it wasn't this. "You mean for the master password?" she clarified, and her eyes narrowed when Sam nodded. "You don't seriously think I would ever let anyone use that?"

"Of course not. Not knowingly," Sam agreed. Glancing to Vivienne's phone, which sat on the coffee table in front of her, they said, "It wouldn't have to be knowingly. If you left your phone unattended, even for a minute, it would be a simple matter of taking a picture of the password while you weren't looking."

"Well, yes. But I don't just leave my phone lying around. And who—" Vivienne's gaze followed theirs to her phone before she shook her head sharply. That curl sprang free of her wrap again, but she didn't seem to notice. "This is ridiculous. I wouldn't let some stranger look through my phone. How would they even unlock it?"

"I'm not talking about a stranger."

"Sam." Her voice was full of warning now, and Sam's heart ached as they saw the realization dawning on her face.

"You know there's only one person who makes sense," Sam said as gently as they could.

"Don't you dare." Vivienne's voice shook with emotion, and Sam winced at the sight of her face twisting with anger. "How could you even suggest something like that? You've met her. How could you . . . How dare you? You know she would never—"

"I know that she's with you all the time," Sam said, speaking right over her sound of protest. "I know I've seen her ask for your phone before, and that you handed it over willingly. And I think we both know how she feels about—"

"Don't," Vivienne repeated sharply. "This is absurd. Look around you." Vivienne's hand slashed through the air, indicating the hard-won opulence that contrasted sharply with that sad apartment she and Sam had known two decades earlier. "You think I could have accomplished any of this without her? She would never do that to me."

"Then tell me who else." Sam's quiet words cut straight through her fierce defense. "Think about it. I know it's terrible. But just think—if not her, then who?"

The words landed like a gut punch. For a long moment there was nothing but silence. Vivienne's breathing became uneven as the truth grew in her mind, and Sam squeezed their eyes shut. They should have been a waiter. Or a cashier, or a janitor, or anything that didn't involve hearing good people have their hearts broken on a regular basis.

Standing abruptly, Sam crossed the room to Vivienne's side and dropped down on the sofa next to her. She looked at them with wide-eyed panic—and anger, and confusion, and all the other emotions fighting to surface inside her. Sam only hesitated slightly before reaching out to take her hand in theirs.

"I'm sorry," they told her, earnest and simple. It wouldn't help, they knew that. But it was true, and it should be said. Squeezing her hand firmly, they repeated, "I'm so sorry, Viv."

"You're wrong." Vivienne's voice trembled.

"I wish I was. But I'm not. And now I have to ask you for something terrible."

"No." The word burst from her lips with violent certainty. Vivienne wrenched her hand away, and Sam let her.

"I'm sorry," they repeated. "But we can't do this without you."

"No. Don't ask me for this," Vivienne snapped. Her hands curled around the edge of the hard sofa like she was stuck between jumping to her feet or collapsing in on herself. In a weaker voice, she repeated, "Please. Why would she . . .?"

"I don't know. I have some theories, but there's only one person who can really tell us why."

They didn't ask for her help again. They didn't have to. Vivienne pressed one trembling hand to her mouth as she choked back sobs. Sam didn't reach for her or try to comfort her, but they did bow their head and let her mourn. They could give her that, at least.

Especially when they both knew that what came next would be so much worse.

CHAPTER THIRTY-SIX

Light spilled out from beneath the office door. The building stood silent and dark against the backdrop of the city at twilight, but the voices murmuring inside the room sounded warm and full of energy.

"Sorry again for making you work late." The female voice was low and playful. Not a boss apologizing, but a lover poking fun at her own romantic indulgence.

"At least the benefits are pretty good." The equally flirtatious reply was rich with satisfaction.

Pale fingers appeared at the door's edge. It had opened just an inch or two to reveal an arm covered in a full sleeve of ink when the first woman's voice came again.

"Aren't you going to clock out, at least?"

The hand disappeared lightning-fast. There were footsteps and then something that was probably meant to sound like kissing. Sam grimaced a little. They didn't expect the two to take things as far as Sam had on their undercover dates—Vivienne was a married woman, after all—but this was all a little melodramatic for their taste.

Vivienne let out a sigh, long and satisfied, and Sam revised that thought. Maybe she did know what she was doing.

"All right. You'd better get out of here so I can call my wife," she told the person who was distinctly Not Harper.

"Don't tell her I said hi."

Footsteps crossed back over to the door. The short blonde woman stepped out into the hallway looking completely at ease in her own skin. It wasn't like *she* was cheating on anyone—although she didn't seem to have an issue leaving a married woman's office in thoroughly rumpled clothing, either.

The woman's heavy boots thumped down the hallway in a satisfied saunter. Sam had to strain their ears to hear Vivienne's voice floating along in her so-called lover's wake.

"Hey, honey. I'm sorry, I know I said I'd be home for dinner. Promise I'm on my way now, I just had to wrap up a few things at the office."

Her visitor's face pulled into a light smirk as she turned the corner into the lobby. Just a person enjoying a casual romantic tryst after hours.

"Detective Novikoff."

Donya's feet stumbled slightly as she turned the corner and seemed surprised to discover the woman sitting in one of the stiff lobby chairs. Sam could see from their vantage point that Beck's head was still slightly bowed, her face hidden behind a curtain of auburn hair. She had appeared just moments after Donya arrived and taken a seat within earshot of Vivienne's office. As the scene played out down the hallway, each salacious giggle and whisper had seemed to weigh on her.

"Uh, Beck, right?" Donya said, quick to recover from her surprise. Beck's pale hands gripped the large tote in her lap even tighter at the sound of her voice. "I didn't expect anyone to be hanging around the office this late," Donya continued.

"I bet you didn't." Beck's voice was flat and unamused. "How was your meeting?"

"Oh, you know. Just touching base about the case. I know how stressful these investigations can be," Donya said with a casual wave of her hand that only made the other woman tense more. "Wanted to make sure your boss was all taken care of, you know?"

"I think it's her wife's job to take 'care of her.' Not yours," Beck said.

Donya's smug expression dropped into a frown.

"Did you know they're trying to have a baby? Five years of marriage, months of couples counseling, IVF treatments—all so they can actually have something good." Beck's chin rose, and she let out a slow breath. Turning her head, she pierced Donya with a glare so frigid that Sam could feel the chill from across the room. "How dare you come here and try to destroy that?"

"O-K," Donya said slowly, with just the right amount of scorn mixed with discomfort in her voice. Offering Beck a concerned once-over, Donya said, "I don't know what kind of caffeine pills they've got you on to keep you working around the clock, but maybe ease back. I was just here to—"

"Don't play dumb. I heard you together."

Beck stood abruptly from her seat, much as she had the day Harper had interrupted Sam and Vivienne's dinner. Only this time, when Beck's hand dipped inside her designer handbag, it emerged gripping the handle of a large butcher's knife.

"Well," she said darkly. The metallic edge of the blade caught the fluorescent lights overhead. "You won't get away with it this time."

"Whoa, whoa. What the hell are you doing?" Donya demanded. She tried to take a step back, but the knife rose in response, and the detective froze in place. Giving Beck an incredulous look, Donya said, "You do know I'm a cop, right?"

"You're a *home wrecker*." The words were a bitter curse, and even Donya flinched a little at the conviction behind the insult. Beck's eyes were wide and glassy. She stared at Donya with undisguised hatred, gripping the knife so tightly that her hand shook a little. "Vivienne and Harper belong together. They love each other," Beck declared. "They just need less . . . distraction before they can be truly happy."

"You're fucking nuts, you know that?" Donya observed. When Beck took a step forward, Donya raised her hands defensively and said a little louder, "Hey. Pretty sure we don't actually need footage of her turning me into a pincushion to wrap this one up. Someone want to get me out of here, please?"

"Who are you talking to?" Beck asked with a frown. Her sharp eyes darted around the room before she took another quick step forward. "What—"

"OK, that's enough." Sam's cool voice split the air as they emerged from behind the lobby's front desk. Beck's eyes widened in shock as Sam raised their stun gun and aimed it straight at their perp. "Beck," they said calmly. "Put the knife down."

"What? Sam? What are you—what is this?" Beck spluttered.

"You should know what this is. You've helped me prepare for enough of them." When Beck still looked confused, Sam stepped out from behind the desk. "It's an undercover op. Donya was here to make you think Vivienne was having an affair."

"No. You're confused." Beck almost sounded relieved, like this was somehow just a big misunderstanding. Gesturing to Donya with the knife, she said, "They were together. I heard them."

"Interesting."

Sam had formed a pretty good picture of what might motivate Beck to do something like this as they dug deeper into her history, but this right here was the real missing piece. The conviction on Beck's pale face. The certainty in her voice, despite Vivienne and Donya's pathetic reenactment of *When Harry Met Sally* earlier. It was apparent that the line between reality and obsession had long ago eroded for the knife-wielding self-proclaimed "cupid."

"You never could resist trying to set things right, could you?" Sam observed. Beck's grip tightened slightly on the handle of the blade, and Sam took a warning step closer. "Come on. Put the knife down. It's over now."

"But you're wrong," Beck insisted. "I heard them together."

"If you seriously think that's what a hookup sounds like, you need to get out more," Donya said, and Sam frowned at her tone. Maybe she really did want some ironclad evidence, though, because she added, "Even if we were getting it on, you still can't stab someone just for sleeping around, you know."

Beck did not seem to know that, because her response was to spin toward Donya and lunge in her direction, blade first.

"Hey!" Sam barked.

Beck froze.

"Don't make me do this." The prongs on the stun gun glinted dully under the fluorescent lighting as Sam aimed directly at Beck's back. "Drop the knife."

Beck's gaze pinwheeled wildly from Sam's stony expression to Donya's unimpressed face. Her grip tightened on the blade, but she finally seemed to accept that she was not going to be able to make a move against the "home-wrecking" detective if she didn't want to find out what 50,000 volts felt like.

So instead, she did the next logical thing which was to turn and start running for the stairwell. Because apparently the older Sam got, the more their perps seemed to think a foot chase was their best chance for escape. But that was a poor assumption.

"Noah," Sam said calmly.

Before Beck had even made it three steps in her stilettos, the door to the stairwell swung open, and Noah stepped out with weapon in hand. Unlike Sam's, his gun didn't shoot electricity, and the panicked look on Beck's face said she knew it.

"No!" she said, the word twisting with frustration as she raised her hands reflexively. The gesture didn't quite convey innocence, given that she was still clutching the knife she had used to stab four other women.

"You don't understand," Beck insisted as Noah silently stepped out of the stairwell and let the door swing shut behind him. "She—I didn't—I had to. Someone had to do something." Tossing an angry glare over her shoulder at Donya, she said, "You can't just let her get away with hurting people like this."

"You're the only one hurting people, Beck," Sam said. They kept their stun gun pointed at Donya's would-be murderer as they circled clockwise to ensure that they weren't in Noah's line of fire and that he wasn't in theirs.

"How can you say that?" Beck demanded. She turned to face Sam properly now, apparently unbothered by having her back to a loaded gun. "I thought you, of all people, would understand. I can't let her hurt Harper like this."

"Detective Novikoff. The elevator, please," Sam said without so much as acknowledging Beck's words.

"Seriously?" Donya's voice complained from over their shoulder. "If you keep her pinned and give me your cuffs, I can just—"

"What? Get yourself stabbed arresting her in your street clothes?" Sam's tone made it clear that this was not a debate. In case there was any doubt, they added, "Elevator. Now, Donya."

"Whatever you say, Supercop." Despite the disparaging words, Donya didn't seem all that put out about the prospect of escaping this tense standoff. Her boots thumped across the tile floor behind Sam before emerging in the corner of their peripheral vision by the elevators. Jabbing the call button, she gave Beck one last look and said, "See you on the stand, crazy lady."

"You won't get away with this," Beck spat. She didn't dare take another step toward her target with Noah and Sam still pinning her between them, but if looks could kill, Donya would have been dead before the elevator doors opened.

"We'll be standing by downstairs," Donya said as she stepped into the waiting car. "Don't take too long, or Vince will come up here to put the cuffs on her himself."

"Yeah. We'll be down in a minute," Sam assured her.

Donya nodded grimly and let the doors slide shut. Beck watched in despair as her would-be victim's face disappeared behind the steel doors, leaving her alone with Sam, Noah, and two weapons pointed directly at her.

"I'm not a monster, you know," Beck said into the silence after a long moment.

"Put the knife down, Beck," Sam repeated calmly.

"It's not my fault that people can't just do the right thing. If he could have just been faithful—if he could have just been *honest*. But no. People always have to hurt each other." Beck's voice was hot with frustration. She certainly didn't seem interested in relinquishing her weapon, which was going to be a problem if this arrest dragged on any longer.

"Is that why you stabbed those women? Because Jason was sleeping with them?" Sam asked as conversationally as they could, given the circumstances. Noah gave them a look over Beck's shoulder, but they ignored him. A little chitchat was far preferable to a violent arrest, if it could be avoided.

"*They* were sleeping with *him*," Beck corrected, because apparently that made a difference in her eyes. "A married man. Who does that?"

"Dude was in an open marriage or some shit, wasn't he?" Noah asked, and Beck spun around to face him.

"There is no such thing as an open marriage," she spat, and Sam took advantage of her distraction to step a little closer. Beck didn't seem to notice. "How would you feel if the man you loved went out every time you were out of town and slept with any whore who would open her legs for him? And then to find out one of them was even . . ." Her voice wavered with revulsion.

"You're the one who threatened Cassie," Sam said. Beck turned again, and Noah seemed to understand the point of this game now. His shuffling footsteps weren't quite so subtle, but before Beck could notice, Sam asked, "Was that the first time you used Jason's account to target his dates? Or did it start before that?"

"I saw the message she sent him. I knew I had to do something," Beck replied. The topic clearly upset her, because Noah was able to tighten the trap with ease this time. "Jason isn't a strong man. If he had found out that he had—that she was—"

"Pregnant," Sam said bluntly. "You can say it. Cassie was pregnant with Jason's baby. That's why you killed her."

"He would have left her. He was so weak and selfish and—" Beck's pretty face twisted under the weight of her emotion.

It was interesting to Sam that she didn't seem to enjoy the killing. They supposed it made sense. It wasn't as though the murders had been performed with any particular showmanship. The master password to get into Jason's account. A couple of messages inviting the victims out for a would-be good time with a familiar hookup. The suggestion of a rendezvous under the cover of darkness. One or two well-placed stabs to incapacitate, followed by the severing of at least one artery to ensure death. Then delete the conversation history and wait to see if Jason would fall back in line.

Or at least, back in the line Beck had decided was right for him.

"Jason wouldn't have made the right choice. So I made it clear to her, on his behalf, that she only had two choices," Beck finally said. Her lip curled at the memory, and she said, "Cassie made her choice. They all did."

"Nikki, too?" Noah demanded. Hearing the anger in their rookie's voice, Sam gave him a warning glance over Beck's shoulder. He didn't seem to notice.

"Noah."

"Just because she slept with some dude you're obsessed with," Noah pressed, ignoring Sam's warning. "That was a good enough reason to kill her?"

"No," Sam said. Noah's gaze shot back to them in surprise. Sam glanced pointedly at his finger, which had inched toward the trigger, and Noah quickly reset his hands into a more neutral position. Beck gave them an uncertain look, and Sam tried to sound compassionate when they said, "This was never about Jason. Right?"

"He was supposed to love her." Beck's words weren't quite so confident in the face of Sam's gentle tone. That disgust had peeled back a little to reveal the festering hurt beneath.

"Like Patrick was supposed to?" Sam asked, and Beck's face blanched at the mention of her ex-husband. "I guess he didn't get the message, either."

"This has nothing to do with—"

"The similarities must have been a little overwhelming," Sam said over Beck's protest. "A man and a woman fall in love. Then the man cheats and knocks up another woman. Only instead of killing her, you had to stand by and watch as your husband left you for someone else." Beck's bright eyes were full of tears now, and Sam could see how much the truth hurt her. "It must have been unbearable to imagine Jen going through the same thing after you worked so hard to find her a soulmate in Jason."

"That was different," Beck insisted, although her wobbly voice wasn't very convincing. "Jason was weak. Patrick was just . . . confused. He didn't mean to—"

"What? Knock up some other chick?" Noah jabbed again. "Seems like you'd have to be real confused to get that one wrong."

"She seduced him. She tricked him." Beck's voice cracked a little on the denial. Sam watched the way her hand tightened on the handle of the knife. The familiar weight seemed to soothe her, because she settled a little before saying, "People make bad decisions. Sometimes they need someone stronger to help them see the right path."

"What, by killing off all Jason's other options?" Noah asked incredulously. Despite his anger over Nikki's death, even he seemed to be realizing the depth of Beck's delusion. "Were you just going to keep stabbing every chick he slept with until he thought his dick was cursed or something?"

Sam felt something prickle in the back of their mind—an uncomfortable friction between the horror of Beck's obsession and the terrible understanding of what had driven her to it.

Beck thought Sam understood her because of their tumultuous past with Vivienne, but Sam's damaged relationship with love had begun long before they had the faintest clue about romance. For a long time, they had only known love by the shape of its absence. And they could understand why that experience in adulthood, without the armor forged by a traumatic childhood, might break a person.

"What else was I supposed to do?" Blinking rapidly, Beck used her non-knife-wielding arm to swipe away the gathering tears. "I put them together. I promised Jen she'd be happy. Now Jason has to keep his part of that promise."

"Love has to be a choice," Sam said. Beck's glossy eyes met theirs, wide and vulnerable to the compassion in their voice. Sam offered her a sad smile and said, "The choosing is the part that makes it good. Right?"

"Man, this is some Dr. Phil bullshit." Noah's voice cut through the tender moment with all the grace of a rookie who hadn't yet learned the difference between a hammer and a scalpel. Beck's expression was already hardening again when he said, "Let's just put her in the cuffs, boss. Let the lawyers deal with this crap."

"You know Nikki actually said she preferred that he was married?" Beck said abruptly. Noah stiffened, and she sniffed lightly before brushing away another tear. "No strings attached. That was how she put it in her messages." Giving Noah a brief flash of that curling smile, she said, "I didn't feel so bad about it after that."

Noah's body went totally still at the sound of her cruel words. It was fascinating, in a dark sort of way. Beck clearly had no trouble understanding what made a person tick. How to find them someone they'd match well with. How to hit them where it would hurt most.

The only thing she couldn't see clearly was the danger of her own convictions.

"Boss?" Noah asked. Sam could see the anger boiling beneath the surface, but Noah's finger had not moved toward the trigger again. Like most rational people, he was able to see that hurting Beck wouldn't do anything to bring his cousin back.

"Go ahead," Sam said. "I'll cover you."

Sam's taser remained trained on Beck as Noah holstered his gun and swiftly approached the pretty young woman. Her face twisted in fear, and she raised the knife to defend herself, but there was a reason she'd had to rely on the element of surprise to take down her previous victims. Designer heels and pastel jumpsuits weren't exactly made for putting up a fight, and despite his two left feet, Noah had her disarmed in seconds.

Beck began to sob the moment the knife clattered to the ground. Noah sent it skittering across the floor with the toe of one boot. Beck tried to back away, but he grabbed her roughly before she could think about breaking for the stairs again.

"Please," she pleaded as Noah wrenched her arms behind her back.

"Her rights?" Sam suggested over top of Beck's tears.

"Rebecca Fisher," Noah said in his most serious voice. Beck cried out like a wounded animal, and Noah flinched a little. Clearing his throat, he tried again. "Rebecca Fisher, you are under arrest for—"

"Stop. You're hurting me," Beck shrieked, throwing her entire body against his restraining grip. Noah didn't so much as sway under the force, but he did hesitate at the sound of her desperation. Twisting toward Sam, Beck whimpered, "Please. He's hurting me. He's going to break my wrist! Please."

"Whoa. I'm not—" Noah's grip loosened at the sound of her accusation, and Sam watched the rest unfold like it was happening in slow motion.

Beck twisted out of Noah's grip so quickly she was little more than a blur of long hair and pale skin. Sam prepared to shoot, but Noah lunged straight back into their line of fire in his attempt to recapture her. Sam only just managed not to pull the trigger, but Beck took advantage of their hesitation to reach for the holster on Noah's belt. He shouted in surprise and smacked her hand away, but it was too late. She was already dancing backward with his Glock gripped in one trembling hand.

"Don't move. Don't you dare move," Beck ordered in a shrill voice when Noah immediately pursued. She stumbled back another step until her shoulders were up against the wall, the gun pointed wildly in Noah's direction. "I'll do it. I swear to god—don't come any closer."

Sam could practically see Noah gearing up to do something stupid, and they swore under their breath. This kid was really going to be the death of them.

"OK. Settle," Sam said before Noah could go getting his head blown off. Keeping their eyes pinned on Beck and the gun, Sam said, "Let's nobody do anything crazy."

Beck let out a sound that was caught somewhere between a laugh and a sob. "It's a little late for that, don't you think?"

Sam took a quick half-step toward their rookie.

"Don't."

Sam froze at the sound of the safety clicking off.

"I mean it," Beck promised in that tremulous voice. "I don't want to hurt anyone, but I will if you make me."

"OK. I'm staying," Sam assured her. "Look." They placed their taser slowly on the ground. Noah gave them a pained look as Sam straightened back up, their hands raised to show Beck that they were playing nicely. "See? We're not going to hurt you. So just put the gun down. We can talk about this."

"Talk?" Beck echoed in disbelief.

Despite her glassy eyes and rapid breathing, Sam didn't think she seemed especially frightened in that moment. There was an awareness in her movements when she flicked her gaze between the two detectives. She seemed to consider her options before taking a step closer to point the gun at Noah's chest.

That was better, actually. Panic was dangerous. Awareness was something Sam could work with.

"You think I'm stupid?" Beck demanded, oblivious to Sam's racing train of thought. "I know there are about a hundred cops waiting for me outside this building. I won't make it a single block if I try to walk out of here."

"Shooting him won't fix that."

"I'm not going to shoot him." Beck swayed a little on her feet, but that didn't make her seem any less dangerous as she reached out to prod Noah with the muzzle of the gun. "I'm taking him with me. They won't hurt me if it'd mean risking another cop's life."

"You really are some kinda crazy if you think I'm going out there as your fuckin' hostage," Noah snapped. He had the restraint not to try and take the weapon from her, but Sam was confident that wouldn't last long if Beck kept pushing him.

"You can be my hostage, or you can be dead. Your choice," Beck retorted, and despite his bravado, Noah flinched at the certainty in that statement.

"How about a third option?"

Beck startled at the sound of Sam's voice, much nearer than it had been before. Her eyes widened and she spun to get the gun on them. Unlike their young rookie, Sam didn't flinch. In fact, they stepped in even closer until the gun was nestled against their sternum and Beck had to lean back so they weren't looming over her. Their hands were still raised, empty and harmless, but that didn't seem to make the other woman any less nervous.

"What the hell are you doing?" Noah demanded. His voice surged with panic when Beck brought her other hand up to support her grip on the gun.

"What does it look like?" Sam could feel the button of their shirt pressing into their skin under the weight of the gun's muzzle. The metal was cold and unnatural through the thin material, but Sam still didn't back down. They looked at Beck. "You wanted a hostage. Now you have one."

"I—" Beck started, looking a little dazed, and then quickly shook her head. "No. No—you're just trying to distract me so he can—"

"He's not going to do anything," Sam said firmly. "Isn't that right, Rook?"

"Sam." Their name was a warning note in Noah's low voice. "Don't do this."

"Come on, Beck. What do you say?" Sam said, ignoring his plea. Despite the gun pressing up against them, they were perfectly calm. Friendly, even. "You and I can walk out of here right now. We can go out the fire escape. My car is parked a block away. We'll walk there together and then I'll take you anywhere you want to go. Doesn't that sound easier?"

"He's just going to tell them where to find us," Beck replied, but that tremor was back in her voice. "The second we walk out of here he'll have every cop in this city tracking me down."

"No, he won't. Because he's my rookie and he's going to listen to me. Right, Noah?" Sam risked a glance in his direction for half a second. The anguish on his face was real, but he remained where he stood. To do anything else would have been suicide at this point.

"Sam, please. Don't be crazy. Just let me go," Noah pleaded anyway. Because the kid really was that kind of stupidly loyal.

Teddy was definitely going to like him if they ever had a chance to meet for real.

"Please," Noah repeated, seeing the resignation on their face. "She'll kill you."

"No. She might kill you. But she's not going to hurt me," Sam said. Beck softened a fraction at the cool confidence in their words, and a momentary flicker of understanding passed between them.

"Sam—"

"She is not. Going. To hurt me."

It wasn't the kind of understanding a kid like Noah could grasp. Maybe someday—but not yet.

Noah fell silent as Sam took a step back from the gun. Instead of trying to escape, though, they turned toward the hallway that led deeper into the building. To the fire escape, and their car, and the endless miles of freeway beyond.

"Now, you'd better run downstairs and tell everyone to settle in for the night." Giving Noah one last glance, Sam said, "Maybe make yourself a coffee or something. Do some paperwork. I'll be back before you know it."

CHAPTER THIRTY-SEVEN

The car was surprisingly peaceful as it zipped along under the streetlights at a cool 70 miles an hour. A little slow for Sam's taste, but they didn't want to startle their passenger by driving like they normally would. She was still pointing a gun at them, after all.

"You don't have to do that, you know," Sam said casually. Their right hand twitched uncomfortably against the wheel, but they ignored the urge to reach for the gear shift. "I'm not going to try anything."

"Keep driving."

Sam's fingers flexed, but they nodded silently and kept their eyes pinned to the road. Anywhere you want, they had said. She'd told them to get on the freeway and drive. So they kept driving.

The radio on the dashboard let out a squawk and the gun's grip groaned when Beck's hand tensed in response.

"I can turn it off, if you like," Sam had suggested the first time it happened.

"Keep your hands on the wheel."

This time the voice on the dispatch was letting local officers know that Travis and Parker would be setting a speed trap at the next exit. There was some razzing back and forth from officers on the scanner about their promotion from meter maids to freeway vampires before the conversation petered out again.

"OK if I get over a lane?" Sam asked. "I know those two—Travis and

Parker. They won't bother us if I don't give them a reason to."

"Sure. Fine." Beck's voice was dull and distracted.

Sam was very aware of the Glock still pointed in their direction, but they had noticed how Beck's eyes had started straying toward the passing exits for the last couple of miles. That made sense. Right about now would be when the regret usually started to set in. The uncomfortable knowledge that life on the lam wasn't quite so easy in the twenty-first century. You couldn't stab a bunch of people and think the authorities would leave you alone just because you successfully skipped town.

Sam's hand reached for the gear shift, which was a small mercy in itself. How other people actually drove with both hands on the wheel was a mystery to them.

"Hey. Don't even think about trying anything." Beck's gaze sharpened a little when Sam's hand curled around the stick. "I know you're too good to stall out."

"Viv tell you that?" Sam asked as they guided the car into the middle lane. Statistically the least likely to draw an officer's attention—the last thing they wanted right now. Beck didn't respond, so they tried again. "Or am I supposed to believe a pretty girl like you actually knows how to drive stick?"

"That's kind of sexist, you know," she replied with a light sniff. Her eyes were dry, but her skin was still blotchy from all the theatrics earlier. Almost as an afterthought, she added, "My husband did try to teach me once. A while back."

"Sounds nice."

Beck didn't expand on that anecdote, but she didn't insist that Sam return their hand to the wheel, either, so . . . that was progress.

Years of training told Sam that gaining Beck's trust right now was critical. They had to keep things comfortable, easy. Just two friends talking. Their ability to be vulnerable was currently the only thing standing between them waking up next to Teddy tomorrow morning or hoping that Noah would be smart enough to track him down and let him know about the funeral.

That was not an experience Sam wanted either man to have, so it was time to put all those Questions of the Day to good use.

"I learned from a guy in my town," Sam announced into the silence. "He was the sheriff, actually."

Beck glanced at them sidelong, as though she was trying to figure out why they were sharing this with her.

Sam forced their expression to remain neutral. This was just one of their nightly phone calls with Teddy. What would he want to know next?

"John wasn't all that friendly," Sam continued conversationally. "He definitely wasn't interested in teaching an annoying kid like me. But he let me mess around in the old pickup out back till I figured it out on my own."

Beck shifted slightly in her seat for the first time in over ten minutes. "Why'd he do that?"

"Don't know, really. Wasn't much of a talker," Sam said with a small shrug. "Mostly I think he knew I didn't want to go home, and I knew he wouldn't make me as long as I kept busy." They hesitated slightly before adding, "Probably would have been a lot harder to steal his truck, too, if I hadn't already learned how to drive it."

"You stole somebody's car?" Beck said, oblivious to the irony of that statement. Sam's story certainly seemed to have caught her attention, though.

That didn't surprise them, really. People always wanted to know.

"Sort of. It's complicated, I guess."

For half a second, Sam was fifteen again, sick to their stomach from their latest treatment and still lightheaded from the eight-mile hike to the station. The old truck's engine was so loud in the deserted lot. You'd have to be drop-dead drunk and passed out to have missed it. Surely John was going to appear on the back deck any second now and order their skinny ass to quit messing around and go home.

The sheriff was a sober man, but the station remained dark and silent.

"Most of the time, if a man leaves his car unlocked, you don't take that as an invitation to drive away in it," Sam explained despite the bitter taste of old memories on their tongue. "But I needed to go, and John knew I wouldn't get far on my own. So he kept leaving the keys out, and I kept borrowing them until one day I didn't bring them back."

"But wasn't he . . . mad?"

"Don't know. Never actually spoke to him again," Sam said. "That was just the way it had to be, you know?"

Beck didn't answer, but given her current predicament, Sam thought she probably did know. There were some things you couldn't really take back. The person you had been before was gone and all that was left was the after.

They drove on in silence, but Beck's gaze was now firmly on the road ahead and not on her talkative hostage.

"I know what you're doing," she said after another three miles had passed by under the wheels. The interstate wasn't empty, even at this time of night, but it still felt like they were the only two people on the road right now.

"What's that?" Sam asked.

"Trying to soften me up so I won't hurt you," Beck replied. Her gaze dropped to the gun in her lap, and she added, "I'm not a monster, you know."

"Never said you were." Sam risked shifting down a gear. The movement would have been innocuous in any other situation, but here in the car's tense interior, Beck's stillness spoke volumes. Glancing at her sidelong, Sam said, "I came with you willingly, didn't I? Would have been pretty stupid to do that if I thought you were going to shoot me."

Beck was silent again. Sam could feel her trying to see through them, and they let her look. That was the trick to this game—it couldn't be a game at all. She could stare them down all the way from here to Sacramento, but she wouldn't find a false note in anything they said.

They hadn't even made it another mile when Beck's quiet voice came again. "I just don't understand why people can't be honest with each other."

"Your guess is as good as mine," Sam replied with another easy shrug. "Why do some people hit their kids? Or spoil them rotten? Why do some people gamble, or litter, or drink?" Beck's face twisted with frustration at their words, and Sam risked another glance in her direction. "Why didn't you leave Patrick when you found out he was cheating on you?"

"That's none of your business."

"Sure. Sorry." Sam nodded agreeably. But after another lull, even shorter than the last, they suggested, "You could tell me anyways. If you want to."

"There's nothing to tell." Beck's voice trembled slightly with that familiar conviction at the mention of her ex-husband. "I made a promise. We stood at that altar together, and we said—" Her voice broke a little, and Sam felt a genuine pulse of sympathy for her anguish.

"We said for better or for worse. He might not have meant it, but I did."

This time Sam waited for Beck to come to them. It didn't take very long.

"What about you and Viv?"

"Well," Sam said, leaning forward to squint slightly at the sign for the upcoming off-ramp. They hit the turn signal and waited to see if Beck would react. "Viv and I weren't married, for one thing. I'm not even sure you could really call it dating. It was more like surviving in tandem." The wheel shifted to the right, and the car silently drifted over a lane. "I don't think what we had would have made a lot of sense to anyone else, but it was what we both needed back then."

"If it was what you both wanted, then why did she step out on you?" Sam's grip tightened on the wheel, but despite the edge in Beck's voice, she didn't try to stop them from taking the exit.

"Needed. Not a lot of wanting involved," Sam corrected gently. "When the need was over, she—I don't know. Maybe she was scared to be alone. I know I was." They shifted down another gear to take the curve of the ramp a little slower. "But it all worked out in the end, right? She's got Harper, and her company, and maybe even a new baby. And she's happy. So that's good."

"But you don't have any of those things," Beck pointed out.

"That's her story, not mine. Doesn't mean I'm not happy, too."

They pulled to a stop at a red light denoting the end of the freeway and the beginning of suburbia. For sixty excruciating seconds, Sam sat there in silence next to the woman with the Glock held limply in her hand. Cars streamed by in the opposite direction. A couple of pedestrians appeared and disappeared between streetlights. Just another Wednesday night in midtown.

The light flipped back to green. Sam's hand flexed against the gear shift, and they let the car roll forward. Beck blinked slightly and turned her head from side to side like she was only just now realizing that they hadn't been moving for the past minute.

"Where are we going?" she asked uncertainly. Her eyes flitted to the signs overhead, and Sam saw a glimmer of recognition there.

"I told you," Sam said, putting their foot back to the pedal. "Anywhere you want. You just say the word."

Beck nodded slowly. If she did know where they were, she didn't seem to have a problem with it, so Sam turned to the right and continued deeper into the maze of scruffy low-rises lining both sides of the street. They weren't sure if this was really where Beck wanted to be, but it felt right. Or inevitable, anyway.

Not five minutes later, Sam was turning onto a sleepy cul-de-sac just off the main road. The houses were bigger here, with more character. The sort of house a young professor and a lawyer of middling success might be able to afford. They were only a ten-minute drive from the place where Sam and Jason had connected previously, but that hotel might as well have been on a different planet from this quaint neighborhood.

The car's interior was silent as Sam pulled to a stop at the foot of the driveway. It was all so quiet here. They could hear Beck's breaths growing shallow as she took in the house with its cute cobblestone walkway and large bay window. The gauzy curtains had been thrown open to let in some air. Warm light spilled out into the darkness, illuminating the happy scene within.

Two people sharing a late dinner. Or maybe dessert. The touch of a hand. The knowing flash of a smile. It was strange to see Jason like this. In Sam's memory, he was an unappealing person with a blunt, get-to-it attitude. But Jennifer Albertalli clearly didn't share Sam's reservations, because she was all smiles at whatever her husband was saying to her from across the table.

It was impossible to know what they were talking about from this distance. What was certain was the genuine smile pulling at Jen's pretty face and the way she leaned in closer to absorb Jason's every word. Not exactly the portrait of a sad, abandoned woman who was heartbroken over her husband's cheating ways.

"I don't understand." Beck's voice sounded small and miserable in the silence.

"I don't think you have to." Gesturing to the happy couple in the window, Sam said, "This is the life Jen chose. It might not be your idea of a good marriage, but it's what she wants."

Beck's pale hand pressed against the window like she wished she could get out of the car and go join the two. Of course, Sam could never allow that—but they could let her have this moment, at least.

They hit the button on their control panel and let the passenger window slide down a couple of inches. Beck's hand dropped limply to her lap. They could just make out the sound of two voices floating out the open window and down the driveway to the car. The words were gone, but the lilts of laughter and cheerful conversation remained.

"She looks pretty happy to me," Sam ventured after a long moment.

Beck sniffed quietly. She was really quite beautiful, with fresh tears shining on her cheeks and such potent longing written across her face. Sam thought, even after all this, that she probably still saw Jen as the victim here, despite the lives that had been lost in her quest to protect the other woman. It was strange to realize that Jen may never find out what had been done in her name. Although that might be better than living with the truth.

It was funny what something as intangible as grief could do to a person over time.

Sam pressed the button again and the window slid shut. Now there was only the shaky soundtrack of Beck's tears and the even sound of Sam's breathing again.

"How did you know I wouldn't hurt you?" Beck asked. She scrubbed her free hand across her eyes, paying no mind to the mascara streaks it left behind. More tears just welled up in their place, anyway. Noah's gun still lay in her lap, but it might as well have been a chunk of plastic for all the mind Beck was giving it.

"Because you're not a monster, Beck. You just want people to be good to each other," Sam told her. She gave them a questioning, watery-eyed look, and Sam found themself smiling a little ruefully, against all odds. "That, and I knew I was busted the second you caught me texting him."

Beck let out a wet, startled laugh at the begrudging confession. She sniffed again, and Sam reached across her to the glove compartment. Beck stiffened but didn't stop them from popping open the lid and reaching inside for a travel pack of tissues.

Beck considered the little packet, then accepted it. "You love him," she said as she dabbed at her overflowing eyes.

"I—" Sam found the words strangely hard to say. It wasn't like they'd never said them to anyone before. It wasn't even like they weren't sure. But it felt wrong for a murderer to hear about it before Teddy did, so instead they said, "Yeah." Being monosyllabic about it didn't seem quite right, either, so they touched a hand to their chest and added, "He's really . . . something. To me."

Well, hopefully if they actually got the chance to spill their heart to Teddy, it would go a little smoother than that. Probably not, though.

Offering Beck a tight half-smile, Sam said, "Was kind of hoping you wouldn't shoot me if you knew I had to get home so he could tell me off for trying to be a big damn hero again."

"I can't imagine him doing that," Beck said, wrinkling her nose at the thought. She sniffled again and added, a little wistfully, "Definitely not with the way he looks at you."

"You're right," Sam said with an agreeable sigh. "With my luck he'll probably cry, and then I'll feel like a huge jerk and have to buy him something to make up for it."

"Something tells me you're pretty good at that part," Beck observed. There was a strange note in her voice. Sam thought it might be sadness, or maybe resignation.

"Apologizing? Sure. Have to be when you're bad at everything else," Sam replied in that same easy tone.

Releasing their seatbelt, they turned to face Beck. The other woman seemed to have forgotten that she was holding them hostage. They could have been sitting at the office, having a chat over coffee between meetings.

"So, in your expert opinion, what's a good 'I'm sorry' gift these days?" Sam asked. "Flowers?"

"For Teddy?" Beck replied a little hesitantly. "No, I don't think so."

"Why not? Too girly?"

"No, I just think—maybe a plant instead. Something that won't just get thrown out, you know? I think he'd like that," Beck suggested. When Sam nodded thoughtfully, she said, with a little more confidence, "And you shouldn't use those paper cups for your coffee all the time. They're bad for the environment."

"Ah, yeah. He does hate those," Sam agreed with a wince at the memory of Teddy's horrified reaction to their overflowing trash bin.

"You should always pay attention to whatever he's working on," Beck continued as though Sam hadn't spoken. Her sad eyes tracked back toward the window. The dining room was empty now. Jason and Jen must have turned in for the night at some point.

A light flickered behind one of the curtains upstairs. Maybe it was a TV. What kind of shows did those two watch together? Did Beck know? With her obsessive matchmaking skills, Sam bet she probably did. Maybe things would have turned out differently if someone had just shown her that kind of attention at some point.

"Maybe" wouldn't change what had happened, though.

"It's important," Beck insisted, even as her lip began to quiver again. "Even if you don't get it or you don't . . . like it. You should still try. To pay attention. I think—I think people just—they don't mean to, but—they forget—"

Her words dissolved into quiet, anguished sobs as Sam quietly lowered the window on their own side this time.

"Hey. It's OK," Sam said soothingly. Reaching across the seat, they placed one comforting hand on her trembling shoulder.

"You should tell him. How you feel," Beck said, a little more frantically, between hiccups. "You have to tell him. Every day."

"I'll tell him," Sam assured her. Their free hand came down to wrap around the gun still balanced in her lap. She didn't even try to resist when they gently tugged it out of her grip.

"Don't hurt him," Beck pleaded.

Safety on. They wedged it between their thighs to quickly eject the bullet from the chamber before releasing the magazine. It was a little harder with one hand, but this wasn't Sam's first rodeo.

"Please. You have to promise you won't—"

"I won't," Sam said firmly. The magazine disappeared into their jacket pocket. "I promise, I won't hurt him."

That was a lie, of course. Nobody could really promise something that big, but Sam surely intended to do their best and would gladly beg forgiveness every time they fell short.

"You have to tell him," Beck repeated.

"I will. Soon as I can. All right?"

The empty body of the gun clattered to the ground outside the vehicle. Something moved in the neighbor's window. If the sight of two strangers lingering outside a nice house like this hadn't done it yet, the Glock lying on the chalk-patterned pavement would certainly ensure that every cop in a twenty-mile radius would be arriving any minute now.

But that was in a minute. For now, they slid over in their seat to pull Beck closer. Her head dipped under the weight of her sobs, and Sam tucked their arm around her firmly so she could cry into their shoulder.

There was a time for being the clever detective, and there was a time for being a human. Sometimes real justice required a little bit of both.

CHAPTER THIRTY-EIGHT

"Jesus fucking Christ, that was a long speech," Noah complained. Shoving his hat back with one hand, he rocked up on the balls of his feet and then winced. "I think my blisters have blisters."

"Cameras are still rolling," Sam replied unsympathetically. Their eyes remained trained on the crowd pooling around the steps leading up to City Hall, where Mayor Kelso had just wrapped up his rousing speech from the podium.

Noah winced again and crammed his hat back in place. Their dress uniforms were stifling in the early afternoon heat, but Kelso didn't seem to mind. He took his time posing for pictures with Donovan and her shiny new medal for the media vultures snapping pictures below.

What a load of bullshit.

Glancing sidelong at their rookie, Sam muttered, "Baby powder." Noah gave them a questioning look, and they subtly lifted the fabric of their slacks to show him the ring of white powder around the top of their sock. "For next time. It'll be one less terrible thing about these press circuses."

Noah jerked his head in a nod, and Sam let the fabric drop again. Kelso finally turned back to face the uniformed officers lined up behind the podium, and that seemed to be the silent cue that everyone could relax again. The cameras went dead, and the crowd reverted back into a chattering mass of curious onlookers and nosy reporters.

Sam could only hope that Kelso's speech had brought some comfort to the families of the victims. They certainly didn't think anyone deserved any applause over the bodies of four dead women, forget a medal. Especially when the last victim had died while Sam was forced to run around in high heels on a wild—

"So what, she gets to go home and we gotta stand here till we melt into the pavement, or what?" Noah's voice cut straight through Sam's brooding thoughts as he squinted out at the far side of the plaza below.

Sam followed his gaze to the spot where Vivienne was wrapping up an interview with three different reporters. Harper put an arm around her wife's shoulders and turned her away from the demanding crowd. It was to Harper's credit that no one followed when she began marching Vivienne toward the parking lot and away from all the flashing cameras. For once, Sam was grateful for the other woman's intimidating presence, if it meant their friend might get a little peace and quiet.

On top of saving the reputation of her business and coming to terms with her former employee being a serial killer, Vivienne was also expected to show up to these events and demonstrate her unquestioning support of the police. Clap on cue. Shake hands. Disown her friend with a smile while trying not to fall apart behind the scenes.

Sam would have liked to go down there and tell the reporters exactly what they thought about them harassing a grieving woman just to get more coverage of this terrible tragedy. But Vivienne's lawyers had made it very clear that public displays of "preferential treatment" from the police would not be a good look for the company.

Sam made a mental note to bring an entire bucket of pad see ew to dinner with "the company" on Sunday.

Sliding their gaze back toward Noah, they offered him a tiny shrug and said, "If you've got a spare million lying around, I bet the Mayor wouldn't care if you left early, either."

"Well, damn. Guess I'm not going anywhere," Noah said bluntly. Nodding to something over Sam's shoulder, he added, "Looks like you could make bail if you asked nicely, though."

Sam spun around to see what he was looking at and sighed in exasperation when they caught sight of their man staring right back at them from the plaza below.

Teddy quickly dropped his gaze back to the coffee thermos he had been faithfully holding through the entire ceremony, and Sam sighed again, a little more fondly this time. When Teddy had sworn up and down that he would keep things "subtle" if they let him attend Kelso's formal address, Sam had already known it would be a losing battle, but still. They hadn't expected his pretense to be quite so painfully transparent. Even in jeans and the least floral t-shirt he owned, Teddy exuded the kind of charisma that automatically drew eyes to him—and Teddy's own eyes might as well have been big red hearts when he looked at Sam in their dress uniform.

Well, if more people had to know they had a gorgeous boyfriend who was incredibly likeable and yet still crazy about them for some strange reason, Sam would probably find a way to live.

They turned back to face the other side of the platform again. Kelso was about halfway through his visit with the troops, with Captain Donovan shadowing his every movement. In another couple of minutes, he would reach Sam and Noah's position, and then Sam would really have to bite their tongue.

Shaking their head at the thought, Sam stepped out of line and headed for the stairs down to the plaza, where the crowd was pooling below. If they had to choose between rich guys to hang out with at this event, they'd pick secondhand sneakers over Italian leather every time.

Sam was vaguely aware of Noah eagerly following in their wake, but they were busy practicing a little unsubtlety of their own. Teddy straightened as they approached, and despite the fact that Sam had been sharing his bed for way too many nights in a row, their heart still skipped a beat when he smiled at them like that.

Sam hadn't made it halfway across the plaza when Teddy began holding the coffee thermos out to them like a peace offering. Sam just rolled their eyes and stepped past the thermos to pull him down for a swift, hard kiss. It wasn't as though a little innocent PDA would make any difference at this point. Anyone with eyes could tell Teddy was only here for one person.

"Hello," Teddy said cheerfully when Sam released him in favor of the thermos full of much-needed fuel. "I thought we were supposed to be playing this subtle?"

"Bro, you could have spray-painted 'Sam's got a boyfriend' across the pavement and it woulda been more subtle," Noah said with a snicker. "You two are worse than teenagers."

"Oh yeah? Maybe I should have gone with 'Sam's got a smart-ass rookie' instead," Teddy retorted. And then Sam's ridiculous boys were slapping each other on the back like best pals instead of two people who hadn't even known each other a month ago.

"Ugh. What is that?" Sam interrupted when they tasted the weak excuse for coffee inside the thermos. They lowered the mug to give Teddy a look of pure betrayal. "Is that . . . decaf?"

"¡Me ofendes, mi amor!" Teddy exclaimed, pressing a melodramatic hand to his chest. "Eso es inaceptable, jamás haría algo así."

Squinting at him suspiciously, Sam raised the thermos to their lips and watched the little smile pull tellingly at the corner of his mouth. Scowling, they lowered it again and said, "You're such a liar."

"You're speaking Spanish now?" Noah asked in disbelief.

"No," Sam said shortly, although they couldn't quite meet his eye when they said it. They *had* been learning to interpret Teddy's Spanglish alarmingly fast—all the good parts, anyway. Scowling harder to make up for the smitten look on Teddy's face, they said, "I just know when he's hiding something."

"Well, it's not decaf," Teddy said innocently. "But half-caf . . . maybe."

"You are the worst," Sam grumbled. They sipped the coffee again in hopes that it had somehow improved, but it had not.

"Mhm. And you're going to be stuck with me taking care of you forever," Teddy agreed cheerfully. Hooking an arm around their shoulders, he dragged them in closer to kiss them on the head. "I'll keep you healthy," he continued before smooching their cheek. "Whether you like it"—he kissed them again—"or not."

"Ugh, enough," Sam complained lazily while putting absolutely zero effort into escaping Teddy's affectionate embrace. "First you want me to eat whole meals, then get at least six hours of sleep, and now—"

"So this must be *baby*." That familiar snide voice snaked straight through Sam's words like a bad smell on a beautiful afternoon.

Sam stiffened at the sight of Vince swaggering toward them with his own rookie in tow. Although he sported the same dress uniform as every other officer in the plaza, the navy blues somehow looked slouchy and unkempt on him.

Looking Teddy up and down with that flat, shark-like gaze, Vince offered the larger man a nasty sneer. "Kind of big for a baby, isn't he?"

"Hey. You'd better watch your mouth if you don't want to be drinking your food through a straw," Noah snapped, and Vince pulled up short.

Noah stood almost a foot shorter than Teddy and probably weighed half as much, but he was still facing Vince down with an intensity that would put most police dogs to shame. Apparently owing Sam his life twice over also meant undying loyalty to their partner, which Sam couldn't say they hated.

"And here I thought I was meeting Sammy's boy toy," Vince said with lazy contempt. Flicking his gaze toward the blonde detective at his side, he said, "I guess we already knew they liked a little variety, though."

"Don't be gross, Vince," Donya said, sounding terribly bored in response to Vince's uncreative needling. The older cop gave his rookie a hard look for daring to undermine his authority, but she didn't even blink as those blue doll eyes drifted right past him to land on Teddy. "Nice to see you again, Teddy," she said almost warmly. "Enjoying the ceremony?"

"What's not to enjoy?" Teddy replied with a grin that said he was not sorry at all for openly drooling over his partner, despite his promises of "subtlety."

Teddy and Donya had only met a week ago, by chance, when he and Sam had ventured over to a mutually agreeable bar for a night out, but apparently even Donya was not immune to Teddy's particular brand of charm.

"Teddy?" Vince scoffed. Jerking a thumb in Sam's direction, he asked, "And what do you call her? Bunny?"

"Ah, so you must be Vince, then," Teddy said cheerfully. Sam could almost see Vince realizing his mistake the moment Teddy's strong hand shot forward to clamp around his in a handshake that looked like it hurt. A lot.

"I heard you needed a lesson on pronouns," Teddy continued, and despite his smile, he didn't seem especially friendly anymore. Without taking his eyes off the other man, Teddy turned his head a quarter inch in Sam's direction and asked, "¿Qué opinas, amor? ¿Le pateamos el trasero?"

"Pórtate bien, mi amor," Sam replied simply in a bad approximation of Spanish, and they were instantly rewarded by a slight softening around the edges of that hard smile.

They didn't need to speak Spanish to know that their passionate man would not hesitate to put Vince in the ground if they just said the word. But after many patient nights spent collecting the bits and pieces of Sam's painful history, Teddy also understood them well enough to know that more hurt wasn't what they needed.

"Well, this is just adorable," Vince said dryly when Teddy obediently released his hand. The unaffected act would have been more effective if he didn't have to flex his fingers to get the blood flowing again. "Should I get out Google Translate, or can I assume I'm supposed to be intimidated by *el luchador* here?"

"Intimidated? Of course not," Teddy laughed easily. "Besides," he continued as his gaze tracked over Vince's shoulder to something beyond. "What could a nice guy like me possibly do to hurt a tough guy like you?"

"What are you—" Vince started suspiciously.

"Theodore Burgess the Third. As I live and breathe," a booming voice proclaimed.

Vince hadn't even made it all the way around before Mayor Kelso was blowing past him to pull Teddy into a handshake so enthusiastic that Sam thought it actually might count as getting to first base. Captain Donovan stood close behind looking slightly bemused by the mayor's excitement.

"What in the world are you doing here, my friend?" The mayor asked. "I didn't expect to see you on land again until Christmas!"

Sam's eyebrows shot up in surprise. Maybe it was shortsighted of them, but they had never really considered what Teddy's bank account, combined with his equally high follower count, would mean to politicians like Mayor Kelso. To Sam, Teddy was just . . . Teddy. Sweet. Talented. In love with his art, and the world around him, and maybe even Sam, too. But based on the way the mayor was eyeing up their man right now, Sam suddenly suspected most politicians really would round the bases if it meant earning Teddy's endorsement.

"Mr. Mayor. You know I love a good surprise," Teddy replied with slightly less enthusiasm but twice the charm. "How's Elise?"

"Good. Wonderful, really, but she'll be devastated when she finds out she missed you today," Kelso said with grave sincerity. "Honestly, I'll never hear the end of it. If you've got a moment before you set off again—"

"Gladly. Mrs. Fox commissioned me to make a tribute for the victims of the case, so I'll be around for a while still," Teddy assured him with all the confidence of a man who was used to being in high demand. "Tell her to come by the boat anytime."

Sam offered him a slightly baleful look from behind their thermos. Not that they could really complain—it was Teddy's boat, after all, and he had always had an open-door policy for friends and clients. But that policy didn't work so well when he had a grumpy, introverted lover hanging around embarrassingly often these days.

"Or maybe I'll call her to set up a time," Teddy quickly corrected, seeing the look on Sam's face. Kelso still looked a little puzzled, and Sam had to fight the urge to roll their eyes when Teddy clarified, "My new, ah, roommate likes their privacy, you know?"

"Ahh, a new roommate. That explains the unexpected shore leave," Kelso replied with a sage nod. "Anyone I would know?"

"Maybe. It's a small world."

Sam hoped the heat crawling up their neck wasn't completely obvious when Teddy shot a self-satisfied and incredibly unsubtle glance in their direction. Donovan narrowed her eyes suspiciously, and Sam made a mental note to have a talk about Teddy's interpretation of "playing things cool" when they got home.

To his home, of course. Not that they lived together or anything.

"Well, you'll have to introduce us sometime," Kelso said with such cheerful obliviousness, Sam suddenly understood how he stayed sane under the pressure of the mayoral office. "Although I suppose I am quite behind on introductions as is," he continued, with a polite nod to the gathered officers. "Claire, if you wouldn't mind?"

"Please, allow me, Mr. Mayor," Teddy said before Captain Donovan could so much as open her mouth. Her expression tightened, but Teddy only offered that charming smile as he gestured to Noah and Donya in their pressed navy blues. "These are Junior Detectives Donya Novikoff and Noah Mariano. Both instrumental in the success of the operation."

"Wonderful to meet you both," Kelso said with the exact same gravitas he had used to address the crowd earlier. He reached out to shake both rookies' hands in turn. "Truly, the city can't thank you enough for your efforts on this case."

Did his gaze linger a beat too long on Noah's face? There was a strained, almost confused quality to Kelso's expression, as though he was trying to place the young man in his memory.

"And you obviously already know Captain Donovan," Teddy continued, drawing the Mayor's attention away from a certain gangster's thoroughly disowned nephew. "And there's also . . ." Teddy's face twisted into a slightly embarrassed expression as his gaze landed on Vince. "Ah, sorry, friend. What was your name again? Officer . . . ?"

"*Detective* Vincent Renier," Vince said flatly. Offering the mayor a smile that was working hard to be charming, he added, "Senior Detective on Vice Squad. It's an honor, Mr. Mayor."

"Right, right. Sorry about that," Teddy said with an easy, self-deprecating laugh. "I've been so tied up in making this tribute, I've really only gotten familiar with people who were involved in the case."

"Detective Renier actually was involved with the Paths case," Donovan corrected. Arching an imperious eyebrow, she said, "He personally trained Detective Sam for undercover field duty."

"Oh, really? How interesting," Teddy said with such bright enthusiasm that Sam suspected Vince and Donovan were about to find out exactly how unsubtle their man could be when he wasn't happy.

"Mr. Burgess . . ." Sam started, a warning in their voice.

Vince was too busy preening for the Mayor to notice. "That's right. I head up a lot of undercover investigations on Vice," he boasted, puffing up a little under Kelso's curious gaze. "Just earlier this year, I—"

"So it was your idea to put a nonbinary officer on an undercover dating case?" Teddy interrupted, and Vince's words instantly choked off. For once, he didn't seem to have anything clever at all to say.

"I—no," Vince finally managed after a long pause. He darted a desperate glance in Donovan's direction. "I was just following the brief. I wasn't in charge."

"Oh. My bad," Teddy said in an equally pleasant tone. Pivoting to stare Donovan down now, he offered her the same hard smile and said, "So you were the one who thought asking someone to be misgendered on a daily basis seemed like a good idea?"

"Teddy," Sam said, more firmly this time.

Every eye swiveled toward them—accusation from Donovan, concern from the mayor, and barely contained anger from Teddy, who probably would have liked to say a whole lot worse than a couple of honest statements in their defense. And they loved him for it. But just the thought of facing the consequences on their own come Monday morning was enough to make Sam feel exhausted.

So instead, Sam ducked their head against the scrutiny and said, "I was just doing my job. It really wasn't a big—"

"Nah, don't listen to them, Mr. Mayor," Noah interrupted loudly. Sam shot him a warning look, but the stupid kid just clapped a hand on Sam's shoulder and declared, "This case was a load of bullshit, and Sam's a fuckin' hero for getting it done anyways."

Teddy laughed openly at Noah's bold assessment, and Noah grinned in the face of Donovan's displeasure. "They've for sure saved my ass at least twice already," he continued. "If anyone deserves a medal for this whole mess, it's Sam."

"He's right," Donya said, and Sam looked to her in surprise. She offered them a small shrug and said, "Sam would take a bullet for any one of us." Flicking her gaze in Vince's direction, she added a little more pointedly, "Can't say that about just any coworker."

"Well, it certainly sounds like there's an apology in order, Detective," Kelso said, looking properly uncomfortable as Sam's colleagues came to their defense.

Or perhaps "colleagues" wasn't the most accurate term for what these people had become to them over the past few months.

"Not necessary, Mr. Mayor," Sam managed to mumble, despite the overwhelming wave of fuzzy feelings that was making it awfully hard to speak at the moment.

"It certainly is," Mayor Kelso said firmly. "Not only have I failed to offer you my thanks sooner, but clearly I . . . misunderstood your personal circumstances." This last bit earned Donovan a look that had her face twisting like she'd swallowed an entire beehive. Turning back to Sam, he asked, "I wonder if you'd accept my apology in the form of a dinner invitation? Your insight would be highly valued in ensuring such situations never happen again under my watch."

"I'm sure I wouldn't have much to say."

"Nonsense," Kelso insisted, almost before Sam had finished speaking. "Anyone who has earned such respect from their peers must be a natural born leader." Offering Sam a magnanimous smile, he added, "Of course, if it'd make you more comfortable, you would be welcome to bring a . . . special someone. If you have a someone. In your life."

"Thank you, sir," Sam said with a sigh.

Kelso gave them a pleasant, expectant look, and Sam felt their gut clench, despite the fact that the mayor was probably the only person left in the entire plaza who was not clued into who Sam's *someone* was yet.

"Well," Sam said after a long moment, "I do have a, uh, partner, I guess. But I'm not sure he'd be interested in—"

Teddy cleared his throat, and Sam winced.

"I mean—I'm just not sure it'd be very—" they tried again, but Teddy gave them such a pointed look that the denial shriveled on their tongue. Donya coughed back a laugh, and Sam could feel their skin positively burning as Kelso grew more confused by their flustered response.

"Hmm?" Teddy asked with a tilt of his head. "¿Quieres repetir eso, mi amor?"

"Oh, fine," Sam snapped in exasperated defeat. "Just say it if you want to say it so badly."

"How romantic." Despite the dry words, Teddy's expression was nothing short of smitten as he tucked an arm around Sam's tense waist. With his eyes still pinned to his lover's neon face, he said, "Sam and I would be happy to join you and Elise for dinner, Mr. Mayor."

"Sam and . . . you mean . . . this is the new roommate?" For half a second, the political mask slipped, and Kelso sounded genuinely rattled by this information.

"Oh yes. Sam and I met during the Paradiso case," Teddy said, tugging Sam even closer to his side. They made a warning sound, which did nothing to dissuade him from dropping an adoring kiss to their temple. "They needed a translator, and, as it turned out, I needed them."

Sam made a face at his flowery words, but the fact that they did not pull away from his embrace said they didn't completely hate Teddy's over-the-top romanticisms.

"Well. This is all very . . . surprising!" Kelso spluttered. "Wonderful. Surprising and wonderful!"

Sam wondered vaguely if he thought ending every sentence on an exclamation point would make him sound less like he was panicking.

"Claire!" Kelso said, reaching desperately for the nearest scapegoat. "How could you not have told me about this sooner?"

"I wasn't aware Detective Sam had a partner, sir," Donovan said. Sam was impressed that she managed to only sound a little sour about being thrown under the bus. Giving Sam and Teddy a cool once-over, she added, "Certainly not one quite so . . . popular."

"Believe me, no one's more surprised about it than I am," Sam said gruffly. "But I'm pretty sure I wouldn't have made it through this case without him, so I guess we should all be grateful that he's got such bad taste."

"I have excellent taste, mi amor," Teddy contradicted. Reaching down to take Sam's thermos in his hand, he gave it a demonstrative shake and said, "I think someone just needs more coffee."

"Oh. Can we do that?" Sam asked with such obvious hope at the thought of being anywhere but here that even someone as oblivious as Mayor Kelso could surely tell that they weren't a threat to his career.

Maybe Sam should have felt bad for not wanting to change the world, or this city, or even just their own department. But that wasn't what they were made for. If anything, Sam thought they hadn't been made to do much except maybe solve murders and be fiercely loved by this beautiful human being.

That seemed like more than enough of a reason for being to them.

"Of course. One coffee, coming up," Teddy promised suavely. He sealed the deal with a hard smooch on the cheek that had Sam reconsidering their mushy thoughts. "Mr. Mayor," Teddy said with a nod to the older man. "Henry will be in touch about arranging that dinner—and in the meantime, please give Elise my regards."

"Will do," Mayor Kelso agreed eagerly as Teddy took Sam by the hand and started turning in the direction of the parking lot. "Take care of our star detective, would you?"

"Every day," Teddy promised warmly, much to Sam's great embarrassment and silent delight. And then, to really drive the point home, he shot Sam's less supportive coworkers one last victorious grin and said, "I don't plan on going anywhere."

CHAPTER THIRTY-NINE

Sam watched with open satisfaction as Teddy focused all his attention on weighing out the coffee grounds on the tiny kitchen scale. They never got tired of the way he prepared each cup like it was a precious gift, and Sam was more than happy to show him their gratitude for his efforts every time. But after all that romantic foolishness down at City Hall earlier, Sam wasn't feeling especially patient.

They prowled across the kitchen to wrap their arms around Teddy's waist from behind. He hummed in acknowledgement, then laughed when they tugged harder to pull him away from the counter.

"What, you don't want coffee now?" Teddy asked as Sam turned him toward them insistently.

"In a minute."

Teddy looked quite pleased with himself when Sam reached up to cup his face in their hands. That probably should have been more annoying, but instead, all Sam felt was the primal urge to kiss him until they were feeling just as pleased. So that's what they did.

It was a damn good kiss. The kind that was meant to leave him weak in the knees and certain above all else that he was absolutely adored. Sam was pretty sure he was getting the message from the way he swayed back against the counter with their body cradled oh-so-tenderly in his warm embrace.

"So," Teddy said, a little breathlessly, when Sam had finally finished kissing their message into his lips, "I guess you're not mad at me?"

"I really should be," Sam replied, although it wasn't very believable when they were pinning him up against the counter like this. "When you said 'playing it cool' this morning, I didn't think that would end with us getting an invitation to dinner at the mayor's house."

"I know. I'm sorry. I wasn't expecting it to be so hard to hear—" Teddy started, sounding properly chastised. Grimacing, he offered them a sheepish look and said, "But I probably could have handled it better. Sorry."

"Well," Sam said with a coy shrug, "I don't know about *better*." They allowed a ghost of a smile when they remembered the sour look on their captain's face. "I guess I didn't hate seeing Vince and Donovan squirm a little. Just this one time."

"Oh yeah? You liked that?" Teddy asked as Sam twirled one of his curls around their finger playfully. "Maybe I really should have punched him."

"No way. Absolutely no fist fights for you anymore," Sam said sternly. They slid their hand back into his hair and pulled him down for another very convincing kiss. When they pulled back, it was only to murmur against his lips, "If anyone else wants to touch so much as a hair on your head, they're going to have to go through me first. And nobody is going to enjoy that."

"Oh boy," Teddy said weakly. "That probably shouldn't turn me on so much."

"What can I say? You make me very possessive." Sam's teeth flashed in a grin against the skin of Teddy's neck, and Teddy swallowed hard beneath their touch. "I just want to protect you, and spoil you, and keep you by my side forever and ever so no one else can . . ."

Sam's words trailed off in a bubble of giddy laughter as Teddy made an adorable growling noise and wrestled them into his arms for an enthusiastic cuddle. The beautiful thing Sam had discovered about being with Teddy was that they could let him take care of them from time to time—because he also wanted Sam to care for him in the same way. Dishes, laundry, cups of coffee—it was all the little things they couldn't do for each other over the phone that Sam hadn't known would make their heart so full now that they were together in person.

"Come on. At least let me put the coffee on," Sam laughed helplessly when Teddy's wandering hands started to get a little frisky.

Teddy didn't release them, but he allowed them to lean over and grab the kettle. His hands felt wonderfully familiar as Sam tipped the hot water into the fancy pour-over coffee maker. The device had magically appeared on Teddy's counter along with the thermos after Sam's second morning in a row at his place. Somehow that had been over three weeks ago, and the coffee maker was now looking as thoroughly loved as Sam felt these days.

Putting the kettle back down, Sam turned back to settle their arms around Teddy's shoulders. "OK," they said. "Now you have five minutes."

"Five minutes, huh?" Teddy said thoughtfully. Leaning down, he kissed Sam lightly on the nose. "I guess that might be long enough."

"I'm game to try if you are."

"Not that, you depraved thing," Teddy said with exasperation. Tugging Sam's shirt back in place, he clarified, "I meant it was long enough to talk about what Kelso said earlier."

Sam froze.

Teddy peeked up at them to gauge their reaction. "About my being around more than usual?"

"Oh." Sam was still for a long moment before pulling away.

Teddy sighed quietly the moment Sam turned their back to him, and they winced a little at the sound. For all the things they were enjoying about each other, Sam knew Teddy did not love their propensity to run any time things got too hard. Or too good. Or too serious—or really too anything that Sam wasn't used to dealing with during their many years of self-imposed isolation.

So instead of making an excuse and disappearing out the front door like they wanted to, Sam just walked over to the dining room table and started fussing with the papers scattered across the surface. Flyers, invoices, half-finished sketches. Sam wondered vaguely how much mail had piled up at their own apartment over the past couple of weeks.

"Well, it's just for a month or two while you finish the piece for Viv, right?" Sam forced themself to say. They didn't dare look in Teddy's direction, for fear of what they might see there. "Then you'll be on the move again."

"That's the part I wanted to talk about." Teddy's voice was careful. He was always so very careful when he was testing their boundaries, and Sam felt a nauseating mix of affection and panic flash through their system in response. "You know I left home straight out of high school, right?"

"Yes," Sam replied shortly. They sorted the last of the papers into their respective piles, but Teddy still hadn't said anything else, and now they were out of distractions. "And?" Sam demanded impatiently. "You went to college, sort of. Then odd jobs. Then you sold your first piece. Then the boat. Which part am I being quizzed on?"

"You're not being quizzed," Teddy said so gently that Sam was immediately ashamed of their irritable response.

It wasn't like they hadn't known this was coming. Teddy was an adult. So was Sam. They each had their own lives before all of this began. Teddy's had always involved being on the open sea, and no matter how much Sam's stupid heart wanted to throw pride aside and beg him not to leave, they knew they couldn't ask him to stay.

"Sorry," Sam muttered. It wasn't a very good apology, but it was sincere. The proof was in the way they couldn't even meet Teddy's gaze when they added, "I just . . . I'm not ready for you to go yet." The words were raw and uncomfortable on their tongue, but he deserved their honesty. "I'm not sure I'll ever . . ."

The words trailed off. Just because he deserved their honesty didn't mean Sam had gotten any better at expressing their thoughts. They were sure they looked miserable enough in that moment that he got the idea.

"Well, that's good news, since I don't really have any interest in leaving."

Sam's head snapped up to pin him with a disbelieving stare, but Teddy's expression was all soft, smitten lines. "Are you seriously surprised that I wouldn't want to go now that I've finally found what I was looking for?" he asked sweetly.

"Don't just say that." Sam tried to remember how to breathe normally, but all the air inside the boat seemed to have been sucked out of the cabin. "I'm serious, Teddy," they insisted as he reached into his pocket to retrieve something. "If you haven't really thought about this—if you're not sure— please don't—"

Teddy tossed them the object, and Sam's hand flashed up to catch it. Their anxious words choked off as they felt the jumble of hard metal and plastic tags biting into their palm.

"Those are for the places I'm supposed to be looking at today," Teddy said, nodding to the fistful of keys they were staring down at like an alien object in their hand. Sam tried to find something to respond with, but they didn't even know where to begin. Thankfully, Teddy always seemed to understand what was happening in their brain, because he just smiled and suggested, "You could come with me. If you wanted."

"Why?" Sam managed. The keys jangled as they tightened their grip on the ring.

So many keys. How did he think he was going to see that many places in one day on his own? The man got distracted every time he walked past an interesting window display. He didn't even have a driver's license, for god's sake.

"You know why, cariño."

Sam was silent for a long moment. The timer went off and they slowly placed the keys on the kitchen counter in favor of removing the drip top. They tossed the grounds in the compost and started washing out the filter. Then they washed it twice more, because they still hadn't figured out how to process any of this.

Teddy's solid warmth pressed against their back as he reached past them to turn off the water. His hand was faintly damp and wholly comforting where it curled around their hip. Sam leaned back ever so slightly and then let out a shaky breath when Teddy nuzzled up against them. They let their eyes fall shut as they accepted his silent comfort in the midst of their confusion. How was it that they fit together so perfectly? It was improbable. Impossible. After so many years, how could they possibly be so lucky that someone like him would just—

"So?" Teddy's voice shattered their train of thought. "What do you think?"

Sam didn't open their eyes, but they felt a helpless smile tugging at their lips when he shifted impatiently against them. "I think it sounds a lot like you're asking me to move in with you."

"Would that be so terrible?"

When they didn't answer immediately, Teddy wrapped his arms around them, and Sam felt their pulse picking up even as they relaxed a little more into his embrace.

"You going to keep making me coffee?" Sam ventured.

"Every morning," Teddy promised.

Sam felt a little dizzy as their eyes blinked open to stare at the fancy little coffee maker on his kitchen counter. They remembered thinking at first that it was such a ridiculous gesture. Buying a coffee maker because they slept over one time? Honestly. Teddy didn't even like coffee that much.

But he had used it to show them how much he liked *them* every single morning since.

"And you won't get annoyed if I need space sometimes?" Sam asked as they reached out to snag the ring of keys off the counter. "Like maybe . . . my own office, or . . . ?"

"Baby, you can have an entire floor to yourself if you want it," Teddy said with a small laugh that tickled their ear and sent a flush scattering across their cheeks. As though sensing their uncertainty, Teddy added, "You also don't have to give up your apartment if you don't want to." His lips brushed against their temple. "Although I hope you'll still prefer sleeping in my bed."

"Mhm," Sam hummed helplessly as they tilted their head to accept more of his sweet ministrations. "And if I let you sleep in my bed, you'll stop calling it 'making love'?"

"I see. So it's your bed now." Teddy laughed again, and this time when Sam's heart stuttered at the sound of those words it felt a whole lot more like excitement than fear. "Sorry," he said, nipping playfully at their ear just to make them laugh, too. "You're going to be stuck making love to me for the rest of your life."

"Is that so?"

"If I have my way, yes."

For half a heartbeat, Sam hesitated. Then they were turning around in his arms so quickly that they nearly tripped over Teddy's feet as he drew them in for a rushed, ecstatic kiss. Sam's heart was hammering, and their hands may or may not have been shaking a little, but their elation at the idea of him staying here, of being together, of never saying goodbye—it was all so good and also way, way too much.

"Teddy," Sam tried, feeling a little overwhelmed as Teddy continued to pepper them with enthusiastic kisses. Obviously, he was not feeling at all concerned about this insane leap, which was great, but also . . . "Are you sure about this?"

"So sure."

"Teddy, please," Sam repeated when he pressed forward against their restraining hands. "Are you really sure?" Pinning him in place with a stern gaze, Sam said, "I know I'm not exactly . . . easy. To be with. So I need to know you've thought this through."

"Sam," he echoed back mock-seriously. Sam started to scowl, and Teddy only seemed more smitten at the sight. "I love that you really think that," he sighed, reaching out to trace the line of their jaw with one knuckle. "Like being with you has ever been hard for me."

"I'm serious. I'm too stubborn—and old. Too old for you," Sam insisted, as though that would hide the way their words got all tangled up when he touched them so tenderly. "You should want to be with someone who—"

"Who what? Who's still messing around and trying to figure out what they want?" Teddy's voice was all fond exasperation. "Who wouldn't love being the only one you wanted too much to walk away from?"

"OK. That's—that's technically true. But I just—"

Teddy pressed his forehead against theirs with no care at all for how rudely he made their heart flutter while they were trying to make a point. Sam sighed, long and slow. "I just know I'm going to disappoint you."

"Sure. And I love that you worry about that," Teddy said agreeably. His nose bumped against theirs, too eager and impatient to leave a single inch of space between them. "I'm going to disappoint you, too, sometimes. That's part of being in a relationship."

"You haven't yet," Sam mumbled, leaning in helplessly for a kiss, only for Teddy to pull back abruptly.

"Yeah? You like it when your clothes are all wrinkled because I did laundry but forgot to fold them?" he asked with a knowing smile when they frowned at his teasing. "You like it when the fridge is empty for the third night in a row because I swore I was going to go shopping 'for real this time' but then I got inspired and, oops, still no groceries?"

"Well, no, I don't like it, but that's not . . . That stuff doesn't matter," Sam protested. "I can just order something in, and you can get back to work."

"Do you even hear yourself?" Teddy demanded. Before Sam could reject his sweet words, Teddy was taking their face in his hands and holding them steady with that adoring gaze. "Sam, I love your prickly, selfless heart. I love your giant, transparent walls, and how intense you get when something really matters. I love talking to you, and going on walks with you, and making coffee for you, and waking up next to you." Teddy offered them that scrunchy-eyed smile that put his whole beautiful heart on display. "I love that you're still surprised when I beg you to stay just one more night because I can't stand the thought of sleeping without you anymore. Eres la razón por la que mi corazón late. Amo todo de ti, Sam."

Sam was pretty sure they had forgotten how to breathe by the end of his over-the-top declaration.

"And this is the part where you say . . . ?" Teddy suggested after a long moment of watching them short-circuit.

"I still don't speak Spanish."

Teddy started to roll his eyes in response to their typical hardheadedness, but then Sam was knocking his hands aside so they could take him in their arms.

"I don't speak Spanish *yet*," Sam clarified, "but you make me want to learn when you say stuff like that." Teddy blinked rapidly in response to their unexpected romantic words, and Sam felt their own smile tugging at their lips. "And I am difficult to live with, but you're very much worth improving for."

They could hardly believe this flowery confession was coming out of their mouth, but Teddy was looking properly flustered now, and that made it impossible to stop.

Drawing in a deep breath, Sam tightened their hold on him and said, "Teddy, I know I'm going to disappoint you along the way, but I swear to god, if you'll let me love you anyways, I will spend the rest of my life trying to make you happy."

"Oh." It actually seemed to take a second for Teddy to figure out what came after that, and Sam was delighted to see their passionate man be the tongue-tied one for once. "Well, I could probably go for that," he finally managed, despite looking awfully swoony. "As long as you're going to let me love you, too."

"I'll probably make it hard," Sam warned.

"Good. It's better when you have to work for it."

Sam stretched up to kiss him firmly on the lips for that one, because damn this perfect man. They gladly would have just given him whatever was left of their battered, flinching heart, but no, of course he wouldn't accept that. Teddy was driven by a passion for making broken things beautiful again—no matter how much work it took.

His sigh ghosted across their lips, long and sweet, when they pulled away. "I love you, Sam," he said so sincerely Sam was certain they had never heard anything so beautiful.

"I love you too, Teddy." He kissed them again in a way that gave Sam the distinct impression that they were going to be drinking microwaved coffee by the time they were finished with the rest of this confession.

Teddy stepped in closer until they were pressed up against the counter and Sam was no longer thinking about coffee at all. Their elbow bumped the abandoned ring of keys on the counter and the jangling sound was enough to break through the lovely, romantic haze.

"What's so funny?" Teddy asked when Sam huffed out a small laugh.

"It's not funny, I just—"

They laughed again when he gave them a wonderfully suspicious look. He, who loved them, which made everything wonderful right now. Nudging the keys again with their elbow, Sam said, "I just love that you agreed to see more places than you could possibly get to on your own, because you already knew I'd be with you." Kissing him lightly, they said, "That's really very arrogant, you know?"

"Is it arrogant that I didn't want to imagine a scenario where you weren't by my side?" Teddy asked, which only made Sam laugh more. He offered them a bashful look at the sound of their amusement and admitted, "I also wasn't exactly sure what you would like. And I really wanted it to feel . . . like home, you know? For both of us."

"Yeah." The word was a happy, satisfied sigh on Sam's lips, because they absolutely did know.

For half a heartbeat, Sam let their eyes slide shut as they enjoyed their first deep breath in thirty-eight long years. Teddy's arms were secure around them, and the air inside the boat was warm from the midday sun, and if they really let the romantic delirium take over, they could swear there was even the faintest hint of that Paradiso magic drifting in on the ocean breeze.

"OK, my love," Sam finally said, taking the key ring in their hand. "Let's go home."

ACKNOWLEDGEMENTS

All my love and gratitude for everyone who has supported me throughout this writing journey. My mom, who gave me Zuma Beach, and my dad who is my number one book peddler. My partner, Alex, who loves me even after I get mad at him for telling me when I need to re-write something (even though he's always right). My friends, who say motivational things like "don't you ever sleep?" and "are you sure it's healthy to drink that much coffee?" And always my early cheerleaders Cathy Clark, Christine Szepesi, and the late, great Evelyn Mee.

Special thanks as well to the small but mighty team that helped make this book something you can actually read and listen to! My copy editor Amy Kruse, Spanish translator Carlos Cohen, narrator TJ Clark, and sound effects artist R.B. Honeycutt. Each of these incredibly talented individuals were instrumental in the creation of this book. There aren't enough pages in the world to write out what their efforts have meant to me.

And finally, to every reviewer who took the time to share their thoughts on book one. I said in the acknowledgements of *Like & Subscribe for Murder* that I would consider it a win if even one person read the book and laughed. Suffice to say, I did not expect so many people to connect with Detective Sam, but I'm so glad their story has brought happiness to so many readers! Please know that every single review lives rent free in my head forever, and I couldn't be luckier to have connected with such a kind and incredible audience.